"*Dragonfly* is a stunningly original novel, by turns frightening, funny, gripping, and moving. This is a major book, perhaps the finest of John Farris's distinguished career. Don't start reading *Dragonfly* on a weeknight, unless you plan to go to work the next day looking like a zombie. It is absolutely riveting."
—Douglas Preston and Lincoln Child, authors of *Relic*

"*Dragonfly* has style, heart, cunning, terror, irony, suspense and genuine surprise—and an absolutely fearless look into the souls of people very much like you and me. This is one of John Farris's best books, and that says it all." —Ed Gorman, *Mystery Scene*

"His paragraphs are smashingly crafted and his images glitter like solitaires." —*The Philadelphia Inquirer*

"FARRIS IS A REAL MASTER . . . A GIANT OF CONTEMPORARY PSYCHOLOGICAL HORROR."
—Peter Straub

"Farris has remarkable ability to jab his literary ice pick into the bone marrow." —Brian Garfield

By John Farris from Tom Doherty Associates

DRAGONFLY

JOHN FARRIS

FORGE

A TOM DOHERTY ASSOCIATES BOOK
NEW YORK

For Mary Ann and Peter John

Cover art by Shelley Eshkar. Cover photo by Waldo Tejada.

A Tor Book
Published by Tom Doherty Associates, Inc.
175 Fifth Avenue
New York, NY 10010

Tor Books on the World Wide Web:
http://www.tor.com

Tor® is a registered trademark of Tom Doherty Associates, Inc.

ISBN: 0-812-55263-6
Library of Congress Card Catalog Number: 95-23246

First edition: October 1995
First international mass market edition: May 1996
First mass market edition: July 1996

Printed in the United States of America

0 9 8 7 6 5 4 3 2 1

PART **ONE**

Still, it taught me something about love. If it's so tough, forget it.

—Derek Walcott, **Blues**

ONE

By seven-thirty on that Saturday evening in June, it was obvious that the wedding of Clare Sumrall Malcolm and Joseph McLaren Tucker, scheduled to begin on the spacious south lawn of the Malcolm estate at five o'clock, wasn't going to happen. Joe was missing.

He had left Omaha forty-eight hours ago, shortly after the wedding rehearsal, on a quick business trip to his home state of Texas. Then he planned to stop by Fort Worth on his way back to Nebraska. His mother, a reclusive sort who also was a determined nonflyer, had weighed her neurotic fears against the prospect of missing her only son's wedding, and had opted to make an appearance rather than watch the nuptials on a cassette. Darly Rae Tucker had always been real sweet to Clare on the phone, and Clare was looking forward to meeting her.

They were due on Friday night at ten o'clock, but Joe called at the last minute, leaving a message on Clare's answering machine. He explained that his mother was suffering an attack of sciatica, but that they could be counted on to arrive by noon the next day. Cutting it a little close, but Clare wasn't worried. In the time she'd known Joe—it was to be exactly five months and four days from "Nice to meet you" to "I do"— he had been the soul of reliability and thoughtfulness. Also she was too caught up in the last-minute fuss of preparations for the small (strictly limited to seventy-five guests) but elegant wedding. And around her head, as everyone could see, there were shimmering clouds of bliss. Clare had been married before, at nineteen, an event she seldom thought about and never associated with this one, her *real* marriage, the only one that would ever matter.

As a courtesy to his sister, Donald Malcolm went to the airport to personally pick up Joe and his mother when they got off the direct flight from Dallas–Fort Worth International. The plane happened to be delayed, so it was one-fifteen when "Brud" found out that Joe and Darly Rae were not on it.

All of Brud's doubts about the legitimacy of Joe Tucker returned in a steaming flood that soon had him red-faced and in danger of losing his infamous temper. He was a stocky, balding pit-bull type who bit savagely when aroused.

An airline supervisor was reluctant to say if Joe and Darly Rae had been booked on a subsequent flight, not due until four-thirty. Brud was not family, there fore not privileged to have that information. Brud got the airport manager on the phone and chewed on him for thirty seconds. The information was given out promptly. None of the airlines servicing Omaha had either of the Tuckers on their manifests for Saturday arrival.

Meanwhile Clare and Brud's cousin Philippa, who Brud knew could be counted on to keep her wits about her and her mouth closed in this emergency, was trying to locate Joe Tucker in Texas.

The number they had for Darly Rae Tucker turned out to be a pay phone at a Christian Science reading room in downtown Fort Worth.

An airport cop reported that the black Maserati which was Clare's wedding present to Joe Tucker was not in either of Brud's VIP parking slots at the airport. It soon was apparent that Joe had not flown out of Omaha following the rehearsal dinner.

By then Brud realized it was going to be bad news all the way. Not that he could blame himself; he'd been very thorough looking into Joe Tucker's background, once he observed that certain light in Clare's eyes whenever Joe was around. Damn it, you couldn't be more thorough, and Tucker had checked out all the way: certified birth certificate, TRW, high-school and college records, IRS returns obtained from agency files—good God, it was virtually impossible to fake some of that stuff! Yet Brud was readily convinced "Joe Tucker" was not the name of the man Clare thought she was going to marry. And all Brud knew about him was contained in an obviously fraudulent financial and business profile. Joe had somehow managed to sucker-punch them. But *how?*

Brud was getting sicker by the minute. The fact that his little sister was about to be jilted didn't bother him so much. She'd had a disastrous history with men almost since adolescence; it was her lot in life, apparently. What he cared about was that he and Clare were about to look like fools to their friends (and Brud's enemies), and obviously Clare was out a lot of money, from some scheme or other she'd been careful not to consult him about.

Familiar with Brud and his reputation, the resident manager of the Horizon Towers condominium had no qualms about opening the two-bedroom furnished penthouse that Joe had leased for the past six months. Joe had cleared out very neatly, leaving nothing behind except possibly his fingerprints; but Brud already had a set of Joe's fingerprints, and he was not on file with the FBI.

There was plenty that belonged to Clare in the penthouse suite, mostly in the bathroom and in a bedroom armoire. Some frilly, baby-doll lingerie, not typical of Clare's taste: Brud had never seen her at breakfast in anything but a sensible plaid bathrobe. Bikini underpants he found in a drawer had the crotch cut out. He saw a book of erotic art on a bedside table, opened to some eighteenth-century Japanese drawings of women astride men with everything showing. Picturing the two of them dallying in the broad bed with the plum-colored silk coverlet, Clare assuming similar lewd postures for Joe—Brud was enraged.

It was a few minutes before sunset when Brud drove through the gates of the country estate where he and Clare had continued to live after the death of their father five years ago. Most of the family fortune, which Brud managed astutely, was from ranch land in the Sand Hills country, and considerable property on either side of Dodge Street, from Westroads Mall to Boys' and Girls' Town. There were twenty acres of windbreak woodlots, a nine-hole private golf course, air-conditioned horse barns, paddocks and show rings. Brud's passion, other than golf, was Arabians, and Clare owned and rode hunter-jumpers. She had her own money, most of which she was willing to let Brud invest for her. But there were a couple of accounts on which he was not a cosigner, money she could draw on when she wanted to buy a horse or invest in little businesses run by friends in Omaha or Hobe Sound, their winter home in Florida. How much money? He wasn't sure. She'd been lucky on a couple of her investments, and stud fees for her champion jumper Roshomon had been impressive the last couple of years. She might have had a million, maybe a million two in cash or cash instruments. That was before Joe came along, and she began sinking money into the gallery they were starting together.

Joe was, or claimed to be, an art historian. He knew cutting horses, and could ride. His golf handicap was a respectable seven. For a young guy, twenty-nine according to his birth certificate, he was damned competent at a lot of things. Good-looking, certainly, confident but without cockiness, well read and soft-spoken, a rock-ribbed Republican. And he had to be a genius at seduction, because Brud knew very well that Clare had had a lot of problems with sex over the years, thanks to good old Tunkie, her psychopathic first husband.

Imposing thunderheads filled the sky over the Missouri River, a dozen miles away; rain had been promised for the weekend, but Clare had wanted an outdoor wedding, in the century-old south garden among the flowering pink dogwoods. In the gathering twilight, the guests were still waiting there, along with the string orchestra and the Episcopalian ministers, four bridesmaids and a flustered wedding coordinator with her crew.

Philippa met Brud at the front door and told him Clare was incommunicado in her second-floor suite, waiting for her brother. Nothing had been heard from Joe, of course. Brud nodded and told her to pass on the news that the wedding had been postponed.

"Give them all a couple of drinks and the buffet if they want it, and get them the hell out of here as quick as possible. Oh, and call Gordon Estes. Number's on the Rolodex in my study. I want him here tomorrow morning, no excuses!" Estes and Associates was the Washington firm Brud had employed to check on the background of Joe Tucker. The associates were all former FBI and Secret Service agents. Brud was primed to give Gordon Estes hell.

He went upstairs and down the hall of the west wing, which had been added when the century-old, classically

Victorian house underwent massive renovation in 1952. The quarters that Clare occupied had been their mother's; Evangeline was devoted, as Clare was, to Spanish motifs. The marquetry double doors were unlocked. Brud passed through an arcaded entrance to the empty conservatory/sitting room, walked past a Miró and a Bécquer and a Tapies abstract on one wall. Tapies was Spain's leading contemporary artist, but the abstract looked like a cow wallow to Brud. His only interest in art was the bottom line, and he knew within a few dollars the current worth of all the art collected in Clare's suite.

"Clare, it's Brud; you in there?"

No sound; he stood back respectfully a few steps from her bedroom door, and called again.

The door was wrenched open. What seemed to Brud like an apparition stood there, staring at him in hope and dread. She was a big woman, five-ten, with the bones of their late father, whereas Brud had inherited the short stature and blunt, pugnacious jaw of their mother. Clare had never been fat, but still there always seemed to be too much of her, even after breast-reduction surgery gave her figure more pleasing proportions. She looked strong and competent, a throwback to her pioneer forebears; but emotionally she was as fragile as a porcelain teacup, and in the hours since her scheduled wedding, Brud could see that she had come undone.

"Now, Clare—" Brud held his hands up in a placating gesture, while his stomach burned with the acids of his hatred for Joe Tucker. "—I want you just to take it easy."

Her wide mouth, with all the lipstick chewed off, worked hard; her throat muscles stood out. She gasped.

"What . . . was it? An accident? Was he badly hurt?" Her normally high voice had a nervous tremolo. "Where is he?"

"Clare, just let me come in, and we'll—"

"He's dead." The dreadfulness of this assumption seemed to grow in force like a bad wind shrieking through her mind. Her eyes lost focus even as her body twisted tight as rope and she screamed out, "TELL ME!"

"No. I seriously doubt that he's dead. Yet." Brud sighed and moved toward the bedroom doorway, guiding his sister back with the flat of his hand against her side. Under his breath he added, "The son of a bitch."

Clare whirled away from him, almost lost her balance—she was wearing only one of her wedding shoes—then straightened and lashed out with a slap he shied from, taking the blow on the point of a raised shoulder.

"How dare you! If you won't help me—"

"Clare, listen. He didn't go to Texas. He drove the Maserati out of town instead of to the airport, and it's probably sold by now. I'm sure that his mother, so-called, was somebody he hired to act the part. Joe Tucker, or Buttcrack, or whatever his name may be, is not coming back to Omaha. Now, my guess is he never intended marrying you. And I tried my best to warn you, Clare; but you never would hear a word of it."

Clare batted her long eyelashes. The mascara had matted from the humidity of her grief. She swayed. She was ashen. It was a mean business and Brud had no wish to torture her, but usually it was best just to bore ahead and get the unpleasantness over with.

"Lying to me . . ."

"I wish to God I was," he said, staring her down.

Now her hands fluttered; she grasped the large heirloom sapphire engagement ring as if she were afraid it would fly off her finger.

"He gave . . . he said . . . in his family . . . almost two hundred . . ."

"Oh, well, it's a nice enough ring, yes indeedy, and it probably did set him back a few thousand at some deluxe flea market. But he had money to invest in you, apparently. Looking to make more money. So, how much, Clare?''

A shudder tore through Clare. Her eyes were growing blanker. ''Get . . . out. Leave me alone, Brud.''

''Whatever share he put up for that art gallery, he probably withdrew it from the bank. We'll know Monday. It was his, anyhow. The crucial question is, did you give him anything? He went off to Texas supposedly to buy some pictures, wasn't that it? Some song-and-dance he handed you about this old-time wildcatter with the fantastic collection of Western art he had to get rid of in a hurry?'' Brud paused; he didn't have to look at his sister to know he'd reached the heart of the matter. ''Yeah, I heard about it from Harley. You can't keep anything from me, Clare, I just wish you wouldn't try.'' He paused again. ''You gave your fiancé cash money to buy those pictures with, didn't you?''

She nodded. Her hands fell to her sides. She looked down, as if she were about to throw herself from the roof of a forty-story building, then straightened with a snap. But there was a faraway look in her eyes, as if she were witnessing a holy vision.

''It . . . it's all right. Something happened. But he'll . . . definitely be here. I think I . . . I need to freshen up?'' Clare looked up with a stark, ghastly smile. ''Just tell everybody . . . to wait. We're going to get married, really, and . . . it's . . . uh . . . he loves me, Brud. Joe loves me!''

''Clare. Darling . . . how much of your money did he leave town with?''

''But it's okay! He's in Texas. Buying paintings. I know all about it. There was probably . . .'' Clare broke off, cringing at the look in Brud's eyes. She crossed her arms over her breast. She was wearing a Dresden-blue wedding suit, and a pearl choker. The skirt was badly rumpled. ''I wish Mama was here.'' Her voice had become feeble and childish. "I wish Daddy . . . You never have liked me, Brud. You never *approved* of me."

"You're my sister and I love you dearly. But I need to know. A couple hundred thousand, Clare?"

When she didn't answer him he stepped closer to her, held her right hand in a forceful grip and ground the knuckle bones together. He hadn't done that since she was a kid. Clare sobbed in pain and misery.

"Don't!"

"How much?"

"Six . . ." Clare choked. He let her go. She turned and limped toward the four-poster bed. Her image swam in his vision. His blood pressure was way too high. *Six hundred thousand dollars.* Brud breathed harshly through his mouth, appreciating the skill and effrontery of "Joe Tucker," an appreciation that did not in the least diminish Brud's desire to kill him.

Facedown on her bed, Clare went into hysterics.

Outside on the south lawn, a violinist had begun to play something lilting and Hungarian.

Brud bounded to the French doors and out onto the balcony, sighted a group of relatives, the women in flouncy spring hats, the men in cutaways, cravats and striped trousers, all of them drinking champagne.

"Somebody tell that asshole to shut up!" Brud bellowed.

His blood pressure was knocking him for a loop. He had to sit on the edge of the bed for a couple of minutes, listening helplessly to Clare scream in heartbreak. It would pass, he consoled himself. Clare would be all right eventually. And so would he. Just another minute or two. Then he would make his way downstairs to his leather-paneled study, close the doors on everybody, sit and recall every little thing he could about "Joe Tucker." He was a clever boy, but somewhere along the line, in the months he'd hung around Omaha screwing Clare and scheming to get his hands on a large chunk of cash, he'd made a mistake. Left a clue as to who he really was.

He just needed to be patient, Brud thought. It would all work out, to his ultimate satisfaction.

TWO

After the Omaha project was completed and he was home aboard the *Dragonfly*, Joe was a long time surfacing from the depths of a complex malaise.

He spent ten days at anchorage in Fajardo, once the *Dragonfly* was back in the water. Immediately after leaving Omaha he had shaved off the inch of beard he wore as Joe Tucker, and he renewed his tan on flawless blue days. He ordered marine supplies and restocked the big galley for the first couple of months of aimless sailing he had in mind. There was always work to be done on the Swedish-built sloop. She was fifty-six feet of teak and mahogany laid over a canoe-shaped hull of fiberglass, Vinylester resin and four coats of epoxy. He had local help with the topside refurbishing, the sanding, polishing and varnishing, but, relishing solitude, he always sailed alone. He was big enough and had the strength and agility to handle the necessary spread of sail.

Many things never seemed to function following *Dra-*

gonfly's extended stays in storage. Despite Joe's careful inspections, a couple of daylong shakedown cruises provided plenty of aggravation. Plugs popped out of teak decks, diodes blew, transducers failed, a bilge pipe valve malfunctioned, clew rings cracked in a fresh breeze, tools were either missing or stowed in the wrong lockers. Much of this was to be expected, and shouldn't have had him in a sullen mood. But, instead of feeling the familiar exhilaration as problems were dealt with and his boat-handling skills sharpened, he couldn't shake the lethargy that dogged him in the lulling tropical twilights when the *Dragonfly* lay at anchor off the marina harbor and the couple of raucous cafés where he customarily spent a lot of his free time.

Isobel Tavarés heard that he was back and came around from the hotel where she worked in Guest Relations. In Puerto Rico, everyone has a nickname and hers was "Puchi." She was a small lively Latin package with flattened Taino features and coarse straight black hair that grew to the tip of her tailbone when she didn't have it in braids. Joe was on shore unloading his Yamaha trail bike from the back of the small pickup truck he rented while he was staying in Fajardo. He wore ragged denim shorts and neoprene flip-flops.

Puchi put on a smile for him, although she was seething.

"Hey, long time, Joe."

"Yeah, I guess it has been, Puchi." He smiled too, willing her to forgive him, but when he offered to kiss her she backed up a step, skeptically.

"So, you just take off like a *sinvergüenza* and I don't hear from you. How am I sposed to feel, I mean, like shit, no?"

Joe frowned. "Didn't hear from me! I wrote you, what, half a dozen times?"

"How the fock should I know? Wrote me where, the other side the moon, maybe?"

"Hey. Hey, Puchi. I told you what I do for a living.

Hydraulic engineering. There was an emergency. I flew out to the Pacific, barely had time to pack. You were up there in Newark with your *mami* so sick, remember?"

"Uh, yeah. What do you mean, the Pacific?"

"Java, babe. Big hydroelectric project, the company I work for sometimes. I was in the middle of a jungle, you know? Got real sick for a while. I spent time in a hospital in Surabaya. Bad fever. I almost died."

"Ay, bendito," Puchi said, but with a slight skeptical twist of her lips. "And you wrote to me—that's the truth, huh?"

"Puchi, you know I'd give up my front-row seat in hell for you."

"Joe, you know what you got? You got lying blue eyes. But I forgive you anyhow." He bent to kiss her, but she leaned back. "What about that Swees girl live in Humacao, she works for Warner-Lambert? I know about you and her, man. She have letters from Java? 'Oh, I miss you, love you only, boo-hoo.' "

"Puchi, God's truth, when I look at you I can't remember any other woman on the face of the earth. How's your *mami?* Was it her gall bladder again?"

"Yeah. They do this operation now, they doan have to cut nobody open so much. They sock out the stones in bitty pieces. She's hokay. Well, I got to work tonight, hotshot. Maybe tomorrow night, huh?"

Joe's face fell a yard and a half. "Puchi, I have to make a quick trip. Four or five days. I'll be back by Sunday."

Hands on her hips, she said, "Quick treep? You know, sometimes I wonder about that big boat of yours. What you carry from island to island that might get you in big troubles some day."

"Do I look stupid to you, Puchi? I'm a recreational sailor. I work hard when I work, get paid well for it, then I take a few months off to enjoy life."

"I can get a little time off myself, Joe."

"That's good, Puchi. Real good. Come Sunday, we'll plan something, just you and me."

On Sunday Joe was in Montserrat, one of the world's tiny snoop-free banking havens. From there it was only a full day's reach to his favorite place in the Caribbean, the anchorage at Bourg on Terre-de-Haut, an even smaller and less-well-known island in the Antilles chain. He had forgotten Puchi and his spur-of-the-moment promises. Joe had made a lot of promises to women all over the Caribbean and in Mexico, a sometime haunt of his. But he had no interest in women right now. Clare Malcolm was still hanging around, in his daytime reveries, in his restless dreams.

He had first seen Clare in *Town and Country*, where he found most of his projects. *T and C* devoted several of its pages each month to society weddings and charity events; sometimes a full page, in color, covered a particularly trendy fund-raiser. The event in Omaha was a ball to benefit pediatric AIDS, and Clare Malcolm was the chairperson.

Over several months Joe could look at hundreds of photographs of elegant women in their thirties and forties without a trace of frisson; then something would stimulate his curiosity bump. Perhaps there was a psychic connection he didn't understand. He looked at the face of Clare Malcolm for a few moments, noting that she was almost a head taller than the other women in the group photograph, and wore a voluminous gown of a green material that reminded him of leftover Christmas wrap. Then he clipped the page from the magazine, folded it and put it away. This was his usual practice. He had a drawerful of magazine and newspaper clippings aboard the *Dragonfly* that he never referred to after his initial tickle of interest. A couple of times a year he emptied the drawer and added the clippings to a bonfire on a deserted beach.

But sometimes, after a week or so of uneasiness that

had a strange, sensuous appeal, he would retrieve the recent article or photograph and look at it again. This was the case with Clare Malcolm. He spent a half hour meditating on her image. She was blond, with her hair pulled back from an asymmetrical, rather long face. A healthy, blandly handsome Midwestern face. There was no stiffness in her pose for the camera. Her mouth was wide, and she was smiling. But he sensed reticence in her smile. Her hands were gloved. He couldn't tell if she was married. Not that it mattered. He had dealt with both married and unmarried women. Often the married ones fell hardest for him. And often their husbands didn't give a damn until they found out, too late, what Joe had cost them.

It was the new year. Joe and the *Dragonfly* were in Cayman Brac. After a day of diving the spectacular vertical walls, he sailed over to Grand Cayman and in Georgetown visited the branch of a British bank where, as a corporate entity called Reef Adventures, Ltd., he did some of his business. A fax was sent from the bank to the detective agency in Atlanta he used on a rotating basis with two other agencies in the States. Within ten days, by Federal Express, he had everything that was available on Clare Malcolm. A few good recent photos were included with the report.

Clare was thirty-three. Born and raised in Nebraska. With her brother Donald, forty-one, she shared a country estate that had been in the family for more than a hundred years and was still a working farm. Just under nine hundred acres, down from about five thousand acres at the turn of the century. The house, built in 1883 at the edge of the Great Plains, had a name: Windward. It was a massive limestone Victorian mansion with a couple of wings added on, not very artfully. Neither she nor her brother was married. Her first husband, T. Bristow Lescoulie, commonly known as "Tunkie," was, according to their wedding photo, a grinning gargoyle with abundant golden curls and a

dearth of character in his face. In the same photo
Clare looked taller than her husband, and poker-faced
from stress. She was nineteen. The marriage had lasted
eight months. Clare got the divorce, and was in therapy
for three years afterward. Two engagements followed.
Both were broken in short order.

Joe began to get a faint but probably accurate impression of what was behind the slight, sad reticence
of Clare's smile.

Two years at Vassar before her marriage, then she
earned a degree in fine arts at Lincoln when she was
twenty-five. No attempt to establish a career for herself.
She didn't travel much. Horses and good works took
up her time. At the moment she was in residence at
the winter house in Hobe Sound, scheduled to ride in
a charity horse show in Boca Raton over the weekend.
They had a major corporate sponsor, so it was one of
numerous events during the winter months on the
gilded East Coast of Florida that anyone could buy his
way into.

Florida. He had done a project in Sarasota nine
years ago, so there was always a chance of an embarrassing and potentially hazardous encounter in Boca
Raton. It was much too small a world in the circles
Clare Malcolm frequented. But the odds were accept-
ably long that he'd run into Lottie Santangelo. She had
to be, what, fifty-five now? And she'd never expressed
an interest in horses during the five months he'd been
intimate with her. King Charles spaniels were Lottie's
abiding passion.

He decided to keep the beard he'd been wearing
since his last project ended, seven months ago in Hon-
olulu. Darken it, and his hair, leaving it full and over
the ears. He had most of the right clothes aboard the
Dragonfly for a social weekend in Boca.

It was not his intention to make a move on Clare
Malcolm at this point. He might not even want to meet
her. With the assistance of the Amiga computer aboard

the *Dragonfly* he did some further research and felt that
he was well enough prepared, if it happened, but for
now observation was all he had in mind. He always
spent a great deal of time taking his time, examining
all projects with a well-educated eye for the probabili-
ties, ultimately rejecting four out of five prospects. The
young ones were too well protected, the old usually
defenseless. He preferred a real challenge. And his
hunch was that Clare Malcolm had pretty well given
up on men.

The well-attended three-day riding event was held at
the Sandalfoot Polo Club on the last weekend in Jan-
uary. There were a lot of striped tents, some of them
air-conditioned, set up around the paddocks, the
schooling rings and the manicured Bermuda of the
Grand Prix course. Auctions and a showing of contemporary artists helped the well-heeled while away their
time. There was a lot of unobtrusive security from
Wackenhut, but anyone was free to wander around the
stable area. On Friday he watched Clare Malcolm
schooling a big black stallion named Roy Bean. The
horse had a very good hind leg and good stamina in
the deep sand of the schooling ring. Miss Malcolm
complemented him with a long, strong back, an assured seat. She jumped to a second-place finish on Saturday as rain clouds moved in.

Roy Bean's owners were from Fort Smith, Arkansas.
At the Polo Club they entertained in a custom Silver
Eagle motor home, the sort of luxury that country-
music stars enjoyed on the road. Joe insinuated himself
into the company of some young horse bums and hung
around with them until he saw Clare Malcolm leave
the Silver Eagle by herself and stroll across the stable
grounds to the exhibits. In one hand she had a foam
cup with the Budweiser logo on it. She had changed
out of her riding clothes into faded Levi's and a ging-
ham Western-style shirt. Her figure wasn't much and
there was no exercise discipline that could change it.

She was tall from the waist up, with a low-slung butt. Ample breasts, and a too-long neck. She had recently washed and combed her hair, but it wasn't completely dry. Without makeup she had a lot of freckles. She smiled and nodded, but joined no groups, making her way a little aloofly past the sponsors' pavilion to the art show. The music of Elton John blasted from numerous speakers. It looked more and more like rain. Joe decided to follow her.

The piece Clare was most interested in, a rectangular oil-on-burlap painting reminiscent of Miró, had a red SOLD sticker on the frame, as did several others by the same artist, identified as Stanley Wax.

"Well, damn," she said softly and regretfully, and swallowed the rest of her Bud.

"I felt the same way," Joe said. When he spoke he was instantly a Texan.

Clare gave him a cursory unsmiling glance. "Do you know Wax?"

"I've never seen any of his work. Is he local?"

She resumed her study of the painting she'd considered buying. It had grown darker outside; thunder rumbled and rain began to fall on the tent.

"I think he lives in Spain now. But he's had a gallery in South Beach, oh, four or five years, since they cleaned up that area."

"I like him. He's not afraid of texture even though his vernacular is the subconscious. Kind of pricey. For me, anyhow. Saw you ride earlier. I thought your big black was getting a little squirrelly before the last grid."

"Squirrelly?" She cocked an eye at him. She had changed from custom-fitted Vogel riding boots to less formal ostrich-skin pointy-toes. Still Joe was able to look down at her. "I guess. He showed a tendency to veer when I schooled him. But he's just a big baby, really. This was his first shot in high prelims. He got all fussed after that tight triple."

"*Very* tight. Two faults on that one is no disgrace."

"Still, I didn't deliver the ride Beaner is capable of. It's only the second time I've ridden him in competition. Deatcy asked me as a favor; the job they did on her hip joint after she spilled in the Ox Ridge didn't turn out right. I'm used to hunters."

"Rocking-chair course, compared to Grand Prix."

"Right." She dropped her gaze, appraising his status as if it were an instinct she'd been born with, powerful as the need to find her mother's breast. Classic two-button blazer; striped Gap shirt open to the middle button, revealing the hand-carved miniature of an Olmec head he wore on a gold chain; Lauren khakis; dusty—but not dirty—Lucchese boots. Difficult to place him on the social scale.

"Miró used to say he painted what he saw. And what he saw were hallucinations brought on by hunger. One meal a week while he was struggling in Paris. *Harlequin's Carnival*?"

She nodded, trying to recall the painting. "I never heard that story."

"I guess I know a lot of them. Too many. I'm an art historian." He did a proper amount of fumbling for his business card. "Joe Tucker."

"You're from Austin?" Clare said, studying the card as if it were a text dense with footnotes. He sensed her shyness, a reluctance to take the next step.

Rain drummed harder on the vinyl tenting. Some people ducked inside, laughing at the deluge. He moved a step closer, isolating the two of them, proclaiming them a unit as the tent continued to fill. Her chin came up. She smiled, then touched her lower lip with a forefinger, a childlike gesture that he subsequently discovered had many meanings. Caution; a question; surrender.

"I'm Clare Malcolm," she said. "Nice to meet you, Joe."

THREE

On a dead-calm morning in the Îles des Saintes, Joe awoke sweaty and with a tingling of dread that became a clonus.

Just past sunrise. A hundred yards from where the *Dragonfly* lay at anchor in the harbor, the village of Bourg was waking up. Voices spoke the soft French Creole patois of the island. Someone whistled cheerfully ashore. He heard the familiar sounds of carts with squeaky wheels, the wooden mallet of a boatbuilder rhythmically tapping a chisel. Frigate birds cried out above the walls of Fort Napoleon. Outside the harbor, beyond the reef, he heard fishermen calling languidly to other fishermen in their orange-and-blue boats. On his own boat the chittering of tiny *sucrier* birds in the rigging underscored giggles and the voices of children sternly shushing one another. It was his first morning in Les Saintes in almost eleven months. But already he had company.

He'd been dreaming about Clare. In the dream they

were at a black-tie affair at Omaha's Joslyn Museum. But the party was somewhere behind them. They were exploring a gallery he'd never seen before. The gallery made him uneasy. There were shadowy portraits in leafy gilded frames on the velvet walls, menacing faces he couldn't quite make out. He was having difficulty swallowing. It seemed very hot to him. He was sweating buckets, but Clare didn't seem to notice. She had him by the hand and she was strong. Pulling him from one side of the gallery to the other. *"Look!"* she said. *"Look! They're all here!"* He didn't know what she meant, but he wouldn't take his eyes off the floor to find out. *"Come on, Joely!"* Clare said, manic with excitement. He had dug in his heels. He wouldn't be budged. She laughed at his stubborn expression. *"Just one more, Joely-Moly. Look at this one."* Her tone changed. *"Joely-Poly! I mean it. You have to look."* But he couldn't. He knew who it was, towering over him in a portrait three stories high, looking down at him with displeasure and contempt. He felt so awful, so guilty, he couldn't raise his eyes from the dirt floor to acknowledge her. A hot wind was blowing. *What did he do that was so wrong?* Maybe Clare could tell him. He looked up, squinting, but the sun was in his eyes. A blazing white desert sun. In the distance, a cloud of dust. Clare was walking away down the middle of the shimmering tar road. At least, he thought it was Clare. But he was terrified that it was not. Clare was the only one who had the answer: *What did I do wrong?* When he ran after her receding figure, he came to a shocking halt. His feet were mired in soft asphalt, which began to lap around his thin bare legs like a dark wave of the sea—he was screaming.

The dream-scream was only a brutal pounding in his temples when he sat up naked on the edge of the wide double berth in the *Dragonfly*'s master's cabin. He heard a scamper of bare feet along a side deck, and giggling. All of the portlights in the stateroom were open; he had slept without air-conditioning. He took several deep breaths, relishing the smell of the sea.

Thirty-two days, almost five weeks, and he was still dreaming about her. Unusual. Once he left them they didn't stay in his memory for long, not so insistently as Clare had. He had learned long ago that memory was a skilled torturer, so he'd also become adept at scouring slates when a project was over. Clare hadn't been the best-looking or the richest or the best in bed of the women he had conned in a fifteen-year career, so why should she still be hanging around where he was most vulnerable, in his sleep? He had liked her, he liked them all, but he didn't miss her. He had the feeling that something wasn't finished, where Clare Malcolm was concerned. And that worried him.

He passed a hand down the underside of the bolt-upright erection he always had on awakening, still unable to dismiss Clare from the morning round of his thoughts. She'd been the most difficult of all his lovers to seduce. Her introduction to sex, age nineteen, had been at the hands of a pathological character whose orgasms could only be achieved as the climax of a whipping. What the hell was she supposed to think? Subsequent liaisons with clumsy or incompetent lovers had turned her off completely. She decided that she was frigid, and it was a loathsome thing anyway. Who needed it?

But she had needed Joe, not that she realized or acknowledged it right away. And needing was the key to wanting, without fear or disgust. Joe wasn't a psychiatrist. But he knew a lot about intimacy; he knew about listening and touching and just being there, a reassuring, undemanding presence. No matter what inhibitions preyed on her, a healthy and vital woman's reaction to those attentions was inevitable. It was like waiting under a tree for fruit to ripen in its season. The first time they made love her nipples were hard in heat, but her stomach muscles quivered whenever he kissed or drew his fingers across a line just above her pubic triangle. An hour, another, yet she couldn't, oh she couldn't. Three hours of repeated, gentle caresses. Opening her thighs, as if they were a heavy book with pages stuck together from years of neglect. When she came, at the moment of his nudging entrance, her spasms were as great as if he'd cut her throat.

The memory made Joe smile, ruefully. His penis drooped. He wasn't interested in women or sex right now. What he wanted was coffee and a fresh baguette from Maman Arcelin's hole-in-the-wall bakery just off the harbor square. He heaved a sigh and went into the head, came out after relieving himself and brushing his teeth, looked for shorts and a T-shirt and sandals, then went topside.

Four young heads turned as he emerged from the companionway. The kids were sitting in close order on the cockpit coaming with their bare feet dangling, all of them as blond as their Brittany forebears, tanned skins still beaded with drops of water from their swim out to his boat.

"Kouman ou ye?" Joe said in his all-purpose Creole. He recognized three of the boys: Christophe, Illion, Providence. The fourth might have been a girl, seven or eight years old: someone's little sister. She had bright elliptical eyes that shone like mirrors from her excitement at being included with the guys. "Long time no see," he said in English. None of them understood him, but Illion, the oldest, repeated it with a snicker, and then they all laughed and tried saying "Long time no see."

The kids, and many others who would show up eventually while he was in Les Saintes, were his local crew, and Bourg was as close to a permanent home as he'd come. He knew everyone on the island, and more people on the sister islands of Terre-de-Bas and Marie-Galante. Cousteau probably made more of a stir when the *Calypso* was in port, but still it was nice to have a welcome.

Joe chatted with the kids for a few minutes, catching up on island gossip. They were off from school until after Fête des Saintes. His hundred-kilometer passage from Montserrat had been mostly against the wind at thirty knots, the skirts of a tropical disturbance that had stalled south of Hispaniola, and he'd taken some seas. There was a lot of cleanup to be done, and he put them all to work washing off the salt while he puttered ashore in the dinghy.

Greetings came to him everywhere, from old men repairing piles of mauve or purple netting on the quay, to the curate of the *ti' église* enjoying his breakfast after the five-thirty mass and feeding his scruffy black dog at his usual table on the narrow terrace of Le Breton. There were a few mopeds on the streets now, young Europeans on holidays scattering from the hotels to the beaches at Pain du Sucre or Anse Rodrigue before the nine-to-noon ban on the noisy scooters went into effect. In a little while the day-trippers would be arriving from Guadeloupe on the JetKat ferry, but there were never hordes of tourists on Les Saintes at any time of the year. They had a small constabulary on what was virtually a crime-free island, but Customs was nonexistent. He came and went as he pleased. He was one of them, and trusted. He played dominoes and drank with the Saintois, but never got drunk. He volunteered for community labor projects. In past years he had made generous contributions to the church and the committees of various festivals. To the small infirmary that served the island. When bacterial meningitis, spread by a sick tourist, threatened the lives of several children including Illion Arcelin, he arranged for the most critically ill to be flown to a children's hospital in San Juan for treatment. He had no business arrangements in Bourg. He did not get serious with the young, marriageable women on any of Les Saintes. He knew what everybody was up to, their indiscretions, complaints and quarrels; but he was never questioned, and volunteered nothing about his own life. In fact, he had no life he could talk about. He was an actor, whose best work would be seen by only a few people. And seldom appreciated, after the fact, by any of them. In those loneliest of times when his gut hurt and he was desperate for a sense of peace that all the sun, sailing and accommodating women could not bring him, he felt shadowless, as insubstantial as a blue-water hallucination, the bugaboo of single-handed sailors on every ocean.

Walking up the street to Maman Arcelin's, past white walls brimming with frangipani and bougainvillea, past the old street sweeper with the dented forehead named Hubert, he thought, You can stay this time. You don't have to do it anymore. He had brought back from Omaha six hundred eighty thousand in cash, from the money that Clare had arranged for the purchase of unavailable works of Western art and from the sale of her wedding gift to him, the Maserati that he unloaded six hours after leaving town, to a dealer in Kansas City. The proceeds from the dealer's cashier's check had by now washed through half a dozen offshore bank accounts. It could not be traced to Joe. The rest of the cash, in new hundred-dollar bills, had accompanied him to Puerto Rico, replacing the picture tube of a twenty-seven-inch Panasonic in its original shipping carton. His expenses for the Omaha project came to a little over twenty thousand dollars. After deducting the twenty-five-percent fee he'd paid for his false identity as Joe Tucker, he had cleared four hundred and ninety thousand dollars.

So his current net worth, counting the eight hundred thousand he had in the *Dragonfly* and its array of electronics, was—Joe shook his head as he turned into Maman Arcelin's. His net worth, after three years of small pickings while he learned his trade, and ten years of ever-more-lucrative payoffs as the breadth and audacity of his cons developed, was comparable to that of rock stars his own age. Maybe better: he had no ex-wives to settle with. And there had never been any taxes to pay to corrupt and spendthrift governments.

Money went, instead, to an orphanage in Honduras, to a public-health facility in Lagos, to a nonprofit manufacturer in Trinidad that employed the handicapped, to college scholarship funds in half a dozen countries. To books for school libraries, to church-sponsored missions for the indigent, and to those medical-research organizations he didn't feel were ripping off the public and private dollar. Employees he'd never met, in an office in Luxembourg—an office he never visited but which was devoted solely to his business and philanthropies—handled all disbursements, based on information Joe provided in his ramblings.

But he didn't have to look for projects anymore. There was enough money, suitably invested, to continue the outflow for the rest of his life. He felt a sense of good cheer at this prospect, and gave Maman Arcelin a hug that lifted her tiny frame from the floor. She had her back to him as she waited on a customer in the bakery, and she let out a whoop of indignation until she realized who it had to be.

She kissed him and scolded him in patois for being gone so long, then sat him down at a little table by the door to feed him.

"Are you married yet?"

"No, Maman."

"Are you wasting your life on frivolous things?"

"I don't think so, Maman."

"This time you will stay forever. You will settle down and marry a beautiful Saintois like Yvonne, who was very sad to celebrate her seventeenth birthday without your company."

"Yvonne must go to Paris and study hard and become a teacher, because Mme. LaRouche will keel over any day now, and then who will educate the children of Terre-de-Haut? When Yvonne comes back from Paris, that is another matter."

"In the meantime you will be discreet with the tourist women, and not break her heart. I will cook wonderful little dinners for you on your boat. Like I cook for no one else since Jacques drowned."

Her husband had been a fisherman, lost off Les Roches Percées in a before-dawn collision with what everyone assumed was a smuggler's boat from Marie-Galante—large, powerful, showing no running lights. She was a widow seven years, with Illion, age twelve, her youngest child.

"You should go to work for Yprés," Joe said, naming the proprietor of one of the best restaurants on an island noted for its cuisine. "To get up at three in the morning and bake bread is no life."

"That rascal. Why should I waste my talent making someone as lazy as Yprés a rich man?"

"With your head for business, you would own his restaurant in six months."

He passed a pleasant hour at the bakery, and the rest of the day slipped by without effort. Only in the evening, as he sat alone under the Bimini awning in the stern of the *Dragonfly* listening to *Achtung Baby* on headphones and watched the sun torch the darkening clouds to the west, did the cold feeling steal back to him: the sensation that something other than clouds was gathering on his horizon.

From their first meeting he had been wary of Donald Malcolm, a killer fruit with a mind as lethal as a spinning saw. Joe had no doubts that once he jilted Clare, Brud would come after him with everything he had. On leaving Omaha, he took extra precautions to cover his tracks. The beard came off in a Holiday Inn by the Kansas City airport; he cut his hair short and changed the color from sun-streaked brown to a reddish shade. Contact lenses darkened his normally bright blue eyes. He wore glasses with amber lenses, even at night, dressed like a European backpacker touring the States, and adopted a German accent. The documentation he'd cached months ago in a mailbox facility in KC identified him as Hans Shuler of Bremen.

He shipped his Panasonic TV by Federal Express to Puerto Rico marked HOLD FOR PICKUP and, as Shuler, flew to Oklahoma City. There he paid cash for a ticket to Denver, where he left Shuler in a Dumpster and took an early-morning flight to Charlotte, North Carolina, via Atlanta. He got off in Atlanta and bought another ticket to San Juan.

Joe changed the CD in his portable player and had another straight shot of the dark bronze *rhum, vieux* he'd been too fond of recently. He was still thinking about his recent getaway. Maybe, if he'd been super-cautious, he could've hitched rides out of Atlanta, made his way south to Miami, and from there wangled a ride on a corporate jet to San Juan. But by then he was content with his precautions and bored with a game he couldn't be certain anyone else was playing. He wasn't sure just how many islands there were in the Caribbean: well over a thousand. And more secluded anchorages than he could visit in a lifetime of sailing. A good many people with something to hide had "retired" to a life of civilized comfort and privacy in the islands. He was safe in Terre-de-Haut, and he didn't have to leave again; he had made up his mind that he wouldn't.

There were a few more ounces of rum left in the small cask, and it seemed like a good idea to finish it off. Which would give him an excuse to sail to Marie-Galante tomorrow and buy more casks of the seven-year-old rum at the distillery. After drinking alone for two weeks, he might be in the mood for a party any day now. But the prospect of a bash aboard the *Dragonfly* didn't stir his blood; he still felt jaded and vaguely unhappy. He'd invested a lot of nervous energy in the Omaha project. He still woke up at odd hours with a pounding heart, not sure that he was alone on the boat. He checked and rechecked the primary and backup alarm systems.

Always there were unattached young women staying at the small hotels and guesthouses; he could have bedded his choice of flight attendants and slightly over-the-hill runway models and footloose college kids with a minimum of effort and no expense. It was what they had saved their money and traveled south for: a single guy with a ready smile and a hell of a big boat. But none had tempted him; the idea of touching any of them prompted a chill of apathy, a tightness in his gut. He was not used to a homecoming like this one. After a project he always made some rapid rounds, burying the memory of one woman in the sun-warmed willing flesh of many others. Now he couldn't be bothered.

His birthday passed, unannounced to anyone. He was thirty-seven.

After a few days his malaise became noticeable, like a ghost that followed him doggedly to the beaches and cafés, to dinner at the homes of friends.

Yvonne Saint-Sauveur was making preparations to leave for school in Paris; she was giddy from equal parts of anticipation and dread and may have interpreted his mood as sadness that she was going away. She had never traveled beyond the island of Guadeloupe. In Paris she would live with a family whose daughter was also enrolled at the Sorbonne. She would be cared for and protected. Joe had set everything up for her through a scholarship fund he maintained. The family knew nothing about his involvement, but they knew he had been to Paris, so they were full of questions about the City of Light.

After dinner he danced with Yvonne to Zouk and Soca music on the paved patio that overlooked the rust-red roofs of the town and the harbor. She was childishly barefoot but pungently female, wearing perfume tonight, and hoop earrings. When the music from Yvonne's stereo stopped and he pretended to gasp for breath, they could hear the strains of disco from a medium-sized cruise ship anchored off the fortress headland north of Bourg.

They sat together on a low wall, looking at the constellated lights of the ship. Yvonne toyed with the gold bangle-bracelet Joe had given her as a reward for her diligence and scholastic achievement. Hers was a tough-pretty face, with high cheekbones and slanted smoky eyes, which she had painted as boldly as the eyes of an Egyptian deity.

"Will you come to Martinique to see me off?"

"Sure I will."

"Because you have a way to disappear, and not tell anyone." She pouted, then looked up at him with sharp speculation.

"Have you ever wanted to kiss me, Joe?"

"Sure," he said again, and planted one on her forehead.

Yvonne glanced swiftly at the interior of the house, but her mother and father were talking, and her brothers were watching "Star Trek: The Next Generation." Gustave Saint-Sauveur was one of the more prosperous merchants in the Îles des Saintes, and they owned a satellite dish.

Yvonne grasped Joe and kissed him back, avidly, her lips apart. In spite of his desire to be cool and correctly distant, the sneaky tip of her tongue aroused and unnerved him.

She sat back, but kept a hand on his wrist.

"I am not leaving for three more days."

"Some things are just not possible, Yvonne. I'm old enough to be your—"

She went from sensual assurance to tears in moments.

"Do you think that matters to me? I'm a woman. And I love you!"

"I love you too, Yvonne, and I want to be very proud of you."

She sniffled, examining the sugar-coated message. "What harm could it do? And we probably won't see each other again for a long time."

"Well—you'll be home for the Christmas holidays. I'll be here. And I'm not leaving Terre-de-Haut again, ever."

The message became confused. "Does that mean—?"

He patted the back of her hand. "Shh. We'll talk about it later."

In the moonlight her young face shone with the purity of one unharmed by life. She made him feel rotten.

"You'll wait for me? You won't go off for months and months, and not let me know where you are?"

"That's a promise, Yvonne."

Yvonne's friend Inez came by on her moped, distracting her. Joe escaped into the house and after a decent interval said his good nights. He walked down the hill to the harbor where he'd left his dinghy. The disco music from the small cruise ship annoyed him; so did the faint sounds of laughter that signaled good times aboard. On impulse he stripped to underwear briefs, leaving his other clothes in the dinghy, and dove in off the quay. He swam in a glum mood toward the *Dragonfly*. As he approached he reflected, dismally, on what it might be like to swim on by the sloop and out of the harbor, into the dark sea beyond. Swim until he was too depleted to lift his arm for another stroke.

That mood passed quickly, but he felt shaken by the unrealized experience as he hauled himself up the stern ladder, crouched there wet and shivering in an offshore breeze.

He had to get it back, somehow. His sense of well-being. Yvonne, the adolescent temptress, had upset him badly. Blame it on the unexpectedly knowing kiss, but it had crossed his mind to bundle her into the

double berth and give her a going-away present to remember. He was opportunistic, but always with women
who had some experience with life, some mileage on
them. He never thought of himself as callous. Could
he really have been sincere, even for a few moments,
about filling his nest with someone as tender and trusting as Yvonne? Just what the *hell* was the matter with
him?

Whatever it was, he resolved to change it. Beginning
first thing in the morning.

FOUR

She was at a table under the awning of Le Breton, well shielded from the early-afternoon sun, absorbed in a hardcover junk novel. She'd had lunch; now she was dawdling. She wore Ray-Ban sunglasses with apricot-colored lenses and her head was tilted down toward the open book, so her eyes weren't visible. But unless she turned out to be cross-eyed, she was one of the loveliest women Joe had ever seen.

When he paused by the table, standing where he cast his shadow across her, she didn't look up. The midday breeze did attractive things to her dark hair, which she wore medium-short, a waif cut. She had on a blue and white boat-neck knit shirt with a Greek key motif, matching shorts, and sandals. Her toenails were immaculately painted; apparently she didn't care for the beach. Her skin was pale for the tropics, but not an unappetizing shade of white; it had a café-au-lait luster, as if she might be one-quarter Creole. Her features, however, were too finely wrought: slender bridge to her nose, a somewhat high, intelligent forehead, full underlip but not so full as to weigh heavily above a small rounded chin. There was a cigarillo burning in an ashtray to one side of the table. She turned a page of her novel with long, shapely fingers. Her one affectation seemed to be a streetfighter's assortment of rings on both hands.

The novel was called *Savannah's Flame*, by Pamela Abelard. It looked like a bodice-ripper, but Joe seldom read any fiction. The author was also a beauty, judging from the color photo on the back of the jacket.

"Any good?" Joe said.

She looked up with a slight inquiring smile, then laid the novel carefully down and raised her sunglasses to the crown of her head. Her large eyes were a shade of violet in the intense light of day.

"Abelard's okay, as long as she sticks to simple declarative sentences. Otherwise it's the literary equivalent of riding a tricycle."

Joe ran a hand across a three-day growth of beard and grinned at her. She picked up her cigarillo and smoked, still looking up at him with a pleasant expression that didn't quite affirm an interest in his presence. She held the cigarillo like a dart thrower.

"I'm Joe," he said.

"So am I." She let that ride briefly, then added, "Josephine." She blinked a couple of times; her gaze was muted by the brightness of the sky behind him. Her smile turned a little dreamy. She lowered the sunglasses and went back to her novel.

"I'll see you tonight," Joe said.

"Oh?" she murmured. "Where?"

"There's only one place. If you don't go to the beach and you're as bored with Techno as I am. The best dinner in the Îles des Saintes, followed by a moonlight cruise."

"To?"

"Anywhere you like, as long as you like."

Josephine turned another page.

"You must be the one who owns that sloop with the tumble-home hull parked out there in the harbor."

Joe let out his breath in a low sound of admiration. "Do you sail?"

"All the time, when I was a kid. Not so much lately. Too busy earning a living."

"Seven-thirty," Joe said. "Should I meet you here?"

She thought about it. "No, in front of the church."

"The church?"

"Shouldn't I thank God for answering my prayers?" Josephine said.

She could talk boats, all right, and she understood the expensive differences between high-end production models and one that had been built to live in at sea by a designer who knew exactly what he wanted.

While Maman Arcelin prepared dinner for two in the fore-and-aft galley, Joe walked Josephine over every foot of the *Dragonfly*, then sat with her in the midships salon, showing her the notebooks in which his concepts for the *Dragonfly* had evolved over several years.

She praised his precise, clear technical drawings, and the realization of his ideas in evidence around them: the molded companionway with angled steps for safer footing when the boat was heeled, the spillproof plastic-coated wire shelving that kept his books in place, the complex jigging of trim and curved, flowing lines of joinery work, the array of electronics at the nav station, which were cleverly concealed when not in use.

When Joe left her for a few minutes to consult with Maman Arcelin about some ingredient for a sauce that should have been aboard but wasn't, the two of them conversing in a highly colloquial French, Josephine scanned his books. He had the usual sailors' bibles; dictionaries in French, English and Spanish; Vasari's *Lives of the Artists*; Emerson, Thoreau and Voltaire, among other philosophers. Books about the sea, of

course, and about music; quite a lot of scholarly soci-
ology and, surprisingly, best-seller psychology—getting
in touch with the child inside of you, and that sort of
thing. But what the hell, Josephine thought, she had a
weakness for Pamela Abelard and Danielle Steel.

His taste in art was discriminating, although there
was little space for display aboard the *Dragonfly*: she
particularly admired a figurative painting by Dieben-
korn, an early Precisionist study of a Lake George barn
by Georgia O'Keeffe, and an Agostini bronze of a galloping horse. In a hand-carved mahogany case she discovered a two-hundred-year-old *Atlantic Neptune* atlas
containing, in meticulously colored engravings, the
first accurate sea charts of the Atlantic Ocean.

Depeche Mode was on the stereo. Her taste. Josephine had brought the CD along, and also the latest
from the Juilliard and a recent recording of the Schubert C-Major String Quintet by a new group in Hei-
delberg she admired, just in case his own musical
favorites were of a kind to give her a raging headache.
Joe was amiable about programming the evening's music to accommodate her.

Josephine had revealed a few things about her own
life, and was content to ask no questions of him. Joe
was unassuming about his lifestyle. No touch of brag.
That would have bored her. Physically he was damned
impressive—the blue eyes that Abelard routinely described as "incandescent" (the author was partial to
strapping blue-eyed rogue-heroes in her novels). His
own eyes were somewhat secluded, but not secretive,
beneath a ledge of brow. A hint of mischief in them,
when he looked straight at you. Most of the time he
didn't; it was a flirtatious trick he employed, flicking
his gaze like a whip into the face of whomever he was
talking to. An actor's trick, but she liked it. Liked her
own, visceral reaction.

"Second violinist?" Joe said, as they shared appetiz-
ers of crisp fish fritters and *boudin de poisson* in the

comfortable canvas sling chairs he brought up to the foredeck. "I know about first violin, but—"

"Second violin is important too. Not everybody knows when and how to get out of the way of the first violin." She smiled serenely. "I've lived a life of seconds," she said. "Second child of a second marriage for both parents. I ran the second leg of my four-hundred-meter relay team at school, and I was salutatorian."

"How many marriages?"

She paused. "My second will be my last. She helped herself to another fritter and gracefully licked her fingertips while looking around the spacious harbor, where there were only half a dozen boats approaching the size of the *Dragonfly* riding on the nearly imperceptible swells. Lights had come on all over the hillsides of Bourg. "This is a lovely place. How long have you been coming here?"

"It's home, really."

"Do you want this last bit of sausage?"

"Help yourself."

"What a treasure she is! I can't believe the odors that are coming from that little stove in the galley."

"To Maman it's routine. All the women in the Îles des Saintes are gastronomic geniuses."

Dinner consisted of soufflé of sea-urchin eggs, grilled lobster nuggets, poached filet of grouper in a savory *court bouillon*, and curried chicken. Josephine's indigo eyes seemed to bulge a little by the time Maman Arcelin offered a plate of warm coconut cakes, an island specialty called *tourments d'amour*. They finished with cups of homegrown coffee while Maman did the dishes and departed in her small outboard-equipped skiff.

The puttering of the engine faded shoreward. The breeze that came through open portlights was delightful but cool; there was rain to the east, accompanied by lightning faint as candleglow in the mountainous clouds. Josephine drew a sweater around her shoulders and sighed.

"Ready to go sailing?" he asked her.

"You've got to be kidding! I can't budge. Besides—isn't there rain headed our way?"

"Could be. The wind's changed a couple of times in the last hour. Well, no hurry." He was completely at ease on the corner of the salon banquette opposite her. Long legs outstretched. He had slipped out of his boat shoes. She took hers off too. The soles of their feet met; toes moved over toes in a leisurely exploratory way, like blind newborns. "Maybe in the morning, then."

She stifled a yawn that surprised her. Then she surprised herself again by blushing.

"For sure. In the morning."

They looked at each other, and listened to the Schubert, and Josephine hummed softly. Their feet crossed and recrossed, comfortably.

"How about a swim?" Joe suggested. "Gets the blood going. Helps the digestion."

"I don't go in the water," she said. "For the same reason W. C. Fields wouldn't drink water."

"Oh, why not?"

"Because fish fuck in it."

Joe laughed. Then he got up, stretched and took her by the hand, pulling her up from the banquette.

"Fish don't know what they're missing, do they?" he said, and led her back to the big double berth in the master's cabin.

Rain hit the decks of the *Dragonfly*, and she rolled on the swells raised by the passing squall. Joe woke up wondering about the bite of the lee anchor. Lightning flashed above the old fort on the north headland. The starboard portlights were half open, but the rain was coming from the other side, the harbor entrance and the open sea.

It was two-thirty in the morning. Above the ham-mering of the rain he heard the engine of a JetKat, which was something he shouldn't be hearing this time of the night; the last ferry to Guadeloupe left Terre-de-Haut before sunset.

The other side of the berth was empty. He wondered if Josephine had been awakened by the rain and had gone into the aft head. He reached up and turned on the reading lamp recessed in the canopy headboard.

The light revealed her in the doorway of the master's cabin. She was dressed. She braced herself against the pitch as the JetKat diesel throbbed closer. Out of the corner of his eye Joe saw running lights; the ferry, a catamaran smaller than the *Dragonfly*, approached and hove to. There were men on the decks, vague figures in the dark and the rain. But his full attention was directed to Josephine, who was pointing a gun at him: a 9mm Glock that might have been his. He kept the automatic where she would have been able to find it without going to much trouble.

"Company's coming," she said. "Just stay put. I'm not into violence, but I had the second-highest aggre-gate in my class on the pistol range at Glynco."

"I might've guessed. Glynco? Who're you with, Josie? Treasury?"

"Not anymore," she said vaguely.

"Could I put some clothes on?"

"No. Don't move at all."

"But I'm cold."

Fenders of the JetKat rubbed against the hull of the *Dragonfly*. Feet thudded on the starboard deck. Joe shuddered. He had goose bumps Josephine probably could see from where she stood. If he was going to make a move, fight his way through the intruders and go over the side, he had to do it *now*. Even as he vi-sualized a bravura exit, he knew it wasn't possible. He was quick, but not that quick. She would probably shoot him reflexively, in self-defense.

"Let me go, Josie."

"No. It's too late."

She said it as if she might be regretting that it was too late. But she was cool, hip-braced in the doorway, both hands on the Glock. The companionway hatch was opened; Joe heard them coming below. Several men. He tried to swallow. The lights in the salon were on. Past Josie he saw dark faces. Islanders, probably. One glimpse of them and he knew with icy certainty that he wasn't going to be placed under arrest, for whatever crimes he was presumed to have committed.

Now someone else was on the companionway steps. Unused to boats, he took his time descending, reaching for handholds. Joe caught his breath again, even before he saw Donald Malcolm's bald crown and rain-streaked face. He had the look of a man stumbling into a surprise party for himself.

Joe's face set in lines of resignation, but he looked forgivingly at Josephine.

"How did you find me?"

She shook her head slightly and backed away from the cabin, flashed a look at the men behind her. Two of them were armed, and one had a walkie-talkie with him. She put the Glock down and exchanged looks with Brud. Not as if they were acquainted. His eyes were red from fatigue; obviously he'd traveled a long way from Omaha since getting the news. He stared into the master's cabin at Joe, who hadn't moved or attempted to cover himself.

"Hey there, brother Brud," Joe said in his Texas voice.

Brud stiffened slightly, then allowed himself an inquisitive smile. He looked again at Josephine, curiously and a little maliciously.

"You ought to have taken a shower. I can still smell him on you."

Josephine said with a glare, "I was told to stay close, that's all. Nobody said he was dangerous."

"Well, all right, all right." Brud patted her shoulder. "You did a fine job. I'll be sure to let Gordon Estes know I think you deserve a big bonus, honey."

"Josephine," she said, in a small deadly voice.

Brud smiled and flushed darkly at the same time. "I mean, bigger than that hunk of Polish sausage Joe's got hanging there. Now stand aside, Josephine." To the black man with the knife scar like a shadow-mouth on one cheek, Brud said, "Drag him on out here."

Joe was getting up slowly from the berth, but they didn't allow him the dignity of walking unmolested into the salon. His left wrist was twisted in a monkey-wrench grip; his right hand was forced high between his shoulder blades. He was thrown facedown on the teak sole in the middle of the salon, pinned there by a knee in the small of his back. He breathed harshly from the pain in his arm and shoulder, but said nothing.

Josephine looked away.

"I don't know what you have in mind," she said to Brud. "But I don't want any part of it. I kind of like the guy."

Brud shook his head in exasperation. "Ain't life peculiar?" he said.

He turned to another of the black men, a Rasta with reddish shoulder-length dreadlocks.

"Moss, see that Miss Josephine gets safely aboard the ferry. Drop her at dockside, and have the captain return in about twenty minutes. I want him to follow us on out to sea."

Joe raised his head slightly, looking at Josephine with a strained smile, as if not being a bad loser allowed him to retain an illusion of integrity.

"I'm going to miss you. In spite of everything."

"I know when to get out of the way." But there was something in her face, a shadow of desolation. She wasn't proud of herself. She turned abruptly from him and hurried up the companionway steps with her rat-sey bag.

"Set him down on the banquette," Brud said, when the hatch doors closed. He looked weak and mumbly around the gills, from the continued tossing of the *Dragonfly*. "Somebody see if you can find a drink on this tub."

"Liquor stores are in the galley," Joe said graciously. "Cold beer in the fridge."

"A little brandy would go down better." Brandy was brought to him. Brud gestured magnanimously. "Pour one for Joe, too. Looks like he could use it. He's shaking. You cold, or scared, Joe?"

"A little of both," Joe conceded. He was handed a crystal snifter of brandy. He was able to drink it without choking, in three swallows. The glass was taken from his hand. There were big men on either side of him, alert to his every move. He didn't look anywhere but at Brud, who fingered the antinausea patch behind one ear. In spite of it he still appeared distressed and unseaworthy when he finished his own brandy.

"Well, Joe, all things considered, I'd rather be in Omaha."

"What did that drink you just had cost you, Brud?"

Brud sighed. "When it's all toted up—has to be over a million. Gordon pays his top people two-fifty a day and expenses. We've had fifty operatives looking for you down here for better than thirty days."

"I'm not easy to find. I didn't think I left any hints behind."

"Guess again. It wasn't anything big, or obvious. I spent a few days myself, going over in my mind every conversation we had during the time you were in Omaha. Talking to others who golfed or rode with you. Of course I knew you met up with Clare in Boca Raton, so that was maybe a starting place. Texas, I never bothered with Texas. I figured you for a boat person, after what I learned from Clinton McBride. You do remember Clinton?''

"The fag Arabian trainer?"

"That's right," Brud said, colder now. "He said you had the habit of playing with a length of rope in your hands when you were around the paddock. Tying and untying that rope while you talked. And he was pretty sure what you were tying were sailor's knots."

Joe looked down at his hands, which gripped the insides of his thighs with his testicles plumped up between the knuckles.

"We knew you'd change your appearance once you left Omaha. Not much use trying to trace you with a photo. Instead I wondered just what you'd do with all that cash. Now, six hundred thousand in one-hundred-dollar bills fresh from the Federal Reserve makes quite a package. Somebody worked it out for me: that's six thousand bills, weighing about thirteen pounds. The package would be as thick as half a dozen bricks stacked together. You don't go into a U.S. bank and drop that much cash on them, not if you're interested in avoiding quick attention from the Feds. You can't carry more than five thousand through airport security because of the implant strips they put in Federal Reserve notes. My hunch was you sent the money ahead, to the Caymans or the Bahamas. But there's always a chance the customs people will intercept that much cash coming into their countries. You probably had a working arrangement with a bank somewhere in the Caribbean, though. The problem being delivery, not acceptance."

The rain and wind seemed to be slackening. Joe heard the diesel of the JetKat winding up as the ferry turned away from the side of the *Dragonfly* and headed toward shore.

"I figured that if you shipped the cash, it was to one of two places where the package wasn't likely to be inspected on arrival. Of course there's always ways you can fool the noses of those dogs trained to sniff out money. Okay, we'll say the money went to Puerto Rico or the U.S. Virgin Islands, where it would be no trouble for you to stow it on a sailboat like this one and distribute it at your leisure to numbered accounts scattered all over the Caribbean. How am I doing so far?"

"I follow you, Brud."

"It was a given that where the money went, Joe would go. Puerto Rico, St. Thomas, maybe St. Croix. If you owned a boat and you sailed those waters, somebody around the marinas would know you. Right again. And the boat was the *Dragonfly*. Once we had that much knowledge, finding you was a matter of showing your photograph, with and without the beard, in a lot of ports. Our girl Josephine spotted you yesterday, living like a prince of a minor paradise. By now I don't suppose there's much of Clare's money left on board."

"I keep enough cash on hand for thirty days' expenses, that's all. You'd have to tear the *Dragonfly* down to the waterline to find that."

"Don't intend to go to all that trouble. I'll just take back what you've stashed in the bank, and we'll call us even, moneywise."

Joe looked up at him. "Here's the way it works, Brud. The account codes are changed every day, by either of two lawyers in the firm that represents me in Luxembourg. If I want to make a substantial withdrawal or shift some money around, I make a collect call to a number where my voice is compared by a computer to the voiceprint on record. When they're sure they know who they're talking to, they send a fax to a designated bank in the islands. It could be here, or in Martinique, or a dozen other places. Wherever it is, I'll be waiting. Alone. When my physical description is verified, the information in the fax is turned over to me. The fax contains account information that is only valid in conjunction with the daily code. Then, while

I'm sitting in a private office in that bank, the transaction is completed with my bank in Luxembourg.''

Brud winced. ''Jesus, you must have a hell of a lot to protect.''

''That's right, I do, Brud.''

''Well, then, I'm hoping you'll just do the honorable thing, and turn that money back to me voluntarily.''

''We don't really have the time, do we? I mean, it's less than four hours to daylight. And I'm pretty sure you don't intend to let me live that long.''

Brud glanced at the impassive faces of the black men, who didn't shift their attention away from Joe. None of them had any questions, but Brud acted chagrined.

''Now, I honestly don't know what you take me for, Joe. A murderer? I suppose I shouldn't be surprised, hearing that from someone like you—an individual with no moral sense whatsoever. A common thief, a—''

''Save it, Brud. I don't steal money. They get what they want from me, I get what I want from them. They can afford it. And I earn every dollar.''

''Listen to you!'' His eyes had turned a deeper red, from more than fatigue; there was a vein acrawl in the hollow of one temple. ''I wonder just how many women there were before Clare, innocent and unsuspecting—''

''I was what Clare had been wanting, and needing, all her life. You saw the change in her. Maybe that's what you resent most about me.''

Brud trembled. ''You tortured my sister! She—she tried to kill herself, Joe!''

Unexpectedly he began to cry, hunching his shoulders; his face flushed with the effort to control his grief. The black men glanced at him, and looked away stonily.

''I don't know why—you didn't have the decency— to stay and marry her. Whatever you got away with—

you could've had more. *Much* more. All you had to do was—marry Clare, go on pretending you cared about her. But you—snuck away. You were so despicable. She couldn't—she just couldn't face anybody. God—how you must hate women!"

Joe drew an unsteady breath, still in shock from what he'd been told about Clare.

"Hate women? I love them."

Brud moved closer to Joe, close enough to touch him. He was still trembling, although the crying had stopped.

"I think you are the most pathetic, contemptible individual I have ever met in my life. It disgusts me to be in your presence. Now you hear me! Nobody—nobody who could do what you did to my sister has any love in him!"

Brud leaned over as if spellbound in his wrath, staring into Joe's eyes. Then Brud savagely kissed him on the mouth. Joe tensed but didn't resist, even when his lower lip was bitten.

When Brud had finished, as he was turning away, Joe said softly, "There were times when I wondered if I got engaged to the wrong Malcolm."

Brud spat on the cabin sole and said, "Tie his hands, but not his feet. You know what I want done. Take him in that stateroom back there. And shut the door."

"You don't want to watch, boss?" one of the black men said.

"No. Just make sure I hear him. I want it to last, and I want it good and God-damned loud."

FIVE

*The brief storm blew itself out and the sea was calmer, al-*though some clouds remained through which the horn of the moon and the closer planets burned mistily from time to time. Kneeling on her bed in front of a jalousied window, Yvonne Saint-Sauveur devoutly watched, through binoculars, the *Dragonfly*.

Since the sloop's return to Terre-de-Haut, her surveillance had been a nightly diversion, then a ruling passion after Joe's visit to her home. Yvonne had been nearly sleepless for the past two nights, sinking into a nervous doze when the emotional pangs of her vigil exhausted her. Awakening with a start, a dry mouth, a wet brow. Her short womanly nightgown, ordered before Christmas from the Victoria's Secret catalogue, sticking to her sensitive nipples. Bolting up to snatch the binoculars. Convinced by the pounding of her heart that he had at last come on deck in loneliness and desire to signal her in the dark.

*Yvonne, I know you're watching. I was mistaken. I want
you now. I can't wait any longer.*

She was familiar with the belowdecks layout of the
Dragonfly; she knew every inch of the master's cabin in
which he slept. A few years ago, before puberty, she
had been a regular member of Joe's in-port crew. She
knew which toothpaste he favored, his preference in
aftershave. No one else in the juvenile crew had been
allowed in his galley. And once—the memory was sacred, she had never told anyone but her best friend,
Inez—Joe had allowed Yvonne to trim the unkempt
beard he had returned with after a weeks-long cruise.

Despite her ravenous love for Joe, which at times she
was helpless to deal with, Yvonne understood his reluctance to marry her—although by island standards
she had been of marriageable age for at least three
years. He had traveled the world. Joe wanted her to
know as much about art and literature as he did, so
they would always have interesting things to talk about.
At seventeen she could cook nearly as well as her
mother. There had been some close calls with boys her
own age, but currently she was a virgin; in spite of that
apparent handicap she had no doubts that she would
make love to Joe better than any woman he had
known. No other man would ever turn her head. In
addition to her fanatical loyalty, she had brains. She
would never disgrace him.

At the moment, although Yvonne had been keeping
watch since before midnight, through all the rain that
sometimes obscured the lights aboard, Joe was nowhere in sight. The JetKat that had appeared in the
harbor twenty minutes ago and tied up alongside the
Dragonfly was now idling beside the quay. Yvonne had
watched a woman disembark and hurry off by herself
toward the small business district of Bourg. Maybe it
was the woman he'd had dinner with. Yvonne had bitten her tongue in outrage when she saw the two of
them at dusk on the foredeck of the *Dragonfly*. After

seething for an hour, she rationalized the woman's presence there. She was a friend of Joe's from the States; or a relative, perhaps. She was not staying the night, a fact that lifted Yvonne's spirits even as she wondered about the appearance of the ferry from Guadeloupe at a late, unscheduled hour.

After a few moments her thoughts returned obsessively to the plan she'd been contriving for days: her best opportunity to seduce Joe before her imminent departure for Paris. Because she was not going to step aboard the Air France jet without having first sealed their implied betrothal.

Yvonne had nerved herself to do it tonight, then had lost both nerve and heart upon seeing that he had a guest for dinner. But the woman was gone; Joe was, as far as Yvonne knew, alone on the *Dragonfly*. It was two-thirty-five in the morning. Sunday morning. The fishermen of Bourg, including her older brother Abel, would not be setting out as usual at four o'clock to net the day's catch for the restaurants they supplied. Through the binoculars she saw a man in the small wheelhouse of the ferryboat that idled beside the quay, but no one else was around at this hour. Abel's twenty-foot Saintois fishing boat was available to her. She could row unnoticed to the *Dragonfly* and tie up at the stern. What would Joe say? He would be surprised. He might pretend to be annoyed—Yvonne smiled. She knew better.

She was not deserving of his love if she didn't have the courage to claim it.

Yvonne put the binoculars down. She felt lightheaded, feverish, but charged with energy. She stripped off the filmy nightgown and put on a turquoise-and-pink jumpsuit, took a little time for lip gloss and the right, jaunty costume earrings.

Night wind stirred the flamboyants along the street, cleared the sky and blew the stars to brilliance like embers on a hearth. Schwarzenegger, the family's black

Labrador, appeared as she let herself through thej gate in front of the red-roofed house. Rather than risk having him bark at her if she tried to make him stay, Yvonne ignored the dog. Schwarzenegger trotted briskly beside her as she jogged down the hill to the cove where her brother's boat was beached at night.

There were twenty boats in the little cove south of the quay. Most of them were equipped with outboards, but none of the boats were chained to the palm trees a few feet away. Theft was rare on Terre-de-Haut. Communal nets were hung up to dry like big spiderwebs among the trees. Schwarzenegger went nose-down along the shoreline, coursing after fiddler crabs, which were hard to catch; they disappeared into the wet packed sand like henchmen tunneling to a bank.

Still ignoring him, Yvonne pushed Abel's orange-and-blue boat backward off the blocks and into shallow water. As she did so, she heard a change in the pitch of the JetKat's engine, and the ferry pulled slowly from the quay two hundred yards to the north, drifted abeam momentarily, then turned and headed toward the mouth of the harbor. Watching the ferry, she saw out of the corner of her eye that the *Dragonfly* was also under way, on its auxiliary engine. Joe was in the cockpit—or was it him? For a few moments she was unsure. But she had sharp eyes, and when she focused between cupped hands she saw that the man at the helm of the *Dragonfly* was broad and heavy, almost fat; the shape of his head was wrong too.

For several seconds she stood barefoot in shallow water holding the boat in place with her hands on the bow gunwale, confused, then annoyed at seeing her plans for the rest of the night thwarted. And then with a change in her heartbeat came a stiffening of fear: it occurred to Yvonne that someone was stealing the *Dragonfly*.

Another moment, and her fear sharpened.

Where was Joe?

The wake from the two boats making for the open sea sloshed above her knees as she stood there, chilly at the nape of the neck, soul-paralyzed. What was happening? Piracy was the worst crime in all the islands. The *Dragonfly*, according to her father, was worth nearly a million dollars. But that didn't matter to Yvonne. She pictured Joe aboard, bludgeoned and bound, helpless. If they were taking his sloop, what would they do with him once they cleared the harbor?

Yvonne trembled; then she gave an all-out push and leaped into the fishing boat as it glided into deeper water. No thought of rowing stealthily to a rendezvous now. She scrambled back to the stern, skinning one shin on the edge of a seat in her haste. The pain made her hold her breath as she tipped the outboard engine upright and pushed the starter button. The thirty-horsepower motor caught with no hesitation.

Yvonne pointed the bow after the two larger boats that were now nearly side-by-side as they left the harbor. Running lights on the JetKat, but the *Dragonfly* was dark topside. Only the portlights illuminated the water creaming away from the hull as both boats picked up speed.

Flustered, but not knowing what else to do, Yvonne continued on a course that kept her well astern of the *Dragonfly*, far enough back so that the helmsman would not hear the muted Mercury outboard on the transom of the fishing boat. She had been going to sea in boats like this one since before she was able to walk. The dark swells beyond the harbor were moderate, occasionally capped, nothing she gave a thought to. The breeze was from the east, eight to ten knots.

When the lights of Bourg fell behind their little flotilla and they cleared the half-mile-long chunk of rock called Cabrit offshore, the heading seemed to indicate they were bound for the much larger island of Guadeloupe, twenty minutes away to the north, where the nimbus of Basse-Terre was plainly visible. Three or four kilometers to port, a lighter was steaming south in the Windward shipping lanes. The wind whipped her hair across both cheeks; she had tears in her eyes. She was frightened now, crouched on the stern seat, all but frozen to the outboard's tiller.

Since the age of twelve she had attended the Catholic school in Basse-Terre, where there was a population of twenty thousand. In Paris there would be millions of people, all strangers. She would be lost there, lost without him. Didn't he realize that?

"Joe!" But she only whispered his name, afraid of being heard above the sounds of the diesel engines in the cat and the *Dragonfly*. There was no moon track on the water at this hour; her own humble boat would be difficult to make out as she followed in their wakes.

Then the two larger boats slowed, and the JetKat closed to starboard. Yvonne cut back the engine of the outboard to near-idle. The ferry and the sloop were dead in the water nearly a kilometer away, side by side. She wished she had her binoculars. By the running lights of the JetKat she saw men leaving the *Dragonfly*. Four in all, including the helmsman. She couldn't tell at the distance if Joe was among them. Intuition told her he was not.

Well, then, maybe it wasn't—

The JetKat pulled away, heading at full throttle for Basse-Terre. The *Dragonfly* seemed to wallow rather heavily in the ferry's wake. Yvonne stayed where she was, staring at the sloop. There were no sails showing, not even a jib. The *Dragonfly* acted rudderless, drifting slowly westward, heeling laboriously.

Once it was difficult to make out the receding lights of the ferry, Yvonne went full-throttle toward the *Dragonfly*, and caught up with it in a couple of minutes. The sloop was still wallowing, much lower in the water than it should have been. The slopping of the wake from her own small boat nearly spilled across the foredeck.

She bumped the port side aft and shipped the outboard, reached up desperately for a grabrail on the *Dragonfly*, hung on while she pulled herself forward and found the cleated tie rope on the bow of the fishing boat. She snubbed the rope to a cleat on the side deck of the *Dragonfly* and jumped aboard. She shouted for Joe through an open portlight of the cabin.

The sloop had settled a few more inches since her approach. With each roll of the decks, she took on seas. The cockpit pumps weren't working. The hatch doors stood open. She knew the *Dragonfly* was in danger of going down.

Yvonne scrambled down the companionway to the salon. The lights were on. Water sloshed across the teak sole. No way to tell where it was coming from. She screamed for Joe, hesitated, then made her way back through the galley to the master's cabin. As she passed through the galley she smelled propane but didn't stop to check the source. She was sickeningly aware that the boat had been thoroughly sabotaged. They had breached the hull somewhere. The men who had abandoned the *Dragonfly* wanted her to sink.

And they had left Joe aboard to sink along with the *Dragonfly*.

She threw open the door to the master's cabin. He wasn't inside.

"Joe!"

A faint, human sound came from the head to her left. Yvonne leaned her slender body against the door, which budged only an inch. She tried to brace herself on the waterlogged sole, straining to open the door against whatever blocked it from the inside. She was wiry, strong for her size. The door yielded, and a hand caked with blood fell palm-up into view.

With one hip wedged against the door so it wouldn't close again, Yvonne knelt and grabbed his gory hand, pulling at him.

"Get up! We're sinking! Get up, Joe!"

She heard him groaning. His hand tightened on hers, loosened. He pulled it away. She heard his efforts to sit up inside. This time he stifled a scream. She was able to force the door open and look inside at his nodding head, at his face, or what was left of it. Joe was almost unrecognizable. Blood everywhere, in his hair, in the matting on his chest.

He was naked. Her heart seemed to stop for a couple of moments; then a leaden calm possessed her. She made herself reach into the water and feel his groin; but he was still intact there.

Then nothing else really mattered, except to get him off the doomed *Dragonfly* and into a hospital.

Yvonne wormed her way inside the head, got an arm around Joe, gripped one wrist, tried to lift him. His eyes were closed. Fresh blood bubbled on his lower lip. He was ice-cold, slippery as a gutted fish, and breathing badly, as if his lungs were shot through with rib bones, like the swords in a magician's cabinet.

"You have to help me," she said, still with the nerve and self-possession that had seen her through other crises: her father's heart attack, her friend David's moped accident when they were thirteen. "You must get up. Otherwise we will both drown, because I will never leave you."

Joe looked at her with the eye that would open, although it couldn't open all the way. Then, incredibly, he smiled, revealing blood-clotted and broken teeth. But his voice was a strangled whisper, the words in English. She knew some English, but could understand only one word of what he was trying to say.

"Angel."

Yvonne began to sob, and was instantly angry. Someday she would kill every one of them, the men who had beaten him. It was her duty. As she made her vow, her limited strength was increased by the size of her anger, and with some effort on Joe's part she heaved him to his feet. Together they stumbled through the swirling knee-deep water toward the companionway. She steeled herself not to hear his screams, and kept them moving.

She had to shove Joe up the steps, laboring furiously behind and below him. They would sink, she thought, in one convulsive gulp the sea would swallow them before they could reach the bobbing boat tied to the wounded *Dragonfly*.

In his nakedness he was too slippery to get a grip on, to move him, even by inches, when he faltered. She found rope in a cockpit compartment and tied it round him, tied his wrists together. She dragged Joe over the coaming into waves breaking over the stern. Maybe she was killing him, had killed him already. He appeared to be unconscious. And she was nearly exhausted, snorting through her mouth, shuddering from effort.

But the fishing boat was still there, snubbed to the *Dragonfly* and in danger of going down with it. The *Dragonfly* was heeled permanently to port, so she simply rolled Joe over the grab rail and into the boat.

Nothing left to do but untie the lines and push off with one foot, tilt the outboard upright. The engine failed the first time; Yvonne groaned. Then it caught, and she pushed the throttle lever hard right. The bow jumped out of the water and they bounced away from the sinking sloop.

Joe lay facedown across two seats, his hands still lashed together. He looked like a drowned man. When she was a hundred yards abeam of the *Dragonfly*, Yvonne throttled down and opened a locker, looking for the fisherman's sweater her brother wore on chilly predawn mornings, a dry pair of denims.

With a prayer to her patron saint on her lips, Yvonne paused to look back at the *Dragonfly*. Oddly enough, lights still shone aboard, although she was down to the gunwales in the sea. Then it seemed to her as if a bright brassy sun was rising from the interior of the scuttled sloop, which disappeared in a seething cloud. There was a concussion she felt more than heard as she stood up in the stern, staring at the conflagration that spread across the water toward her quicker than she could draw a breath.

From the darkening cloud something huge and glowing materialized, writhing madly in the air like a fiery ghost: Dacron ejected from a sail locker as if it were the mouth of a cannon, and instantly ignited in the superheated, hurricane wind from the explosion. It was burning to pieces even as it passed over the fishing boat, and part of the falling sail engulfed Yvonne like a flaming shroud.

Yvonne screamed, swallowing fire and charring her lungs. She toppled overboard in a sizzle of sparks. Beneath the water she fought free of the burned sail and broke the surface frantically; but her lungs were closed and she could no longer draw a breath. The fishing boat drifted a dozen feet away. She flailed with seared arms, attempting to swim. She had a last glimpse of Joe in the diminishing light; then her eyes closed. The sea took her down.

SIX

*The slight rocking of the boat on the open sea; calm of mid-*day. The sun.

He was not conscious enough to know where he was, or why his hands seemed to be bound. Or why he should feel such terrible pain at every motion of the drifting boat. Better not to think about it: where he might be going, how long it would take him to get there. Try to ignore the power of the sun and his sear-ing thirst, and sleep . . .

"Joe?"

No need to open his eyes, to acknowledge her. But he'd dozed and lost track of where they were. Maybe they were coming to a town, some place where they had a Dairy Queen.

Big for his age. His eyes were above the level of the windowsill in the car, his face turned away from her. He peeked. It was the same old dry, baking landscape. Barren mountains that didn't seem to be any closer

than the last time he'd looked. Hot wind poured into
the car. His lips were so dry they had been bleeding
for two days. The air conditioner didn't work anymore.
And it had been a long time between drinks of water.
You're going to love California. Not if it was like this.

"I wish you'd wake up," his mother said, the note
of complaint in her voice. She'd never been a com-
plainer, before this trip. "I can't get anything worth
listening to on the damn radio. Talk to me and keep
me company. This is no fun for me either, Joely-Poly."

He was scrunched against the door in the front seat
of the Studebaker, and when she spoke he shut his eyes
tightly, out of pique. No, he wasn't going to talk to
her, because it was her fault they had to be moving
again.

When he thought about leaving New Orleans, he
nearly convulsed from unhappiness. He forced himself
to be very still in his corner of the front seat, clenching
his hands between his knees.

She'd been bad again, he knew that much. The po-
licemen never came to the house on Dauphine Street
unless she'd done something real bad.

This time there were two of them, and there was a
police car parked half on the sidewalk in front of the
little frame house in Vieux Carré. He saw them when
he turned the corner from Ursuline Street with Tante
Berthe, who had taken him this Sunday morning to
the Farmer's Market for beignettes and strips of fresh-
cut sugarcane. Tante Berthe wasn't a relative; it was
what she'd asked him to call her. She owned the house
where he and his mother lived, in two rooms on the
second floor.

Joe pulled free of Tante Berthe's hand and ran calling to his mother, who looked around with a distracted
smile. She was wearing her black leather pirate's vest
with a rope of pearls, a short black skirt and parrot-
green high heels. There were crumbs of mascara on
the tips of her eyelashes.

"It's okay, Joe," she said, holding him and touching a fingertip to the sticky corners of his mouth. "They just want to talk to me. I'll be back in a little while."

But she was nervous, pale and snatched from sleep. He looked at the faces of the two cops. There was nothing likable in one of the faces—it was florid, mean, indifferent. But the younger of the two smiled at him.

"Your name's Joe? Do you go to school?"

"He finished the first grade at Saint Philip's," his mother said, and held him tightly, as if she felt confused by the morning light, punished by the sun. The rapid beating of her heart made him anxious. The last time police had come to the house, she'd been gone for three days. "He's the best reader in the class," his mother went on. "But he could read before he started school. I taught him myself."

"Let's go," the older cop said.

"I don't have anything to say! I told you. I didn't even *know* the guy." She seemed to be making a last-second pitch for clemency, as if Joe's presence somehow might prompt in them a change of heart.

"I guess you didn't know a lot of them," the older cop said, with a sour smug twist to his mouth. "But this one's dead. Okay, do I bring out the bracelets?"

His mother shook her head quickly. "Shit," she said, almost inaudibly, "there's a little *boy* here." Then she whispered in Joe's ear, "You stay with Tante Berthe, and I promise I'll be home by suppertime."

Joe nodded. She smelled this morning of spritzed cologne, sleep-sweats, the pomade she used on her blond duck's-butt haircut. There was a peachy bruise on the side of her throat he hadn't noticed before. He usually didn't see much of her in the daytime. She worked all night, at a place on Bourbon Street. He'd walked by it and had been both curious and repelled by odors that came from the dim interior, that were repeated in her hair and on the clothing she left strewn around the bathroom floor: sweet and sour, like crushed fruit and gin; stale and salty, like old cigars.

She let him go. Joe's throat was closing. He touched the delicately drawn, blue-and-green dragonfly tattoo on her right shoulder. She had often claimed that touching it would bring him luck, but nothing so far. Then he stepped back into Tante Berthe's protective embrace. Her thin fingers were always cold, even in the swampish heat of Louisiana June. She said something in French to the older cop, who shrugged. The doors of the police car closed, and his mother, knees together, hands locked in her lap, twisted around to look at him wanly as she was driven away.

Tante Berthe was still muttering in French; he looked up at her.

"Don't worry, you," the old woman said. "They make big mistake about you mama. I know her for a good woman, she. You come on in my house, help me clean out them parrot cage this morning. Give you a quarter, yes." Both of her hands were on his head, fingers moving slowly through his hair, which was as short and bristly as the fuzz on a caterpillar. She might have been reading his fortune from the contours of his skull. The back of his neck prickled, which felt good. Tante Berthe read his bones, she read tea leaves, she read the strange-looking old cards with hanged men and royalty on them, like the royalty on the floats of Mardi Gras. She dipped snuff and kept parrots who talked back to her and made Joe laugh, and she did him small kindnesses his mother had little time for, in spite of her good intentions.

For once true to her word, his mother was home by suppertime. She looked drawn, distressed. She said the cyst in her ovary was acting up. He didn't know what she meant by that, guessing when she pointed to where it hurt that it was probably like a stomach ache. His mother took him out to eat. They had po'boys at the Express, half a block from the cathedral on Jackson Square. She barely touched her sandwich, or sat with him for very long at the sidewalk table; she was busy making phone calls. After the last phone call she smoked a cigarette and sat looking at him with a tense smile.

"We have to leave," she said finally.

"You didn't finish your po'boy."

She shoved the neglected fried-oyster sandwich across the tin table.

"You eat it. Want another soda?"

"No'm." Joe smiled at one of the street artists he knew, who saluted him as he walked by with his folded easel and paint box. Pigeons waddled along the curb of the cobbled street, alert for crumbs, their eyes like coals in the long shadows of a summer evening.

"I mean, we have to leave New Orleans."

He sat there, with a lump of oyster in his throat that wouldn't go down, and heard the hoot of a tourist sternwheeler on the river, which was uphill behind the levee on one side of the square. He loved New Orleans and loved his school. He loved his mother, even when she disappointed him.

"What for?" he said, after he swallowed the oyster with some Coke.

"Well—I may have a chance to be in the movies, like in California. Hollywood. You know."

"Don't you like working here?"

"Yeah. It's okay. I mean, it beats hell out of Buffalo. Remember all that snow?"

He did. Vaguely.

"I don't want to go to California."

"Joely—it's kind of a question of—self-preservation."

"What?" His face began to hurt from the strain of not showing how much he wanted to cry. "Did you— do something bad here?"

"Oh, Joely. Now look, I didn't do nothing! That's a promise. But I—may have stepped in something, like,

by accident, and there are these people who don't believe me."

"The police?"

"Yeah, them. But some other guys too, strictly low-
lifes. I had—something to do with one of them once."
She made a bitter face. "You wouldn't remember him.
His nickname's 'Checkout' and believe me there's a
good reason why they call him— The fact is, I hear
the guy's making noises about me. Like I don't know
how to keep shut about stuff even when, I swear to the
Lord Jesus—" She crossed herself. "—I don't know
anything to talk about! It's all a big mistake, but this
guy—he could definitely hurt me, just to be mean.
Which you don't ever want to happen to your mom,
right?"

"No'm." Then the tears started rolling. He wiped
them away, leaving grease tracks on his cheeks.

"You know, you'll *like* California. There's this guy,
he lives right on the beach. Redondo Beach, I think
it's called. He says I should come out, that I'm wasting
time in New Orleans when I could get into the movies." She leaned toward him with a determined, win-
some smile. "He could help me out, Joely. He drives
movie stars around. He could introduce me to Debbie
Reynolds. He *knows* her personally. Wouldn't that be
terrific?"

Terrific or not, she didn't solicit his opinion again.
They were packed up and on their way within three
hours, his mother driving all night deep into Texas, as
if she was anxious to put New Orleans well behind
them.

At every stop she left him for a few minutes to make
phone calls, thin and tall and leaning like a mantis in
a jar inside the phone booths at the lighted peripheries
of gas stations, holding her free hand over one ear,
staring out at the whizzing headlights of traffic on the
Interstate, turning her back and lowering her head
whenever a car approached the station. He ate fruit

and cookies packed for him by Tante Berthe, and had diarrhea twice by the side of the road until his mother gave up and rented them a motel room. There was a thunderstorm before dawn, the glare of lightning through venetian blinds. His mother tossed in her panties and bra on top of one of the narrow beds, moaning in her sleep.

In the morning his bowels had dried up, so his mother let him have pancakes for breakfast. She was tired and uncommunicative in the café across the street from the motel. She drank black coffee and ate Tums, but her stomach still hurt her, he could tell. It was the sips that she was always complaining about.

The men in the café all wore Levi's and cowboy boots, and kept their straw rancher hats on while they ate at the counter. A couple of them would look from time to time at his mother. She never looked back, just picked at some flaking polish on a couple of her nails.

"I don't know," she said, gazing out the window at the wide street at the tag end of the small Texas town, "maybe we should've gone home to Buffalo instead." There were two mud-splattered cattle trucks parked in front of the café. Joe could see the tufted white muzzles of steers pressed against the slats that made up the sides of the trucks. A fly buzzed their table. He tried to bring it down by spitting milk through a soda straw. Usually he got a stinging slap on the back of his hand for such behavior, but his mother was oblivious this morning.

"Is Daddy back yet?" he asked, feeling as if another fly was buzzing in his heart.

She said impatiently, "Joe, I have told you too many times already. Your daddy took off two weeks after you were born, and hasn't been heard of since."

"Well, maybe he's back there, how do you know he's not?" The buzzing had turned to sharp little stings. He felt short of breath, as he almost always did when he dared to bring up the matter of a father he'd never known. His mouth turned down. He bent his straw into a pretzel shape.

"Take my word for it."

"Wasn't he a nice man?"

"Joe, look at me." She had to say it again, until his eyes rose reluctantly. "Your father was a very nice man. I wouldn't never say a word against him. But he—couldn't stand any kind of obligation. I know you don't know what I mean by that. I can't explain it any better. That's just the way people are sometimes. Let me tell you—wherever he is, Pete don't know what he's missing, having a smart, good-looking little boy like you."

"Pete," Joe said, hearing the penned-up lowing of cattle in the trucks outside the restaurant. He wondered where they were taking the cattle. He wondered if he would ever see anybody he knew from school again. And if his grandmother in Buffalo would know where to send her Christmas card and the five-dollar check for him which his mother had cashed at the bar on Bourbon Street where she used to work. He still had three dollars left from last Christmas, plus quarters Tante Berthe had given him when she was in the mood. He was thrifty. When he got older he would go and find his father and give Pete all the money he had saved to stay with them and never go away again. Joe was six years old, but already he understood that you had to have money so that people would do what you wanted them to do.

"Gila Bend," Joe said, reading the name of the town from the gas-station map. He pronounced "Gila" with a hard *g*. He had made up with his mother because he never could stay mad about anything for very long.

"How far? Look at the little numbers between that last excuse for a town we came through, and Gila Bend."

"Okay. There's a three and a two."

"Thirty-two miles. Are you squinting? I hope you don't need glasses."

"Something's in my *eye*. I wish we could close the windows."

"We'd roast, boil and bake."

"Can't we get the air disher fixed?"

"Maybe. Anyway, we'll stop in Gila Bend for a cold drink and a sandwich, and I'll make a phone call. It's *air con-dition-er.*"

"That's what I said," Joe muttered, rubbing both eyes. "Who are you calling all the time?"

"Just people I know. I've been trying for two days to get hold of Keg. He's the one I told you about, in Redondo Beach."

"What's he like?"

"Keg? Well, he played two years for the Saints. Isn't that something?"

"I don't know. We don't have to stay with him, do we?"

"Maybe for a couple of weeks, until I get on my feet and find a job."

"In the movies?"

"Yeah, in the movies. Or maybe, like, I might have to wait tables for a while until the movie thing happens. We'll see. Stop rubbing your eye, you'll just make it worse. Blink a lot and make tears, wash the grit out."

He sat on his hands and for the most part kept his eyes closed until they reached Gila Bend. What he saw when they got there wasn't impressive. They stopped at a garage that looked busy. Next to the garage a man with long black hair who looked like an Indian to Joe was throwing old tires into the back of a pickup truck. His mother parked their red-and-black Studebaker beside the café and stared bleakly at the garage while Joe stared at the first real Indian he'd seen.

"What's the matter?" Joe asked her. "Are you going to get the air disher fixed?"

"Later," she said. "Let's grab a bite first."

The café was big and crowded. Their waitress was a
skinny girl with lively eyes and large uneven teeth in a
small mouth. She smiled at Joe and said, "Hi, handsome. Where did you come from today?"

Joe ducked his head. His mother said, "We're from
New Orleans. How about a couple of cheeseburgers,
that sound good, Joe? He wants a chocolate shake,
would you bring it right away, and I'll have a Coke.
Can I buy some aspirin here?"

"Sure thing. Up front where you pay. I always take
the Goody's Headache Powder myself. In fact I'm
gonna take me a couple soon as I get to the kitchen,
my feet are sufferin' like sin. How do you want those
burgers?"

After the waitress left their booth his mother got up,
slowly.

"You stay put till I get back. I need to use the telephone too."

"Does your sips hurt?" he asked, studying her wan
face.

"Not so bad. But all the driving's hard on my back."

When his milkshake came he drank it slowly, without
a straw; the cool foam felt good on his parched lips.
By the time he reached the bottom of the tulip-shaped
glass the burgers were on the table, but his mother
hadn't come back. He ate most of the potato chips on
his plate, then started in on the cheeseburger, looking
up every few seconds.

His mother was a long time returning. When she sat
opposite Joe she had an expression he'd never seen
before. Close to tears, defeated.

"Guess we won't be going to California," she muttered, opening a package of headache powder and stirring it into her tepid Coke. She glanced at Joe for a
response. "Keg said—well, it doesn't matter. I'm just
too hot for anybody right now. Shit, how did this *happen* to me?"

"Not supposed to say—"

"I know, bad word." She did the familiar panto-
mime. "We'll put it in the 'sorry' box and leave it for
the garbage man."

She put her face in her hands, hiding from the sight
of a newly devastated life. When she looked bleakly at
him again Joe said, "Where're we going to go, then?"

"There's probably lots of places he can't find me,
so—"

"Who?"

His mother looked through him. "Or maybe he can.
No. I can manage it. Make sure it's safe, then I—" She
refocused. Her face squinched from grief for a few moments; then she smiled. "Ketchup on your chin, Joely-
Moly." Without waiting for him to react, she dabbed a
twist of paper napkin in her water glass and reached
across the table to clean him. "You'll be all right," she
said, speaking more to herself than to Joe. "Nothing's
gonna hurt you." She nodded emphatically, seeming
on the edge of her control again. "Nothing."

"Oh, is something wrong with your cheeseburger?"
the waitress asked.

Joe's mother looked up. "No, I—my appetite's just
gone away. Must be the heat."

"I sure can sympathize." She looked approvingly at
Joe's plate. "*You* can put it away, Joe. How about a
piece of homemade pie to top off that burger?"

His mother spoke up for him. "He likes cake."

"Me too. We got applesauce cake, chocolate layer
cake—"

"He loves chocolate."

"You don't say! We must be distant cousins or something, right, handsome? I'm one of those, you know,
chocoholics myself. One big piece of chocolate cake
coming up. And I'll just take that cheeseburger off
your bill, ma'am."

"Thank you." She smiled at the waitress. "People
sure are friendly here. What's your name?"

"I'm Rhonda. Rhonda Pott. Would you believe, I'm

still not used to saying 'Pott' instead of 'Waldrup'?''

"How long have you been married, Rhonda?"

The girl held up her diamond and the gold wedding band to show off the set. "Seven months. My husband's at Camp Pendleton and I was gonna go out there to be with him, but what happened, his regiment just got their orders, and it looks like they'll have to ship out to that country where LBJ's been sending all the troops lately. I'm scared to death, but mostly I try to look on the bright side and trust in the Lord."

"I had Joe when I was eighteen," his mother said, proudly he thought.

"Well, I envy you. Let me hurry up that chocolate cake for this starving fella."

"She talks a lot," Joe said, when Rhonda Pott had left them alone.

"I think she's a good soul. Lots of good people in the world, Joe," she said, upbeat, and he started to smile at her. Just as unexpectedly, her mood crashed. "How do I keep getting mixed up with the wrong kind?"

She looked intently at Joe, as if all the answers were there in his innocent blue eyes; then she smiled ruefully and gave a shrug. The smile was gone, replaced by a look of remorse as she bowed her head over joined hands. They had attended Mass at the cathedral in New Orleans on Christmas Eve and Easter Sunday, and on such occasions he had observed her looking like this, eyes closed and prayerful, although his mother explained to him that they weren't Catholic.

"Do you know what?" she said, before she opened her eyes and looked up again. "There's lots of good stuff in the souvenir shop next door. Arrowheads and petrified wood."

"What's that?"

His mother lifted her head and fumbled with her purse. "Oh, it's wood so old that it's turned to stone, then they take it and polish it and make it pretty." She hesitated, then took a crumpled five-dollar bill from her purse.

"You know how much this is, don't you?"

He stared at the five-dollar bill. "Uh-huh."

"How many dimes?" she said sternly. Joe chewed his lips and did the math on his fingers, showing her. "That's *right*. Well, take it, but don't spend more than half on arrowheads or junk, just buy a little something to keep in your cigar box and remind you—"

Alarmingly, her throat constricted and she gasped softly, as if she was about to cry. Joe froze. The moment passed before he could ask her if it was the cyst again. She pushed the five dollars across the table in the booth and said, "Go ahead, take it."

The offer of the money was so attractive, it over-powered a pinching qualm. "Where're you going?"

"To see about the car."

"Can't I go too?"

"Oh, no, Joely, eat your cake and—then look at all the pretty arrowheads. I don't want you in that dirty garage. Your father worked in a garage. Did I ever tell you that?"

"No," Joe said, suspensefully mulling this new bit of information regarding his father and hoping for more. "Did he fix cars?"

"Trucks. Big trucks. He was good at it, too, but then he had an accident. I've never liked garages since. And the smell always gives me such a bad headache. Anyway, the car—"

She was standing. She leaned toward him to kiss his forehead. "Here comes your cake. I'll pay the check when I go out."

"Wait—" But his mother was already halfway to the door, walking quickly past Rhonda Pott. Joe was half-inclined to slip out of the booth and follow his mother, but Rhonda was in his way before he could decide. Maybe his mother just wanted to be left alone for a little while. Sometimes she was like that. He looked at the slice of cake as Rhonda set it in front of him. He was still hungry, so he dug in. Rhonda lingered.

"How's that for chocolate cake?"

"Um." He ate with a spoon in his right hand, the five dollars clenched in his left fist.

"I know it's good, the way it's disappearing. You don't make a mess of crumbs, like my little brother. How about another glass of milk? I guess your mom went and paid the check already. But we won't worry about that."

Joe finished his cake and half of the glass of milk, and needed to go to the bathroom bad.

Except for a large man in bib overalls whose wispy white beard reached as far as his bulging stomach, the men's room was empty. He smiled at Joe as Joe slipped into a vacant stall, then reached up to lock the louvered door behind him. His mother had told him not to talk to strangers in public bathrooms, and always to lock the stall door behind him.

He had to do number two, which took a little time, forcing out marble-size constipated balls. When he left the men's room he was attracted to the souvenir shop adjacent to the café and went in to wait for his mother. He had decided he wasn't going to spend any of the five dollars she'd given him. If his father had worked in a garage, maybe he still fixed cars. That, Joe reasoned, would make it easier to find him when Joe was old enough to go looking. And had more five-dollar bills, more than he could count on the fingers of both hands.

But there was a lot of attractive stuff in the souvenir shop. Feathered Indian headdresses, tom-toms with tightly stretched rawhide drumheads, and scaled-down but real-looking bows and arrows. Tomahawks were $1.50 each. One dime per finger, ten fingers made a dollar. Five more fingers, $1.50. He was tempted to buy one of the rubber tomahawks. His mother had a rule about shopping. There's lots of things to like; buy something you *love*. The question was, what did he love most, the red-and-orange tomahawk, or his father? He kept the five dollars in the button-down change pocket of his shorts.

After a while he became bored with walking up and down the aisles of the souvenir shop. He glanced often at the entrance, but his mother hadn't come back from the garage. The café was a lot less crowded, and he saw Rhonda Pott standing around chatting with one of the other waitresses. "Pott" was a funny name for somebody. His mother called the toilet a "pot." Joe suppressed a giggle; then suddenly, not aware of any reason for it, he felt like crying. What was she doing at the garage for so long?

Outside the sun was lower in a blue-gray sky, but still intensely bright, a shock to his eyes. The hot gritty wind blew almost without letup across the gravel apron of the frame-and-shingle buildings by the highway. Tires whined on the blacktop as trucks sped by. Joe looked where the Studebaker coupe had been parked, then at the garage. He couldn't see from where he stood if his mother had pulled the car inside to be looked at. He trudged that way, his mouth drying up.

Before he reached the garage he saw his footlocker, sitting by itself next to a drink box on a concrete slab in front of the garage. They had bought it at an Army-Navy store on Poydras Street, and his mother had helped him letter his name on two sides with red fingernail polish. He could spell "Joe" easily enough, but his last name, which had a lot of letters, was very hard for him, both to spell and to pronounce. Also he had misspelled "Kep out." His clothes and all of his personal possessions were in the footlocker, which had been in the trunk of the Studebaker.

He ran into the garage.

There were two cars up on the lifts, mechanics in filthy overalls working underneath them. Neither car was a red-and-black Studebaker. He ran past a jacked-

up station wagon, fenders lacy with rust, glanced into
an office cubicle beside which a big wall-mounted fan
was roaring, and found himself at the open back door
of the garage.

A tall man with bad posture and grease-smeared
cheeks was having a smoke in the slant shadow of the
overhanging corrugated metal roof. Beyond him there
was nothing to see but treeless flinty ground, cool
stripes of irrigated farmland in the hazy distance, then
the jagged mountains of western Arizona.

"What're you looking for, kid?"

Terrified, Joe turned and ran back through the
noisy, sweltering garage, out into the glare of sun. He
hesitated, then ran toward the road, the glitter and
growl of California-bound truck traffic.

"Hey!"

He was stopped at the edge of the highway by
Rhonda Pott, who dragged him, writhing, back a few
feet.

"Look out, Joe! Where're you going, there's been
people killed trying to cross the highway here!"

Joe stopped fighting her. He breathed through his
mouth, searing his throat and then his lungs.

"What's wrong, Joe? Where's your mom?"

His head jerked one way, then another, as he looked
for her, for the missing car. He scarcely noticed the
tall man who had been smoking behind the garage.
The remainder of the cigarette was spit-pasted to his
lower lip as he approached them.

He said to Rhonda, "There was a blond woman,
maybe half hour ago, took that footlocker over there
out of the trunk of a Studey and drove off. Never
looked back."

"Oh, my God," Rhonda Pott said softly, and felt Joe
slip from her loosened grasp.

She looked down and saw him lying faceup in the
gravel, eyes rolled back in his sunstruck head, a little

bloody froth on his lips. His arms and legs were thrashing uncontrollably.

"Oh, my God," she said again, kneeling to shade Joe from the light, to touch him consolingly, helpless to stop the brutal grinding of his tongue between his teeth.

The rolling motion of the sea near sunset; a gull crying on the wind.

He couldn't breathe through what was left of his nose. The air he dragged in through his mouth tasted of seawater and old blood. Not fresh blood. So he recognized that he was alive, and probably not bleeding to death internally. It was all that he knew, or could remember. His predicament was a blank to him. Adrift, hurt—something had happened to him, to the *Dragonfly*. An accident?

The image of a woman recurred. Looking up from her book under an umbrella. Who? And where . . .

Dancing with pert lovelorn Yvonne on the terrace of her home. Some occasion or other. *When?*

He couldn't breathe, couldn't smell. Taste of salt, of blood. Too painful to drag in another breath. Broken bones. But the body wouldn't give up, not yet.

Slap and sting of a wave in his face. The wind rising, the boat pitching. Whose boat? His eyes closed, images of the mind no longer tinged redly by the sun on tight, glued-down lids.

The water moistened his matted eyelashes. He was able to open his eyes, slits, a second at most. Sky of pastel blue, washed with sunset pink. Clouding up. Thunder, far off. Nothing wrong with his hearing, then. But he'd heard the gulls earlier, off and on. So not completely at sea. In a channel between islands, or a Windward shipping lane rich with tramp-steamer garbage. The wind coming from—

He raised his head. The effort caused him to black out again. When he came to, perhaps only a few sec-

onds later, he was shivering, in horrible pain. Hard to
bear, but his pain was better than numbness, the profound trauma that calmed the spirit before death. His
body was alive, wanting to survive.

The boat lifted, fell. A small wave broke over him.

This time when he sat up, hands clutching the gunwale for support, he remained conscious—groaning,
then crying out as the pain cut him like a quick dull
saw. He nearly strangled, trying to breathe without disturbing his broken ribs. His head lolled with the motion of the boat. He was nauseated, but he forced
himself to open his eyes and try to appraise his situation.

The boat he was in appeared to be one of the beautifully crafted, always dependable Saintois fishing
boats. There was a motor on the transom. And, on the
horizon, he saw the mountains of an island large
enough to be Basse-Terre or Dominica, its identity
partly shrouded in storm and spidery lightning.

When he looked again at the bow, lightning revealed
the face and breathtaking form of a woman seated
there.

Her hands were clasped just above her smooth pu-
denda, hairless as marble, and she was posed, un-
adorned, with her face in three-quarter profile, as if
she were having her portrait painted. Her brown hair,
in soft full waves undisturbed by the wind, had russet
highlights. Her exposed breasts were tipped with glancing flame like St. Elmo's fire. Her nakedness was chaste
enough, but her cheekbones had a sensual tilt to them,
and her eyes flashed according to the whim of her
flame; shades of blue and holy gold. She was familiar,
but he couldn't place her. He might last have seen
her within the halls of an elegantly archaic middle-
European art museum, or a cathedral. She was ghost,
hallucination, a temperate angel. His heart was seized,
roughly engaged, in a way he'd never felt. Her pres-

ence subdued his pain; humbly, he wanted her to love him.

Am I going to die? Joe said, or thought he said. Nothing else could explain this visitation on a dark sea, at a dark hour.

She smiled slightly, as if that were a foolish idea. Then her long fingers described arcs of atmospheric, spectral fire as she held out a hand to him.

Then I'm going to live. Why?

The question in his mind excited her flame; there was red in it, and in her eyes, and for a few moments he thought he'd made the wrong interpretation of who had been sent to him. But it was just a flash of spirit, a comment on his obtuseness, for which she forgave him with another mute arc of the hand. He felt, without substantiation, that he was still all right with the angels. The reasons he would have to fathom for himself, if he cared.

SEVEN

Beckham, Georgia, is a small place, the seat of a county slowly becoming urbanized as the metropolitan area of nearby Atlanta expands east along Interstate 20. There is a courthouse square favored by moviemakers looking for authentic small-town Southern atmosphere, a plain, four-room farmhouse with a rust-red tin roof that the Virgin Mary reportedly visits from time to time, a cherry blossom festival held in the early spring, light industry sufficient to hold down the unemployment rate, and a very expensive private hospital in a greatly expanded antebellum mansion on a hilltop, facing away from the loading docks of a Kroger and a Wal-Mart in the strip shopping center just off Exit 42 of the I-20.

The hilltop acreage features so many large vintage magnolias, dogwood and longleaf Georgia pines that the southern-exposure veranda and lofty Doric columns of the original mansion, still locally known as Jasquith Hall in spite of its decade-old conversion into a hospital and outpatient clinic, are barely visible for much of the year from the interstate lanes a few hundred yards away.

McCarter Langford specializes in reconstructive and plastic surgery, from faces so severely damaged that anthropometric analysis is required, to routine tummy-tucks for the forty-something crowd that can afford the best. They also do ("for the sake of our immortal souls," one of the group's younger surgeons remarked to Joe) some charity work, specializing in the correction of horrendous birth defects in children.

Laddy Langford performed almost all of Joe's required surgeries, as soon as Joe arrived from the Caribbean after a week in the Pointe-à-Pitre hospital with his face clumsily wrapped in smelly bandages, running a high fever in spite of antibiotics.

"How bad?" Joe asked when the bandages came off and Langford had a chance to assess the damage. He could barely talk. He had been shot full of Dilaudid, but even the slight effort needed for articulate speech revived the pain.

"Both cheekbones, a couple of subcondylar fractures. The chin is shattered, and the bone between the eye sockets is fractured. I'll probably want to remove the back wall of the frontal sinus. That'll allow the brain to fill the cavity and prevent mucoceles formation. What that is—"

"Potentially fatal abscess. I've read Grabb and Smith."

"Oh, you have an M.D.? I didn't know."

"Never finished school. What about the nose?"

Langford was a large, ungainly man with a bass voice so low it tended to rumble. When he wasn't piecing bones back together he sang with a well-known barbershop quartet.

"Not much to work with, I'm afraid. We're looking at three to four months. I'll do a cantilevered nasal-dorsal rib graft with an expanded forehead flap. Sili-

cone bag, hundred-cc device, say about ten fills al-
together. You follow?"

"Yes."

"It'll be a work of art. But we don't know exactly
what you looked like before. If you could think of an
old girlfriend who might have a snapshot or two—"

"Everything went down with the *Dragonfly*. Ad-
dresses, phone numbers."

"Damn shame. You still don't remember how it happened?"

"Maybe it'll come back to me, one day. I'd at least
like to know—"

Langford respected his silence for a few moments,
then murmured, "About the girl? What a tragedy."

Joe opened his suppurating eyes, looking up from
the examination table. His mourning contained, his
depression intact. "Her body came in with the tide,
right . . . to the mouth of the harbor at Bourg. I didn't
know what to say . . . to her family. I don't know if
Yvonne was with me on the *Dragonfly*. But it wasn't . . .
like that. I mean, she was a kid. I was sending her to
university in Paris."

"Joe, I'm going to crank up the team and we'll get
started in an hour. Once we've got the microcompres-
sion plates screwed in you should be able to see an
oral surgeon. Like I said, four months, you'll be as
good as new."

The patients at McCarter Langford usually didn't so-
cialize. A good many of them were celebrities who
didn't want it known they were there, jacking up their
faces to prolong careers before the unforgiving cameras. Joe passed the time while his nose was being rebuilt speed-reading by day on his balcony when the
light was good, exercising in the well-equipped gym,
and watching television at night, suffering from insom-
nia as he was weaned from medication. Late-night
channel-surfing, trying to find something that would

engage the mind, if not his blunted emotions.

Quick flicks of the remote control: antique movies with leading men in the style of their day, trim little mustaches, hair glossed hard as a turtle's shell. Then pale, beefy Mae West—if sex were food, she'd be a bowl of three-alarm chili. Blink. A preacher with a full head of glittery paralyzed hair, kissing ass for Jesus, and—blink—a stand-up comedienne complaining about her bad sex life. He'd been better entertained by Rorschach blots. Blink-blink, semi-porn women wrestlers who looked like the photos in every truck driver's wallet were softening each other up with body slams. Commercial. They were selling kitchen knives that would cut through the Koh-i-noor diamond. A rerun game show featuring heavily tanned bimbos of both sexes. Larry King, and an actor who used to be big in the movies. He was on TV now, his show probably not doing so good in the ratings. He was heftier, with sober gray in his mustache, wisecracking as if his heart could break, wearing the albatross of waning celebrity like a farm dog wearing the chicken it killed on a string around its neck. Knowing—as they all must know, sooner or later—how easily they could be banished: they were all lighter than air, thinner than ghosts, no more substantial than figments of the public's imagination. It was what killed them all, in the end. The public was fickle, and easily bored.

"Do you know what TELEVISION is?" the frail but still imperious voice asked him. "Television is MOTHER, with electronic tits."

Joe turned his head toward the partially opened door of his suite. He would have smiled, but his face still felt stiff from the shrinkage of a scar on his upper lip and another at one corner of his mouth.

"So I guess you need mothering tonight," Lark Worship said. "Turn that damn thing OFF and invite me in."

Joe muted the sound on the TV instead and got up

from the sofa in the suite's sitting room. "How are you tonight, Lark?"

"Perishing for a cigarette," she complained, coming across the Aubusson carpet with her four-footed walker, gold slippers on her child-sized feet. They matched the gold cloth of her turban and the pendant on the gold chain she wore on the outside of her batik sari. "Of course that isn't ALLOWED around here. You have to be devious as hell to cop a smoke. Your AMARYLLIS are wilting."

"Sorry about that," Joe said, glancing at the vase of flowers on the round library table in the center of the room. "How about a drink?"

"Suds, if you've got any."

"Carlsberg?"

"Dandy." She abandoned her walker and lowered herself with suspenseful slowness to one of the matched pair of Regency sofas. Joe went behind the bar to open the refrigerator. He poured beer for both of them. Lark Worship took her stemmed glass with a little grateful nod. Her bones were osteoporetic and without the walker to lean on she would bend almost double in no time. But her hands, with a fine, nearly translucent pallor like porcelain, didn't tremble. She was past eighty years of age, so the wrinkles were there, but looking at her in the soft cream light of a single lamp behind her right shoulder, he was reminded of that lovely, eerie face from the early thirties that he'd seen from time to time in the late hours on AMC and TNT: the narcotic tenderness of eye and the understated stoicism of a waif, the pale but still luminous tone of a slightly suffocated jonquil.

She watched him as he watered the amaryllis with what was left in a bottle of Evian.

"You could use a haircut."

"I know."

"But your Z-plasty has been a real success. I'm DYING to know how you turn out. You a rich kid, Joe?

Have to be, to afford this place week after week. I'm doing all right, myself. My third, and thank God my LAST husband, was a banker. One of his ruling passions was telephone bonds. The other, I belatedly learned, was pederasty.'' She gave it two beats, then said, ''Unfortunately my UNERRING artistic judgment never carried over into my personal life. Love, Joe. By the time we're smart enough to figure out what love is all about, we're too feeble to protest what it's DONE to us.''

Joe nodded appreciatively.

Lark Worship looked at the books piled on the floor beside his sofa. Most of them were medical texts.

''Do you actually READ all these?''

''I'm afraid so.''

''Not a doctor yourself, are you?''

''I had two years of medical school at UCLA. Didn't stay the course.''

''Oh. Why NOT?''

''I found something else that interested me more.''

''Boats?'' she said, looking across the room at the drafting table he'd set up, the sketches that were the bare beginning of a new *Dragonfly*.

''And the women who bought the boats for me.'' He didn't mind talking this way to Lark Worship. He felt safe from her, from everyone, behind the healing, tightening skin of his not quite familiar face-in-progress. And he enjoyed her reactions as she played to him like a debutante.

''You're a gigolo!'' She paused to savor the revelation. Joe knew a few things about the acting game, and he especially liked her pauses. Her timing was still impeccable, although she probably hadn't acted professionally for twenty years. ''I suppose you don't go in for older women,'' she said, with a little hopeful smile that was delicious malarkey.

''They're usually the ones who have the money.''

''God, but you remind me of Kyle! You wouldn't

know about Kyle. He's not EVEN in my autobiography. Kyle belonged to the Soloflex generation of young men: Day-Glo deltoids, HAIR too blond for his eyebrows. He was gorgeous, semitalented, fun to fuck, and as shallow as the cat's saucer.''

Lark Worship laughed, mildly at first, then with enough bawdy energy to cause some beer to slop from her glass onto her sari. She didn't notice.

"Come sit here beside me, Joe. I promise I WON'T fibrillate. Tell me how you hook the big ones.''

During the weeks before his recovery was completed, Joe spent a good part of his free time in the evenings with the actress, who, like many in her profession, talked a lot about herself. Lark Worship was as salty as old pork, and her vanity had more miles on it than a Sunday-school bus. But she also was good at listening, analyzing, absorbing character and exploring, often with great accuracy, the labyrinth of a complicated psyche.

"What happened after your mother abandoned you, darling?''

"I was a ward of Maricopa County, Arizona. They put me in a foster home until they could find—her. But they never did. She left the car by the side of the road in a place called Buckeye, which was forty miles north of Gila Bend. Nobody ever knew where she went from there. Probably she caught a ride. I had pictures of her, of course, snapshots, in my footlocker. They weren't any help.''

"Did you EVER think of looking for her yourself?''

"No. She got good and lost, and she wanted to stay lost.''

"MY mother was a real stinker. Religious to a fault. She would NOT allow me to tap-dance. I bluffed my way onto the Lot and lied about my age, and signed with Metro when I was sixteen. The Lot became my home. I made THIRTEEN pictures in three years.

That's how you learned. But your fate was decided by the fan mail you received. I wore my fingers down to the second knuckles writing fan letters to myself, hired other girls at fifteen cents an hour to write MORE letters, sent them off in cartons to be mailed from different parts of the country. I was given better parts in bigger pictures. Occasionally a director would be assigned who gave a damn. The first one who gave a damn about me, I MARRIED him. Directors had such panache in those days. Marty was a great philanderer, of course, but he told wonderful lies. I love an inventive lie. But stubborn lies, pathetic lies, pointless lies, all are little rotten toadstools of the mind.''

Joe thought it was probably a line from one of her movies, like *The Ushery Women*. Nevertheless she had a point to make.

"I couldn't—I didn't—talk for a year after she left me. Obviously I was a mental case, but some people named Pachek took me in regardless. They'd never had children, but they were good parents. Vance Pachek had eighty-five acres of lettuce and made a good living most years. Vance believed in the therapy of hard work, and that's how I grew up, working hard on the ranch, going to Sunday school. Vance taught me to ride and read the greens at the public golf courses in Phoenix. Until I was almost thirteen not a day went by that I didn't think it was a mistake, that she was going to come back for me. Then I discovered girls. I mean, they discovered me. An Arizona State cheerleader seduced me when I was in the ninth grade, behind a pile of irrigation pipe way out in one of the fields. She was blond, a little bucktoothed, and I remember how red her face got, inches away from mine as she was going up and down on me like a monkey on a flagpole, how the sweat ran down her cheeks, how she dug into my shoulders when she came. I'd been scared silly when she took my pants down, almost paralyzed, but by the time it was over—I—it was a revelation. What's the buzzword nowadays? *Epiphany*. Around that time I stopped thinking about my mother. Completely. Just stopped. Until—"

"Until what, darling?" Lark Worship said, after he'd stared and flexed his hands and stalled.

"I was working on a project in northern California. This was right after I'd made my biggest—" He stalled again.

"Score?" she suggested. "Darling. I am far too old and have led MUCH too sinful a life to be judgmental."

Joe nodded. "Anyway, I was—going with a woman named Adrian. The family was old-money shipping in San Francisco, and she was a year or two away from menopause. Bored with her husband, disliked her children; she was hot for an adventure."

"I know too well."

"I had a treasure-hunt scenario worked out. Honduras. While I was getting Adrian interested in gold and emeralds off the Bahian Islands, she was trying to interest me in consciousness expansion. She'd been through Freudian analysis and flirted with wacko LSD and peyote-based cults, but—"

"There ought to be a penalty box for faddish people," Lark observed, blowing a cloud of smoke from her illicit cigarette toward the ceiling.

"When I met her, Adrian's latest thing was holotropic breathwork—therapy that utilized Eastern breathing techniques, percussive music and hypnosis. It was supposed to realize the benefits of LSD without the risk of frying your neural circuits."

"Rather dangerous for you to be hypnotized, given the circumstances."

"I knew that. I had . . . a lot of confidence in myself then. I felt in control of every situation, even group sessions like the ones Adrian talked me into attending. I was going along with the gag, you know, feeling . . .

untouchable. I didn't realize what breathwork and even mild group hypnosis can accomplish in the right setting. You're mostly naked, body lightly oiled, and you're sitting in a circle with the other oiled bodies on a redwood deck under a starry sky with the eucalyptus swaying in an offshore breeze, waves crashing on the rocks, vapors from the hot tub keeping everybody warm and cozy. I know a lot more about the power of groups than I knew then, since I was, out of necessity, a dedicated loner. The group took over; all the constraints of consciousness faded. The screaming started. It seemed a natural, primitive, necessary thing. Others were screaming, screams of terror and guilt and grief. I screamed too. Such terrible things about my mother. All the little rotten toadstools of the subconscious were popping up and exploding. See, I never had the chance to know. Her. What she wanted. From me. What she *expected*. I felt like a raw, just-born thing, writhing on the deck, screaming pitifully but getting no answer."

After a long time Lark Worship put out her hand in a way that suggested she was breaking a bad spell.

"Later . . . Adrian took me to bed and fucked me like the cheerleader from Arizona State, pounding away as if she were doing CPR, desperate to bring me back to life, or something. I wasn't performing at all, and she couldn't—bring me back to the life I had lied about. I told her what I was up to. I'm not sure she was surprised, or shocked. She said she wanted to marry me anyway."

"I would've assumed that, had you not told me. Poor Adrian. She JUST didn't get it, did she?"

"No. She didn't get it."

"Well. I hear it's almost TIME for the champagne. You're clearing out of this place soon."

"Couple of days."

"What are you going to do then, Joe?"

He smiled; the unfamiliar stretching of the smile muscles hurt.

"You know. It's what they say about acting. Not enough to want it—you've got to need it."

"God bless," Lark Worship said.

EIGHT

Flora Birdsall was late leaving the office; after she stopped at the Tysons Corner shopping center to pick up a prescription and some dry cleaning, she pulled her Camry into the town-house driveway at seven-twenty. One of the Lillis twins from next door had left a pink Big Wheel on her flagstone walk. End of summer in northern Virginia. The sun was setting but the temperature had hit a muggy 94 and the heat of the day lingered: she could feel the hot slate flagstones through the thin soles of her office shoes as she walked up to the sentry-box-size porch.

The shoes came off first thing inside the door; Pumpkin, her declawed Himalayan, made passes at her toes as she hung up the dry cleaning in the entrance-way closet. She took off her dark blue skirt and jacket and draped them over a ladder-back chair in the breakfast nook, paused to undo her bra and slipped it off under her blouse, took a seven-ounce Silver Bullet from the fridge and drank most of it while leaning against the counter between nook and kitchen. Pumpkin leaped up from the seat of a chair and posed beside the telephone console for the nightly replay. That got the Congo Greys going in their twin cages. Flora unbuttoned her blouse partway and went through the largely unconscious ritual of checking for lumps while she chatted with her birds. She belched mildly, feeling frumpy but contented, happy to be out of the pressure cooker on a Friday evening.

Then she checked her messages. Miller had called, from the Senate cloakroom and not his office; they were putting in late hours on the bill he and Hamrick of Minnesota were trying to get through the Senate Finance Committee. He had, he confided, news about the divorce. Flora couldn't be sure from his harried tone of voice if it was good news or bad. Why bother to say anything until he was able to see her? I'm forty-nine, she thought. Fifty coming up—oh God—a week from Sunday, and I'm going to go crazy if this thing drags on much longer.

Mikki at the travel agency, confirming reservations to Bermuda for her birthday weekend. The cottage near the Elbow Beach Club belonged to a friend. Miller had never visited Bermuda. They traveled separately, they met in out-of-the-way, off-season places for a couple of days, sometimes for just a few hours.

Gabrielle at Cuts 'n' Curls, confirming tomorrow's appointment with Giles.

Would they be able to meet this weekend? Flora wondered. Eight days tomorrow since they'd last been together.

In her half-unbuttoned blouse and panty hose, Flora went to the fridge again for another Silver Bullet, ignoring the Weight Watchers' calorie chart magnetized to the door. Miller didn't mind if she was a little full-figured. He loved her eyes, her intellect. She knew how to take good care of him. He was a Bridge widower: Alicia was a slave to Master Points. The marriage had been over for years; all five children were grown. Why couldn't Alicia just let *go*? Southern women were so damned clinging and manipulative. It was bred in the bone.

A caller who hung up without comment.

Flora nursed her second and last beer of the evening, while watering her African violets in the greenhouse window over the kitchen sink. Pumpkin lazed against an ankle, then paused for a couple of bites of cat chow on his food-and-water caddy next to the laundry alcove.

Flora had no illusions about the secrecy quotient of her affair with Miller Harkness. She'd grown up with the Company. The Office of Security had had a year to pick up something: fact, rumor, it didn't matter to them. Her position with DS and T required the highest security clearance. The scrutiny of her behavior, her private life, didn't stop with fitness reviews, a yearly polygraphing, informal but de rigueur conversations with company shrinks. Her town house was swept every few months for bugs. In Pops's day the OS didn't bug Company personnel, but now she could never be sure. And how much of Official Washington knew about her love affair with a married senator? Probably, through mutual tact and watchfulness, they'd had better luck there.

Flora felt like having a chat with her mom, whose farmhouse and studio in rural New Hampshire had from the beginning served as the lovers' chief trysting place. Bessie had no more use for Southern women than did her daughter. Bessie's dry humor and droll fits of vituperation would make Flora laugh, and then she could while away the rest of the lonely evening without feeling too heartsick and nervous about the state of her yearlong love affair.

Another caller, who hung up. Was it the same caller? End of messages.

As the tape was rewinding, the phone rang. Flora picked it up hopefully.

"Hello."

"Hi, Aunt Flora."

It had been a while; but she would never forget his voice. Flora hesitated, now feeling just a little buzz from the beer. Her nerves prickled. She didn't know whether to be happy, or hang up the phone.

"Yes?"

"It's your nephew Eddie, from Seattle."

"Oh, Eddie. Yes, hi." She hesitated again, drawing an inaudible breath. Then she said, committing herself, "Long time no see."

"Long time no see," he repeated cheerfully.

"Well, what brings you this far east, Eddie? Are you still in computer sales?"

"In a manner of speaking. The company I work for now manufactures arcade video games. I'm on the road a lot, but I really like it."

"Uh-huh. I see. So you're on a sales trip?"

"I'm just passing through. Called on a client in Arlington this afternoon, but my flight for Seattle doesn't leave Dulles until eleven-thirty. I was wondering if you'd like to have dinner?"

"Dinner? Yes, that sounds—where are you calling from, Eddie?"

"Birchfield Mall. Do you know where that is?"

"About twenty minutes on the Beltway from my house. I could meet you there—say, around eight? From Birchfield it's only a half hour to Dulles."

"Swell! I'll be at the arcade in the mall. Oh, Aunt Flora? Dinner's on me. I'll put it on my expense account."

Still the actor, she thought, perhaps having hoped for better: doing a word-perfect impersonation of a junior-executive boob trying to impress a seldom-seen relative. "Wonderful. Looking forward to it, Eddie."

* * *

Time for a bath, then a nubby linen pantsuit and date-night jewelry and—still not too late in the season—sandals, although she would have preferred jeans and walk shoes for the mall trekking. Her mind churned as she fussed a little with her appearance; it was almost as if she'd accepted a blind date. How long since he'd last called? About eighteen months. Well, that part of their relationship was over with. No need to put herself in jeopardy again, because of a long-ago affair with the most inappropriate man she'd ever met.

Then why see him at all? Flora wasn't sure, although she wasn't squeamish about analyzing her own, worst flaws. She'd always been too eager to please the men in her life, from her father, a cofounder of the CIA, to her infrequent lovers, one of whom, a law professor at Georgetown, had characterized her affections as "thinly disguised demons of possessiveness." But he had been a weak man, easily fazed by any demands made of him outside the confines of the academy. As for the boldest, most liberating of her lovers—did she want to go to bed with him for old times' sake? *Wild Flora*, his name for her. Crazy in the sack for such an outwardly staid person, but the heat of it—unimaginable, then irresistible. Her nighttime passion had bled into her other, orderly life. Wild Flora, risking everything. She was dry in the mouth and, to her chagrin, a little too easily aroused, thinking about the possibility of spending the night with him. No. There was Miller now. It would be a cheat, even though she was lonely. She couldn't do that to her self-respect.

Still—she had to know if she could see him, end on a pleasant, nostalgic note and walk away. The sex part was over, and she had pressed her luck too far with the business relationship. No matter that the risk-taking had been as satisfying to her as their highly charged sex.

*   *   *

Flora seldom went to Birchfield Mall; she preferred the more upscale mall in Tysons Corner Center, which had Bloomingdale's. She parked at the wrong end and had to walk the length of the mall to find the video-games arcade, by the entrance to the theater complex. On Friday night this part of the Mall was crammed with teenagers, like a cattle pen for young consumers. She felt slightly intimidated by the arcade itself, a cavelike place on two levels, provocatively lighted in lush blues and dusky reds like a high-tech brothel. No music, except for the expressionistic lilt and percussive rhythms of the electronic machines. Robot voices gave instructions or commented on the progress of the mostly young players huddled in shared rapture in front of the cartoon screens. It was mania elevated to an art form. There wasn't much about computers Flora didn't understand or couldn't use to her advantage, but she felt ridiculously out of place, out of touch with an entire generation while she looked around like a mother searching for a strayed child.

Her eyes went over Joe three times before she concluded, with a shiver of shock, that it could be him.

Even then she didn't budge, but stared at him until he turned away from a martial-arts fantasy massacre and, observing her watching him, smiled and beckoned.

"Hi, Aunt Flora."

Amazed, she almost said his correct name before catching herself and, instead of speaking, lifted her heels an inch to kiss him on the cheek.

"You look—different."

"I am different." He looked past her, casually sweeping the entrance to the arcade with his eyes, at the same time holding her hand, holding her close to him. "But you look wonderful."

"You—I can't—your face—"

"A good man put it back together for me. But he didn't have photographs to work from."

"My Lord," she said, her pulses pounding.

"It's okay, no permanent damage." His smile, she realized, hadn't changed, except for a little gleaming scar that impinged on his upper lip. He had one other scar she was sure hadn't been there the last time they'd met—and his hair, shorter than he'd customarily worn it, was shot through with silver now. It looked really good with the deepwater tan.

"What happened?"

"I'll tell you about it. As much as I remember. Let's get something to eat. Is there a decent place around here for Chesapeake oysters?"

"Let me think. I *can't* think in this place. Come on. Do you have a car?"

"Yeah."

"Rental? We'll take yours."

"Cautious is as cautious does," he said, again with that lazy, insinuating half-smile she'd seen in her dreams a few times since they'd last met.

"I was raised that way." Damn it, she would have to be tough with him, that was all. Not let him get away with it: the smooth persuasion, the old come-on, the confident tease and calculated tricks she resented even as she fell for them. Get a grip, Flora. You know what he is. Just a cheap womanizer for all the smoothness. The emotional depth of a barracuda. There's not an ounce of true caring in his body. He could get you killed, and it wouldn't bother him. So get this over with. Be brutally frank. Shoot from the hip. And try to ignore the pressure behind the eyes, the girlish urge to shed tears. The numbing desire just to have his arms around you, for a few seconds. *Flora, you asshole.* Let go of his hand!

In the postcoital dark of 3 A.M., she awoke from a satisfying nap to see him standing naked by the windows of their second-floor room in the Annandale Red Roof Inn.

"Joe?"

He turned his head. "Hello, luscious."

"Joe."

"Did I ever tell you I'd give up my front-row seat in hell for you?"

"Stop it, Joe. My fault, wasn't it?"

"I don't know." A slight catch in his voice. Real or improvised, she wondered.

"Well, I do. You jumped a foot when I—I mean, you always liked it before when I massaged your prostate. Come and be with me, please."

He lowered his head and rubbed his brow as if chastened, then returned to the bed and lay down in her arms. She kissed the lobe of an ear, sealed tense eyelids with the tip of her tongue. She sensed the nervous movement of his eyes beneath closed lids. This resonance of secret vision gave her a naked tingle. The rest of him seemed emptied, ready for burial.

"Easy, Joe," Flora whispered, now thoroughly convinced of his distress.

"Sorry. Sorry."

"Don't be. It's a perfectly natural thing, for a man— tell me something. How many times have you made love since the hijacking?"

"Once. She was a surgical nurse at the hospital. Same story. No problem getting an erection, couldn't hang on to it. Neither could you." He laughed, but it felt like a seizure; his body stiffened.

"That means it isn't a physical thing. And you didn't cause me any distress, I came in two seconds. Joe, you took a horrible physical beating. I've heard stories of what that does to a man emotionally."

"Yeah . . ."

"Count it as a blessing that you don't remember."

"Should I?"

"What's the last thing you *do* remember?"

"I was talking to a woman at Le Breton. That's a restaurant on a little island called Terre-de-Haut. It was, I think, about two in the afternoon. She was reading a novel. I remember everything in sharp detail—what she had on, the brand of beer she was drinking: Corsair. I remember the title of the novel. *Savannah's Flame*, by Pamela Abelard. I was particularly struck by the author's photo on the back of the book jacket. The next thing I remember seeing was *that* face. I was adrift between Marie-Galante and Dominica. She was sitting big as life on the transom of a Saintois fishing boat like a vision of heaven. Or hell, I'm not sure."

"You were in shock. The mind does strange—"

"I've seen her since then, too," Joe murmured.

"Pamela Abelard? She's popular. I noticed one of the girls reading an Abelard paperback in the cafeteria at Langley the other day. Thoroughly engrossed in that twaddle. Joe, how badly do you want to know what really happened to you and the *Dragonfly*?"

"If it was pirates, then it doesn't matter."

"And if it was someone from your recent past, an irate husband or—"

"That doesn't matter, either. I'm not looking for revenge. I'm not the violent type. I just wasn't careful enough. It's the one thing that I can't forgive myself for. Flora—"

"Yes?" Flora said, slipping down in the bed to nuzzle the small of his back with her lips.

"That feels good."

"You bet."

"Flora? I should have told you this. I was raped."

Her lips parted, closed. Her hands were quiet on his groin and slowly swelling penis. "Oh, no."

"It's okay, I was tested, I'm not carrying anything."

"I didn't think you'd get into bed with me if you were. That's why you jumped when I—but do you remember it being done to you?"

"Physical evidence only."

"Poor lamb." She kissed him again, at the base of his spine. "Now, don't do anything," she said. "I'm making love to *you*. Let it happen. Don't think about it. Turn on your back, baby."

"Flora," he said, a few minutes later, "I need an identity."

She paused and lifted her head, blew her warm breath into the hollow of his scrotum, which she held in one hand as tenderly as the fuzzy brown chick of a giant raptor.

"Isn't it too soon?"

"I hope not."

"You can't need the money."

"It's not that."

She massaged his groin with the gentlest of touches, turning up the heat and the pace of her activity, tongue flickering to the niche in the apricot-size head of his now-firm penis.

"What are the rules again?" she said, her own eyes closing, feeling the bliss of his fingers invading her as she humped over him, seamy but febrile, her large breasts pressing down on his belly.

"I don't kill anybody. I don't take everything they own. I leave the young ones and the emotional misfits alone."

"And you never, never, *never* tell anyone about Flora. Because they won't reprimand me, and they won't fire me. Never mind who my father was—they'll assassinate me."

"I know."

"I'll bet you didn't know this. I've never touched a penny of my end. It's all just sitting there in the bank in Madeira. I converted everything to gold, like you said. I'll give it all back to you, Joe, if you promise me you'll quit."

"You know I can't do that."

"Well, *I'm* quitting, Joe. This is the last time. I mean it. I'm getting married to a hell of a nice guy. I know I am. It's gonna work out. Who—are you going to be this time?"

"Joseph Bryce, M.D. Specialist in pediatric oncology."

"A doctor? That's a—tough one, you ought to know that. I'll have to—set you up with the AMA, and other—professional societies. That means maximum exposure on my part. My involvement could be traced. Oh, God, Joe! Yes, right there, that little spot. Nobody could ever find it like you can. *Fuck* me, dearest. I'll need—uh, uh, *uhhhhhh*, recent photos."

"They'll be in the usual place. How long, do you think?"

"Joe, honey, I'm almost there!"

"I mean for the documentation."

"We have new procedures. Computer codes change every fifteen seconds now. It's so—fucking difficult. Oh, *why*?"

Flora began to cry even as she came. Afterward she was slack and upside down on him in that awkward—now that the passion was done—position, her head between his legs. She shook with bitter sobs while he caressed her spread hips. The worst of it was, she hadn't done Joe any good, and she realized she was never going to see him again.

"Hey," he said shyly.

"Oh, what?"

"Congratulations on your forthcoming marriage."

Flora drew a deep, shuddery breath.

"Thank you. This moment will always be fixed in my memory. I will never erase from my mind that you said 'congratulations on your forthcoming marriage' while you were looking straight up my ass."

"Isn't there an all-night waffle house across the street? Do you want to go out for something to eat?"

"I want to kill myself. But because I'm mature enough to know that that isn't a viable alternative, I guess food would be the next best thing."

PART **TWO**

T*he truth that can be told is not the truth.*

—*Lao-tzu*

NINE

There were no suites at the Planter's House, but the double room Joe was given on the fourth and top floor of the best hotel in Nimrod's Chapel proved to be more than adequate. It had a private bath with copper pipes on the wall that rumbled when the hot water was turned on, and a balcony overlooking the pleasantly shabby park that extended for six blocks along Pandora's Bay, parallel to the main street of town. In the park were live oaks dripping with Spanish moss, a turn-of-the-century brick-and-latticework bandstand, and a small covered carousel, also an antique. At the south end of the park was one of the better harbors on the Intracoastal Waterway. There was a pier, a marina, a fish house, and a large anchorage by the fish house for both commercial shrimpers and charter fishing boats. At the north end of the park a causeway with two swing bridges crossed the blackwater rivers that came together above Nimrod's Chapel to form an estuary teeming with blue and green herons, osprey, and other aquatic bird life.

Neon signs were not allowed within the town's Historic District. Many of the small commercial buildings displayed bronze plaques that denoted a listing in the National Register of Historic Places. The town had a weathered, durable, old-fashioned appeal without being self-consciously cute. Before the shops along Front Street closed for the evening, Joe bought a good pair of binoculars at a camera store in a narrow arcade paved with cobblestones that had come to Carolina as ballast in English merchant ships.

From the balcony of his room he used the binoculars to look southeast across the bay, its surface shining like hammered copper in the sunset, to the Barony on Chicora Island. The distance was about three miles. Barbara Ann, the assistant manager of the Planter's House, had told him that on most days the main house of the former plantation could be seen with the naked eye. "It was practically a ruin, but they have done a *lot* of work on that old place in the last few years. Charlene, that's Dr. Luke's third wife, she was Miss South Carolina when I was a senior in high school? Well, she's good at restoring and decorating, or so I hear; I've lived in Nimrod's Chapel most of my life, except when I went to Clemson, but I have yet to set foot in the Barony."

Barbara Ann was a giggler and a chatterbox; he probably could have learned a great deal more from her, over drinks and maybe later in bed. But it was a small town; he knew better than to ask a lot of questions. And Barbara Ann wasn't the one he'd come to Nimrod's Chapel to seduce.

Still, he was curious. He had assumed, from the unusually sketchy reports he had on Pamela Abelard, that she was the owner of the Barony. Now there seemed to be a "Dr. Luke" in the picture. Medical doctor? That might serve to complicate his project. At least he wasn't Abelard's husband. But the caution light was on, even as Joe focused his binoculars on the house across Pandora's Bay.

What he saw, through huge live-oak and chinaberry trees that undoubtedly had survived a couple of centuries of bad storms off the nearby Atlantic, was a Tudor house with two one-story additions on either side. Ivy grew on the brickwork. The main house was not as imposing as he had anticipated from the name. There were two full stories and a smaller, judging from the size of the windows under the eaves, third or attic floor. The original Tudor architecture and the Queen Anne façade had been bastardized with the necessary addition of hurricane shutters, which for now, on a calm early-October evening, were open. There was a veranda with a gazebo at one end, gardens with brick walls and hedges, a modern pool house, an old cemetery and then a dock on an inlet off the bay. The last light of day glittered on the corrugated zinc roof of what might have been a boathouse, but he couldn't see much of it for the cypress trees rising from the shallows of the inlet like knobbly old fishermen calling it a day.

He listened to the music of the little carousel in the park, the nougat-rich Southern voices of strollers below his balcony, and thought about his project. Qualms were not unusual at the start. They came and went until he was well established in the lives of those who had been strangers. That might take days, or a few weeks. Until the half-life of the one he was pretending to be changed from shadows to flesh. It was like learning a foreign language. He was not yet thinking like Dr. Joe Bryce, lately out of Africa and having a hard time adjusting to the change. .

Joe went back inside, closing the balcony doors. He drew the lacy curtains but not the drapes and lay down on the four-poster bed, glanced at his reflection in an oval mirror on the opposite wall, then turned on his side and picked up a Pamela Abelard novel, her latest, which was called *Honor's Flame.* The novel had been number two on *The New York Times Book Review* hardcover best-seller list the previous Sunday. There were 585 pages, which he'd read in an hour and a half. *Honor's Flame* had to do with a rice planter, a sea captain, and a tempestuous young widow in Charleston, South Carolina, who, in the 1790s, seemed to be two hundred years ahead of her time with her feminist sensibilities. The sea captain raped her, the rice planter could only get it up with slave women, and Honor, the title heroine, made a fortune in the indigo business before marrying a Scottish laird with strong shoulders and "tawny hair that curled thick as liquid gold over the high collar of his lace shirt."

Her prose was as boring as a minuet, and she had never met a cliché she didn't like. But she could write good dialogue, which gave her characters more flair than the predictable story lines merited.

Honor's Flame was, according to the brief biography on the back flap of the book jacket, the author's sixth novel. She had published her first at the age of twenty-three. Pamela Abelard still looked very young in the color photo on the back of the book. She'd been born and raised in the Palmetto State, and now made her home in Nimrod's Chapel.

There was more from a recent *Publishers Weekly.* Her first five novels, all international successes, had sold thirteen million copies. A new contract with her publisher called for four more *Flame* books, with an advance payment against royalties of fifteen million dollars.

The carousel went round and round. In the gathering dark Joe heard a fragment of song from some minstrel of riotous feeling. The soft night wind was as seductive as ether. Joe was hungry, but not ready to go out yet. He stared at the painted tin ceiling of his room, pondering what he knew about Pamela Abelard from the reports of the investigative agency that had done his homework for him.

It wasn't quite enough to say that she was a very private person. Pamela Abelard was literally reclusive. Her publishers and literary agents had never met her. She never gave interviews. The president of her fan club (Pam's Pals, eight thousand members) had spoken to her only a few times, on the telephone. She didn't have a passport, or even a driver's license.

Five years ago, when her earnings from the early best-sellers began to accumulate, she had purchased from a local bank the deed to two hundred acres of the heart of what was known as the Barony, an original land-grant plantation established by her ancestors in the early 1700s, and which once had taken up most of the seven thousand acres of Chicora Island. There she now spent nearly all of her time, turning out a new historical fiction approximately every two years.

He studied the jacket photo of Pamela Abelard again, although he'd done this so often since initiating the project that he could have drawn a likeness from memory. It was not a heavily airbrushed studio portrait; in contrast to other women authors in her status bracket whose aging faces had been transformed for the camera by hours of makeover and accomplished lighting techniques, Pamela Abelard seemed appealingly natural. Probably the photo was a blowup of a snapshot taken by a friend. Sunlight was hot on her brow and cheekbones; her eyes were slightly, tantalizingly narrowed as if from glare as she looked into the camera lens. She had gray or very light blue eyes. Her eyebrows were much darker than her hair. There'd been a strong breeze, and her hair glowed with red highlights in the strands whipped across her forehead. A few freckles were visible. She had good facial planes, a strong Scots chin with a hint of a crease, and a wide mouth—not smiling, but quizzically amused. And she might have been a little shy about being photographed.

Something unaffected, raffish in her appearance. Her only flaw was a pair of jug-handle ears, but they didn't detract from her casual beauty, the Huck Finn sincerity and naturalness.

Abelard's image on the back of *Honor's Flame* fused with the vision Joe had had of her on the transom of the fishing boat at sea. And as always this made him uneasy, feeling a little out of control of the project before it had begun. He felt inadequately prepared and, even worse, impulsive, drawn to her for reasons more tragic than sentimental. As if their lives had already intersected, and her appearance had been more than a hallucination—he pitched the novel away and groaned. That was the kind of nonsense he didn't subscribe to, but which Abelard apparently found of interest, having fashioned a book around the theme of reincarnation. *Eternity's Flame*, number three or four in her oeuvre. He'd read them all so fast, the story lines became a jumble of hot-blooded, resourceful heroines and men with great bodies and shady pasts. Women loved bastards, as a movie producer of Joe's acquaintance had once remarked. It was one of the secrets of the success of his pictures, and it probably had a lot to do with the popularity of Abelard's books.

Joe smiled. There were all kinds of bastards, and probably she had known her share. She was too good-looking not to have had a lot of men around. Even in a backwater like Nimrod's Chapel, where she'd chosen to sequester herself to pursue her art. She wasn't married, but undoubtedly she was engaged to or sleeping with someone. Joe wondered how long it would take for him to get rid of his rival. But that had never been a problem, and it didn't worry him now.

TEN

From a piece she had contributed to a writer's magazine, Joe knew that Pamela Abelard liked to get cranked up at about nine-thirty in the evening, after an eight-o'clock dinner. She dictated for two, sometimes three hours, almost without a pause. The dictation was transcribed daily by her assistant, but the author never looked at the pages until the first draft was finished. Then she put in three or four months of rewriting, until she was satisfied. Given her work routine, Joe thought that the best time to find her at loose ends might be in the morning, so he left Nimrod's Chapel after a breakfast of pecan muffins, soft-boiled eggs and hominy grits and drove across the causeway to the Barony.

Barbara Ann, at the Planter's House, had told him to look for a general store and ask for directions, because there was a nearly total lack of road signs on the island. The hard road, as she called it, went north and east toward Chicora State Beach. The other roads were little more than sandy lanes mixed with shell, and sometimes it was difficult to make out the turnoffs for all the palmetto thickets and hardwood forest.

He had rented a four-wheel-drive Jeep Laredo at the Myrtle Beach Jet Port on his arrival the day before. There had been some rain on the short drive down the coast to Nimrod's Chapel, but today was clear and mild, the estuary steaming as the sun burned away layers of morning mist thick as cake icing, revealing fishermen in their small boats among the dark cypress snags, great birds floating through the mist in a silence as profound as the moment before the dawn of time.

The general store he'd been directed to find shared a crossroads with a roadside market that sold pecans by the bushel basket, pumpkins and colorful calabashes. A barefoot local artist had set up a display of his work in front of his dilapidated Volkswagen van: oil-on-velvet paintings of Jesus, Elvis Presley and unicorns, the complete canon of redneck spirituality. The store had fish-bait boxes on the porch, and smelled musty-sweet inside from the dozens of sugar-cured hams hanging from six-by-six beams.

An old Negro man with a liver-spotted bald head the color of beeswax and an old white man whose eyes were magnified by glasses the size of automobile headlights interrupted their checkers game by a luminous front window and told him, more or less, how to reach the Barony. There were forks in the road to reckon with, they couldn't agree how many, and marshes to cross, and then keep an eye out for the old 'Piscopal cemetery. "The church, of course, burnt to the ground in 1915. That's not right, Henry? How would you know, you wasn't born then. Anyhow, you take the right-hand fork at All Saints', and—I'm the one telling him now, Henry, would you give me a chance to finish—and not more'n half mile, pert near the cutoff to Mariah Beach, there's a grove of live oak planted straight as a stitch 'longside the road to the gatehouse of the Barony. Where that book writer woman lives, and be damned if we don't get half a dozen folks a day stop in here wanting directions. But that's the summertime, mostly. Ain't had nobody, it's three-four days now, asking about her. Where you from, son?"

"Africa."

"You don't say. That your home?"

"No, I was working there."

"Henry here, his great-grandmother come from Africa."

"She did. That's a fact."

"What did you do there, in Africa?"

"I'm a doctor. Children's doctor. I worked with a French group called *Médecins Sans Frontières*. Doctors without borders."

The high-yellow Negro, Henry, looked at his partner for a few seconds.

"Reckon we ought to tell him the right way to go, Allard."

Allard nodded. "If he's a doctor, then it would be okay."

Joe said, smiling, "That's some routine you fellas have for the tourists."

"Well, you know," Henry said. "Can be a bother, they walk around the plantation without they be ask. Look in windows with them cameras. Don't care for nobody's privacy. Dr. Luke, he ask us to kindly misdirect as many folks as we can. We ain't got nobody so lost they have to call out the bloodhounds. Sooner or later, they all winds up down at the beach."

With what he hoped were the right directions in mind, Joe followed a mule-drawn wagon for half a mile, made a little better time on a hard-packed dirt road to a three-story freestanding chimney of fire-blackened brick that was nearly overgrown with Carolina jasmine. He crossed a blackwater slough on an old brick bridge, heading southeast with the sun in his face. The air was sultry. There were a few shacky houses along the wandering road, mailboxes; abruptly he came to a marsh beyond which the bay was visible in a hazy light through islands of cypress. He was going due south, with live oaks on the east side of the improved road, which was a mix of dirt, sand and crushed shell. The road was only about a car and a half wide but it had been graded recently to smooth out potholes and allow for good drainage.

Within sight of the bay again, in an area of fallow fields and woodlots, he came to the Barony. A couple of black men were at work repointing the formidable brick gateposts. The iron gates stood open. Along the road to the house, which had been built with its back to the widest part of Pandora's Bay, a couple of dump trucks were parked at a lean on one side of the roadway embankment. Men with chain saws were clearing a stand of longleaf pine near the road, and a stump-grinder added to the racket.

Someone who might have been a foreman glanced at the approaching Jeep, then left the men in hard hats he'd been talking to and stepped onto the drive, gesturing for Joe to stop. He was a big black man. For October the humidity was high, and his blue work shirt already was sweat-stained. The tab on a sack of tobacco hung from one breast pocket. Instead of a hard hat he wore a black baseball cap with a red bill. He had bad knees and walked as if hampered by leg irons, but he looked to be the sort of man who'd been a juggernaut in his youth: hard, fast, merciless.

"Good morning, suh," he said, in a voice that might once have been plush velvet, but now had a few snags in it.

"Morning," Joe said. "What's going on?"

The big man leaned on the sill of Joe's window, dripping sweat. Scar tissue pulled tight the corners of his eyes, the pupils of which were a burnt-almond color. "Oh, Dr. Luke, he's lately taken up polo. We're clearing out all the slash growth to make room for a practice field and a new horse barn."

He looked past Joe at the copy of *Honor's Flame* on the other seat. He smiled gently, like a bouncer sizing up potential trouble.

"You ain't the decorator fella from Charleston, is you?"

"I'm from Chicago. I've been out of the country for a couple of years. I was hoping I could get Miss Abelard to sign a book for me before I go home. It's a birthday gift for my sister in Fond du Lac."

The man nodded thoughtfully, took his hands off the windowsill, straightened and reached into his pocket for the sack of smoking tobacco. He had tissue-weight wrinkled papers in his other shirt pocket. He began to roll a cigarette for himself. His hand movements were graceful for someone who looked as if he'd broken every knuckle at least once.

"Yes, suh. She'll gladly do that. But you needs to leave the book with me. I'll see that she gets it, and sends it on to you."

Joe glanced in the rearview mirror, saw a Range Rover on the road outside the gates of the Barony, making time, leaving a cloud of dust behind it. The decorator fella from Charleston?

"You sure are hard to find out here," Joe said pleasantly.

The big man finished rolling his cigarette, sealing it with spit, and felt for matches.

"Reckon I couldn't find my way round Chicago, if I chanced to be there." He also looked at the oncoming Range Rover, and started to frown.

"As long as I've driven this far," Joe said, "I'd like to say hello to my favorite author. I've read everything she's written."

"Sure, sure, I understand. But Miss Abby, she can't take the time, sit and chat with everybody, wouldn't get no work done." He heaved a sigh. "So if you'll just let me have your copy—"

He was distracted by someone yelling in the field. "Yo, Walter Lee!" He turned and stared, trying to make out what was being said to him, but the smoky stump-grinder roared again like a badly tuned motorcycle.

"Be right back," Walter Lee said to Joe. He tucked the cigarette he hadn't had the chance to smoke between an ear and his baseball cap and went down the six-foot embankment to the field at a hobbled lope, waving his arms.

The dusty green Range Rover was coming up fast behind Joe, and the driver didn't seem to be in a mood to stop or even slow down. The Range Rover's horn sounded.

Joe pulled out around the first of the dump trucks, intending to make room for the oncoming vehicle. As he angled past the high fender of the other truck he misread the slope of the embankment and the back end of his Laredo slid in the loose shell and sand. Nothing he couldn't handle easily with four-wheel drive. Then he saw at the base of the embankment the stumps of some pine trees that had been felled but not removed, recognized an opportunity and seized it as the Range Rover blasted by him.

He gave the wheel a sharp turn right and the slide was accelerated. Instead of shifting into low and pulling out of it, he pumped the brake, shifted into reverse, and went bumping backward down the embankment, stopped with a crunching jolt atop a couple of the jutting stumps and switched off the ignition immediately. He didn't know where the gas tank was, but the crash might have ruptured it. The Laredo was tilted slightly to the driver's side. He opened the door and stepped down into some mud from a recent rain. He sank into it just past the cuffs of his khaki Dockers.

The Laredo was hung up firmly on the stumps, the

right rear tire a foot off the ground. The gas tank seemed to be okay. The bumper had been bent slightly in the collision, but provided there was no damage to the rear axle or ball joint, the Laredo might be drivable once it was yanked up off the stumps and set down on the road. But that would take a while, even if there was a tow truck in the vicinity.

The stump-grinder and the chain saws had stopped as the men working in the stand of pine trees paused to consider his predicament.

"Lord, Lord," Walter Lee said in a weary voice.

Joe shrugged, looking baffled and a little angry.

"I was just trying to get off the drive to make room for that Range Rover."

"I know. I allow it wasn't your fault, mister."

"My name's Bryce. Dr. Joe Bryce. Who was that driving the Rover?"

Walter Lee said reluctantly, "That was Mrs. Thomason. She don't have a whole lot of patience, you see." He added, almost under his breath, "And not much sense sometimes." He rose from his examination of the undercarriage of the Laredo. "Muffler's about tore off. Look here, I'll get some of the boys, and we'll try to lift the back end up off them stumps."

"I'd appreciate that. But I don't want to risk driving it until I'm sure there's no real damage. Could I find a phone somewhere?"

Walter Lee looked at Joe's mud-covered Nikes. "You want to call a tow, take it to the garage? Sure. Listen, I'm real sorry what happened. Say you is a doctor?"

"That's right. And you're Walter Lee."

"Walter Lee Clemons. I looks after things round here."

Joe offered his hand. He could palm a basketball, but Walter Lee could probably have palmed a wrecking ball. "Nice to meet you, Walter Lee."

"What I'll do, I'll walk on up the house with you and call the rental-car people. They got their own arrangements with a garage in town. Bring that rental agreement along, if you please." He turned to one of the hired hands. "Y'all see what you can do while I'm gone."

Joe reached into the Jeep for the rental agreement fixed to the sun visor, and picked up his copy of *Honor's Flame*. Walter Lee didn't say anything about the novel. They walked up the drive toward the house, with Joe squishing every step of the way. He would have been more comfortable barefoot, but the crushed-shell drive would have shredded the soles of his feet. Walter Lee labored, breathing through his mouth.

"What weight did you fight at?" Joe asked him.

"Oh, two-fifty. Two thutty-five, when I could get down to it."

"Did you ever fight anybody good?"

"No. I was on the hamburger menu, worked the training camps some. Archie, Jersey Joe, Floyd. Well, there was this Puerto Rican boy, he got a shot at Ali one time. I know I whupped him, but they done give it to him on points anyhow. That was in Ponce, Puerto Rico, you see, and they wasn't about to let the hometown boy lose." Walter Lee squinted at Joe in a shaft of sunlight where the shell road became a circular brick motor court arranged in a herringbone pattern around an old magnolia tree and a marble fountain. "I allow you been in the ring some yourself."

"Amateur bouts. I had quick hands. But I never had the desire."

The dog came out of nowhere at them, swift as a cloud shadow through leathery magnolia leaves lying on the Bermuda lawn in front of the house. Joe's blood ran cold when he saw it, because of the lather around the brute's muzzle. But Walter Lee whistled sharply and the dog stopped a few feet shy of them. A moment later they heard a girl's voice calling.

"Bruiser! You get back here, finish your damn bath!"

The dog appeared to be some kind of mastiff, bulky at the shoulders and with a flattened black muzzle on the order of a boxer dog. But Bruiser probably weighed twice what the average boxer would weigh. He'd been in his bath, all right, which accounted for the suds Joe had momentarily mistaken for hydrophobia. Then he shook himself all over, showering both Joe and Walter Lee. This made Bruiser happy, and he sat back with tongue lolling, heedless of the young girl who now came charging after him with his collar and chain leash.

"Bruiser!"

The mastiff lay down and wormed his way through some fallen leaves.

"Now look at you! We've got to start all over again!"

She was about thirteen, and tall, with no real shape apparent yet in her Grateful Dead T-shirt and frayed denim shorts. Her hair was a frizzy strawberry blond. She had red-rimmed blue eyes and sun-raw cheekbones and a nice curvy mouth to go with a pugnacious jaw.

Joe brushed suds from the front of his knit shirt and said, "Do you have room in Bruiser's bath for me?"

She took him in with a slightly startled expression, from the mud on his shoes to his hairline; still looking at him, she stooped to wrestle the now-accommodating Bruiser into his choke collar.

"You are a mess, aren't you?" Her voice was high and tended to sound aggrieved. "Are you the decorator from—"

"Charleston? No, I'm Joe Bryce from Chicago. What's your name?"

She pushed and pulled until Bruiser was on his feet.

"Elizabeth Abelard. You might as well call me Lizzie, everybody else does." She expressed her distaste with a squint and wrinkling of her nose. "What happened to you?"

Walter Lee said, "His car got stuck off the road there."

"I was trying to get out of the way of—"

"The Queen Crab?" Lizzie looked at the Range Rover, parked beside a pristine '62 Cadillac in beige and black, its engine still ticking in the sun. "I heard her pitching a fit about the driveway being blocked, or something."

Bruiser, belatedly, began to growl at Joe.

"Oh, shut up, he looks okay to me."

"What kind of dog *is* that?"

"Neapolitan mastiff. If you tried to sneak in here at night he'd kill you."

"Oh, come on, Miss Lizzie," Walter Lee said.

"Well—" She gave the dog a hug, wetting down her T-shirt. "He bites a little, but he can't chew. Walter Lee, you gonna help this man with his stuck car?"

"Yes, I'll take care of it."

Lizzie looked soberly at Joe, then at the book he was protecting under one arm.

"Okay. He'll be with me." To Joe she said, "Let me hose down Bruiser, and we'll do something about your shoes. Are they washable?"

"I think so."

"Let's go, Joe."

He followed Lizzie and Bruiser across the motor court and along a brick garden walkway chinked with moss. There was a vine-covered trellis overhead. Tree ferns, Spanish moss and mistletoe grew in the great boughs of the oaks that shaded the garden. Water trickled into a pool edged with red and purple impatiens. They came to the spigot and a garden hose where Lizzie had been bathing the dog.

She tied the chain leash to the spigot and went back to work. Joe sat down on a stone bench nearby and put his book aside.

"That yours?" Lizzie said, squinting in the sun that shone through hollies behind Joe.

"Uh-huh. I was going to have it signed and send it to my sister."

"Oh. I didn't think you were the sort to be reading that stuff. Ninety-nine percent of her readers are either old maids or sex-starved housewives. You ought to read some of the fan letters Abby gets, are *they* a piss."

Joe unknotted and took off his shoes. "Is Abby your sister?"

"Hold *still*, Bruiser. No, we're second cousins. My stepfather got a snootful and fell off the back of his boat down around Daufuskie Island last year. Drowned. My mother's never been able to handle adversity, which includes me, so I'm staying here until she gets her wits together. Which may or may not ever happen. It's okay. But the damn school bus takes an *hour* each way." She swatted a mosquito that had alighted on the back of one thigh, looked around at Joe for the third or fourth time and said, "Did anybody ever tell you you've got really terrific eyes?"

"Lots of times. Do you always say everything that comes into your head?"

Lizzie shrugged. "Sure, why not? Who's gonna sue me, I don't have any money."

A station wagon had pulled up in the motor court, and a slim young guy up to date on manly fashions got out with blueprints under one arm, looked at the front of the house with a calculating eye.

"That must be the decorator from Charleston," Lizzie said. "We've had 'em from all over, believe me. They last about a week."

"Lot of work going on inside?"

"The Queen Crab's never satisfied."

She stood back to spray the soap off Bruiser, waited until she was sure the decorator from Charleston was safely in the house, then let the mastiff off his leash to roll on the mossy ground. Lizzie coiled the hose neatly. By now she was soaking wet, from the hose and the humidity in the garden.

"Come on, let's find something to put on. We'll throw those running shoes in the washing machine. Pluff mud doesn't stain, like the red clay where I come from. I guess you want to meet Abby while you're here."

"The word is she's kind of hard to see."

Lizzie offered a knowing smile, and flipped a few soggy curls off her forehead with the back of her hand.

"I can arrange it for you, Joe."

ELEVEN

There was a service porch tacked to the house off the kitchen; it was not heated and there was no air-conditioning. The walls were old brick, in a lattice pattern to allow for the passage of breezes on the sweltering Low Country days. A glass storm door opened to the gardens that surrounded the house on three sides, but the porch had no windows. The laundry and ironing were done by girls who came in three days a week.

It was an in-between day for laundry, so Lillian, the housekeeper, attended to Joe's running shoes and muddied clothing. Joe, not quite at home in his boxer shorts and a white terry-cloth pool robe, glanced at the sports section of the previous Sunday's *Columbia State*, waiting for Lizzie to return with some clothes for him to wear while his own things were in the wash.

"Have you worked here long?" he asked Lillian. She was a thin mannerly woman, Gullah-black, her skin as lightless as a seam of buried coal, her forehead popped with small wens like fleshly afterthoughts. She wore thick glasses. Her feet were in such poor shape from age and the climate she could only wear carpet slippers.

"For the family, twenty-eight years. We move ourselves to the Barony from Beaufort, let's see, it's five years now. This house was falling down before then. Would you like some coffee?"

"I can't drink coffee. It's hard on my stomach lining."

"Some grape-juice lemonade?"

"That sounds like a winner."

While Lillian was in the kitchen, Lizzie came bustling back and tossed him a folded T-shirt.

"I got this one at the State Fair last weekend. Extra large, I like to sleep in 'em." Lizzie had changed from the skin out, and brushed her hair. In the diffused morning light it looked as pink and fluffy as cotton candy.

Joe unfolded the shirt, which had a block-letter inscription. MY BODY IS AN OUTLAW. IT'S WANTED ALL OVER TOWN.

Lillian, shuffling back from the kitchen with an old-fashioned metal soda-fountain tray and a pitcher of lemonade, looked at the shirt and said mildly, "Lizabeth, that don't hardly seem appropriate."

"What's wrong? I think it's awesome." She smiled at Joe as he turned his back to take off the robe and slip the shirt on. She wore orthodontic braces, the transparent kind, which he hadn't noticed before. "I don't have any pants that would fit you, and we're kind of short of men around here. I could look in Luke's closet, he's in Columbia today sucking up to the state legislature. Luke's a little taller than you, probably, but he keeps himself in good shape for somebody as old as he is."

"Don't go to any more trouble, Lizzie."

She shrugged. "You look incredible in those boxers anyway. How old are you, Joe?"

"Over twenty-one."

"Are you married?"

"No."

"Divorced?"

"No. No kids, either."

"Mind if I ask you what you do for a living?" she said with her nonchalant nosiness, sitting on the corner of a laundry-folding table next to Joe, who had sat down again in a wicker basket chair.

"You are giving us both the earache," Lillian grumbled, looking into one of the heavy-duty driers where Joe's Nikes were tumbling around.

"I'm a doctor."

"Hey. No kidding. Brain surgeon?"

"Pediatrics."

"Oh," Lizzie said, a little disappointed. Then she brightened. "I have the *worst* rashes. It's because I'm so fair. I've got one now, in the middle of my back where I can't scratch—" She twisted her upper body like a soul in deep torment, then hiked the loose-fitting shirt she was wearing. "See it?"

"Doesn't look so bad."

"But it's driving me nuts! Is there something you could put on it?"

"Baby powder."

"*Baby* powder?"

"Same remedy mothers have been using forever. Cornstarch and a little talc."

Lizzie dropped her shirt just as a blond woman walked onto the porch from the kitchen. She gave Lizzie a sharp look and did a slight double-take at Joe, who smiled, but not quick enough to catch her eye as she turned to Lillian and said, "Lillian, I can't find my new swatches anywhere!"

"What new swatches?" Lillian said, in a voice that was on the edge of indifference, but still polite.

Lizzie leaned over to Joe and said in a low voice, "Hold on to your *cojones, señor.*"

Charlene Thomason whirled on her. "Excuse *me*, Lizzie?"

"Nothing. I was just talking to Joe in Spanish. I'm taking Spanish this year."

Without getting up, Joe said, "Mrs. Thomason, my name is Joe Bryce. I'm sorry to intrude like this."

"*Some*body," Lizzie said, "ran him off the road this morning."

"Oh," Charlene said with a slight frown, "was that you in the Jeep? But I—I thought there was room. I was in a hurry, I needed to—"

"Pee?" Lizzie suggested.

Charlene ignored her. She was very blond, and so pale she looked as if she had no body temperature. Her paleness made the beauty mark on one cheek stand out as hot as a sunspot. Her eyes were large and dark and round and when she looked directly at Joe he could see a rim of sclera beneath each pupil, which gave her a sensuous, unearthly look, like a high priestess of conspicuous consumption. She reveled in gold jewelry, and, even if her suit was a Chanel knockoff, she had the figure to wear it superbly. The Carolina accent was a delightful, earthy touch, but the pampered face, the type, was very familiar to Joe. They were seen most often getting into or out of Rolls-Royces. They congregated at the fringes of show business like fleas around a dog's muzzle. Most of them seemed to have the longevity of Dracula. And they all could get alimony from a stone.

Joe stood up slowly, the hell with the boxer shorts and the T-shirt, and saw her expression change in just the way he knew it would. He was wary of Charlene Thomason, but he said in a relaxed, easy manner, as if it were his house and she were visiting, "What happened was my fault. I got a little too deep into the shoulder and—"

"I see. Are you a friend of my husband's?"

"No, I—"

Lizzie, perched on her corner of the table, swung a long thin leg back and forth and said, "He came to see Abby. He's a fan."

"Oh." Charlene half-closed her eyes, conserving on power. "I'm afraid that Pamela is—"

Lizzie said in her high, hostile voice, "It's okay. I already talked to her."

Charlene looked at her with a deliberation that returned the hostility. This family was getting more interesting all the time, Joe thought.

"Lizzie, you haven't been with us very long, but it really is time that you learned not to impose—"

Lizzie ducked her head, one side of her face scrunched as if she had a toothache. Then she said, more rapidly than most Southerners can talk, "I've been here long enough to know that if it's what Abby wants then it's what *everybody* wants. And I already told you, she's dying to meet Joe."

Charlene's chin came up a millimeter, the only expression of annoyance she allowed herself. Lizzie kept her head down, reached out and plucked at a ragged nail on her big toe. Her face was flushed.

Charlene turned to Lillian and said, "Lillian, if you can possibly spare the time right now, I need for you to help me locate my swatches. I can't keep Mr. Loeffler waiting the rest of the day."

"Yes, ma'am."

"One other thing."

Lillian took Joe's Nikes out of the drier and straightened slowly.

"We're having barbecue for a hundred people tonight, and this house is nowhere near ready to receive guests. That's *your* fault, Lillian."

Lillian's jaw worked, as if she were chewing this bitter pill before swallowing it. "I'll see to it, right away."

Charlene cast around for an opportunity to vent a little more spleen.

"I hate this tacky porch. It's such an eyesore. I'm going to tear it down at the first opportunity and build a nice orangerie with lots of glass." Then, refreshed and on top of things, she turned to Joe.

"So nice to have met you, Mr.—"

"Bryce. Dr. Joe Bryce."

Her smile tilted more in his favor. "Oh, you're a doctor? My husband's a doctor."

Lizzie made a small but negative noise through flubbering lips.

"I'm sorry you won't have a chance to meet him," Charlene went on, getting a visible grip on her patience, but not as if Lizzie meant any more to her than a dead fly on the table. "He won't be home until late this afternoon."

"I'm glad to have had this opportunity to meet you, Mrs. Thomason."

She nodded and turned blithely, with a signal to Lillian that she wanted to be followed. "Enjoy your little chat with Pamela. Bye now."

Lizzie said, after Charlene and Lillian had cleared the kitchen, "I usually win bigger than that. But it was getting to be embarrassing."

"Thanks for sparing me."

"I'll see if your pants are dry yet," Lizzie mumbled, springing from the table and rubbing the back of her thigh where the edge of the table had left a welt.

"What have you got against Mrs. Thomason?" Joe asked her.

"Did you notice the way she was looking at you?"

"I didn't mind it."

"Well, men wouldn't," Lizzie said scornfully. "But that's one of the reasons I can't bear her. There's others."

"I see."

Lizzie glanced over her shoulder. "You don't, and I

can't tell you. Even if you are a doctor." Immediately after this testimony to her integrity, Lizzie added, "But you probably noticed anyway."

"Noticed something about Mrs. T?"

Lizzie took his Dockers and knit shirt out of the other drier. "I ought to run the iron over these before you put them on. Won't take a second."

"Thanks."

"Aren't doctors supposed to be able to tell when somebody's on drugs?"

"Depends on the substance, usually. Are you still talking about—"

"Oh, well, let's skip it. Doesn't matter. I'm probably going to go nuts too, it's so isolated here. I think that's why Charlene puts up wallpaper, and takes down wallpaper, and goes around obsessing over her *swatches*. Either she's hyper, or she stays in her room for a couple of days at a time and won't talk to anybody. Maybe they'll go live in the governor's mansion next year, and she'll get her act together. He could get elected. Really, that's what I heard. Stranger things have happened in South Carolina politics. We have all kinds of relatives up there in the legislature. My great uncle Woodrow T. Plover ran on what he called the Truth Platform a long time ago. He's famous for making a campaign speech and saying he foresaw the day when only the living could vote."

"Dr. Thomason's running for governor?"

"*Yes.*" Unexpectedly, Lizzie had a fit of the giggles. "I'm telling you, Joe, everybody in this house is certifiable. Lillian sees ghosts all the time. Knows their names too. I'm afraid I'll start seeing them. That'd freak me so bad I probably never will get my period."

"And Abby?"

"Oh, Abby. I think she's the most courageous person I've ever met. But how long can it last?" Lizzie's eloquent face was screwed up again, either from dismay or concentration as she pressed Joe's pants. She set the iron upright and brought the Dockers to him. "She's probably about finished with her morning swim. Let's see if we can catch her in the pool house."

TWELVE

The gardens behind the house were more extensive, and for mal, than anything Joe had seen yet. There were hedges of thickly budded camellias, stone and brick portals covered with ivy and jasmine, fruit trees, huge beds of roses, trickling fountains and shady moss-covered banks beside a pond. Serpentine brick walkways went in all directions—to a gazebo with a stone and bronze sundial in front of it, to the gated entrance of the walled cemetery, to a converted carriage house, and to a larger, newer building designed with the power and simplicity of a Cistercian church: it had a high, gabled roof, clerestory windows and window-walls at each end. The pool pavilion was connected to a wing of the main house by a glass conservatory. Through the middle of the gardens there was a visual passage to the sparkling bay a few hundred yards away. *Fifteen million*, Joe thought. On top of perhaps ten or twelve million she'd earned so far. The portion of Pamela Abelard's royalties that had gone into the revitalizing of this venerable estate had been well spent.

Gardeners were at work, pruning and planting, moving shrubs to new locations. An old black man was down on padded knees patiently cleaning bird droppings off the bricks, which varied in shading in a crazy-quilt pattern from dark red to pink. In a mossy area under a live oak that would have spread its most ancient boughs half the length of a city block, two caterers had lifted a wrapped steaming package from a firepit to check on the progress of the intact pig inside. Smoke was in the air, flavored with the aroma of cooked pork.

"Those have been cooking since yesterday afternoon," Lizzie said. "Shorty and Bum cater all of the big cookouts around here. I guarantee by ten o'clock tonight everybody'll be in a barbecue coma." She smacked her lips ecstatically, like Hannibal Lecter rhapsodizing over a human liver. "I can hardly wait."

Lizzie was carrying her CD Walkman, listening through one earpiece of a headphone to whatever-it-was while she talked to Joe. The music that leaked through the dangling earpiece clashed violently with the tranquil, sun-dappled gardens.

"What group is that?"

"Pig Vomit."

"You're making it up."

"I swear! Some of the nastiest stuff I've ever heard. Masturbation and peeing and coming and so forth. I mean, it's *vile.*"

"So why listen to it?"

Lizzie shrugged. "Because it's happening. They're expressing their rage and disgust at the world we live in. That makes it kind of interesting, in a way—if you think about barf as, you know, sort of a metaphor. Cool. Anyway, I have to know what's happening, or I'd just be some kind of drupe at school, totally *lame.*"

"How come you're out of school today?"

"Teachers' meeting. Lucky for you I'm here. I mean,

nobody gets past Walter Lee ordinarily. That old carriage house? It's Abby's workshop. Really neat. Maybe you'll see it later."

She stopped and turned off her Walkman, hung the headphones around her neck.

"Could I ask your medical opinion about something?"

"Sure."

"I'm thirteen, almost thirteen and a half, and I haven't got it yet. Isn't that abnormal?"

"Not if you've been under a lot of stress."

Lizzie scratched an ear, then scratched a bare shoulder. "Well, I guess I have been stressed. My stepfather; and then my mother's been making me crazy since I can remember." She looked down critically at herself. "Nothing much is happening up front, but I've got pubic hair. I had to shave some of it already. Should I pick out some kid in my class and do it with him? A friend of mine says that's how she got started."

"I doubt it. Very bad idea, Lizzie."

Lizzie shrugged, not as if she were disappointed. "Okay. There aren't any guys at school I'd want to give my body to anyway. They're all a bunch of hicks. What *should* I do, then?"

"Hang on another two or three months, then if you still haven't menstruated, see a gynecologist."

"The only one in town is so old he's positively creepy. I can't imagine letting *him* touch me." She gave Joe a speculative look, but said nothing more about the matter. "C'mon. Abby's swimming. This way, Joe."

The sweet smell of roses and tang of baking pork gave way to muggier, lightly misted air as they entered the pool pavilion. There was no odor of chlorine; the swimming-pool water was cleaned by ozone filtration.

At the shallow end of the pool, the size of a basketball court, a man and a woman stood waist-deep in the churned water watching a swimmer go from one tiled side wall to the other, breast-stroking, working hard.

"One more lap, Abby," the woman said encouragingly; her voice had a slight echo in the navelike space. "Can you do it today?"

Lizzie put a hand on Joe's arm. They paused in the colonnaded lounging area, where tanning lamps in the low ceiling alternated with conventional lighting for cloudy winter days.

"Abby had this built about a year ago," Lizzie said. "She was putting on too much weight. But she's looking great now."

Joe studied the swimmer. About all he could see of her was a bright orange cap and goggles.

"That's Abby in the pool? Who are—"

"The one with the hairy chest is Norse. He's Norwegian or something. I thought he was to die for, but he goes on and on about muscle groups. He said he could help me develop my bustline. Uh-huh. He gives Charlene massages, and I don't think that's all he gives her. She's Tonya. What an airhead, but look at that body! They're physical therapists."

As Pamela Abelard reached the end of her cross-pool lap, the strapping Norse reached her and held her up. Joe had a sudden chilly feeling. He looked at Lizzie again, but she was watching something that had flown in through an open window, cringing a little as it seemed about to dart near her head.

"Terrific, Abby," the therapist named Tonya enthused. "Sixty laps today. How do you feel?"

"Out of breath," Abby managed to say, "Great. No problems. Help me out now."

It was obvious to Joe, as the physical therapists combined to carry Pamela Abelard up the steps at the shallow end of the pool, that she was paralyzed, at least from the waist down. A flotation collar held her ankles together.

"Hey," Lizzie said softly, jolting him out of his own paralysis. "What's the matter?"

"My God. I had no idea."

"It was a hit-and-run driver. Abby was nineteen. The boy she was going to marry died after a week in a coma. I don't think she's ever gotten over him."

Abby was coughing up some pool water. When she could speak, she said in a squeaky voice, "Jaysus. Cramp. Left shoulder."

Norse went to work on her immediately as she sat on a poolside bench. Abby reached up with her other hand and pulled off the orange swim cap, letting her abundant auburn hair tumble. For a longtime paraplegic she was well preserved and proportioned.

"Hey," she said, regaining full use of her voice, "I *was* good today, wasn't I? I'll be ready to try for a mile before the year's over. Ouch!"

"Really knotted here," Norse explained as he eased up on the pressure.

Tonya unwrapped the Velcro flotation collar and covered Abby's legs with a beach towel. Abby groaned again, spat another mouthful of water on the pool apron, then straightened up and waved Norse away from her shoulder. For the first time she noticed Lizzie and Joe.

"Lizzie, hey! Did you see me?"

"Great!" Lizzie called back.

"C'mere, sweetie. Who's with you?"

"Joe."

"Joe, who's Joe? C'mon, both of you."

As they walked toward her Abby leaned over again, this time pressing both hands on the quadriceps muscle of her right leg. She grimaced and flipped the towel back. Her leg was trembling violently, thigh and calf muscles jitterbugging, the foot kicking as if she were about to leap up from the bench and hit the dance floor.

"God damn it," Abby said grimly.

"Do you want your Lioresal?" Tonya asked her.

"No. That stuff makes me stupid," she complained.

The absurdist motions of her leg were already quieting.

Abby was still trying to get her breath when the drag-onfly appeared in sunlight over her shoulder, hovering in radiance like an insectile Tinkerbell. Abby didn't notice until the dragonfly sailed down to alight in the crook of her left arm. She didn't react badly. She seemed to be used to insects.

"Look at that! Isn't it a beauty?"

"Don't they bite?" Tonya said, timidly preparing to whisk the dragonfly away with her golfer's terry-cloth sunshade.

"No, they don't bite," Joe said. "Actually they bring good luck."

They all looked at him. Norse stepped back from Abby, flexing his strong hands, and kneeled to take a bottle of lotion from a gym bag. Abby wiped away water dripping down her tanned face from the goggles she had propped at the hairline and smiled critically at Joe. Her two front teeth had space between them and stood out slightly from the even line of her other teeth, like alabaster gates about to open. The effect lent expec-tancy to her smile.

"Tell me another," she challenged him. The drag-onfly continued to rest in the crook of her arm, the wings, colored like oil on water, moving slowly.

"My mother had a dragonfly tattooed on her left shoulder."

"Yeah? What kind of luck did she have?"

"She had me," Joe said.

Abby demonstrated a rollicking, living-it-up-in-a-barroom laugh.

"When a dragonfly lights on you, it means you've been touched by good fortune."

"I'm already famous, rich and good-looking," Abby said, holding his gaze, amused by all the conceits. "What else do I need?"

"You'd have to be the one to answer that."

Norse began working on the shoulder that had

cramped with a milky lotion, glancing at Joe as he kneaded and stroked in a professional but still proprietary manner. He had three small diamonds in the lobe of one ear, like awards to his sexual ego. His smile was tight and guarded. He paid Joe a lot of attention. Joe already had seen all he needed to see of Norse.

Abby dwelled on the motionless dragonfly.

"They're all over the garden," she said. "But I haven't had one come this close. He's not afraid of me, is he?"

She looked around for confirmation. Lizzie said disdainfully, "Bugs is bugs."

Abby made a face at her, then glanced up at Joe. Her slightly brassy gray eyes were partly veiled, eyelashes delicately enhanced by tiny waterdrops.

"Joe? Joe what?"

"Bryce."

"*What?*" she said, in disbelief. "B-R-Y-C-E?"

" 'Son of the Ardent One.' At least I think that's what the name Bryce means."

"You bet it does! God, is this *incredible?* In my first novel I named my hero Joseph Bryce!"

"The Confederate blockade runner. I know. It's quite a coincidence, isn't it? *Flames of War* is still my favorite of all your books."

"Come on. You haven't read *all* my books."

"Yes, I have. Ask me something."

"Okay. Ten bucks says you can't tell me the name of the Ku Klux Klan infiltrator in *Mercy's Flame.*"

He pretended to have to think about it while her smile broadened, mockingly.

"Peter Langtree."

Abby laughed gleefully. He knew he would have liked her from the sound of her laughter, even if he had never set eyes on her.

"You look like Captain Bryce, too." She had been out of the water for a couple of minutes, and now she was getting gooseflesh. Tonya helped her put on a striped terry pool robe. "I mean, you're almost the way I pictured him in my mind when I was writing the book."

"Where's my ten bucks?" Joe said. He felt it was safe to show a little attitude.

"God, you *sound* like Bryce."

"Who sounded a lot like Rhett Butler, by the way."

"Okay, okay, don't pick on me, it was my first novel, you have to steal from somebody. Anyway, I always pay my debts." She leaned forward on the bench as if to shake his hand. The dragonfly took flight, soaring in a magically quick, zigzagging pattern over the surface of the quieted turquoise pool.

"Oh-oh. There goes my good fortune," she said, almost as glum as if she believed the story.

"Once you've been touched by the dragonfly, you'll always be blessed."

Her grin was a little cock-eyed. "Mon, you can talk the talk. Not a writer, are you?"

"Just a fan. It's been a real pleasure meeting you. I've looked forward to this for a long time."

Norse, with a sulky glance at Joe, said, "Abby, you should change."

"Yeah. If you guys will excuse me; I can't afford to take a chill. I'm allergic to antibiotics. Hey, don't go anywhere!" she said, concentrating on Joe. "Can you spare the time?"

"I hadn't planned—I just wanted to have my book signed—"

"No problem! Tonya, take the book for me and leave it in the office box with a note. Lizzie, I'm deputizing you. Don't let Cap—Mr. Bryce—get away. Somebody fetch Rolling Thunder for me."

Norse brought the mechanized wheelchair, which was flying a miniature Confederate flag, and Abby adroitly maneuvered herself into it, zipped off to one of the changing rooms.

Lizzie sneezed. "Ozone wrecks my sinuses. I never use the pool. Can we go outside, Joe?"

"Sure, Lizzie."

He smiled at Tonya, handing her his copy of *Honor's Flame*, and walked with Lizzie into the garden. The day was heating up, but there was an unexpectedly spanking breeze from the northeast, the quarter from which most storms came to this coast. On the Weather Channel, an early-morning habit of his, Joe had seen the satellite shot of a big bulge of tropical storm off Africa's west coast. A little late in the season for one of those, but like any good sailor he'd filed the information away instinctively.

Bruiser wandered over to have his head scratched. "Thirteen years," Lizzie said broodingly. "She's thirty-two now. If it had been me I'd've killed myself, but I don't have any talent. I guess that's what keeps Abby going."

They sat together on a low brick wall. The batteries in Lizzie's Walkman had gone dead. Birds were chipper in a clump of hackberry nearby. Lizzie juggled the dead batteries in the palm of one hand. "No legs," she said, "but that's not all that's going."

"What do you mean, Lizzie?"

Lizzie looked uncomfortable. "I don't like talking about Abby. After all, she's the one who's been decent to me around here. I don't think Dr. Luke likes me. Charlene, forget it. Anyway, maybe Abby'll tell you, when you two get to talking again. You really took her over, Joe. Did you see Norse's face? He'd like to put you in the firepit with tonight's dinner."

"Is he Abby's boyfriend too?"

"Ha. Doesn't he wish. All that money. But he's never got anywhere with her. No, Abby likes you, Joe. But I bet that isn't a big deal for you. I bet a lot of women like you."

He smiled at her melancholy, slightly miffed expression.

"I haven't had much time for women, Lizzie. Let you in on a little secret?"

For a few moments Lizzie looked shocked. "You're gay?"

"No. The fact is, women kind of scare me."

Lizzie's face scrunched on one side again, and her finely-haired eyebrows rose skeptically.

"Tell me *another*," she said, bringing her voice down in a good imitation of Pamela Abelard's own husky contralto.

THIRTEEN

Abby had changed into a free-fitting white jumpsuit with an elastic waistband and top; the suit was cinched with a woven fabric belt that had a Western-style, turquoise-studded silver buckle. Whatever her weight problems might have been before the pool pavilion was finished, she looked to be in excellent shape now despite her confinement to a wheelchair.

"I spend most of my mornings in the garden when the weather's good," she said to Joe. "Would you be interested in a tour, Mr. Bryce?"

"*Dr.* Bryce," Lizzie corrected her. "He's my new pediatrician." She appealed to Joe again. "Couldn't I take shots or something to speed up my development?"

"Lizzie, behave," Abby said, with a trace of annoyance. "Puberty will catch up to you." Her face in the sun showed crinkles at the corners of her eyes. Her thick sable eyebrows were darker than shadows. "So

you're a doctor. You must play a lot of golf, with that
tan."

"Haven't played for a long time. And white men in
Equatorial Africa tend to pick up a tan."

Abby aimed Rolling Thunder down a garden path
and took off. "Excuse me, they're putting the Euryops
in the wrong places. Hey, Raymond! Aldous! Hold on
a minute!"

Joe and Lizzie walked beside her, off the path, with
Bruiser behind the wheelchair.

"Africa, huh? Whereabout?"

"Burundi. *Médecins Sans Frontières* had a grant to operate a clinic there. The misery level in Burundi is just
about one hundred percent, and also we were dealing
with Tutsi refugees from Rwanda." The improvisation
came easily; he was able to clearly picture himself in
the stark settings he described, from pictures in news
magazines he remembered in every detail. "Then the
political winds shifted, and we were given twenty-four
hours to get out of the country. I had a six-year-old
patient with cerebrospinal meningitis I just couldn't
leave; so I stayed past the deadline."

"What happened to you?"

His voice was matter-of-fact, a little gritty from the
pain it was so easy to feel.

"I took a beating and was thrown into a stockade for
six weeks, until some officials from the UN and the
Catholic bishop in Bujumbura negotiated me out."

"I'll bet you've had enough of Africa," Lizzie said,
studying his face with an intensity akin to worship. She
was walking backward and tripped over a raised brick.
Joe reached out and caught her.

"I don't know, Lizzie. I honestly don't know the answer to that. I put in two years of eighteen-hour days.
We were always short of everything: vaccines, antibiotics, plain old rubbing alcohol. More than half of all
the supplies shipped to us were stolen as soon as they
came into the country. I spent a lot of precious time

buying our own supplies back on the black markets, for three times what pharmaceuticals go for in the States." He paused and cleared his throat, a thoughtful, distant look in his eye; the bogus memory had become as real to him as the sweat on his brow.

"Where did you practice before you went to Africa?" Abby asked him.

He shifted gears effortlessly. "Winnetka, Illinois. That's just north of Chicago. I guess I could go back to my old group. It was a comfortable life and, yeah, I got to play some golf. But I can't stop thinking about that little six-year-old girl. When she knew they were taking me the light in her eyes slowly died, like ... matches falling into a dark well." He thought the imagery would be appealing to Abby's literary mind.

Lizzie sighed hugely, biting her lip. Abby smiled sympathetically, then stopped to explain to the gardeners what she wanted done with the Euryops, which were small trees with profuse yellow flowers like daisies.

"Well, suppose we start our tour with the cemetery," Abby said cheerfully, when she'd finished giving precise mulching directions. "Oh, see this flower bed? The peonies came from the garden of the Emily Dickinson house in Amherst, Massachusetts. They were a gift from the president of the college. His wife is a fan, and she loved what I wrote about Emily in *Honor's Flame.*"

"The subplot involving a secret mission for the Union Army? That never happened, did it?"

"No, I made it up. Emily was just a shy little mouse all of her life. 'Home is a holy thing—nothing of doubt or distrust can enter its blessed portals ... here seems indeed to be a bit of Eden.' I guess that's how I feel about the Barony, and I really empathize with her. I got run over by a maniac; Emily was psychically paralyzed, you might say. But when I was writing *Honor's Flame* I imagined that just possibly there could have been a supreme moment in her life, during the period of the Civil War when she was strongest and most passionate and writing all that good poetry, when she conquered her fears and had a real honest-to-goodness adventure. But the great romance of her life could not be consummated, so she withdrew forever."

Abby looked at Joe to see if he was bored with the way she was rattling on; his smile encouraged her.

"So, do you read Dickinson?"

"Let's say I've been exposed to her."

"Hate poetry?"

"No, I read a lot of poetry when I was in isolation in Bujumbura. I had a tattered copy of the *Oxford Book of English Verse.* Hopkins, Yeats, Tennyson. They kept my mind off the pain and probably kept me from going crazy too."

"Africa," Abby enthused. "I have *dreamed* about Africa, ever since I discovered Blixen. How I would like to be able to write like that! 'Out on the safaris, I had seen a herd of buffalo, one hundred and twenty-nine of them, come out of the morning mist under a copper sky, one by one, as if the dark and massive, iron-like animals with the mighty horizontally swung horns were not approaching, but were being created before my eyes and sent out as they were finished.' Is that fantastic? I like to read something that brilliant before I get to work, it raises the ante. Gives me something to shoot for."

"Your work is very good."

"Tell that to my critics."

"Where did you study writing?"

"Study it? I just did it. Schools are okay for fish, but they're bad for writers. Excuse me, but most of them give master's degrees for jerking off. Okay, here's the old campground for the Thomasons and the Abelards, among others."

"I am *not* going in there," Lizzie said firmly. "Do you know what she does, Joe? She comes down here to dictate. After dark."

"After dark is when it's most fun," Abby said, with a mischievous grin.

"Yuck. Even Stephen King's not that weird. C'mon, Bruiser, let's go down to the beach. See ya."

Joe followed Abby into the graveyard.

"Probably not much of this would be here if Hugo had come ashore a little farther north. That was, what, in eighty-nine? We were still living in Beaufort then, and it was plenty rough down there. My great-great-great-grandfather's buried over there in that little marble house. He's almost as famous in these parts as the Swamp Fox. But I really need to have this place cleaned up. Oh, and you might enjoy seeing this. Can you give me a push, Joe? I can call you Joe?"

"If I can call you Abby."

"Nobody ever, ever refers to me as Pamela, except Charlene. I can't get her to *stop*. I do think she thinks she's being respectful, and not just acting like a bitch. See those little markers? Westminster Abbey has its Poets' Corner. This is my Critics' Corner. Whenever I read something I don't like and the perpetrator signs it, I get out my woodworking tools and burn in a headstone and bring it down here. Over there's *The New York Times Book Review.* Zap! Lie down and eat dirt, book reviewers! Oh, and here, God rest, is the snide little shit who said in *Vanity Fair* he'd rather spend an hour in the bathroom throwing up than read a chapter of one of my books. I'd rather he would, too." Abby smiled through Joe's laughter. "*Vanity Fair!* Hell, I was crushed. I subscribe to that magazine."

"Do you read all of your reviews?"

"Yes, and any writer who says he doesn't is a liar, in my opinion. But when a bad one comes along, I just get back up and dog away. The English reviewers have been good to me. They praise me for the authenticity of my research, but how would they know? It's true, though. I feel like if I make a mistake, get a date wrong, my whole life is invalidated. Compulsive-neurotic, that's me."

The moment arrived, then, when she couldn't think of any more to say, and they simply looked at each other. Abby nibbled her lower lip.

"Just passing through, huh?"

"Well, I was in Atlanta visiting a colleague at the Centers for Disease Control. Laddy said I should take a week at Hilton Head to try to relax, get in some golf. So I got there, and—just stayed in the condo for three days. I couldn't move. I didn't want to eat. Sort of a panic attack, I think. Because I didn't know who the hell I was anymore, or what I wanted to do. I guess it's like coming back from a war. The sleeping's bad, the nerves are shot . . ."

"You hide it well."

"I'm trying to be on my best behavior," Joe said, with just the right note of rueful charm.

"You don't have friends in South Carolina? Don't know anybody here?"

"Nobody. Well, I should say—now I know you."

She nodded.

"But in a way," he said mildly, "I feel like I've always known you."

She nodded again, as if, listening to gospel, she'd had a vision.

"Sometimes people meet, and—"

"Yeah. Right from the beginning. Is that called empathy?"

"Empathy is when there's nothing left in your glass and you go, 'Hey, bartender, one more thtinger.' Don't say it! I can't help myself sometimes. Maybe 'serendipity' is closer. I'll look it up in my Funk and Wagnalls."

She turned her wheelchair in a slow circle, returning with a smile for Joe.

"Joseph Bryce," Abby mused. "I just can't get over that. I am so glad you went to the trouble to look me up. You probably didn't know I'm supposed to be an *isolato*."

"Like Emily, baking gingerbread and eavesdropping on their visitors' conversation from behind the parlor door?"

"Good Lord, I'm not *that* bad. I get to town once in a while, hit the bars. But it's such a— Look, I live in a totally different world. For one thing, everybody except for little kids is two or three feet taller than I am. I get a neck ache at parties, looking up. At those people who have the courtesy to acknowledge I exist. The handicapped are not treated as badly as lepers used to be, in polite society. But," she concluded, with a hard, perhaps resentful look, "almost as badly."

"Is that why you don't give interviews or do book signings? You don't want your fans to know you're a paraplegic?"

"As Robert Murphy said, my paraplegia represents a contamination of identity. I want my readers to think I've had all the lovers I write about, that I'm an adventuress—let them use their imaginations where I'm concerned. Envy Pamela Abelard for who they *think* she is. And keep coming back for more, keep those cash registers binging away." She laughed, a little edgily. "I hope I haven't been doing an interview without knowing it."

"It's a private conversation, Abby."

"Where're you staying in Nimrod's Chapel?"

"The Planter's House."

"Food's good there," Abby said, summing up her opinion of the Planter's House. "Speaking of which, it must be getting on to lunchtime, and I need to check into my office. C'mon, I'll show you where Pamela Abelard writes her masterpieces."

There was a small white marble statue on a pedestal to the side of the path as they approached Abby's workroom. The statue, worn down from centuries of

weather, had wings and a round face tilted toward
heaven: a little fool's angel, snowblind with innocence.
The double entrance doors to the renovated carriage
house were fourteen feet high. They were from a Spanish monastery, and each door with its intaglio of doves
and sloe-eyed saints weighed several hundred pounds.
But they glided open noiselessly upon verification of
Abby's palm print.

"Better than a padlock," she explained. "I guess I'm
overprotective of my work space."

Inside, on two walls paneled in speckled bamboo,
were blowups of the covers of Abby's six novels, two
abstract canvases—a Frankenthaler and a marvelous
sunset-colored Hofmann—and a carved seventeenth-
century Pegasus. Joe identified the two artists before
she could tell him.

"You know something, Cap'n Bryce? You're not the
uncouth, tobacco-spittin' fast-and-loose blockade runner I always heard about. There's an artistic side to
you, sir."

"When there's a war on, Miss Abby, it doesn't pay
to show your sensitive nature to the enemy."

She loved the game, raising an eyebrow in response.
"And how do you see me, Cap'n? As an enemy, a prize
to be taken?"

He hesitated, but only for a moment.

"A beautiful woman can be my adversary; but never
my enemy."

Abby blew him a kiss and with a sudden change of
heart or mood wheeled herself to the Palladian window that framed another view of the gardens and,
down an avenue of cypress trained on arches, a blue
orb of Pandora's Bay.

"I was born out of my time and place, Joe. My true
place. I love the Old South. Oh, I know. The slaves
and the cruelty and the absolute abysmal folly of people who thought that time changes nothing. Their
sense of grandeur was delusional and look what it got

them—the bloodiest war in history. But still—I can't get the old romance out of *my* blood. Silly, aren't I?"

"No. You're honest and unaffected and you have a talent millions of people respect. A tragic accident might have turned you into a mean-spirited, unhappy, unevolved adult. I'm a doctor. I know what you had to go through to be where you are now."

"I keep to myself too much, I know that. But I was always a loner; I liked to find a pretty place no one else knew about and just sit there and think. It's who I am, I don't apologize. I can't bear to watch what's going on in the world most of the time. I hardly ever look at a newspaper."

She came back toward Joe, reached for a Sotheby's catalogue among many on one of a pair of round tables.

"This is what I like to read. I must look at a couple of hundred catalogues of estate sales a year. I love wood. These tables are inlaid with thirty-two kinds of wood from Jamaican forests. Oh, and I love bronze and pewter and old silver and ceramics, but there's nothing I love better than the smell of a new book, just off the presses."

She showed him the bookcases that revolved like a jeweler's display case so that she could retrieve, in only a minute or two, any one of fifteen hundred volumes, most of them works of biography and history. Some of them were rare editions. She communicated her passion for research by touching his hand, not once but several times, as she showed him book after book. He thought of her fingers as the roots of a starved plant, drinking him in. The more she drank, the more sluggish his heart felt to him. Because he'd already made up his mind that it wasn't fair, it shouldn't be.

There were manuscript files that contained notes and every page of her revisions. Her fan mail she preserved on microfilm.

"How many letters do you have here?"

"I don't know. I've averaged about 150 a week over the last seven years. I answer every one."

"Form letter?"

"We have stock replies to the most-repeated questions. Otherwise I dictate a personal response, enclose an autographed bookplate."

"I'd say you're as good a businesswoman as you are an author."

"I'm fanatical about taking care of the people who take care of me: my readers. As for the money—Luke looks after my investments."

"How are you related?"

"He's my uncle, my mother's brother. The Thomasons are all Low Country people. My father was an insurance man who loved the political jousts. He was mayor of Orangeburg when I was a little girl and had large ambitions, but he never lived long enough to go very far in state politics. A horse kicked him, and he died of a blood clot that went to his brain. My mother had a sore on her breast she was careful not to tell anyone about until it was too late. I went to live with Dr. Luke when I was ten. He was devastated when I—after I was crippled. We've always been real close. I'm only sorry he's never been able to straighten out his love life. Anyway, he's so proud of me now. I guess we're doing good financially. I ask him when I want to spend big on something like a little Degas bronze which I'm currently lusting after, and he almost always says, 'Go ahead, you can afford it.' "

A phone on one of the Jamaican tables chimed, and Abby glided across the pegged-board floor to answer it.

"Yes, Lillian. Ummhmm. Joe, you're staying for lunch, I hope? Yes, we have one guest, and would you ask Charlene if she'd like to join us? Thanks."

As she hung up, the entrance doors opened in their spookily quiet way and a slender black woman with a cocklebur haircut came in, breathing hard, carrying a cardboard carton piled high with mail and packages. She looked curiously at Joe.

"Let me give you a hand with that," Joe said. He took the box from her and put it on one of the tables, next to a computer workstation.

"Frosty Clemons, Dr. Joe Bryce."

Frosty gave Joe another exacting look through round glasses rimmed in gold wire.

"You must be the one Daddy told me to be on the lookout for. Says they towed your Jeep Laredo back to town, on account of something was wrong with the transaxle. Whatever that is."

"I don't know, either," Joe confessed. "Pleased to meet you, Frosty."

Abby said, "Don't worry about it, Joe. We'll get you a lift to the hotel later on."

Lizzie came in looking a little sulky.

"You all went off and left me. Hi, Frosty."

"Playing hooky today?"

"No school." Lizzie flopped into a Colonial-style bamboo chair that looked fragile, and Frosty frowned at her.

"Break the furniture if you don't sit down in it right."

"Bamboo's as strong as steel, isn't that so, Abby?"

"One of the things I like about it. I wish bamboo could survive some of the winters we have here, I'd plant it all over the garden. Frosty, when you catch your breath, how about whipping up some brandy, Kahlua, and cream for us."

Frosty was bending over a legal-size folder containing contracts. "Abby—"

Abby made the wheelchair tires squeak on the floorboards. She had narrowed her eyes at this hint of opposition, like a cat suddenly exposed to bright light.

"Now don't tell me what Luke said. It's not like *real* drinking. It's the same as having dessert before we eat lunch."

Frosty straightened, turned briskly, thrust the folder of contracts at Abby and said, "Better look these over and sign them so I can get them in the mail today. You know it takes almost a year to get any money from your Polish publishers, once you get the contracts back to them."

"All right," Abby said meekly. "And *please* fix us a picker-upper."

Lizzie, yawning in her chair, said, "I'll have a glass of champagne."

"Shoot. What is this, a holiday I didn't know about? You call your mother today, Lizzie?"

"No. It's Friday. I call on Wednesdays and Saturdays." To Joe Lizzie said, "My mother's in a sanitarium. A sanitarium's where you go when you can afford to be crazy. Only I don't think she's crazy, really. Luke says she's just a very spoiled overaged brat."

The bar and refrigerator were contained in a Sheraton-style walnut breakfront that looked too perfect to be anything but a copy. Frosty Clemons opened the doors and began taking out bottles, which she placed on a sideboy with a spillproof top of faux marble.

"Can I give you a hand with those drinks?" Joe asked her. Frosty smiled just enough to be polite. His presence didn't exactly offend her, but she seemed wary of him.

Abby said to Frosty, "How's the new book read so far?"

Joe was close enough to see Frosty react; there was tension in her face, and for a few moments her hands forgot what they were supposed to be doing.

"Well—I think—it's bound to be your best one." She shot Joe a look, as if she suspected him of eavesdropping on her true thoughts, and took ice from the small fridge. Joe turned to Abby, whose face glowed in the light from the big Palladian window.

"Honestly? I have to admit it's been like wrestling a bear." To Joe she said, "I only read my own work once

I have a complete manuscript to look at. Otherwise I might get discouraged and throw it all in the garbage. But if Frosty says I have nothing to worry about—"

"Nothing to worry about," Frosty murmured, "except your eatin' and your drinkin'. Not enough of the first, and too much of the second."

Abby didn't respond. There was a slight fixed smile on her face and no movement at all. It was as if, posing for her portrait in the good north light, she had turned into the portrait itself: dusty, a little faded, neglected. She didn't blink when the telephone chimed again. Lizzie stared at her. Frosty sucked in a scared breath.

And then, suddenly she was out of it, stirring uneasily as if the shadow of something unspeakable had coldly fallen over her. Her teeth chattered; her head sank toward her breast.

"Oh, shit," Lizzie said softly, begining to uncurl from her chair, but Abby raised her head almost immediately and looked at her in an unfocused, dreary way.

"Was that the phone?" she said. "Would you mind getting it for me, Liz? It might be Frosty. I can't understand what's keeping her today."

FOURTEEN

Driving home from the state capital in his recently pur-chased Dodge Ram pickup, Dr. Lucas Thomason took the interstate south to Charleston. There he stopped at Ridler Page on King Street to view a hand-colored seventeenth-century French map of the Carolinas he'd put a hold on. Seeing this rarity for the first time, he felt it was well worth the three thousand dollars the dealer was asking. Then, across the street at another antiques dealer's shop, he picked up a flawless nine-teenth-century painted sideboard Charlene had or-dered, and, on impulse, a gift for his niece he thought she'd like: an Italian porcelain birdbath, complete with porcelain birds perched around the rim.

"Delightful," Rembarto said of the birdbath, a min-iature just ten and a half inches in diameter. "Nothing in the store has attracted quite as much comment since the day it came in. Believe me, Mrs. Rutledge, it's the younger Mrs. Rutledge I'm referring to, is going to be *very* disappointed. But I always tell them, just a small deposit if you're interested." Rembarto shrugged delicately. "The recent reversals in the markets have affected so many more Charlestonians than would care to admit to the fact."

Thomason said, "I was long interest-rate futures the day they changed the furniture in the Oval Office. I haven't suffered any regrets, either."

"In our business the really fine things always sell, of course. It may take a little longer. But the import duties we must pay now . . . and the sales-tax bite is discouraging to the small-business person like myself." Rembarto steepled his fingers as if he were considering a devout petition. "Perhaps we can look forward to some relief from the recently applied surtaxes when you become governor."

"My advisors and I are working on a completely new revenue plan that will make our state the envy of the other forty-nine. Or is Puerto Rico a state now? That would give us fifty-one, wouldn't it?"

"You know, I'm not sure about Puerto Rico. Well, you certainly can count on the King Street Merchants' Association for their endorsement, Governor."

Homeward bound to the Barony on U.S. 17 north, Thomason anticipated the billboards he'd be seeing in a few months along this very route, with his likeness on them. A two-day visit to Columbia had been highly profitable in terms of the support he'd picked up from, among others, the long-entrenched Speaker of the House, Pierce Folsby, and Luke's second cousin on his daddy's side from Gaffney, who was their party's newly elected chairman. It was a tight little community up there in the North, as Low Country people thought of the state capital, an interlocking directorate of lawyer/politicians, businessmen/politicians, banker/politicians, and the old-money squires whose opinions and desires were more important than a cemetery full of repeat voters . . . although the old way of doing things, except in the more backward rural hegemonies high and Low, was riskier in an age when all candidates for office were obliged to wield a double-edged sword called the Media.

His own use of the only two newspapers in the state that mattered and the local television stations had been, to date, selective and beneficial, thanks to the guidance of his press secretary and the PR firm she'd hired a year ago to make him a presence, on his way to becoming a force. Five years as a state representative gave him a beginner's luster; his failed run for Secretary of State had largely been forgotten. He'd put in his time as a local party hack and delegate to the national conventions, necessary for interior strength and useful contacts. He was, like so many other prominent South Carolina men, a graduate of the Citadel. Although he hadn't been in general practice for twelve years, he was a physician, which added to his stature. And he was currently married to a former Miss South Carolina and second runner-up in Atlantic City a dozen years ago. Charlene had maintained her looks and she knew how to deliver a winning sound bite. She would be a source of strength, as long as he kept her in line.

Thinking about Charlene depressed him slightly, but a letdown was inevitable after all the energy he'd expended over the last couple of days. What he needed was a bourbon-and-branch and a good horse under him for a long run up the beach at twilight.

By the time he got home, the work crew clearing land for his new polo field—a recently acquired passion his political handlers frowned upon but hadn't actively condemned as being elitist—were calling it a day. He stopped to chat with a tired, sweaty Walter Lee, and asked him to call the stables to have Diacono saddled and ready when he got there.

"All right, Dr. Luke."

"The crate back there has to be handled real careful, Walter Lee. It's a five-thousand-dollar table. Have Aldous and another boy see to it.''

"Yes, sir.''

He parked on the motor court beside the restored Cadillac he drove locally and the caterers' trucks. He'd momentarily forgotten about the barbecue they had on for tonight. In the house, one of the day girls was running a vacuum cleaner, the sound of which gave him an instant headache. Tired now after the long drive, he trudged up the stairs to his second-floor bedroom.

He was pulling off his boots when he heard Charlene. Her room was separated from his by the bath, but she hadn't closed her door all the way. He sat in his rocking chair holding the boot, listening. Then he took off the other boot, breathed deeply, got up and went into their shared bathroom.

Charlene was entertaining someone. He had a good idea who, without glancing through the crack in the doorway to verify his guess.

Thomason ran cold water in one of a set of sculpted gold-and-onyx washbasins, soaking a bath towel for twenty seconds. There was a paperback open on Charlene's crowded side of the sink top, one of those pseudo-fact books about encounters with space aliens. She read them religiously. Such input seemed part of the paranoia of the half-educated, those credulous people who could not accept life as a random walk, subject to human failure and the follies of nature.

"Oh, God, oh, God,'' Charlene raved, and her satiny old gilt bed rocked.

Thomason wrung out the towel and carried it, lightly twisted, into Charlene's bedroom, looked gloomily at the soles of her bare feet locked on either side of Norse's trim waist, and at Norse's bare taut heaving ass, as suntanned as the rest of him.

Charlene let rip with a string of passionate obscenities that inspired Norse to ever more frantic effort. He was a fucker, not a lover, Thomason observed. A pile-driving asshole. Neither one of them had any notion of his presence.

Thomason grinned and twirled his wet cold towel, remembering the old locker-room hijinks when he was a student at McCallie Prep in Chattanooga. Then he reached back and slashed the tip of the towel at Norse's clenched buttocks just as he was pumping.

Norse let out a scream that was somewhere between real pain and the ecstasy of release. He collapsed on Charlene, grabbing for the spot where the towel had bitten him like a horsefly. He saw Thomason standing at the foot of the bed. Charlene's eyes were still closed; white tooth gleam showed against her underlip. She was groveling and panting like a run-over dog.

Norse sat up suddenly, clutching his parts in both hands as if he were afraid for their safety. Thomason had fleeting thoughts along those lines—his straight razor was open and in plain sight twenty feet away in the bathroom—but he didn't pursue the notion. He only castrated horses, not pigs.

"I realize it's a hell of an inconvenience, Norse, but I'd like to talk to my wife. Get lost, will you?"

Norse crabbed his way off the bed. Charlene groaned, not opening her eyes.

"Luke, how *could* you?"

"Try locking your door when you're in rut." To Norse he said, "Don't put your clothes on in here. Do it in the hall outside."

Norse swallowed hard, gathering up his things from where they lay strewn on an ottoman.

"And don't dribble on the carpet, it cost more than the annual budget of the country that's well rid of you."

"Give me a break," Charlene said, covering her eyes with a languid hand but not bothering to pull a sheet over herself. She sniffed a couple of times. Her nose was running.

Thomason didn't look at her. He knew what the sniffing meant.

"Norse, if you bring any more coke in this house for my wife to pound up her nose, I'll stake you out on my new polo field and practice on-goal shots with your balls. *You're not getting out of this room fast enough, goddammit!*"

Four seconds later the hall door closed behind Norse. Thomason sat down on the bed.

"Charlene, you know what the three stages of a failed marriage are? Stage one is separate bedrooms, stage two is 'He's fucking my wife,' and stage three is 'I've got to get a new wife.'"

"So we're at stage two," she said. "We've been there practically forever."

"I sure God didn't get the pick of the litter when I married you, did I, Charlene?"

She struggled upright, her humid breasts swaying, ran the back of one wrist under her nose and said coaxingly, "Could you fix us both a drink?"

"I mean this very sincerely. No more coke. I'll ship you off to Hobjoy Hill again, I swear to Jesus."

"I don't need to be in detox! Besides, what would that do to your chances if it got out I was there?"

"Seeing you fall apart on a campaign junket would be a hell of a lot worse for my political future."

"I'm not going to fall apart! I haven't been doing much, and that's the honest truth. What you don't understand is, I got a little depressed today." Bedding wadded beneath her, she fondled her slummy cunt with a catch in her breath, looking unsatisfied. "You got turned on watching, I bet. Do you want me now?"

"Yes," he admitted, treated to a glissando of erotic expectation. "Take a shower first, and take a bottle of that Summer's Eve in there with you, I don't much care for sloppy seconds."

"But pour me a drink. Please." She leaned toward him for a kiss. He turned his face aside.

"You don't have to do that," Charlene said, her feelings hurt. "I never let anybody else kiss me on the mouth. That's a rule I have."

"It's a whore's rule."

She kicked him, not really in earnest. "Grab any ass I know while you were gone?"

Thomason got up from the bed, walked to the windows and threw the drapes open, blanching in the sudden light. When he could see again he noticed Abby in the garden, with someone he wasn't familiar with. They were going down a path toward the bay. He watched them for a minute, until the angry pulse in his throat had subsided. Then he went into his bedroom, opened the bar, poured Black Jack over ice for two and carried the glasses into the bathroom.

Charlene was in the Jacuzzi shower, a fancy affair with nozzles that attacked the body from a dozen angles. He'd never been partial to it, preferring a lazy warm downpour. She was sitting, outside the crosshatching jets of water, and he thought from the way her downcast face was set that she was crying. But it was hard to tell with the water gushing every which way. Her blond hair was tucked into a bouffant shower hat like those that children wore to bed in illustrations of eighteenth-century country life. Her face was a perfect oval beneath the cap, innocent of makeup. It occurred to him that women always seemed more defenselessly naked when wearing only a shower cap. Her shoulders were turned in; her previously rosy breasts with their agitated nipples were virgin-pale again. As if her sins were washing away.

"Who's that with Abby?"

When she didn't answer he opened the shower door and stepped inside, clothes and all. Charlene raised her head, sullen eyes dripping.

"I SAID, SOMEBODY'S WITH ABBY! I'd like to know who he is."

She blinked; she was unable to track his behavior

with any accuracy today, and her fingertips were nervous on the tops of her sleek thighs.

"Must be that doctor. Name is Bryan—Bryce—I was supposed to have lunch with them, but I— He is some kind of good-looking, don't you think?"

"Doctor? Where did he come from?"

"I don't know. Pamela might have called him. You know how she's been lately. Maybe your adoring niece doesn't trust you as much as you—"

He had her by the throat before she could finish. Both hands. For a dreadful instant he thought of crushing her larynx so that he would never have to hear her speak to him in that tone again. Her eyes popped lividly in terror. He turned around and dialed the shower to ice-cold while still holding her immobile with one hand. When the riveting slash of cold water penetrated to the molten heart of him and turned it to slag, he found a reasonably dispassionate voice.

"Never, never say a thing like that to me again! Abby owes everything to me—and she's grateful. If you think spending your life in a wheelchair is bad, it could be worse for you, Charlene. *Much worse.*"

FIFTEEN

With a note of apology in his voice, Joe said to Pamela Abelard, "I suppose I'm not making much sense to you."

She looked up at him. They were moving slowly along a breastwork that was roughly paved with tabby, a rocklike composition of ground oyster shell, lime and sand, twelve feet above the tidal swell of Pandora's Bay. She had pinned her hair up before leaving the house and wore Revos to shield her eyes from the lowering sun they faced in a still-cloudless sky.

"I'd be afraid, if I were you."

"I didn't say I wasn't. There's no protection for us in most of those countries, although the UN makes an effort. But when wretched conditions and tribal antagonisms at the government level reach a flash point, the result is wholesale, indiscriminate slaughter. There are at least a half-dozen Central African republics that are little more than huge running sores. Starvation, disease . . . a journalist I respect said this about African self-determination: 'How quickly ideals in the wrong hands become oppression, heartbreak and murder.' We worked for nine months out of a clinic cobbled together from a couple of abandoned Romanian buses. There were days when we saw a thousand patients. Four doctors, three nurses. You pretty much work in a fog of exhaustion.''

"And you can't wait to get back."

"I need to catch up on what's been happening in my speciality. Fortunately I have some flexible and understanding partners at home."

"And an understanding girlfriend?"

"She was going to wait, when I volunteered the first time. I said I'd be gone a year. It stretched into two. She wrote me that she was marrying an oral surgeon in Winnetka." Joe looked appropriately regretful. "I guess I still owe them a wedding present. What are these, cannons?"

They paused next to a corroded old Columbiad, one of several still patiently aimed across the channel after more than a hundred and thirty years.

"This was called Grayson's Battery," Abby said. "The Union Navy came down the coast, bombarded the saltworks along the Atlantic, then sailed up the bay to make life miserable for the planters on both sides. It was a much more ambitious battery once—a dozen earthworks, forty ten-inch cannons. Slaves built the battery, but when Sherman got close to the sea all of our boys were pulled out of Grayson's in a last attempt to stop him. Not one shot was ever fired from Grayson's Battery."

" 'Our boys,' Miss Abby?" Joe said teasingly.

"I told you. The stork may have been late and dumped me in the wrong century, but I am a true daughter of the Confederacy. 'Gray falcon fell in the northern weather/vengeance was exacted beyond any taint of mercy/and the Belle Epoque of Carolina swoons/to a colloquy of gruff bassoons/that soothes the qualms of evening.' I write poetry too, Dr. Joe. Hey, let's break out that shaker of martinis now, and some of the hickory-smoked cheese? We don't eat for real until about eight-thirty.''

"You hardly touched your lunch."

"Oh, I had a stiff headache, but I'm better now.''

Joe opened the hamper he'd been carrying, spread a large checkerboard napkin in Abby's lap, shook the martinis in the silver thermos, poured for both of them into crystal glasses.

"Ummm," she said, tasting. "*This* is living."

He used the hinged top of the hamper for a cutting board, sliced cheese wedges and opened a box of herb-flavored crackers.

"What would it cost, Joe, to build a really decent clinic in one of those countries?''

"Why bother? We couldn't defend it against the thieves and drug addicts. It would be a ruin in a matter of months.''

"But you maintained a clinic—"

"It didn't look like much. It blended with a generally devastated landscape. Shacks and rusty hulks.''

"Oh." She looked across the bay at a flight of egrets, rising like a tidal wave above the shoreline cypress of an island wildlife preserve. "I guess that's one of the major frustrations. You're there to help, but they destroy what will most benefit them.''

"Mobile clinics work, usually. Like the buses we scrounged. But we couldn't keep them running. No parts available.''

"I can't imagine what it's really like. Do you have any photos with you?''

"No. I mailed photos and my diary to my sister when I had the feeling civil war was close.''

"I'd like to read the diary of Joe Bryce.''

"All doctors have terrible handwriting, didn't you know that?''

"The only doctor I've had much to do with is Luke.''

She reached up slowly and massaged her forehead.

"Too much sun?"

"No, I worship the sun. I don't know, I just haven't been feeling all that great."

"For instance?"

"Oh, headaches. And . . ."

She took another swallow of her martini.

"Dr. Luke says it's this stuff, but I swear to you I'm no boozer. I like a couple of cocktails during the day. Maybe wine with dinner. I don't drink at all after eight-thirty or so, because I have to work."

She sipped again, handed the glass to Joe, then turned the wheelchair to face east and took off her sunglasses.

"Joe."

"Yes?"

"I was spacey this morning, wasn't I? In the workshop."

"What do you mean?"

"I mean I—did a fade. I was there, but I couldn't—say anything. As if the paralysis went to parts of my brain. When it happens I drift way, way off. The strangest feeling. I see myself sitting there in Rolling Thunder, but it's as if I—I'm dead. Then, when I come out of it, I don't remember what's going on, what we've been talking about. Scares me."

She turned again in the wheelchair, eyes narrowing.

"*You're* a doctor. What do you think is wrong?"

"I—it's difficult to say. I'd need a history, and—"

"Do you think you could help me?"

"I'm not a neurologist, Abby. I think you need—"

"I need *you.* Because, Joe—let you in on my little secret. As soon as I saw you by the pool this morning, I knew that my life was about to change, that something wonderful was going to happen to me. Then there was the dragonfly! That's not just coincidence, my friend."

He was looking at her, trying to think of an amiable

protest, to back away from her conviction, when they both heard the horseman coming through the woods below the breastworks.

"It's Luke," Abby said. "Maybe you ought to put that thermos and the glasses away, Joe."

Bruiser the mastiff, trailing the man on horseback, barked and came quickly up the breastwork toward Joe and Abby. Joe gave the dog a friendly smile. Bruiser remembered him and turned to Abby, tongue lolling. She seized him by the ears and Bruiser laid his head in her lap.

"Hey, Luke!" Abby called, as the horse and rider lunged up the breastwork. "Who do you like Sunday, the Panthers or the Chiefs?"

"What's the over/under?"

"Twelve."

"Chiefs, and the over."

"You're on," Abby said, and under her breath added, "patsy." To Joe she said, "Do you like pro football?"

"Yes, but I'm out of touch."

"I bet on three or four games a week. I've even got a bookie in Vegas. So far this season I'm ahead. I still owe you ten bucks, don't I? Remind me. I always—"

"Pay your debts," Joe said, smiling. He glanced at Dr. Lucas Thomason as he was getting down from his thoroughbred black gelding.

"Luke, we need casino gambling in South Carolina," Abby said.

"You know I won't touch that one." He hitched his horse to a cannon ring and walked over to Abby, smiled at Joe in passing. He leaned down to kiss his niece on the cheek. "I'd never get you out of the casinos. What have you been up to this fine afternoon?"

"Just having a good time. Luke, I'd like you to meet Dr. Joe Bryce."

"A pleasure, sir." Lucas Thomason gave Joe the sincere, but not the excessively flattering, politician's one-handed, one-pump shake. A big hand but unexpectedly hard, even callused; not soft from scrubbing up like the hands of most doctors. He was a tall man of late middle age who kept himself reasonably in trim. His hair was gray and cut short, to minimize the fact that he'd lost about half of it from the crown of his head. No one would call him handsome, but it was an oddly attractive face, from markedly triangular, blueberry eyes to a commanding jaw to a humorously crimped mouth, the long upper lip protruding slightly and wavy like the edge of a dogwinkle shell. It looked as if he had once caught his mouth in a can opener.

"Bryce? I was acquainted with a slew of Bryces up Walterboro way when I attended the Citadel."

"I don't think we're related. I'm from the Chicago area."

"I recognize that in your voice." His own voice was soft, breathy and fluent, with the cadences of one of the more sophisticated, politicized preachers like Robertson or Falwell. "I had a good friend, Dr. Blaine Conacher, a cardiologist, who practiced in Chicago. He was Chief of Service at St. Mary's of Nazareth. Died an untimely death about sixteen months ago. He liked to build and fly those little airplanes, what do you call them—?"

"Ultralights," Abby said.

"Well, a bolt sheared off, or something, when he was at twelve hundred feet over an Illinois cornfield. You will never convince me that air is man's element. Give me a good horse with four feet on the ground, any day."

"How's the campaign shaping up, Luke?"

"As you can probably tell, my throat's a little raw. Pierce Folsby and his damned cheap cigars. He won't smoke anything better, even though I offered him one of my contraband double coronas. But we got down to cases, in a four-hour session. The upshot is, I can count on Pierce.''

Abby clapped her hands, startling both Bruiser and the black gelding.

"You're in!"

"Next year's primary is looking better all the time," he agreed, and twinkled somewhat at Joe. Not quite a smile. "Excuse us for talking politics, but that's about all we *do* talk around here these days. What hospital are you affiliated with, Dr. Bryce?"

"North Shore, in Winnetka."

"Oh, yes, I've heard that's a very fine facility."

Joe got out a card for Lucas Thomason.

"I see. Pediatric oncology. Welcome to South Carolina, Dr.—"

"Joe."

"Joe. Are you on vacation?"

"In a way. Trying to make up my mind about a couple of things."

"He helped run a clinic in Africa," Abby said. "And he's lucky to be alive, what he went through."

Thomason gazed at Joe with heightened interest. "I'd like to hear more about it. Is there a chance you might be staying for the barbecue tonight, Joe?"

"I already invited him," Abby said smugly.

"Good. Look forward to chatting with you. Right now I need to get Diacono back to the barn and put my party clothes on. Abby, got a joke for you."

"One that's fit for mixed company?"

"Surely. Can you tell me the difference between an evangelist and a rabid dog?"

"No," Abby said. "What's the difference?"

"You can shoot a rabid dog."

Abby groaned. "I like the dirty jokes better."

Thomason untied his black horse and swung up into the saddle. It wouldn't have been effortless, at his age, but he had the height to make it look effortless, perhaps for Joe's benefit. He saluted casually with his left hand and rode off down the breastwork to the woods.

"One great guy," Abby said, watching him. "I don't know how I would have made it through the bad times, without Luke."

"He's late getting into the political arena."

"Yes, but the desire has been there for ten years or more. It's not an ego thing." She looked into the air as if the question had always been hanging around, like an insatiable mosquito. "Ask Luke anything—mental health, the budget, education, the environment, he's studied all sides of the issues. See, Luke and I are a pair of insomniacs, up until all hours, and we're both indiscriminate readers. Every night I insert a book into my brain like a suppository. Greasing the talent, I suppose?" She wrinkled her nose amusedly. "But Luke concentrates on reeducating himself. He took graduate courses on economic and political theory at USC this summer, driving back and forth, back and forth, so I wouldn't be alone too much."

"What about the rest of his medical practice?"

"Oh, he's only had one patient for a few years now."

"You?"

The look in her eyes was pure adulation.

"He does the required work to maintain his medical license. But to tell the truth, I don't think he ever enjoyed medicine. It was a family thing—his father, his father's father, both prominent doctors. Luke always felt he had a higher purpose in life. Now I'm sure it's going to happen."

"A political campaign can be a big expense."

"I don't care what I have to spend! I've told Luke that. The literary business is a lottery, Joe. Four thousand new novels were published in this country last year. So I hit on my first try. Why me? Maybe God said, Okay, you don't walk again, you don't have a husband or children, but here's the good news. Two million people are going to buy your first novel."

She bowed her head for a few moments; then the

tears welled up. Her face was a study in joy and anguish.

Joe took her hand. "You shouldn't devalue yourself sexually. Paraplegic women get married. They have genital sex. And they sometimes have perfectly healthy babies, by C-section."

"I know, but—would I live to see them grow up? Or even make it to Lizzie's age?"

"What do you mean, Abby?"

"I have this horrible—this ontological nightmare sometimes. That I'm going to drift out of my body to a place where there are demons. Things made of fear, as Rilke put it. They will ask me who I am, and I won't be able to remember. Then they'll claim me as one of their own."

With his other hand Joe cradled her cheek, wondering if her demons were of guilt or shame. Abby pressed hard against his palm.

"Sorry. I don't know why I'm like this lately. And I don't know you. Are you sure I won't be reading about myself in the *National Intruder* next week? Sorry again. That was very paranoid. But there's only the thinnest of lines separating paranoia and genius, isn't there?"

Her lips parted when she looked at him. Her anxiety had sensitized her in a predictable manner. He liked the way her lips were shaped. All of her curves were complementary, from her breasts to the whorls in her large ears, the smoothed-down sable thickness of each eyebrow. He kissed her.

Abby didn't move or close her eyes. But she had stopped crying. Their faces were close, hers in shadow. The gray eyes seethed with doubt, and, finally, approval.

"Why did you do that?"

"It seemed a shame not to."

"Yes. I know exactly what you mean. I was thinking it too. I'll be sorry if he doesn't kiss me, because tomorrow—he could be gone."

SIXTEEN

After twice calling Walter Lee to eat, Frosty Clemons fi- nally sent one of the twins outside to the covered front porch to wake him up from his nap. Taura looked at him, sprawled and snoring in a patio lounger, a stadium cushion with the Clemson Tigers' logo propped behind his graying head. She wrapped two hands around a convenient finger and tugged until the snoring stopped and he cracked open an eye.

"Mama says time for dinna."

He smiled at her. "Help me up, Taura."

"*Granpa.* You know I'm not big enough to move you."

Sabina appeared behind the door screen. "Is he coming? Mama says he has to eat old fish heads if he don't come now."

"I *like* old fish heads," Walter Lee said, turning on the lounger and pretending to go back to sleep.

"Granpa!" they screamed in unison. Walter Lee

jumped up, as spry as his knees would permit, and looked around in bewilderment.

"What's the matter? Are we burning down? Cat catch a booger bear?"

Sabina turned her head and called to her mother at the rear of the house, "Granpa's being silly!"

"I want everybody sitting down to the table *right now.*"

With a twin on each side of him, leading him by the hand, Walter Lee made it to the kitchen and pulled up a chair.

"What do we have here? Umm-hmm. Baked beans and ham. Slice tomato. Umm-hmm. Them good tomatoes just keep comin' and comin' this year."

Sabina, the bookish twin, pushed a crayoned drawing toward him.

"I made this for you at nussy school."

"Well, that's something. It sure is. What is it, a booger bear?"

"No such thing as *booger* bears. It's a dragon."

"Oh, yeah. Look at that fire come out of his nose."

"I made you a Popsicle-stick clown," Taura said, nuzzling up to his side. Then she said, in a doleful voice, "I left it."

"Oh, that's okay. Bring it home next time."

Frosty, wearing an apron, carried a pan of corn bread to the table.

"Where's my stinky old fish heads?" Walter Lee inquired, making the girls giggle.

Frosty gave him a kiss on the forehead. "You got to get out there and catch me some fishes first."

"Tomorra morning," Walter Lee promised. "Early."

"You working tomorrow, Daddy?"

"Part of the day, I reckon. Dr. Luke's looking to buy polo ponies, and he want me along. You know he ain't got a good eye for horseflesh."

"He's too old for that game. He'll fall off and bust his head. Like Prince Charles did one time."

"It was his arm, I think. They all wear helmets any-how, and Dr. Luke, he can ride with the best of 'em."

Frosty made sure the girls were served without get-ting any food on the oilcloth, then sat down with a sigh at her end of the table.

"Hard day?" Walter Lee inquired. "—Reach me the ice tea pitcher, Sabina."

"Well, you know. I got to do more and more of the business with the agents nowadays. She plain don't want to talk to 'em. I tell Abby, 'Gal, you're not just a business, you're a whole *industry* to yourself.' She say, 'Well, you handle it, Frosty.' "

"That's what it's like, to be such a creative person. God love her."

Frosty took off her gold-rimmed glasses and rubbed her eyes. She had a dour, moping expression.

"You don't want to eat?" Walter Lee asked her.

"Not yet. I'd like for you to hear something."

From her apron pocket Frosty took out a Walkman tape player, and a cassette. Walter Lee looked at the cassette with a wary eye.

"Why do I think this is no business of mine?"

"Daddy, please. What's on the cassette here, it's part of the trouble that I have been trying to tell you about. I'm at my wits' end. Don't go deaf on me again."

"I just want to eat my dinner in peace."

"Why you so stubborn? Why do you refuse to see there is something *wrong* in that house?"

Walter Lee had trouble swallowing a forkful of beans, and reached for a napkin to cough into. Sabina was patiently buttering all sides of her corn bread, care-ful not to get any butter on her fingers. Taura ate while alertly watching first her mother, then Walter Lee.

He put down the napkin and sipped iced tea. His massive shoulders were hunched as he stared at his plate.

"Why you looking to get fired from your job? Which is what it will come down to, if you meddle."

"Meddle? I'm telling you I am worried out of my head over Abby. She is not *right*, Daddy. And getting worse all the time."

Walter Lee scraped at his plate with his fork, listened to the sink faucet drip and the wall clock tick.

Frosty said to Sabina, "Time to stop buttering and eat some of that."

"I like butter."

Walter Lee said, "You tell the doctor what you suspicion?"

"I mentioned it to him."

"What did Dr. Luke have to say?"

"Says, 'Thank you, Frosty. But you know, she is a *creative* person, and she does have these sinking spells.'"

Walter Lee breathed easier. "What I said too. Everybody knows creative persons is different from the rest of us."

"What does that word mean?" Taura asked.

"Sinking spells! My Lord! I have worked for Abby nearly four years now, think I don't know the difference?"

"Mama! What does 'craytiff' mean?"

"It's like when someone has the talent to write or draw or sing. Creative."

"I can play the piano at nussy school."

"I know you can, darlin'. One of these days, we're gonna have a piano right here in this house."

"Let me dig a little more ham out of that bean pot," Walter Lee said. Taura offered him a bite on her fork instead. He leaned toward it, making gobbling noises. Frosty put her head in her hands.

"Do we have to *play* at the table?"

"Sorry," Walter Lee said, and smiled at Taura. He took the bean pot down from the lazy Susan in the middle of the table.

Frosty straightened with a new resolve, and put the cassette into the Walkman. Walter Lee looked disgruntled.

"Told you I don't want to hear—"

"Hush, Daddy! Just—hush."

She turned the Walkman on. They heard tape hiss, then Pamela Abelard saying, in a rather mournful voice, smaller than her normal speaking voice:

" 'Last night I dreamt I went to Manderley again.' " After a short pause, she repeated it. Then a third time.

" 'Last night I dreamt I went to Manderley again.' "

Frosty switched the Walkman off. Walter Lee scowled, because Frosty was staring at him.

"Well, that don't mean a thing to me. What is it supposed to be?"

"It is *supposed* to be a chapter from Abby's new book that she is dictating." Frosty paused for breath and touched her breast, as if she felt a panic rising there. "What it *is*, is the first line from one of Abby's favorite novels, which happens to be *Rebecca*, by Miss Daphne du Maurier."

Walter Lee swallowed, and sucked at a tooth that was giving off twinges lately.

"Don't have the foggiest notion what you're driving at."

Frosty nodded, acknowledging this. "Listen, Daddy, the tape goes on for almost an hour, and that's all she *says*—over and over. 'Last night I dreamt I went to Manderley again.' In that tone of voice, like she don't know *what* she's saying! When she's supposed to be writing her own book! And I'll tell you something else—nothing she's dictated in the past couple weeks makes much sense either. She forgets the names of her characters—she repeats herself."

Taura, for no discernible reason, was down from her chair and looking under the table. Frosty reached out and sat her down again. She looked at Walter Lee.

"It's like she just can't concentrate anymore."

"It'll pass. It's bound to pass."

"I think what's causing this problem is something

Dr. Luke's been giving her. I'd swear to that. One of those injections he's always—''

Walter Lee slammed his hand down on the table hard enough to make the plates jump. The girls got stiff and quiet and looked at him in fearful surprise.

"Don't you know," he said, glaring at his daughter, "what kind of trouble you can get this whole family into?"

Taura looked at Sabina and murmured, "Granpa's mad."

Frosty shot back, "No, I don't know! What are you talking about? All I care about is Abby—"

Walter Lee might have been inclined to back down, but he glanced at the children's faces; old grievances boiled from his heart, and he leveled a full-bore gaze at his daughter.

"You think that low-life Delmus is ever coming back from Dee-troit City, help you raise these sweethearts, see that they get the education they deserve? They ain't a black woman in ten counties makes the kind of living you do—but you want to just throw it all away, 'cause you gots to meddle, get people stirred up against you—against *us*—"

Whether his words were fair or not, her eyes brimmed with frustrated tears.

"No, Daddy—!"

Walter Lee put both hands on the table, and made fists.

Sabina said, "I need to go to the bafroom."

"So do I."

Walter Lee shook his head grimly, and the twins were like stone, watching him out of the corners of their eyes.

"What else you been up to?" he accused Frosty. "You been up to *something*."

"No, Daddy."

"What's that?"

"I swear!"

Walter Lee's hands relaxed. He slid them off the table. He did not look at his loved ones.

"I'm just so worried—" Frosty had difficulty coming up with her next breath. "—and I been afraid for her the longest time, Daddy."

"All right."

"Poor lamb. I suffer for her."

"All *right*," Walter Lee said again, with the stern finality of a hellfire preacher slamming shut the Good Book in his pulpit. "My advice is, worry about your ownself. And these children. That's all I gots to say." He pushed his chair back and rose from the table as if he were climbing a cliff that had just been put in his way, his eyes raised to heaven. "Fine supper. If they be any of that hand-cranked peach ice cream left, I'll have mine on the porch, when y'all ready."

SEVENTEEN

Politics was on everyone's mind, and entered into almost every conversation, at the Thomasons' barbecue Friday night.

An elderly woman who got around with the aid of two black canes and cataract glasses said to the gubernatorial hopeful, "Well, now, I hope you're gonna run a *clean* campaign, Lucas. None of that *character* assassination."

"Bless you, Meemaw. But I think you got to admit one thing: in the case of our incumbent governor, character assassination is justifiable homicide."

"Oh, honey," Meemaw protested. "Claiborne's heart has always been in the right place."

"His heart, but not his pecker."

Meemaw wheezed with laughter, leaning on him.

"And his brain is the rock of ages," Charlene said, leaning against his other side, looking up at him for approval of this rare witticism, which she had overheard at the beauty parlor. Lucas glanced at her, as

bemused as if she'd spoken Sanskrit: there was no humor in her bones, and most punch lines left her gaping like a fish. Nevertheless he tightened his grip
comfortingly on her right hand. They had been inseparable, at Lucas's request, since the party started. Sex
in the shower had resulted in forgiveness, particularly
since she'd gone down on him; his favorite turn-on,
although she'd always felt that fellatio was undignified.
And rather hard on the jaw muscles. But it had been
an act of penance, not for the infidelity, which she long
ago had learned was part of the excitement he craved
from her, but for popping off about Pamela. His genuine fits of anger were rare, so something was amiss.

Meemaw's renewed laughter had exposed them to
really bad halitosis; Charlene avoided it by turning her
head and raising her glass. She was still nursing her
first bourbon on the rocks, also at Lucas's request. She
didn't know whose grandmother Meemaw was, or if
the title might be honorary at her age: to Charlene the
Thomason and the Abelard family trees were a hopeless tangle of branches. But the social antennae she'd
been born with enabled her to know that some of the
elderly ladies in attendance were as rich as Croesus,
and Lucas was courting them all.

The guests who had arrived punctually were min-
gling in the large front parlor of the Barony, a room
to which Charlene had devoted a lot of time—bringing
it off beautifully, she liked to be told—from the gilt-
and-bronze wall sconces to the Italian oval-back chairs
and the eighteenth-century mirror-front cabinet, also
Italian, which she'd found herself in one of the Royal
Street shops in New Orleans.

Desiring a little praise, Charlene directed Meemaw's
attention to the cabinet.

"Honey, I can't see that far. I promise to look at it
up close later on. But I must say the whole place seems
so cheerful and invitin'. I remember when it was nothing but a termite pantry. I suppose it was pound-foolish

of Pamela to invest her writin' money in faded glory; but I hear she's got plenty of writin' money. I guess it's true what they say: there's a blessing for every adversity."

"Amen," Charlene said, breathing only as deeply as she had to and wishing for a handkerchief dabbed in perfume, secreted inside the cuff of her bell-sleeved blouse. A necessity in the old days for masking unpleasant odors. Sachets, and plenty of gin or West Indies rum to deaden the sense of smell, and it was well known their genteel predecessors at the Barony and other Low Country plantations had used a lot of cocaine, too, in various forms, to pull them through bouts of malaria and tooth abscess and every sort of skin disease known to mankind, drugging the senses during interminable pestilential summers.

The thought of cocaine made her edgy. What she'd had earlier was wearing off, too soon.

"Speaking of investments, Lucas," Meemaw said, "you ought to see the monstrosity of a marble mausoleum Edgar wants us to buy. I said to him, Edgar, what *for*? I'm not fussy about final resting places. An already-occupied grave site will do for me, as long as one of us has a deck of *cards*. Charlene, could I impose on you to fetch me a glass of sweet tea, with just a little ice and some crushed mint?"

"Why, sure, Meemaw."

"Might see what's keeping Abby," Lucas requested, letting go of her hand.

"I can't imagine; maybe the elevator's stuck again."

"Oh, that's *right*," Meemaw said. "I hear she's got a little elevator now for gettin' upstairs and down in. Well, tell the child I do want to see her, but it'll be past my bedtime by and by."

Charlene crossed the entrance hall, which she had turned into an Italianate gallery with busts and urns and greenery, reflooring in a deep green marble that had the tranquillity of a woodland pool. (The original randomly sized heart-of-pine boards had been warped by decades of rainwater leaking in, and from the urine of horses stabled there by a plantation overseer during Reconstruction.) Charlene had the feeling she was going to need a couple of more sniffs to make it all the way tonight. No need to aim for high-high, just enough to be pleasantly on top of things, coping with the hostess role, which Pamela always ceded to her. While remaining the center of attention herself. Even Luke the up-and-coming politician or his prize guest of the evening, United States senator Miller Harkness, couldn't compete with Pamela Abelard's celebrity status among family and friends.

She saw Joe by the fireplace in the small library off the gallery, and impulsively detoured. He was chatting with Spence Labèque, who had taken a leave of absence from the University of South Carolina, where he occupied the Titus Mercer Chair in the poly-sci department, to manage Luke's campaign.

"Hi, Spence. Dr. Bryce. Off all by yourselves; are you having a good time?"

Spence only nodded politely, but Joe responded with a generous smile.

"Yes, thanks. You look terrific, Mrs. Thomason. I'd give up my front-row seat in hell for you, anytime."

Charlene's eyes fixed on him as if on a startling event. "Charlene, please. Actually I've always liked Charly, since I was a kid, but nobody but my brothers calls me that anymore."

"Charly it is. And I'm Joe."

There was another door to the library, open to a hall that ran the length of the house on the east side to the kitchen in back. The wrought-iron elevator cage that had been installed for Abby was in the snug well of the stairs in the hall. The elevator itself was just large enough to accommodate Abby and Rolling Thunder. It wasn't occupied.

Charlene sighed. "Has anyone seen Pamela? She's always late for these things."

They shrugged and shook their heads.

"Well, I'll just take the elevator up and knock on her door."

Her smile for Joe lingered; then she whirled with a little waggle of her fingers and walked briskly out into the hall. She was wearing high-waisted black silk pants with very wide cuffs that swirled around her ankles like miniature tornadoes.

Spence Labèque was one of those men who whistle a breathy tune to express an opinion.

Joe smiled noncommittally. "Dr. Thomason did well for himself."

"Too good-looking," Spence advised. "Don't get me wrong, I like Charlene. She's a talented decorator, apparently, although I don't go for all this overpainted Eye-talian stuff. But Charlene's not— I shouldn't say any of this anyway." He knocked back more of his vodka martini, his third since Joe had struck up a conversation with him. Spence was overweight, with a small beaked nose in a jolly Buddha face, a nap of silver-gray hair around his ears, the chins-down, close-to-the-chest air of a man who is a collector if not a storehouse of secrets, and small inquisitive eyes.

"Like a lot of really beautiful women," Joe said, "she doesn't have a lot of self-confidence."

Spence looked at Joe, respect and a trace of envy in his eyes.

"I think you're a man who has known his share of beauties. I mean, if I handed her the line you did, I'd sound like a genuine horse's ass. From you, she loved it."

"I don't go out of my way, but—"

"Sure. It's a talent. Like pitching. Set them back on their heels with the heater, get them to nibble at the slider, low and outside."

Joe sipped his draft beer and inhaled the tang of

pork barbecue, which permeated the house. The air had cooled, sheer curtains luffed at the windows like the sails of romantic old schooners, the night was alive with the creaking and peeping of tree-dwelling creatures. Laughter in the parlor; women with shawls across their bare shoulders strolled on torch-lit garden paths. There were four coldly sweating steel barrels of Samuel Adams on the brick-paved veranda, and a big bar staffed by young black guys who looked like college basketball players, natty in their white Ike jackets and hickory-striped trousers. He was nearly moved to fall in love with the Barony. That was all he needed, with his objectivity already in tatters. The project was busted, he'd known it from the moment he saw Abby being carried helplessly up the steps from the shallow end of the pool; long legs inert, toes dumbly skimming the turquoise surface, she seemed like a statue being salvaged from an undersea wreck. A lovely paraplegic, and despite her tough talk so without real toughness or any reading on life outside her reclusive homestead she'd be writing checks to his favorite charity with only a few more hints on his part. He couldn't deal with that much innocence. But he hadn't walked away yet, either. He felt baffled and apprehensive, an actor in a dream play listening for a cue that might already have been delivered. The other actors unaware of his lack of status in their midst. There were ghosts here, who didn't approve of him. There also was trouble, as undefined as fog but still threatening. He'd always owned a fine instinct for knowing when to bow, and sidestep, and get out gracefully. But Abby, that other strong presence on his stage, wouldn't let him go yet. He had to continue with his lines while concealing panic, ignoring the sensation that there was a flimsy trapdoor with a bad latch beneath his feet.

Spence whistled tunelessly between his spaced front teeth.

"When I'm speaking of Charlene, what I'm saying

is, she may have too much of one asset for a political candidate's wife, and not enough of the other assets, such as people skills. I don't know just how she's going to turn out to be a liability along the way; but it'll happen.'' He peered at the bottom of his glass as if looking into his heart, and appeared to discover betrayal. ''You didn't hear it from me,'' he added.

Joe said soothingly, ''You must like Dr. Thomason's chances, to take a a year off from your own profession.''

''I do. He's smartened up in the past few months; he's ready now. I convinced him not to know too much. He was studying economics up at the college, slaving away to be informed. I told him, God's sake, Luke, cut it out. You don't need to know all that shit to tell a good bill from a bad bill. *Economics.* They call it the Dismal Science, but it's more of a mystical calling, like the priesthood: all canonical theory, evaluation of pertinent Mysteries and glosses on fiscal catastrophes. From these economists construct models of probability as if they're scenarios from heaven, then issue portents so well hedged almost any future economic event can go into the win column. In Washington they're kind of a stabilizing caste, I guess, but 'economics' has little to do with policy, just as prayer has no discernible impact on events. What the hell, even a politician has to believe in something. Since 'economics' has always had more answers than there are questions, it fulfills this need admirably. What say we stroll outside for some more alcoholic assistance?''

Joe never made it to the bar with Spence; Abby was descending in her elevator when they stepped out into the hall, and she called to him.

''Better late than never,'' Lizzie observed, coming down the stairs in flats and a blue knit sheath dress, and keeping pace with Abby's slow approach. ''Abby was taking pains. Hello, Mr. Lebèque.''

"Hello, Lizzie. You look special tonight."

But Lizzie was looking at Joe for his benison; she paused in profile on the last step, her shoulders back to make the most of her beginning bustline.

"What do you think, Joe?"

He shook his head regretfully. "You're too much woman for me, Lizzie."

She grinned and then blushed a shade of sunset pink. The elevator gates opened and Abby goosed Rolling Thunder into the hall.

"Hi, guys."

Spence kissed Abby's cheek. Joe kissed her hand, finding it unexpectedly cold. But paraplegics often were cold. Some of her color was artificial tonight: eyeliner in a shade between rose and apricot, lip gloss in a bolder pink, emerald earrings that looked like the real thing, about two carats apiece. Away from the sun, her tan appeared sallow. She was wearing one of the sleeveless chiffon jumpsuits she favored, probably because with the elastic top they were easy to get in and out of. This one had gold embroidery. Over the jumpsuit she wore an unconstructed jacket with a crest that might have had some familial significance. Her hair was up in a topknot with a few errant amber tendrils that touched the tips of her hayseed ears and her high forehead.

"Luke mad at me?" she wondered. "I'd better put in an appearance. Lizzie, what became of Charlene?"

"Powder room, I think."

"We won't wait. Come on."

She was holding a large beaded clutch in her lap, unzipped. Joe noticed the top of a silver flask protruding. He reached down and zipped the purse closed. Abby winked nonchalantly at him.

"Mind pushing?" she said to Joe. "My fingers are a little numb tonight, no idea why." She flexed her hands, looking at them curiously. He was aware of the pulse in the side of her throat, a slight nervous tightening of her eyes.

Spence said, "If you'll excuse me, I'm going to duck out to the bar. Can I get you a drink, Abby?"

"Double vodka, rocks. And a bottle of Fresca, so Luke won't know."

"You already had one upstairs," Lizzie reminded in a confidential tone.

"I know, Lizzie. And you know, but we won't let the whole world know, right?"

"Okay," Lizzie said, glancing at Joe but mum already.

"Straight ahead to the kitchen, Joe. There's a ramp for me to the veranda."

Caterers who moved quickly but with balletic precision had taken over Lillian's kitchen; she sat gnomishly on a high stool in one corner, wearing a go-to-meeting dress but with her lumpish feet still in brocade carpet slippers, occasionally advising where some item of cookware or cutlery could be found. The caterers careened and danced effortlessly around Rolling Thunder and Abby's coterie as she passed through, calling out greetings.

On the veranda she was soon surrounded. Joe fielded introductions and filed names: Aunt Ruby Mae, Cousin Caroline, Cousin Portia; Blake and Percy and Leona.

"How many relatives do you have?" Joe asked Abby.

"You mean in South Carolina? There's about a hundred and seventy-five I keep regular track of," Abby said, perhaps a little overwhelmed by the attention. "Hallie, this is my friend Dr. Joe Bryce, who is just back from Africa—"

Hallie was a lean smiling girl with the guileless eyes and high coloring of a calendar Virgin. "Africa! You swear! Were you doing the Lord's work?"

"I'm not a missionary. I'm a pediatrician."

"Oh—you must've been takin' care of those pitiful,

starvin' chirrun we see on television all the time. I think that is so *selfless* of you! Elizabeth Ann, I hardly recognized *you*, darlin'. How's your mama these days?"

"Still crazy as a pet coon," Lizzie said with a wry mouth.

"Oh, Puddin', you know how it is. In some families insanity appears every other generation; in our family it's every five minutes."

Spence brought Abby a bottle of Fresca for one hand and her vodka for the other. A woman toting a bulky camera case caught his eye and sauntered over. Joe had noticed her earlier, going from group to group with her Camcorder, encouraging everyone to smile and say a few words. She was a gaunt, deadpan, thin-lipped woman with sardonic black eyes and an unfiltered clove-scented cigarette dangling from one corner of her mouth. It smelled bad enough to be French. Her style, including the cigarette, was almost defiantly outré.

"Hi, babe," she said to Abby.

"Hello, Adele."

Adele held out her hand to Joe. "Adele Franklin. I'm Dr. Thomason's press secretary. Heard about your travels from Luke. Central Africa?"

"Yes."

"Still a lot like hell these days, or so I imagine. I've been all over the dark continent myself. The blowfly countries, where nothing cuts the dust like warm gin. That's when my ex-husband was writing a column for the *Atlanta Journal.* When we split over his African Queen—she was a Cape Town heiress, actually—I did PR for Coke in the old hometown. I mean Coca-Cola, of course. The perfect nonproduct, an ad man's wet dream. The stuff is a triumph of expectation and imagination over reality." She tipped ash from her smelly cigarette to the brick floor of the veranda. "Like most politicians, hey?"

"Are you talking about me, Adele?" Lucas Thomason said, in his smoothly-paced, slightly breathless pulpit voice.

Adele turned, exhibiting a twinkle. "Just giving Joe here my provenance."

He denied her twinkle with a pinching-together of his injured-looking lips.

"Will Senator Harkness be a no-show, do you think?"

Adele placed a hand over her heart. "Bury me in an unmarked grave if he doesn't make it. Fact is, I talked to him not ten minutes ago in his limo. ETA seven-fifty. Hold the ribs?"

"Hold the ribs," Thomason said, now beaming. Good humor took years off his face. He leaned over to kiss Abby's cheek. She covered the glass in her lap with one hand, as if she'd forgotten that vodka has no odor.

"Luke, I love the birdbath! How did you ever manage to find something so cunning?"

"Walked into Rembarto's, and there it was. Of course I had to snatch it away from a couple of old biddies." Her delight at his impetuosity resulted in another kiss. Thomason raised satisfied eyes to Joe. "The good Lord never saw fit to reward me with a daughter. But Abby's all I could've asked for in this life. Are you a married man, Doctor?"

"I'm still trying to get my priorities straight," Joe said.

Thomason unlimbered to his full height, a hand remaining fondly on Abby's shoulder.

"Good-lookin' fella like you? I was twenty-one when I took the plunge for the first time. Most young men are light on their feet, but their heads can't keep up. And so they are married."

Abby said in a soft, amused voice, "Now, Luke."

A florid woman as shapeless as a beanbag in a green-and-yellow flowered dress said to Thomason, "Luke, I'd like to know what you can do about all the little special-interest groups that are holdin' the rest of us hostage to their whims. I'm speaking of those homosexuals wantin' a nude beach for themselves, right there on Calisto? Do you know they'll be flauntin' their bare butts one dune over from my screen porch! I don't think it's right. My family owned property on Calisto before there *was* any such thing as a homosexual!''

Abby rolled her eyes. "Get to work, guv."

"Tilda, if there's a law on the books, which I am dead certain there must be, I'll enforce that law to keep our beautiful beaches decent for our families."

A very tall elderly man, his head bent as if from the weight of a helmet of brilliantly swirled white hair, said, "I was shurf of Varney County for twenty-three years. I'd be interested to know which side of the death penalty you come down on, Lucas."

"Ed, I still think the best justice is a hanging judge with a short attention span."

"If you're not a man after my own heart."

"Don't forget me, come next August."

Spence Lebèque said, "That's a good answer for a party, Lucas, but before you speak out in public on the subject of capital punishment, we need to formulate something a little less from-the-hip."

"I hear you, Spence. I know that sometimes I just can't resist going for a voter's tickle spot. But I don't intend to be stiff-necked on the stump, wasting energy devoting myself to keeping a civil tongue in my head. That's the trouble with politics today, and what do we get? Up there in Washington, government is nothing but a damned robot that builds other robots. Lord have mercy on us all. Who's pouring the bourbon around here?"

Lizzie said, "I'll get you another one, Luke."

"Thank you, Lizzie. What is that you've got on tonight? Looks just like a squeeze of my toothpaste."

She cast down her eyes self-consciously. "It's a tube dress. What brand of bourbon are you drinking?"

"Just ask Bernard," Thomason said with a wave of his hand, and then, as if bored with carrying the conversation, he turned to Joe.

"There's a lot of polo up your way. Oak Brook, I believe. Do you play?"

"No. I've only seen the game on TV. I ride enough to respect the difficulties."

"Well, you know, it's not so much a matter of equestrian skills as it is the quality of your pony. I own a couple of surefooted little quarter horses, the kind they use for barrel-racing at the roDAYos. Those ponies will pick up the ball and run with it between their teeth, they love the game so much. Like for you to have a look-see, if you're going to be around very long."

"I haven't made any definite plans yet."

"Not anxious to be home, after spending all that time in the wilds of Africa?"

"Not really," Joe said, as Abby looked up quickly with a hopeful smile.

"Come ride with me in the morning, then. We'll get ourselves better acquainted. By the way, what was that hospital again?"

"My affiliation? North Shore, in Winnetka."

"Now I remember."

"Lucas, come over here and settle this argument for us, before Wilmer makes such a doggone nuisance of himself you got to show him the door!"

"Coming," Thomason said, with a temperate smile just beginning to show a little weariness. He nodded in a courtly manner to Joe, winked at Abby, glanced at Adele and walked away. Adele, having absorbed a message not apparent to the others, followed right behind him.

"Adele," Thomason said, when they were out of earshot of Joe and Abby, "call up the administrator of the North Shore Hospital in Illinois and see what he has to say about Dr. Joseph Bryce."

"Why do I say I'm curious?" Adele asked, with a covert glance at Joe.

"Just tell him you're with the State Board of Medical Examiners. Make up a reason, you're good at this."

"What do you want to know about Dr. Bryce?"

"Just enough to give me a high comfort level."

"Oh. Do you think Abby's got eyes for the doctor?"

"That's obvious, isn't it?"

"I'll get on it. First thing in the morning."

"No," Thomason said, with a jutting of his lips that might have been a pout, or a reprimand. "Call him tonight. Unless there's something more important on your schedule."

"There's not," Adele said promptly. "Let me double-check on Senator Harkness, who ought to just about be at the front gate, then I'll make that call."

EIGHTEEN

Adele was waiting on the motor court when the limousine bearing the Hon. Miller Harkness, the senior senator from the Palmetto State, arrived from the Myrtle Beach Jet Port, accompanied by a woman who was not his wife.

It wasn't news that Harkness, his presidential ambitions abandoned for good, had finally worked out the details for a divorce from Alicia Harkness, to whom he had been married for thirty-three years, and was planning to marry for the second time. Adele was abnormally curious, even for someone of her profession, to meet his intended, who remained inside the limo while Adele introduced herself to the senator.

"I'm Dr. Thomason's press secretary. Welcome to the Barony, Senator Harkness."

He was a man of medium height, bespectacled, quite boyish-looking for his sixty-odd years, with the casual yet stately air of one long accustomed to the deference of the people he served. He looked from Adele to the façade of the mansion with approval and a hint of Old South nostalgia. His accent was as thick as peach butter.

"I've heard many stories from my stepmother's half-brother, who of course was a Thomason, the McClellanville Thomasons, about the great days of Chicora Plantation. It does my heart good to see the old place revived and flourishing. Would you allow me—?"

He stooped half inside the limousine again, emerged holding the gloved hand of the woman who was currently the love of his life.

Adele wasn't impressed. She'd expected a Washington lawyer or social firecracker in her late thirties, perhaps, one of those women for whom grooming is a sacrament, as vivid as the senator was plain. But the woman to whom she was introduced was also plain, on the stout side, probably around fifty, and seemed to be a little cowed by her sudden eminence as the next wife, someday, of Senator Miller Harkness. Or maybe she just didn't travel well.

"So very nice to meet you, Ms. Birdsall. I hope the flight down wasn't too rough."

"The smaller jets seemed to get tossed around more when there's turbulence," Harkness said. "Flora was just asking, if there's a room available to freshen up in and change—"

"Helloooo!"

Jesus, Adele thought, but her smile didn't flicker as she turned toward the front door and a vision of Charlene Thomason, blond enough to make the sun look dingy, gold bracelets flashing in the light from the entrance gallery behind her as she waved to the new arrivals, then came down the outside steps to greet them. At least she didn't have a drink in one hand, Adele thought. But Charlene could put an antic spin on things very quickly. Adele knew that Senator Harkness was attracted to the vapid, the artificial and the ridiculous like a mongoose is attracted to a cobra.

"Senator Harkness, I'd like to introduce you to—"

"But we've met!" Charlene interrupted, extending her hand, the artificial nails too red for her pale skin— by moonlight it looked as if she had been careless with a cleaver at a chopping board. "At the Kennedy Center, last February! The black-tie tribute for the composer, what's-his-name—*damn*. I just don't know a thing about music, and care less."

"Oh, yes," said the senator, who probably spent a hundred nights a year at black-tie rites of tribute or charity, "so nice to see you again—"

"Mrs. Thomason," Adele said, with discreet emphasis, "I'll just send one of the boys to let Dr. Thomason know his guests have arrived from Washington."

"Wonderful, thank you, Adele," Charlene gushed while holding fast to Harkness. Charlene's disturbingly high spirits, along with the prominence of the new moons under her dark, starry pupils was one indication to Adele, who had a history of substance abuse herself, that Charlene was coked.

"Mrs. Thomason, this is Flora Birdsall."

"Hello!" Charlene ran Ms. Birdsall's appearance through the status-perceptive neurons of her brain and concluded with a hopeless faux pas: "Do you work for Senator Harkness?"

Flora Birdsall smiled glumly and shook her head, at the senator rather than Charlene.

Adele stepped in and said, "Charlene, Ms. Birdsall was wanting to freshen up after her trip, so I thought I'd take her upstairs now and—"

"Oh, use my bedroom, *please*! I know you'll love it, if you like Louis the Fifteenth." She added, with a touching lack of assurance, "The French king?"

Flora Birdsall found her voice. "Thank you, that's very kind, Mrs. Thomason."

"Charrr-lene," said the third Mrs. Thomason, tripping over a giggle.

"Charlene."

"Borrow *any*thing you see in my closet that you like."

Flora nodded pleasantly, overlooking the implication that she was a snoop. To Adele Flora said, "I have an overnight bag in the car."

"I'll see that it's brought up to you. Lonnie?"

He was one of the young men parking cars for the guests. "Yes'm."

"If you'll come this way, Ms. Birdsall? Oh, Lonnie, would you also run and tell Dr. Thomason that the senator is here? I believe he's on the veranda with Abby."

"No need to *bother*, he's coming with *me* right now!" Charlene was at the senator's side, a hand inside his elbow to implement this act of social arrest. To Harkness she said, "I guess the grand tour will have to wait, because supper should have been ages ago. But before you leave I want to personally show you everything I've done to restore the Barony! When I first set eyes on it, *pigeons* lived inside. It was disgusting. Now I'll bet we wouldn't take two million for this house."

Adele escorted Flora Birdsall inside.

"I want to apologize," Adele said as they went up the curving stairs. "Charlene looks delicate, but—" She smiled wryly, girl to girl. "—socially she can be a Porsche without brakes."

"I found her very—agreeable," Flora said, refusing to be unkind. She glanced at the trompe l'oeil paintings that added depth and perspective to the gallery. "Are these Mrs. Thomason's ideas? It's a wonderful-looking gallery; such clever use of space."

"Well, with the counsel and guidance of thirteen different decorators Charlene did accomplish all this."

"The old saying about a book and its cover."

"Would you like for me to have something sent up, a glass of wine?"

"No, thank you, Adele. I'm afraid wine would put me straight to sleep. If I could have some tea—"

"Right away." Adele showed Flora to the door of Charlene's room, knocked once, prudently, then opened it. "Here we are."

"Oh, my."

"And here we have the bath—" Adele closed the door to Lucas Thomason's room, looking with disfavor at Charlene's side of the bath: glob of toothpaste on the golden bill of one of a pair of swan's-head faucets, snarls of platinum hair like little tumbleweeds on the sink top. She gathered up a handful of discarded towels from the floor, and some of Charlene's slightly gamy underwear, all of which she dumped into a hamper. She took fresh towels from a cabinet, and a folded terry robe with a makeup stain on one sleeve the laundresses hadn't been able to remove. But it wasn't too noticeable. These things she laid out on a padded bench for Flora Birdsall, in case she wanted to bathe.

"Thank you, you've been awfully kind," Flora said, taking the trouble to make eye contact and sound as if she meant it. Her eyes were her best feature: they were like fine English china in a rather ordinary cabinet.

Adele knew that she was tired and wanted to be alone long enough to collect herself before facing a gang of her husband-to-be's cousins and constituents, but Adele's curiosity bump needed massaging.

"Do you live in Washington, Ms. Birdsall?"

"Near there."

"The reason I asked, your name is familiar. Not from a political family, are you?"

"Well—my grandfather was a federal judge in Philadelphia, where I was born. My father was a co-founder of the Central Intelligence Agency. Andrew Birdsall."

"That may be why I know the name."

Flora smiled patiently and volunteered nothing more. Adele excused herself and went downstairs to the library. She was dying for a smoke, a guilty act in this house where none of the others craved cigarettes and Charlene, defending the purity of her carpets and drapes, deplored a smoldering butt as an act of criminal negligence. So when she was caught at it Adele felt as if she'd been masturbating. Outdoors she could relax and practice her spicy smoke rings, her aimless thoughts also eddying in the honeysuckle air, ripples of brain gas floating home to the primordial stars. But there was something she needed to do first.

Charles M. Froelich, Jr., was at home in Highland Park, Illinois, helping his ninth-grade daughter cope with first-year algebra, an effort that usually had her in temperamental tears (it was the age, he kept reminding himself), when the business phone in his study rang. There was no machine on that phone; he had to be available to the hospital at all hours.

"You don't want to fight it," he said soothingly to Kristi. "The problem is, you're closing your mind to the whole idea of algebra."

"Because I *hate* it," Kristi said, with a vehemence that forced more hot blood into her cheeks.

"When you carry on like this, you're only reinforcing a negative progression: I don't like algebra, so that means I can't *do* algebra. But we both know you're a very bright girl, so—"

"So?"

"What we have to do is find a reason for liking algebra."

"God! I just *told* you—"

"Let me pick up the phone, and I'll be right back."

"I'm going outside."

"Kristi, you're *not* going outside. Wait for me right here."

He got up from the floor of the great room, favoring the knee that was aching from raquetball that afternoon, and limped into his study.

"Mr. Froelich?"

"Yes."

"My name is Adele Franklin. I'm co-chairperson for

the Nominating Committee of Pandora's Bay Regional Hospital here in South Carolina?"

He heard the back door slam, and frowned in annoyance.

"Yes, how can I help you, Ms.—"

"Well, now that funding is complete for our new Pediatrics Department, we're considering candidates to head the department. We feel it's important that our choice be in on the ground floor, so to speak, involved with the actual planning and construction of the Pediatrics Wing."

"I see. That might be a good idea."

"In our discussions, the name of Dr. Joseph Bryce has come up more than once. And that's why I'm calling you."

"I'm not sure I understand."

"There *is* a Dr. Joe Bryce on the staff of North Shore Hospital, isn't there?"

"Would you excuse me for just a moment, please?"

Charles M. Froelich, Jr., lowered the receiver of the telephone, holding it cupped against his chest where his suddenly accelerated heartbeat might have been picked up by a pair of sharp electronic ears, who knew how many thousands of miles away? For that matter, how could he possibly know how many others might be listening to this conversation, alert to any hint of duplicity in his reaction to a seemingly harmless inquiry? He snatched the receiver away from his chest, looked past it at the books on the built-in shelves of handsome cherry veneer, which he'd carpentered himself in his basement workshop. Novels by Fleming, Forsyth, Follett, Ludlum, Greene. And especially Le Carré, the modern master of the spy novel.

So the moment had arrived. *His* moment. They'd told him it might happen, but not how: that a woman on the telephone with a cheesy Southern accent (not nearly good enough to fool him) would be asking for validation of the false identity of a covert agent of the

CIA. Who was she, anyway? Iranian? Iraqi? Korean? Or a terrorist of no specific nationality, a gun for hire, telephoning him from the international shadowlands of violence and treachery? All he knew was, somewhere the life of a man, a double agent, perhaps, depended on him. It was not too farfetched to assume that the future security of the United States was resting on his shoulders *right now*.

He took a deep breath, tugged at the middle drawer of his desk with his free hand but remembered that the envelope was locked in the middle drawer of his other desk, in his office at North Shore Hospital. The envelope containing the bona fides of the fictitious CIA agent, Joseph Bryce. And a photograph. It had been brought to him by a prominent vascular surgeon in the midwest, chief of his service at Chicago's most prestigious hospital. And, it became obvious, a man with ties to the Central Intelligence Agency. You could have knocked Charles over with a goose quill. Everything he'd read about interlocking alliances of powerful individuals in all walks of life, secret confederations of movers and shakers, was embodied by the personable, graying, renowned surgeon in a two-thousand-dollar suit. Asking a favor of him, Charles M. Froelich, Jr., a *personal* favor, although they'd never met. It was a matter of patriotism, really. Charles was assured that neither he nor his family would be at risk. He was reminded that it took a man of moral integrity and deep love for his country to step up when needed. Lastly he was assured by the surgeon, a man of unquestioned integrity himself, that he never forgot a favor.

"Hello, Mr. Froelich? Are you there?"

"Oh—sorry. I thought I heard—one of my kids crying outside. What were you asking about—about Joe? The fact is, he's been on a leave of absence from his practice for the past couple of years. I believe he's still in Africa. I received a nice letter from him, I think it was about four months ago."

"Africa? I wonder if we're talking about the same Joe Bryce, I may be confused here. He's about five-six, going bald—"

"Oh, no. Obviously there's some confusion. Joe's tall, at least six-two, and the last time I saw him, he had a full of head of hair."

"Well, I feel foolish. So there must be two Joe Bryces in the medical profession."

"More than that, I'm sure. Why don't you check with the AMA?"

He wasn't so sure that he should have volunteered this suggestion. But if the Agency was thorough in setting up a false identity, then they probably had means of inserting "Joe Bryce" into the medical association's computer file.

"Thank you very much for your time, Mr. Froelich."

"Well, purely for selfish reasons, I hope you don't locate *our* Joe Bryce. He's a wonderful doctor, and we'd like to have him back at North Shore."

When he hung up, his heart was pumping blood hot enough to sear his cheeks; his scalp tingled. He'd done well, he knew that. He'd carried off *his* moment, and he could only hope that "Joe Bryce," whoever he was, wherever he was, would be successful in completing his own vital mission.

Kristi was on the back porch with Carol Ann from next door when Charles walked outside. His thrill continued, intensified by the sight of the spectacular sunset, clouds in rosy galactic spirals, which they'd been treated to this evening. God bless America.

"Who was that on the phone?" Kristi asked. Her posture was hunched and forlorn on the top step.

He smiled and then hugged her so hard she squirmed in dismay. The light of his life. Safe, protected. *I wish I could tell you that*, he thought. "Oh, nobody. What do you say we just forget about the algebra and we'll all go over to Dairy Queen for a treat."

NINETEEN

One of the women at the barbecue was saying, ". . . On Wednesday nights in the Community Room at the library. We've had some fascinating speakers for our series on Children in Crisis; but no one quite as capable as yourself, I'm sure, to bring the reality of the suffering nations of Africa close to our own lives. Would you have any slides?"

"Sure," Joe said, but then he shook his head, warningly. "It's pretty nasty stuff. Close-ups of AIDS-related sarcomas, lesions from sexually transmitted diseases, swollen joints the size of baseballs, twisted limbs—"

"Ohh," the woman said. Her name was Daisy. Her own petals were graying at the tips, becomingly, and her large brown eyes were filled with concern. "These are all *chil*dren?"

"I'm afraid so. Half the babies we see have been born HIV-positive." He sipped his drink. He had moved on from beer to Glenfiddich, neat, provided by an extremely thoughtful host from his own, not the bar stock. The whiskey was thirty years old, and almost worth its weight in gold. Scotch, even the best, eventually gave Joe a headache like tiny bees buzzing inside his temples. But it also controlled a tendency for his mood to swing toward the colder reaches of his heart, to that region of disappointment and failure as he continued to play to an audience captivated by the character he couldn't shed. "I'm a doctor," Joe continued, in a wearier tone of voice. "I photographed what was pertinent to me, not mood shots of giraffes gathered around a water hole at twilight. In fact, I never saw a giraffe all the time I was in Africa. Or an elephant. Or cattle that were fit to eat."

Daisy nodded, responding to the mood of his eyes, his slight tone of bitterness in the face of appalling catastrophe. Daisy was enthralled. She was fortyish, as full-breasted as a setting hen. He'd met her husband, one of those loud boozers whose face is an atlas of dissipation, his life a ship on the rocks. Joe didn't know what her extramarital stats were, but he knew just how she would play it if, a little later, he took Daisy off to a private corner for a communion of lonely hearts. For every woman desirous of a tame love affair there are ten who want to be trampled by a wounded god in rut.

An iron triangle, beaten with a long-handled spoon, rang like a fire bell in the night.

"Ribs, ribs!" cried the chef of the catering crew, whose name was Shorty. He wore a tall cook's hat and a nearly floor-length apron covered, like an artist's palette, with dabs and smears of sauces. "Y'all come get 'em, right now!"

Daisy touched Joe lightly on the back of one wrist. "I do want to persuade you to come and see us. We're not at all a frivolous group, Dr. Bryce."

"Joe. I'm sure of that, Daisy."

"Are you staying at the Barony while you're visiting?"

"No, I'm at the Planter's House in Nimrod's Chapel."

"I would like to give you a call."

"By all means," Joe said, with a measure of gratitude in his smile while at the same time he was thinking, and she must have seen this in his eyes, *Come naked, bitch.* He had to turn away from Daisy because of the rage, storming out of nowhere, that accompanied the thought. He was like a ship on the rocks himself, battered, engulfed, sinking.

Where was Abby? He thought he heard her voice, but she was below his line of sight in her wheelchair, somewhere on the veranda, cheery and vitalized by good company. The crowd outdoors, eighty or more guests, with still more guests in the house, murmured appreciatively at the promise of feasting and began to move toward the twin tents set up on the strip of Bermuda lawn between the low wall of the veranda and the garden hedges. It was a kind of slow sideways falling-out, as if the brick-paved veranda had been tilted slightly in that direction. Daisy's husband claimed her; his eyes, when they focused on Joe, were swarmingly infected with envy and dislike. In the open-sided tents caterers were loading the tables with platters of steam-wreathed baby-back ribs, succulent pulled pork and corn on the cob; great wooden bowls of salad and baked beans; loaves of just-baked bread; crocks of butter; sparkling dishes filled with savories both hot and cold. Joe stayed where he was, nodding and smiling as the veranda crowd thinned around him. He had a glimpse of Abby, operating her wheelchair at trolling speed, looking up and back at Lucas Thomason a couple of paces behind her.

"These days the Second Golden Rule seems to be, Somebody had to get screwed before you could be born, so carry on in the grand tradition."

"Luke, you don't believe that!" Elaborately drawling the last syllable as a remonstrance. Her voice a South-

ern woodwind of infinite notation. There were women
whom you couldn't bear to hear more of after a single
sentence. But Abby's voice both defined the person
and invited the listener to audit another, wordless language as subtle as the tidings of the blood.

"Didn't say *I* believe it. I still hold sacred the original
Golden Rule. But, present company included, I'm
afraid we find ourselves a rapidly shrinking minority."

"It's a *de*pressin' view," said Senator Miller Harkness. "But not at all inaccurate. When people ask
what's wrong with their government, they ought to be
acquainted with the fact that seven out of ten Americans belong to some group or other that has what can
be defined as 'special interests'; and a good many of
them belong to four or more such groups. With so
much indiscriminate pressure, the institution of government, like any other institution, may eventually be
persuaded to make a mockery of its best intentions by
serving only to codify the flaws of the governed. Ig-
norance and greed are the pettiest of evils—until they
attain the stature of law."

The novice politician and the distinguished senator,
who were related in some complex manner, seemed to
be hitting it off. Joe realized that Abby was looking for
him. He waited a few moments for several old parties
to move slowly out of his way; Lizzie then spotted him
and said, "Here's Joe." He started toward Abby as they
all turned and, while Abby paused to wait for him, Joe
saw Flora Birdsall coming from the house with Charlene and Adele Franklin.

He had nowhere to go. The veranda was nearly
cleared. In the next moment Flora took him in, and,
possibly not believing her eyes, stopped and stared.

Joe reacted by devoting all of his attention to Abby,
turning his back and ignoring Flora. His confusion, the
threat her unexpected appearance posed, he concealed with an old-fashioned gesture, taking Abby's
hand and kissing it. What the hell, as Spence Lebèque

had observed, he could get away with such corn as few men could. It wàs the Old South—*her* Old South— after all.

Lizzie almost spoiled it by tittering, but the blush on Abby's face, the delight in her eyes, made all the difference.

"Oh-oh, is this *serious?*" Lucas Thomason said, his tone lower than his normal speaking voice, and without any shading of humor.

Abby glanced flippantly at him. "Oh, Luke, it's a *game* we've been playing today. How could you miss the connection? Joseph Bryce? *Captain* Joseph Bryce, doesn't *that* ring a bell?"

"Hey, now. Sure does. *Flames of War*, that's the right book, isn't it?"

"Yep. You're back in my good graces, mon. Joe, have you met Senator Harkness?"

"A pleasure, sir." Joe shook a stubby hard hand, looking him in the eye; then he looked confidently, reassuringly at Flora, now standing at the senator's side. However she'd managed to suppress her own surprise, or shock, the effort had left her looking shrink-wrapped, stored like the future meal of a spider, alive but without a glimmer of animation. "Hello," Joe said, bearing down with his smile, bearing down psychically as well—*Remember me, we were fucking in the Red Roof Inn not six weeks ago*—and alertness returned none too soon, first with a flicker in her eyes, then a tentative smile. She swallowed; she was calm. She extended her own, cold hand.

"I'm Flora Birdsall. Captain, ah—"

"No," Abby said, "that's *my* Joe Bryce, purely a figment of my imagination. This Joe's a doctor, from Zillionois or some Midwest place like that."

"Oh, silly of me. I'm sorry." She smiled at Abby, still gathering strength, recovering her poise. "And you must be Pam—Pamela Abelard."

"Yes, I am. Welcome to the Barony, Ms. Birdsall. Someone said you weren't feeling well?"

"Oh, it was nothing. Just a bumpy plane ride, but I'm over it now."

The senator put his arm around her, murmured something intimate in her ear. Flora seemed comfortable in his embrace. Lovebirds. She was over Joe, too, at least for the moment. And so they all went to dinner.

TWENTY

Senator Harkness was a man who tended to raise a sweat when drinking. It couldn't have been the humidity, which was low this evening, or the temperature, which had fallen into the low sixties: cool enough for most of the women to be wearing wraps. The senator was drinking Jim Beam on the rocks and he'd also taken in a massive amount of pork tenderloin with baked beans. There was a dab of barbecue sauce on a lens of his glasses. He had loosened the knot of his tie.

"I believe it was Gore Vidal who once remarked to me that the world was governed by deeds, not motives. A simple truth, plainly spoken. But of course not all of us have Gore's ability to speak so well. The truth *is* always simple. It is language that makes difficulties for truth. As for deeds: they are far too often governed by flimflam, mischance, cronyism, crackpot ideology and plain old-fashioned bad faith. That the world works at all may be evidence of some sort of divine intervention. Or, at least, the occasional spark of divinity in those ordinary men we find in the ranks of leadership who are determined to muddle through regardless."

He bowed his head momentarily, one hand on his half-filled glass. The little fleck of barbecue sauce seemed a spot of pain near the iris of his eye. It was obvious how drunk he was, and a wonder, Joe thought, that he could still be so fluent. A matter of habit, presumably, as well as lifelong practice. He liked Harkness, and hoped it was going to work out for Flora. And that Flora was going to work out for Joe, although it seemed unlikely he would have a chance to get her alone and explain his feelings, the revision of his plans. Joe knew what she was thinking, every time she looked at Abby, who in her wheelchair was one of their party of eight at the table. She had refrained from looking at Joe, had not looked at him once since they had seated themselves. Furious that, from all appearances, he'd broken their covenant by stalking a crippled woman.

Flora said, covering the senator's other hand protectively, "God has always sent us great men when we need them."

He raised his glass and drained what was left. The additional infusion of Jim Beam seemed to be just enough to get him out of kilter. He continued to hold the glass as if he were about to propose a toast. Nothing came to mind. So he smiled and said, "I should have been president. Should have been." His eloquence had worn thin, his hair had slumped toward his eyebrows and seemed grayer, he groped to express his dismal regrets. "So we shuffled the deck in the primaries, and what popped up? This wild card, this political stud muffin from the Muskrat State with his horny little Phi Beta Kappa wife, looks like everybody's kid sister. Yessir. The two of 'em just as earnest and eager to please as little old mongrel puppies beggin' for a home. Tooth enamel! Goddamn tooth enamel, that's all we're sellin' on television these days."

The senator half rose from his chair and smiled in a complex way at Abby.

"You're so delightful. So talented. I apologize for airing what grievances I may still have at your lovely party."

Abby raised her own glass to him. "Senator, I understand. And *I* think the president is a prick, too."

"Now, if I can just find my way to a bathroom before it's too late—"

"Use *mine*," Charlene said, as if she loved the idea of a real United States senator urinating in the exact place where she did hers everyday.

Flora also was on her feet, making her best effort to appear at ease.

"I'll just go with you, Miller, I know the way."

"There's peach shortcake for dessert!" Charlene said, with the unengaging smile girls learned for preteen beauty pageants, startling and almost gruesome in its failure to convey any real emotion. She was sitting next to Joe, and she'd given him the lowdown on the pageant hustle. Her good cheekbones had come from her mother, who otherwise had not realized her own potential due to a birth trauma that had left her with a withered arm and mediocre marriage prospects. Her father had been an aggrieved and testy man who worked as an engineer for a radio station; his hobby was logging thousands of solitary miles on the Appalachian Trail until, one summer, he disappeared in the vicinity of Waynesboro, Virginia. Charlene was pretty well convinced that her father was an alien abductee whom the aliens hadn't given back yet. She didn't go deeply into her reasons for believing this was so, but it might have had to do with the fact that her father was a rare blood type, thus qualifying him for extensive analysis by intelligent beings from another world. Charlene had been born luckier than either her father or her mother: type O, flawless and adorable. But, after working her way up to Atlantic City and finishing out

of the money, she had left home and the sting of her
mother's disappointments. In New York she survived
the modeling game for a couple of years, where her
look never became *the* look, cast her lot with a succession of interesting but ultimately unmarriable men—a
manic-depressive director of off-Broadway plays, a Wall
Street trader who slept on a rag rug in an otherwise
empty apartment and never spent a dime on her, the
scion of an English distillery family whose lovely manners in public didn't carry over into the bedroom,
where he dislocated her shoulder one night applying
some antique device of torture while laboring to get
an erection.

Seven weeks after arriving back in South Carolina
she was married in a civil ceremony to Lucas Thomason, whom she met at a medical convention where she
was working as a decorative sales rep for a manufacturer of ultrasonic surgical equipment. She had more
or less patched things up with her mother, who was
dying of a life-long affection for unfiltered tobacco,
and she was still waiting for her father to be dropped
off at some crossroads minus his memory of years spent
as a guinea pig on a spaceship. She loved decorating
and wanted to make it her life's work; she had begged
Lucas to buy an interest in a shop in Charleston so
that she could put her talents to wider use. But he was
so wrapped up in the political thing he wouldn't in-
dulge her.

"Of course, it's not *his* money," Charlene confided.
"I don't think he ever had a pot to pee in, even when
he was in family practice. You know, that's what doctors
do when they don't have any real talent. Write pre-
scriptions for sore throats and stomach aches and *refer*
everything that looks like it might be the least bit
tricky. I saw his grades from medical school once, and
he just *did* scrape through."

Her voice had become a little too loud, following
the departure of Miller Harkness and Flora Birdsall.

Abby heard her, in spite of the recorded music by Jimmy Buffett that had been in the background all through dinner.

"Charlene," Abby said, her own voice harsh from the night air, "I don't think Joe is interested in hearing a lot of who-shot-John about the next governor of the Palmetto State."

"Well—that remains to be seen, I suppose," Charlene said, smiling but snippy.

Abby's chin came up, as if she might be in a fighting mood. Her eyes looked tired, the whites fuming. Joe, seated between Charlene and Abby, said to Abby, "Got a bad joke for you."

"Hey," Abby said, brightening somewhat. "The badder the better." She moved a hand slowly to the glass she'd been drinking from while ignoring most of the food on her plate. The ice had mostly melted. She dumped out what was in the glass next to her wheelchair and put the glass in her lap. She unscrewed the top from the silver flask that had accompanied her to dinner and emptied the remaining ounces of vodka it contained into her glass. The vodka, as far as Joe had been able to tell, was all that she'd had to drink for about an hour. An untouched flute of red wine stood beside her plate.

Joe said, "What's this? 'Clippity-clop, BANG! Clippity-clop, BANG! Clippity-clop, BANG!' "

Abby grinned delightedly, raised her glass to her lips. "No idea."

"Amish drive-by shooting."

Abby tossed her head back abruptly with a show of teeth, in a mime of laughter. But all that came from her throat was a strangled gasp.

No one realized that she was in trouble until the hand holding the glass trembled. Vodka sloshed across the tops of her breasts. Then a second, more violent tremor hit her like a cattle prod.

"Oh, my lord!" Charlene said shrilly.

Joe bolted to Abby's side. He was trying to pry the glass out of her grip when it shattered, cutting them both. She stared at him, her mouth working. Her skin was turning fiery red. She seemed to be all muscle and errant energy, no way to hold her still. Joe looked around and saw Lucas Thomason coming, knocking over empty chairs like a clumsy hurdler.

Saliva mixed with blood slid down Abby's chin. Her eyes were rolling back in her head; they looked faded and glum, as if her soul had been locked into the mechanism of a carnival thrill ride. Her dusky-rose eyelids fluttered. She had begun to sweat, and the pale hairs of her forearms were erect, spiky as the spines of a tiny cactus. He picked her up in his arms as if she were a large, awry ventriloquist's dummy, very heavy and inert from the waist down compared to her whiplash arms and jittery torso.

Thomason reached them, his livid face wrinkled like a walnut.

"Help me get her into the infirmary, Doctor!"

"What?" Joe said, confused; he was intent on maintaining his grip, not dropping Abby. One of her hands, the bloodied hand, lightly slapped his cheek as if she were begging for surcease.

"Follow me, damn it! The house."

Joe trailed the older man to the veranda, past the shocked dark faces of caterers and bartenders. Abby's head was hanging facedown and she was retching. He held her so that all of the vomit spilled out of her mouth and none of it was swallowed as he maneuvered her through a doorway and carried her beyond the kitchen. Abby coughed a couple of times, and began wheezing ominously as she fought for breath.

"Is she epileptic?" Joe asked.

"No." Thomason threw open a door and turned on some powerful lights. What might have been servants' quarters at one time had been converted to a home-treatment room with a padded table at the center. A cylinder of oxygen stood beside the table. There were OR lights overhead.

"Put her on the table," Thomason ordered. He caught his breath and, after a stunned glance at her face, began feeding her oxygen. Abby was still thrashing about, but the vomiting had stopped.

"Hold her for me, Doctor."

Charlene appeared in the doorway. "Luke—!"

"Not now."

"Is she going to—"

"Get *out*, Charlene." Instead of waiting for her to obey, he put the heel of his hand against her diaphragm and shoved her into the hall, saying, "Tell 'em it's okay. Tell 'em she'll be all right." He slammed the door in her face and locked it, went to a cabinet with glass doors, stooped and took a key from its hiding place, a magnetized box beneath the sink next to the cabinet.

"How is she?" he said to Joe, sorting quickly through ampules on a shelf, seeming momentarily uncertain as to what he should give her.

"Breathing easier now. Her blood pressure must be sky-high."

"Right." He seized an ampule, opened a shallow drawer and took out a packaged sterile syringe and a package of latex gloves.

"Has she done this before?" Joe asked.

"No." Thomason pulled on gloves, looked sharply at Joe's hands. "Whose blood?"

"Both of us, I think. She was holding a glass that shattered."

"I hope to God you weren't screwing the nigger women in that pesthole you're lately from."

"Give me a little credit, Doctor," Joe said.

Thomason's forehead was pebbled with drops of perspiration. "Yeah, you're right. I'm sorry. Uncalled for. Just keep a grip on her." He fished for a pair of half glasses in an inside pocket of his Tartan-plaid blazer and put them on.

Abby was quieting down, her wet scarlet breasts heaving as she dragged in the oxygen. Thomason sterilized a spot just above the elbow on her right arm, then picked up the ampule, which contained Procardia. He withdrew half of the contents into the disposable syringe, and injected her.

He took over from Joe, continued to hold her while the spasms eased to barely discernible tremors. He used a gauze pad to wipe the saliva from her face, checked inside her mouth to see if she'd bitten her tongue.

"Doctor, why don't you wash up and bandage any cuts. Then, if you wouldn't mind, I need one hundred twenty milligrams of Luminol and four hundred milligrams of Dilantin from the drug safe."

Joe washed quickly, found the cut on the heel of his right hand. It was easily covered with a large Band-Aid.

"Abby, Abby," Thomason said in a whispery voice, "gave us a real scare this time. Doctor? Help me turn her."

He had stripped Abby while Joe was washing, and placed sheets over her. Her face was still inflamed. She was trying to open her eyes, complaining like a newborn, but even the diffused light from the overhead fixture seemed too punishingly bright for her. Her tongue worked thickly in her mouth.

Together they placed Abby on her left side. Thomason redraped her, leaving only the upper hemispheres of her buttocks and her lower back exposed. There were small scars near the tip of the spinal column.

"Is that a reservoir implant?" Joe asked. He had seen a similar implant done at the UCLA Medical Center, in those days before his attention wandered from a respectable career.

"Put it in myself. She's always hated the needles. But there's no alternative, as you may know. With the reservoir, nowadays I only need to do this once a week. If you'll kindly prepare the injections, there's some 25-gauge spinal needles in the first drawer there.''

Joe looked for the drugs Thomason had requested. "Was the cord severed?''

"No, sir, but it might as well have been. The contusion was severe, and I've been fighting a holding battle against inflammation since her injury, which was thirteen long years ago."

"What about her spasms? When was the last time she had a scan?''

"You were in the bush too long, Doctor. Severe spinal cord contusions are not likely to show up on a CT scan."

"But a tumor would," Joe said. He picked up an ampule labeled Solumedrol and contemplated it.

Thomason said with unconcealed annoyance, "There's no tumor, and I'll stake my life on that. I won't be needing the Solumedrol right now, Doctor, she's not scheduled for another three days.''

"You're treating the inflammation with epidural steroids?''

"Which I will continue to do, until someone comes up with a better method. What's the matter, Doctor?''

"I don't see any Luminol," Joe said, putting the Solumedrol down on the sink counter.

"May have run short. The Dilantin will have to do for now."

"Got it." Joe filled a syringe and took it to Thomason. "She was in an accident, wasn't she? How did it happen?''

"Well, she was run over in the street. Corner of King and Pinckney streets in Beaufort. That's not a brightly lighted area at night. Abby . . . and her boyfriend"— the young man seemed an afterthought to Thomason—"were on their way from a party at the old Tripeer house, at the bend of the river. Not a witness in sight. Paul, Paul Huskisson was his name, lingered in a coma for a week, but there was never a chance for him. Abby suffered a severe cord compression in the lumbar region and lost the use of her legs. There's some spasticity, but she has no pain.''

"Did she see who hit them?"

"We don't know. The accident, if you call it that, has long been blocked from her conscious mind."

Thomason injected the Dilantin into Abby's right buttock; she reacted with a mousy squeal. He straightened and raised the half glasses to the crown of his head. They put Abby on her back again, and Thomason meticulously arranged the sheets over her body. She was still sweaty and restless, but the harsh red tone of her skin was fading. One emerald stud earring gleamed on the left lobe; the other had been lost in transit.

"Get a towel for me, Doctor, while I take her blood pressure."

Joe went to the sink. There was a roll of paper towels on the counter. He failed to notice the ampule of Solumedrol he had placed there, and accidentally brushed it to the floor reaching for the towels. When he stepped back to look for the ampule his heel came down on it, mashing it flat with a little crinkling noise.

"Damn, I'm sorry!"

Thomason glanced at the flattened ampule, the silver-dollar-size spot of clear fluid on the floor. He shook his head and pumped up the pressure collar on Abby's left arm.

"Don't fret about it, Doctor."

"Joe, please.."

"Joe. I do appreciate all the good help you've given me." A few seconds later he reported, "BP's one-eighty over ninety. I wish I knew what caused it to shoot up like that. I'll have to keep an eye on her the rest of the night."

Joe placed the wetted paper towels on a stainless-steel tray pulled out from the table. "Are you taking her to a hospital?"

Thomason said, a little edgily, "I don't think that will be necessary. You can see I'm well equipped to take care of Abby right here. Now, if Charlene is still hanging around outside, have her bring me some of Abby's nightclothes. Are we riding in the morning?"

"I'd like to. But I think—it's time for me to head on home."

Thomason made no protest for the sake of Southern hospitality. Joe looked at Abby while the doctor listened to the murmurous filling and emptying of the tidal chambers of the heart. Her free hand stirred weakly; she seemed to be trying to signal him. Her voice sought to make words, but her tongue still wouldn't work properly. Thomason came to the end of the table, a distant look in his eyes, and stripped the latex gloves, which he dropped into a waste pail. He was standing between them, monolithic in meditation, and Joe couldn't see Abby's face anymore.

"Give her my best," Joe said. It seemed, somehow, bad faith to be leaving her at this critical time. But he had come in bad faith. He let himself out.

TWENTY-ONE

Fingering his long, curiously crimped upper lip, Lucas Thomason studied his niece on the padded table in the small and windowless room, included originally as a storehouse for the adjacent kitchen, and later used as a servant's room. The overhead light cast no shadows.

Under the influence of both Valium and Dilantin Abby's eyes were fixed steadfastly, in a variation of twilight sleep, on a frieze of the mind: a smoky battleground, cannons flaring, soldiers in forage caps in arrested fall; distant voices whispered sadly, as if at a funeral. She correctly supposed that something had gone wrong with her. Her mouth felt excessively dry, and soured. She could feel her heart beating, and a tingling in her fingers. Her nipples were puckered.

"It's the drinking," Thomason said. "Bound to be. My fault for not keeping closer watch over you."

"Luke . . ."

"You'll be all right. I'll take you up to bed in a little while."

"Where's . . ."

"Don't talk." He moved into her line of sight, still lightly stroking his lip with the side of his finger. Probably getting a fever blister there. They popped up when he was overtired.

"But he's . . ."

"Your young doctor friend said to give you his best."

"Oh . . . shit."

"Now, don't start fretting. It's bad for you. It'll lead to a sinking spell, which is worse."

"I wanted . . ."

"Need to stay in a positive frame of mind. Because that's what good health is all about."

"Joe."

"He makes quite an impression on the ladies, young and old. No reason for you to be immune. But some things just can't be. I know you accepted that, long ago."

"Sometimes . . . wish . . . I could die."

"No, no, no, we're not gonna talk that way, missy. I forbid it. Hell, I know it's just the booze; you think you're getting a lift when all it does is work against you physiologically and emotionally. You simply don't have a drinker's constitution. If there is such a thing."

Abby tried, unsuccessfully, to raise herself up. She only succeeded in dropping the sheet from her breasts before lying back in a daze.

He stared moodily at her exposed breasts, at the fine tracery of veins around aureolae that remained as small and pink as a child's. But in more ways than the physical she would always be his child, his special child. He tucked the sheet up around her collarbones and placed a hand on her forehead, until the slight pressure of his palm caused her eyes to close.

Time to clean up. He glanced at the flattened ampule on the beige tile floor of the infirmary, kneeled to retrieve it.

Something jolted him, like a black wasp flying off the floor and nailing him between the eyes.

The label clinging to the fragments read Solumedrol, that was plain enough. But the ounce of liquid on the floor was clear, not chalky.

His heartbeat ran up alarmingly. He dipped a finger into the spill and held it to his nose. Then he tasted it, cautiously.

Distilled water. And not at all what was supposed to be in an ampule labeled Solumedrol, containing epidural steroids.

The label was wet. He lowered his reading glasses and saw the shadow of words on another label beneath the first one.

He tried to pry the two labels apart, but they tore like wet tissue paper.

Thomason straightened slowly, put the fragment of ampule with labels attached on the sink counter, and opened a drawer of the drug cabinet. He was looking for his magnifying glass when someone knocked timidly at the door.

"It's Charlene."

"Just a minute." He glanced at the table where Abby had begun to snore lightly. Opened a second drawer and located his magnifying glass in the back. With it he studied the soaked labels clinging to bits of glass until he was certain that someone had carefully removed the Solumedrol label and placed it on the ampule filled with water.

Which meant that an ampule, once labeled as Solumedrol, was missing from his drug cabinet.

"Luke?"

"I'm coming! Don't bother me."

Pure and simple, someone had come into the infirmary, *his* infirmary, with suspicions in mind, and had taken the one ampule, from among nearly three dozen available on two shelves of the cabinet, that could in the future cause him a problem. A very serious problem. Someone too goddamned clever for their own good.

Charlene flinched when he opened the infirmary door.

"What's wrong?"

"Get in here."

Charlene quick-walked into the infirmary with pajamas and a robe for Abby. He closed the door behind her and locked it again.

Charlene was staring at Abby. "Is she—"

"Abby will be good as gold. Charlene, there's a thief in this house."

"What?" She looked around at him slowly, the word *thief* sinking in, and she crossed her arms protectively over her breasts.

Familiar with the gesture, Thomason said dismissively, "I'm not blaming you. But *somebody* got into my drug safe in the past, it would be three days since I gave Abby her last injection."

"Of what?" Charlene ventured.

"What she has to have on a regular basis," Thomason said, ending her inquiry with a scowl. "Now it's gone and I'm out of it and I'll have to get another shipment from Switzerland right away. Abby's on a course of medication that requires strict scheduling, or else."

Charlene nodded. "But I don't know who—"

"Never mind. I just had a notion. Should have occurred to me sooner."

"I don't think . . . it was Norse. What use would he have for Pamela's—"

"No, it wasn't him. He's too thick between the ears. I said never mind. Help me get Abby into her pajamas, will you?" He glanced at his wristwatch, and flinched. "Jesus. Where'd the time go? What happened to everybody?"

"The party broke up. There's a ton of peach short-cake left, nobody wanted any after Abby's fit."

"Where's Senator Harkness?"

"He passed out, and they're in the guest room to-night."

"Oh, good. We'll have a chance to talk at breakfast. If he's not too hungover." Thomason pressed both hands to the back of his neck. "I've got a bitch of a headache."

"Are you going to come to bed after we take her upstairs?"

"No, I'll sit with her tonight. I have some thinking to do."

"I really would like for you to come to bed with me after a while, Luke." A shudder rippled through her. "I'm kind of on edge? I got scared when Pamela—did that."

"She had a severe convulsion relevant to her ongoing neurological syndrome." But he looked doubtful, even as he provided the diagnosis.

"Don't you think she ought to be in a hospital for a specialist to check her out?"

"The convulsion ran her temperature up but didn't do any lasting damage. And this won't be happening again. I'm cutting out the Happy Hours and keeping her on Dilantin for a while."

"You know what? I just think she's very unhappy."

"Don't be ridiculous, Charlene."

Her lips pressed together tightly. Her eyes brimmed.

"I'm not *ridiculous*. I try real hard. I do, Luke. I just wish you could appreciate that."

"Charlene, I know what you want and I'm sorry; it's a sad but true fact of life that at age fifty-six I can manage only one decent hard-on a day."

Charlene sucked wind as if she were about to take a long fall.

"That is such an asshole thing to say. Sometimes I only want to be *held*. A sad but true fact. Go ahead

then. Play with your Abby doll the way you like to.
Catheterize her and give her her enema and stick needles in her. Your favorite pastime, right? Then when
you're all worked up you can come to my room and
use me to masturbate while there's nothing on your
mind but AbbyAbbyABBY. I'm smart about some
things, Luke. And I wouldn't want to have your con-
science.''

His shoulders squared in anger, but he had sufficient grace in spite of the provocation not to slap a
crying woman. Throbbing from stress, he turned his
back on Charlene instead. On the table Abby's fevered,
dopey eyes were open, but not as if she were really
awake, or even aware of her surroundings. Looking, he
thought, with a sympathetic pang that slowly dispelled
his anger, just as he had discovered her in the emergency room of the hospital in Beaufort on a September
night thirteen years ago.

TWENTY-TWO

*The caterers were packing up the bar when Joe walked out-*side on the veranda. One of them glanced at him and said, "Could I fix you something, Doctor?"

"If there's any beer left."

"Got it right here." He had long hands and wide shoulders; up close he was taller than Joe had thought.

"Play any ball?"

"Yes, sir. Three years at Coastal Carolina." He glanced toward the house as he was filling a glass from one of the steel beer barrels. The question was on the tip of his tongue, but he was reluctant to ask.

"Miss Abelard's going to be okay. Sometimes these seizures happen when there's spinal-cord damage."

The young caterer straightened with a look of relief and happiness, and handed Joe his beer. It was no longer very cold, but Joe drank it gratefully. A three-quarter moon surfaced in a boil of cloud over Abby's workshop, like a blunt bone separated from a galactic skeleton. The lights were on inside; possibly someone was there. The caterer rose from the brick veranda, a beer keg on each shoulder, and walked them gracefully to a five-ton truck parked beneath the ageless oak on one side of the house. The breeze coursing through the garden carried with it a bouquet of sea life and tangy cold combers.

The doors of the workshop stood open a couple of feet, framing the images on a big-screen TV. Lizzie, solitary, lounged on a tufted floor pillow watching a wrestling match. She glanced back at his footsteps and bit her lip wordlessly.

"She'll be okay." He shrugged and offered an explanation. "Probably too much to drink."

"Bull," Lizzie muttered, and fixed her eyes on the expanse of screen, which featured human equivalents of Gothic architecture. "I let Bruiser out to do his business. Did you see him anywhere?"

"No. Lizzie, I guess I came to say goodbye."

She looked around in shock. "Goodbye?!"

"Lizzie, there are things I have to—"

"Joe, you don't understand! Abby will die—he'll *let* her die—if you don't help her!" She scrambled up from the cushion and reached him in two long strides. "She's the only friend I've got in the world! Please don't leave her like this!"

"Lizzie, aren't we exaggerating—"

Inches away, Lizzie rose on her toes to almost equal his height. Eye to eye she said, "Sometimes I exaggerate but I don't tell lies. It's no lie what's happening to her! Luke doesn't have a clue. He's a *bad* doctor! They should take away his license!" She seemed to lose her balance, and Joe put an arm around her, then realized, when she went slack, it was what she'd had in mind. He almost grinned, but he didn't know what Lizzie would do if he belittled her; she needed calming down so he hugged her, as paternally as possible.

"Lizzie, let's just sit and talk about this."

"Okay." Her face was pink and her eyes misty. "But

all you have to do, honest, is take her to a hospital, I mean a good hospital like in New York, where they can find out what's really wrong."

Lizzie made a process of sitting again on her pillow, hampered by the tightness of her blue tube dress, which caused her to look as if she were popping from a chrysalis at both ends. She had taken off her shoes. Her little toenails were lacquered the color of candy apples. She scrunched over, offering Joe a corner of her pillow. He sat with his legs cantilvered and his hands clasped between his knees.

"Lizzie, for one thing, Abby's not my patient and I can't take her anywhere."

"You can if *she* says."

"I'm afraid that would cause some problems around here."

"So *what*?" Lizzie said, going from simmer to boil again. "All that really matters is her life!" She turned her face away from him, angrily. "I hate the way you're talking. I thought—"

"Thought what?"

"She really likes you, Joe. Abby would trust you."

"And I like Abby. A lot. Can I think about this without you going off like a rocket?"

Lizzie hunched her shoulders and wiped her eyes.

"I don't know what there is to think about. You took a Hippocratic oath to help people who need help. Didn't you?"

Trying to distract her for a few moments, Joe said, "Are you a big wrestling fan?"

"I like it, I guess. Abby's the one, though. She says it's a . . . a diversion for the mentally arrested, but you ought to hear her holler when they get to going at it. She hates that guy," Lizzie continued, indicating a big fellow with wild blond hair who wore a muzzle like a fireplace grate, presumably because if he were unmuzzled he would bite off someone's hand. But it didn't restrain him from bellowing dire insults at a nearly naked, baby-oiled behemoth, who bellowed back as they strove to raise the excitement level a little, the sluggish bloodlust of the assembly.

"Do you play a lot of sports?" Lizzie asked.

"I boxed until I got too old for it."

"How old is that?"

"See these gray hairs, Lizzie?"

"They're silver, not gray. They look really neat." Lizzie put her arms around her knees and rocked, a little unsteadily, on the pillow, looking sideways at him. "I'll bet you played football."

"Not my idea of a good time. I did some junior rodeo in high school. Calf roping, bronc riding." He thought about Vance and Patty Pachek, whom he hadn't seen in years. Cards and letters mailed from various points of the compass. *I'll make it soon.* But by now they knew better, no matter what hopes they retained.

"Rodeo? In Illinois?"

"I wasn't born there, Elizabeth. I was raised in Arizona, in the lettuce belt outside of Phoenix." Just telling her that much made him feel firmly grounded, someone with an honest if modest heritage, whereas for most of the evening he'd felt as if he were splitting in half, right down the middle of his clouded psyche.

"Do you own any horses?"

"No. I like boats better."

"Your boat is named the *Dragonfly*," Lizzie said excitedly, as if she were subject to periodic fits of ESP.

"You bet. But I don't have her anymore. She was pirated." He wondered if he'd said too much. Not that it could matter now. He felt comfortable talking to Lizzie, wanting to linger even though he knew he should be on his way back to town.

Her ESP was still ticking. She turned her face sharply to him. Joe smiled reassuringly at her, but with an almost unendurable heaviness in his chest that would have sunk him like an anchor in the ocean. Her own smile trembled.

You know what, Lizzie? I'm just Goddamned tired of lying to people.

"Lizzie, I'll see what I can do."

Joyous and starved for affection, she threw her arms around him. Her eyes dripped a few more tears. He held her comfortingly, although he felt the one in need of comfort, and stared at the big screen. Tag-team match. The preliminary motions that the wrestlers were going through betrayed the ordeal of lions in a cage: boredom, even apathy. He imagined Abby sitting here, often alone, whiling away another insomniac's interminable night watching a similar, sullen ritual of strength with its climax of thudding, groaning, orgasmic fakery. Consummation, however routine. Which may have explained why Abby, isolated from and deprived of the raunchy, gory, tasteless-but-filling excesses of life, found the wrestling matches so appealing.

Lizzie, not unexpectedly, raised her head, her lips tenderly parted, and kissed him with a touching awkwardness. Her eyes were closed, her fledgling body tense. Still, for Joe, the experience had no sensual content; it was like being nuzzled by a pet rabbit.

He put a thumb beneath her chin and lifted it slowly. Lizzie looked out at him from the erotic midpoint of a rosy fantasy and said with a quaver, "It's okay. Nobody's here." She took a breath and quoted him inaccurately. "You said I was the woman for you. I mean, you can kiss me—all you want. I'll never tell anybody about us. Never."

"Elizabeth Ann, I'm not afraid of going to jail; but I am concerned about perdition."

She closed her lips on the translucent braces, and lowered her eyelashes like shades of disappointment; yet it was not exactly a full surrender of the fantasy that worked its druggy lull between her pale temples.

He extricated himself casually and with good humor and was rising from his corner of the pillow, hearing his knee pop, when someone said from the doorway, "Dr. Bryce, there's a limousine waiting to drive you back to town."

It was Flora Birdsall.

TWENTY-THREE

"It's such a lovely garden, don't you think?" Flora said to Joe, in the sort of neutral-friendly voice of one who knows she will be overheard, and wants no gossip made of the moment. "I wonder if you'd mind walking with me for just a few minutes. I have a headache, and the night air would do me good."

"Certainly, Ms. Birdsall," Joe said, wondering what she was up to.

They were well away from the lights of the house, on the path that led to the old cemetery, when Flora detached them both from amiable chitchat and spoke her mind.

"You son of a bitch."

"Now, Flora. This isn't how it looks."

"Oh, really, 'Dr. Bryce'? Let me tell you how it looks: as if you're screwing everything in sight down here, including that—that *child* I found you with." Indignation caused her to hiss like a serpent gliding over a grass mat. *"She* can't be a day over fourteen!"

"Give me a break," he said irritably. "Lizzie has a little crush on me, that's all. She's scared and, except for her cousin Pamela, nearly friendless. Also she's convinced herself Abby is going to die."

"Oh, my God," Flora said, in a hushed, graver tone, passing a hand over her eyes as if she were actually praying, "what have you done? What are you *involved* in here? The poor woman is crippled. I suppose she's in love with you, too. All wrapped around your little finger. I've thought a lot of things about you, Joe; but I never let myself believe that you could be so heartless."

"Do you mind if I explain?"

They had come to an open place; she turned. Her face by moonlight appeared to have sagged from fatigue and stress; her jawline was like the crimped crust of a pie. There was injury in her deep-set eyes. Wounded, they seemed even more beautiful than he remembered. To their left the Spanish moss on a broad twisted oak looked like the gray rags of Confederate men hanged more than a century ago. To their right Pandora's Bay was as bright as the pearls Flora wore in a double strand at the base of her throat.

"What can you possibly explain? How long have you been here—operating, Doctor?" She licked her lower lip, as if her unaccustomed malice had settled there, like a glowing spark.

"I arrived in Nimrod's Chapel late yesterday."

"Yesterday?" She seemed not to believe him. "My God, you're already like one of the family."

"I'm good at what I do," he said, looking patiently into her eyes.

"Oh, obviously." But her mood was losing ire, and his gaze, mildly amused, made her uneasy. Flora looked around, clasped and unclasped her hands. "You have to leave," she said. "It's over. I won't permit it to go on."

"Okay."

She hadn't anticipated this response. She continued, as if an argument were called for, "Because if you don't leave, I—I will take matters into my own hands. I'll *erase* you, Joe. Faster than I created you."

"Flora, I need another day. Maybe two. That's all, then I—"

"Aren't you listening?" she said fiercely. "Your *project* here is finished. You're not taking one penny—"

"I don't want money. I only want to help Abby. It may be that Dr. Thomason has missed something about her condition. What happened tonight could be an indication that she's in serious trouble. I think she had an allergic reaction, not a seizure: the spasms, the vomiting, the way her muscles were writhing—her electrical circuits were overloaded. But it couldn't have been an insect sting, and most spider bites block nerve signals, which would cause an opposite reaction."

"As if you knew anything about it."

"I do know some medicine, and I read a lot. Thomason's a garden-variety GP. I'd like to convince Abby to see a specialist in neurological disorders, have a complete set of skull films and a myelogram done. I know who to call for a referral. If she agrees, I'll take her myself, and then I'm out of it."

Flora started to shake her head. Joe, on the alert, said suddenly, "Let's walk."

"What's the—"

"And we need to keep our voices down. Do you smell it?"

"I don't—"

"Come on. Back to the house."

Fright nipped at Flora's heart as she walked beside Joe, and she was startled by the sight of Bruiser, the Barony's mastiff, noiselessly crossing the path ahead. But Bruiser was no bolder than a shadow, ignoring them as he went about some nocturnal errand of interest only to a dog. Still, she resisted the urge to link arms with Joe.

"I don't understand," she complained, in a low tone.

"Somebody's outside for a smoke. Behind us, near the big oak tree."

"Who?"

"I didn't see anyone. Whoever it was didn't want to be seen. I'm trying to remember what we've said that might get us into trouble."

"Us?"

"I exist only through the good graces of a CIA spook who can wipe me out with a few keystrokes on her supercomputer. You made me, out of less than even God had to work with when He made Adam. But the process also works in reverse, doesn't it? Your continued existence depends on *my* good graces. We're quite a pair, aren't we, Flora? Inseparable, when you think about it."

Flora thought about it. Her steps dragged. Joe watched her. She raised a hand to rub one temple.

"Is your headache any better?" Joe asked.

"You shit."

"I'm not making any threats, Flora. I wish you all the happiness that Miller Harkness undoubtedly will bring to your union. But I need to go on being good old Doc Bryce for a while."

"To help Abby, you said. Your motives are pure, you say. For once in your life. Your respective lives."

"I have a shady side. And I like to think I have a good side, Flora."

She stopped abruptly. "You have *nothing*. You *are* nothing, except when you're pretending to be someone else."

It was his turn to be wounded. "I know who I am, Flora."

Her eyes flashed, contradicting him.

"I see you as scared, Joe. Yes. Right now, you're very frightened. Because it won't be so easy without me. Oh, you can call yourself by a hundred names: birth certificates, Social Security cards, driver's licenses, all those phony things you can buy for yourself. But they don't give you the *identity* you crave. The deep sense of security *I* gave you. A foolproof background to build on, with your photographic memory and your actor's tricks. You've spent a great deal of time on Dr. Joe Bryce, haven't you? And you are *so* convincing. You just don't want to give him up."

"I can give him up."

She put a hand on his arm, fiercely. Then withdrew, as if the reciprocal tension she tapped into doubled her shock: like disturbing a ghost in a forbidden closet.

"Oh, Joe. I couldn't get enough of you. When we were together it was like I had no mind of my own. But what have I done to us? So foolish. Joe, I'm begging you. Give up Bryce. Find your own life, before it's too late."

"I had a life." He spoke reluctantly, with weighty effort, as if he were rolling a great stone of grief away from the mouth of a cave in which the trials and despair of that life lay in deposit. "And it was smashed all to hell. I'd like to go back to try—and fix it, but I can't. Go back. Because it's dark. It's very dark back there, Flora. And I never want to get close enough to see. What's in the darkness."

The weight of the stone rolled back against him; he shuddered. This moment of nakedness recalled to Flora the last night they had been together, his confession of the humiliating violence that had been done to him.

"It must have been so *awful* for you."

"Don't be sorry. I'm okay, Flora." His tone lightened, just when she thought she wouldn't be able to bear any more of his self-torture. "I'm in control, I really am. Just don't do anything to hurt Dr. Joe Bryce." He spoke cheerfully, but his expression laid a glacial chill on her heart. "He's not a bad guy. The more I understand of him, the better I like him."

In spite of herself, she wept.

"Baby. I see now. I should have seen, all along. You need to get help."

He shook his head and smiled in amazement.

"Hey, nothing to worry about. I'm going to have a few drinks tonight, more than a few, maybe, and in the morning it'll be great. I'm not hurting anyone. I'll never hurt anyone, the way I was hurt."

Her voice, already low, had dwindled to a whisper. "Oh, God. There's nothing I can say, is there? God, I'm shaking like a leaf. Go on. Just go, Miller's driver will take you to the hotel."

The wind was up, the moon was out of sight. He bent to kiss her cheek but she drew away from him, almost in horror. The black mastiff padded past them silently and unexpectedly on his way to Abby's workshop. The huge dog seemed, in Flora's freezing mood of remorse and fear, loosed from a deep pit of hell, unpredictable and perhaps dangerous. Flora couldn't move for trembling.

Joe said nonchalantly, as if unmindful of the state Flora was in, "Good night, and thanks for the limousine. I sincerely hope we'll see each other again, Ms. Birdsall."

TWENTY-FOUR

The phone in his room at the Planter's House rang for a long time until Joe was sufficiently conscious to make the attempt to answer it.

"I just knew if I was persistent it would pay off. Have a late night last night?"

"Uhh." The voice wasn't immediately familiar. Her Southern diphthongs were muffled, as if one side of her mouth were packed with gauze after a tooth extraction.

"Hey, Cap'n Joe. This is your writer friend. How you be?"

"Um. Wow. Hungover, I'm afraid."

"Where did you go after you left here?"

"Some place in town. Where they park the shrimp boats at night."

"The Dead-Cat Bounce lost its liquor license, I hear; so you must have been at the Lost Sea Turtle Café. That's where we all go when we're lonesome for sea turtles and other pets. What were you drinking?"

"I stuck to beer." He coughed, gently, so his head wouldn't fall to pieces. His right hand felt sore and was swollen; he couldn't make much of a fist. "I got in a fight."

"You did? Who with?"

"Norse."

"Did you punch him out?"

Joe thought about it. "I hit him twice. Mostly to calm him down. But he can't take a punch."

"He likes to brag that he's a black belt something-or-other. I gotta hear about this."

"Not mad?"

"About Norse? Huh-uh, why should I be?"

"You sound— How're you feeling?"

"Headachy. My tongue is sore. Luke wants me to stay in bed, but I'm not gonna. We both could use a dose of sea air, right? Can you get packed and be ready to move in an hour?"

"Packed? Move where?"

"You'll see. You'll like it. I'll be around to get you at one-thirty."

"Abby, the room is spinning, I kid you not."

"Poor guy," she said. "So we'll make it two o'clock sharp. Be down front, would you, I can't come up. Bye now."

Joe put the receiver of the phone back and lay there rubbing his sore head. He'd slept in his boxer shorts. Slept alone, no reminder of lost sea turtles or other pets in his bed. He dreaded the next two hours, although he was usually quick to sober up. Sea air sounded like a good bet. And Abby's determinedly cheerful mood made him feel better too. He wanted her company.

As far as Norse was concerned, he couldn't decide if he'd behaved badly.

Before Norse had come into the café with two girls and his alpha-wolf posturing, Joe had been all right, sitting quietly by himself at a bend of the horseshoe bar, drinking long-neck Buds slowly and methodically, watching a playoff game from the West Coast on ESPN. His mind and emotions were frozen in neutral. The Dodgers were playing the Mets, 3–2 in the fourth.

Norse's minipack consisted of a stoned-looking red-head in a black cowboy hat and a petite blonde with hot-pink hormones who looked to be, just barely, street-legal. She had a rough complexion and one eye that was noticeably smaller than the other; a mere but-tonhole, it gave the left side of her face a surreptitious look. It was the little blonde who eventually was the cause of his beef with Norse. Even before she sat down she had scanned the room like a Nazi submarine com-mander looking for unescorted shipping and had man-aged to catch Joe's eye, although he turned his head immediately. Norse didn't notice him right away. He had a big laugh and hearty greetings for everyone he knew.

The sound on the dual TVs was turned off when the midnight show began.

The featured artist was a jockey-sized young man with long hair that lay on his shoulders in ringlets, and a tattered black muleskinner's hat. He was not intro-duced; they all seemed to know him, as if he was a long-time favorite at the café. Confined to a motorized wheelchair with rubber tires like those on a small mo-torcycle, he played guitar with a semiclenched and crooked right hand and also blues harp. Once he sang a capella, a nearly whispered, enthralling version of "Nearer My God to Thee." His repertoire was a mix of Piedmont blues, rockabilly and gospel.

The stool next to Joe at the bar was vacated; twenty seconds later the blond girl who had come in with Norse and the redhead claimed it.

Her perfume was a little loud. Joe turned and she smiled at him. Her feet couldn't touch the floor; she sat with one shapely leg across her other knee. She was wearing a miniskirt that, in the pose she'd adopted, covered virtually nothing.

"Hi, I'm Dayna. You looked like somebody who wanted to be left alone, but I said to myself, What-thehell, I'll take a chance."

It was instinctive for him to smile back. She was not pretty but interesting, with the small eye, a lot of lip to her smile and a nose that had been broken and remained bent in a way that didn't mess up her face but gave it a quixotic, sensual appeal.

"Joe."

"Niceameetcha, Joe." She wasn't a Southerner; snowbird, lower-middle-class Pittsburgh, to Joe's educated ear. She kept her voice way down, leaning toward him to speak out of deference to the performer on the small stage, which was steeped in rose-colored light between the entrance to the kitchen and the hall that led to the bathrooms in back. "Isn't he great? Name's Reggie. Somepin or other. I got a thing for the blues, not metal, not Techno. Why I like it down here. Hard to get a good job, though, they pay you dick. Where're you from?"

"Midwest."

"Jack, gimmee Bud?" she requested, turning briefly to one of the bartenders. She turned to Joe again, speaking to the back of his head. "Reggie's, in my opinion, he's better than Sleepy La Beef, when I caught him at Blind Willie's in Atlanta this summer. It's a bitch about Reggie, though. He's incurable. Scur roses, or somepin. All of his joints are falling apart, which is what it is mainly, but after a while you can't swallow or breathe. They named the disease after a ballplayer, Gary, I don't know. Cooper? *Gary's* disease. Probably Reggie won't be playing the twelve-string a whole lot longer." She subsided during an impassioned blues harp break that had her writhing on the barstool. "So-ooo good," she crooned, reaching around to pick up her beer. "Hey, you wanta join us? Norse says he knows you from someplace."

"No, thanks."

"Be that way," Dayna said with a false pout, not conceding a thing. "Ohh, look who's here tonight! This is gonna be good. She can really get it on."

Reggie the blues man had been joined on stage by a woman whom Joe recognized, after a few moments, as Frosty Clemons, demonstrating a calorie-conscious figure in a ribbed cream tank top, tight fawn-colored corduroy pants and brown high-heeled patent leather boots. She kissed Reggie on the cheek to a smattering of applause and verbal greetings from the regulars, whom she acknowledged with a casual wave.

Frosty and Reggie conferred. He found a chord on his amplified guitar, and began to wail.

"Low-down mama
Got a fist like stainless steel.
Ain't nothing sweet about her kisses
Lips just like a lemon peel."

Joe reached for his beer and discovered, on tilting the bottle to his lips, that it was empty. Dayna, alert to his every move, slid her bottle toward him.

"Have some of mine."

"Thanks." He tasted her lipstick on the rim. The beer wasn't very cold; they'd been selling a lot of it at the Lost Sea Turtle Café since he'd come in. He was relaxed and still lucid; the tangle of nerves he'd brought with him to the café had, almost unnoticeably, unraveled into cooled-down strands. He had begun to feel grateful for Dayna's previously unwelcome and barely acknowledged presence. "I owe you my front-row seat in hell, Dayna."

"Hey," she beamed. "My treat." She put a hand in the crook of his elbow, all but leaning on him now.

> *"Well she come down that road from Macon*
> *Borned there in a hollow log.*
> *Lord you know she ain't a bit good-looking*
> *She give points to a mangy dog."*

"Reggie oughta have a recording contract," Dayna said. "That's what I think. Before he gets, like, too bad off to play anymore."

"Lateral sclerosis," Joe said.

"Yeah, that's what he's got, how'd ja know?"

"I'm a doctor."

"I knew it would be something like that! I said to myself, 'He's a cut above the usual kind of guy they get in here. You gotta meet him, Dayna.'"

Until now Frosty Clemons hadn't sung; but after another harmonica break she joined in, with a voice reminiscent of Aretha Franklin's.

> *"But she sister to the Fisher Man*
> *Four winds in her cheek*
> *When she blow a mean old trumpet*
> *All us sinners howl and weep."*

"God, this really gets me going," Dayna said, taking the beer back from Joe. "I've got a real good collection of CDs, including the whole Alligator series, if this is your thing too."

> *"And when she barefoot to her navel*
> *Walking round and round my hall*
> *You know she hand me palpitations*
> *She stop my heart like a pistol-ball."*

The applause was close to frenetic; Frosty stepped back, deferring to Reg, who was breathing hard, smiling abashedly, nodding his thanks. Then Frosty stepped forward and spoke to Reggie, her mouth close to his ear. He looked around at her, as if something she had said shocked him.

"Do you live around here?" Joe asked Dayna.

"My pad's on Calisto. I mean the pad I share, but one of my roommates went home for a wedding and Brenda's visiting her boyfriend at Camp Lejeune, so, you know, I'm just rattling around up there all weekend."

Frosty and Reg were conferring again. He nodded to her, blew a few notes on the blues harp he wore around his neck to signify that it was break time and followed her down a ramp to the hall beside the stage. Frosty had retrieved her clutch purse from atop one of Reggie's amps.

Joe turned and said, "Excuse me, Dayna. Have to hit the nature trail. Why don't you get us a couple of Buds while I'm gone?"

"Hurry back."

The Lost Sea Turtle Café was across the street from the commercial fishermen's pier, occupying an oblong of asphalt between a marine-supply company and a two-story brick building with a sagging second-floor balcony. The parking lot was enclosed on three sides by a weathered cypress-board fence. There was an additional enclosure for a Dumpster outside the kitchen door.

It was raining, lightly, a blowing mist off the bay. Reg had paused to open an umbrella, which Frosty held over both their heads as they passed through a narrow alley of parked cars and sports vehicles to a minivan shining like forsythia against the gray fence at the rear of the lot. Joe watched them from the doorway of the emergency exit. He could hear their voices, but wasn't able to distinguish much of what they were saying. A couple of words were unmistakable: "Abby" and "scared." Somebody was arguing loudly on a pay phone behind him about visitation rights. A kitchen worker unloaded garbage cans into the Dumpster ten feet away.

The rain misting his face felt good to Joe. There was

a line for the men's john. He stepped outside and went
to his left, glancing a couple of times at Reg and Frosty.
She had opened the sliding door of what he assumed
was her van. Joe crossed the drive that was marked off
with white lines and walked between a sixties pickup
truck with a custom paint job and a Jeep with a fabric
top. He came to the fence four vehicles removed from
Frosty's yellow minivan and heard Reg say, "I'd do anything for Abby, but—"

"No, no, there *is* something you can do." Frosty
slammed shut the door of her minivan.

"What's that?" Reg asked, a few moments later, as
if he was referring to something she'd taken from the
minivan.

Joe had unzipped his pants, but decided to wait before wetting down the fence. He moved cautiously
around the high chrome bumper of the customized
pickup, just far enough to see them beside the minivan. Frosty's back was turned to him, her tightly curled
dark brown hair gathering mist and gleaming like a
spider's web in the floodlights mounted beneath the
overhanging roof of the café. Reggie was looking up
at her face, the umbrella at an angle that screened him
from Joe.

Frosty had something in her right hand, holding it
so that it gave off a silvery flash.

"This is the new drug Dr. Luke's been giving her. I
took it from the cabinet in his infirmary."

"Did what? Frosty, I don't want to get into trouble."
When he wasn't singing the blues there was a simplis-
tic, adolescent tone to Reggie's words.

"You won't. I'm the one, if he wants to make trouble! But I fixed it so he can't know. All you need to do
is—"

She reached behind Reggie, opening a backpack he
had hanging from his wheelchair, and put the stolen
drug into a zippered compartment.

"—find out what's in that little bottle when you go

up to Duke University for your checkup next weekend. Because I'm telling you, what he's injecting into her bloodstream has got to be the reason she's fallen off lately."

Reggie, clearly puzzled, said, "Why would Dr. Luke give Abby something that's bad for her?"

"I didn't say that! It don't even make sense, he'd want to hurt her. Abby's given Dr. Luke everything he owns. But he's always ordering these new drugs he hears about. They come by Fed Ex from pharmaceutical houses in Switzerland or Puerto Rico. Maybe he's looking to cure her with some new miracle discovery. *I* know for sure it ain't working. No, sir. But you can't tell him. He's stubborn. *He's* the doctor. Don't want her to see any other doctors, don't listen to nobody else's opinion. Well, I took that mean drug away. The next shot he gives her from the ampule he thinks is the right one can't do Abby harm, it's nothing but a little squirt of distilled water. That ought to give us time to get another doctor's opinion on why that stuff I just put in your backpack is so bad for her."

"Okay, okay, Frosty. I'll take care of it. Let's get back inside, I got another set to do. Hey, you want to sing some Bessie tonight? How about 'Empty Bed Blues'?"

"Hmmm. I'll be okay on part one, anyhow."

"Then we'll do 'Walk Around, Jesus,' to close. Brought my tambourine."

"Man, I am ready to rock the house down."

They were laughing together on their way back to the café.

Joe turned his attention to the fence in the nick of time, and began with childlike fascination to write his name with his stream. He had almost enough to write the Gettysburg Address. Greatly relieved, he returned to the café, where Reg and Frosty were joking around on stage before beginning the last set of the night.

Dayna perked up on her bar stool at his approach. "Must've been a long line."

"You said it." He picked up the beer she'd ordered for him. Dayna had nearly finished hers. She leaned complacently against him, fingers at the nape of his neck.

"What'd ja do, take a shower? You're all wet, man."

"I used the outdoor facility."

Joe drank beer and listened to the good music that Reg and Frosty were making. Dayna took an occasional slug from his bottle but told him she didn't drink much and didn't do drugs, she was high on life. He wondered how many times, in how many bars, he'd heard that particular cliché from personable young women, each of whom was convinced that she was somebody pretty damned special. Hip, smart, always ready to party, wise in the ways of men. Sexually adept but certainly not promiscuous. In truth they laughed readily, but lacked real wit. They were sufficiently undereducated, despite college degrees, to keep them in a rut for most of their lives, always a little behind on the credit cards and the rent, working at jobs that required no more ability than does autoeroticism. Their sophistication was packaged for them by the media manipulators who published popular magazines and produced endless hours of glossy empty programming for the electronic asylum. They eventually married, once or twice or three times, men who were male twins of themselves. The prevailing propaganda about the accessibility of the Good Life that swarmed through them daily like neutrinos from space kept them sufficiently anesthetized until they reached that age of no return when there were too many cards missing from the deck to hope for a winning hand.

He decided he was being an asshole, dumping an unrealized rage at his own transitory state on Dayna, who at the least was vital and not jaded, and appealing in her desire to be thought interesting.

Norse came over after the music stopped. Joe renewed his dislike of the physical therapist with a glance at the diamonds in Norse's earlobe.

"Hello," he said to Joe. Hello and goodbye. To Dayna he said, "Ready to go?"

"Joe and I made some plans," Dayna said.

"Oh. What does that mean?"

"It means I don't feel like another night of sniffing glue and skinning cats with the two a ya's. Tell the truth, it's been kind of boring."

"Why don't we all go somewhere together?" Norse said. "If that's the way it is."

"The way it is, Norse, is that Joe and me are going somewhere separately."

"But we have no car, Dayna."

"Glad to drop you, Norse. If you can get Freddie on her feet long enough to walk her outta here."

The other girl's cowboy hat had fallen off. She was sprawled half across the table, the cheeky valentine of her face resting in the crook of a forearm, lips parted as she enjoyed chemicalized rapture.

Dayna said, "Nice. What've ya been feeding her tonight? So here's the revised plan. You take Freddie out to the car and Joe and me'll see she gets home okay, and you can take a hike."

Norse's mood fell, like a hammer on his thumb. "I don't like that plan."

Joe said, "Do it anyway, Norse."

Dayna looked gratefully at Joe. Norse attempted to stare him down. Joe focused on the bulge between Norse's blond eyebrows and smilingly waited him out. Meanwhile Dayna got down from her stool and went over to the table, sat Freddie up and put her hat on her head. Freddie was as boneless as a cuttlefish, a goofy smile on her face.

When Norse failed to move, Joe got up to give Dayna a hand. Together they walked Freddie down the hall and out the back door of the café.

Mist and fog obscured everything around them; the

license plates of the remaining vehicles parked by the fence were unreadable, and the floodlights had no power to define the geometry of the building they graced. Joe had put away a lot of beer, but his perceptions were okay. In spite of the sensation of being in a fishbowl, he felt reasonably well focused and in touch with his body. He saw that Frosty Clemons's yellow minivan was gone. Dayna drove a pink Jeep Wagoneer.

They leaned Freddie up against the Jeep and Dayna said, "Are you gonna be sick? If you are, do it out here."

"M'okay."

"All right, sweetie. In ya go."

Norse showed up while they were stowing Freddie in the backseat. He watched them with his arms folded, then said to Joe, "Now *you* will take a hike."

Joe shook his head.

Dayna said, "Chrissake, Norse, grow up, why don't you?"

Joe indicated an empty expanse of parking lot.

"How about over there?"

"I should warn you," Norse said. "I have a black belt."

"For what? Wrestling your own dick?"

Norse smiled condescendingly and stalked Joe, who backed off. Another couple who had come out of the café stopped and stared at them. They were all but faceless in the misty drifting murk. Threat produced valuable moments of total clarity. Joe put his hands up and studied Norse's movements closely while he circled, making Norse follow him. He would want to show off, Joe thought. And, knowing from Joe's stance that he could at least box a little, Norse probably would want to finish him without getting in range of Joe's fists. That meant a kick. Right or left foot? Joe feinted twice, giving Norse the opportunity to gauge his quickness. Norse wasn't impressed. He squared up, shifting his weight smoothly, his left—back—shoulder coming forward. Round kick. The only way to go was inside. He caught Norse with his right foot coming around as fast as a power hitter can swing a baseball bat and hit him twice: short left to Norse's solar plexus as his torso was twisting away from the torque of the round kick, right hand crossing to the exposed jaw, just under the ear. The two punches dumped Norse as hard as if he'd fallen off a roof. He lay stunned on his stomach with his jaw dislocated, making small sounds of distress.

"Good Lord, I didn't even *see* that," Dayna said excitedly. "It was like, boom-BOOM! What did you do to him?"

"I worked him like a heavy bag, that's all. It's basic boxing."

"Are you some kind of pro?"

"I'm not even a dependable amateur anymore, I don't work at it enough. He's fast, and I was lucky." He sounded angry, as if he felt he didn't deserve his luck.

She looked glumly at the fallen Norse.

"Well, we can't just leave him lie there."

With the help of a couple of wide-bodied men who had come out of the Lost Sea Turtle, Joe packed Norse into the front seat of the Wagoneer. Norse and the slack, snoring redhead in back took up the available seating. Norse's eyes were open; his head lolled woozily. He sighed painfully several times, but was disinclined to speak.

Joe felt the angle of Norse's swelling jaw, and wondered how hard he'd hit his head on the asphalt parking lot.

"Better drop him by the emergency room at the local hospital," he said to Dayna as she was getting in behind the wheel. "Just to play it safe."

"I could come back for you."

Joe smiled regretfully at her across Norse's slumped body.

"If not tonight, maybe tomorrow night?" There was

a bareness to her lower lip, where she'd eaten most of the lipstick off, as far as the crimson corners of her mouth. She haggled with little flash glances, the smaller eye Oriental in its tightness; her fingers tapped the steering wheel. He failed to bid. She seemed to realize how dispirited he felt about the brief fight, and the fact that Norse was hurt.

"Guess it turned out to be a lousy evening for you."

"Not your fault, Dayna."

"Dayna with a *y*," she said. "And Smith. Easy to remember, huh? It's kind of a small place. We'll see each other again."

Joe faked enough enthusiasm to coax a smile from her. "I'll count on it."

TWENTY-FIVE

Abby arrived at the Planter's House forty minutes past the time she had anticipated, in a customized van with a lowered floor and an automatic sloping ramp to accommodate wheelchairs. Her driver was a young black man whom she introduced as Niles, one of numerous part-time employees at the Barony involved in maintenance and transportation. Most of them, Abby explained, were related to Walter Lee Clemons.

The van was equipped with a dual-control lever: pull down to accelerate, push forward to brake, while steering with the left hand. "I would've driven myself," Abby said, "but I felt too frazzled."

Her hair was bound up in a designer kerchief and she wore aviator-style sunglasses; through the green lenses her eyes looked nocturnal, condemned to lightless depths, like those sea creatures destined to explode upon reaching the surface. On their way out of town Abby was seated beside Niles, and Joe was in the back with his two pieces of luggage. Most of the time, when she turned her head to talk to him, he couldn't see her eyes at all.

"I thought you didn't have a driver's license," Joe said carelessly.

"Who told you that?"

"Lizzie may have said something."

"Oh. It's true, I don't have a license. I let it lapse—a couple of years ago. Maybe three or four years. I used to drive more. I went places. Then I—got too comfortable, I guess. Or lazy." She forced back a yawn. " 'Scuse me. I can't seem to wake up. What did you guys give me last night?"

Joe told her. She said, "When we get to the beach house, I want to hear all about it. Don't spare any of the gruesome details, because I don't remember a thing." In spite of this request she sounded tentative, and frightened by the episode.

"What did Dr. Thomason tell you this morning?"

"Nothing. I was still out of it when he looked in on me. He left the house early, with the senator and what's-her-name, Florence—"

"Flora."

"She seemed nice. They're two peas in a pod, really." Abby held her head at the temples, and took a deep breath. "It's a pretty day, and I've got this *fog* inside me. Anyway, Luke wanted to show off his polo ponies; then they were having lunch with some party pros at the Rod and Gun Club and after that I think the senator was heading on back to Washington. Luke won't be home until late. I don't know if Charlene's with him or not. Lizzie helped me dress. She has piano and jazz ballet today. God's in His heaven and all's right with the world, except my pulses are jumping like crazy. I haven't written anything in two or three days now, and I feel guilty about that. Jaysus, as if it really mattered. Writers are incredibly neurotic—I bet you didn't know that, did you? What did you and Norse beef about?"

"Some ego thing." Without the wealth of her eyes, the rest of her face seemed flat, her expression impoverished; they weren't really communicating, just bouncing words off each other.

"Any good-looking women involved?"

"Not really."

"It's a pretty good crowd at the Sea Turtle. I always like going there. Was my pal Reggie on last night?"

"He's a hell of a talent."

"I love Reggie. He's only thirty-six. We're probably gonna lose him. Lou Gehrig's disease."

"You ought to go see him more often."

"I know. To cheer him up. Except I'm not feeling so cheery myself lately. How about a good bad joke?"

"Do you know why blind people don't sky-dive?"

"Scares the hell out of their Seeing Eye dogs. Heard it. Sorry."

The beach house on Chicora Island faced the Atlantic Ocean across a twenty-foot dune thick with tufted grasses and sea grape and a stretch of grayish sand swagged with olive-colored strands of beaded kelp cast ashore by the modest squall of the night before. In midafternoon the sky was blue chalkboard crisscrossed with contrails from military jets flying the coastline, but so high their silver ships seemed transparent; low clouds floated on the horizon like gardenias in a cut-glass punch bowl. Two thousand two hundred miles away, northwest of the Cape Verde Islands, the tropical depression that Joe had been watching on the Weather Channel was sucking huge amounts of energy from the warm seas and had developed into a hurricane, the ninth Atlantic hurricane of the season, with winds of up to ninety miles an hour at its center. The hurricane had been dubbed Honey. Honey was moving slowly, for now, at ten to twelve miles an hour, on a course that would take her across the sunken Atlantic Ridge to the Bahamas in approximately a week, depending on how big she became and the unpredictable whims of any hurricane traveling through the horse latitudes.

The two-story Gothic house, set on a tabby foundation, had a steep roof of hand-cut wooden shingles and a widow's walk, with jigsawed wood gingerbread trim around the open front porch. Recently updated with a heat pump and improved plumbing, the beach house was three miles from the Barony, connected to it by lines strung on telephone poles, no two of which leaned the same way, standing precariously along a crushed-shell road that wound through a treeless intertidal marsh over a series of small bridges. The nearest human neighbors were a third of a mile away, to the north. Birds were plentiful on the dunes, and above it: gulls, ospreys, some shy sandpipers, an occasional pelican or an eagle, hovering like a Chinese kite in the lofty silence.

A young woman from Lillian's kitchen had prepared an early-evening meal for them: bite-sized fritters of fried grits and oyster pieces, a browned-down hen with corn-bread dressing made from the fat drippings of the hen, and Frogmore stew, which was a dish of sausage, shrimp, crab, tomatoes and corn on the cob, boiled in beer. They ate on the broad front porch of the house, with a long view of the island beach as the sea turned from gunmetal blue to the brassy sheen of old nickels. Joe pulled beers from a half-barrel packed full of shaved ice to wash down his first meal of the day; Abby, returned to Rolling Thunder, drank only a California chardonnay, and that sparingly, as if in atonement for her indulgence the night before. They listened to her collection of oldie 45s on a portable record player that was a decade away from qualifying as an antique. She hummed along with the listener-friendly voices. Ricky and Frankie and several Bobbys. The Coasters and the Miracles and the Supremes.

"I got most of these from my aunt Becca. She graduated from high school the year I was born.''

"How does she qualify as your aunt?"

"My mother's youngest sister. Change-of-life baby. I haven't seen Becca in donkey's years. I need to give her a call. Becca's one of the blue-star numbers on my Rolodex. That means, 'Call anytime, three in the morning if you're feeling lousy, she'll understand.' ''

"Good listeners are hard to come by."

"Now that you've stumbled into my web, I'll have to add your phone number. Doctors are used to calls at all hours, I suppose."

"You don't need a phone number. I'm here."

"But for how long?"

Joe reached out to pull another beer from the barrel. "How strong is your web?"

Abby rested her chin on her folded hands. "I've just begun to weave."

Joe twisted the cap off his beer, stretched, sighed, walked over to her and with his free hand gently removed her sunglasses. She dropped her eyes, as if he might be intruding.

"Time to stop covering up."

"I know I look like billy hell," she mumbled.

"No, you don't. Let's talk about it."

"Don't you want some chocolate cake first?"

"I never eat chocolate cake."

"Are you allergic?"

"No." He pulled over a rattan footstool and sat beside her, one elbow on an arm of her wheelchair. "It was the last thing my mother ordered for me before she drove away and abandoned me in a place called Gila Bend, which is approximately the same as the ass-end of nowhere. I was six years old."

Abby blinked mildly, puzzled, then dismayed, thinking of her own extended family, the love and protection she had always enjoyed. "But—mothers don't do things like that—to their children."

"It happened, Abby."

"*Why?*"

"I'll never know. My best guess is that she was in trouble, something so bad she thought she wouldn't be able to take care of me anymore. She didn't explain. She ordered chocolate cake for me, and drove away while I was stuffing my face. To this day, the odor of chocolate nauseates me."

"Where was your father?"

"That's another story."

"Tell me."

"I had no father. That I remembered. She would say, once I was old enough to miss having a father like the other kids, that he left us both when I was less than two years old. We were living then in Buffalo, where I was born. It was a half truth. His name was Pete. He left by jumping off a bluff into the Niagara River, just before it froze for the winter."

"Killed himself?" The old threat recalled to her the fresh horror of immobility at an early age, the sensation of being little more than half a woman, her naissance as a mermaid with no kick to her heavy anchoring tail, lacking the lightness of the salt sea for buoyancy. "How old was he when he did it?"

"Twenty-one. Two years older than my mother."

"Something really terrible must have happened, for him to do a thing like that. I don't think about it anymore, but there were times when, if I'd had a gun . . ."

Joe placed two fingers lightly on her furrowed brow, at the place where the occult third eye of intuition, undeveloped in the maturing fetus, supposedly lay, infinitesimal, buried like a pollen grain in amber.

"Hey, now."

She said in a brisker voice, "I'm not suicidal. I think I'm brilliant and I know I'm famous; I've had good luck to go with the bad. I love my life. I don't risk aggravating the Powers by pissing and moaning over a lousy twist of fate. I don't ask for more. Not much more, anyway."

"I'm glad to see you smile again."

His fingertips traced a curving line past an eyebrow, to the outer parabola of cheekbone and then the angle of her downy jaw. Her eyes closed slowly; her smile was firm and sweet. He stroked the line of her jaw, and lingered on the pulse in her throat. The last platter from that American age of innocence brought to an end by gunfire in Dallas plopped down the changer onto the little turntable. Bobby Vee sang in his mournful prom-night tenor "Devil or Angel." Shh-boom, shh-boom. The wind from the sea tangled her hair around his caressing hand and wrist. Sand sifted across the worn planks of the porch floor, adding to the Lilliputian dune where the porch met the front wall of the house. Her shoulders had relaxed; she breathed so deeply he thought he had put her to sleep until she blinked mildly and asked, "Did you ever learn why?"

"I took a long bus ride back to Buffalo the summer I graduated high school. Looked up some relatives who almost had forgotten I existed. The Petruskas. Working-class neighborhood. Narrow frame houses on high terraces. A few rosebushes to dress up corroded old chain-link fences. Kids drinking beer and working on their souped-up cars in the street. Two elderly aunts of mine lived together in one of those houses with about twenty cats, and most of the family memorabilia: albums, Bibles, faded wedding triptychs. They even had a picture of me with my mother when I was just beginning to sit up in her lap. They were Aunt Flossie and Aunt Bernarda. Flossie Petruska was almost blind and Bernarda had arthritis so bad her hands looked like toads bloated in a poisoned pond. But her memory was intact. So I found out from her that there had been some good in the marriage of my mother and father, even though it was a forced marriage because of her pregnancy. And my mother had lied to me because the truth—well, she must have been saving it for the time when she thought I would be old enough to understand.''

He took his hand from Abby's face and sat back on the footstool. She frowned slightly, eyelids flickering, and held out a hand in protest. The little fingernail was ravaged to the quick, as if it was the only one she allowed herself to chew while in the throes of creation. He grasped the hand lightly, and she pulled him toward her again, locking him tighter, his knuckles resting in the space between her collarbones.

''Pete Petruska was a mechanic who worked for a big trucking company. He had an accident on the job, not an uncommon type of accident. There's a machine they use to help lever the big tires back onto the rims after they've been patched. Tremendous compression, a couple of thousand pounds per square foot. If you're not careful, a tire weighing sixty pounds can blow back off the rim and into your face. The damage it causes is almost unbelievable. They do the surgery, over and over again, years of it. But there's no surgeon skilled enough to make one of the poor bastards look human again.''

She raised his hand and kissed it with a solemn tenderness.

''Do you look most like your father, or your mother?''

''I have the face he would have had. He was a very good-looking kid, before his accident.''

''But it was too much for your mother. His disfigurement. The pain. I know. I feel so sorry for her.''

''The smell may have been the worst thing about it. That's what Bernarda thought. The smell drove my mother away, and him to the brink of the Niagara River.''

Abby opened her gray eyes inquiringly, pressing their joined hands lightly against the underside of her thrust-out chin.

''Pete was scarred, of course. But his face just sagged,

because there was no muscle tone. His lips were twisted and didn't meet, so there was no way to keep the saliva in. Because some of his teeth were always exposed to the air, he had to coat them with glycerine so they wouldn't dry out and rot. He had to wear a towel around his neck to soak up the constant drool, just buckets of it. That was the worst of the smell, which the strongest men's cologne couldn't hide. His voice was funny; without a mobile tongue and the right lip movements he couldn't pronounce words very well. You can imagine the kind of—freak he thought himself to be. The injury was terrible, but the—the indignity, the humiliation, had to be worse. That was what destroyed him. There are deficits in life no one can be expected to deal with."

"I know that to be true," she said, looking past him as another of the several gulls called to supper by the savory airs of hot stuff on the brazier floated in off the sea to clutch at the porch rail and tilt its black bill hungrily in her direction. She released Joe's hand to break bread and fling a hard crust well over the heads of the gulls. They all scattered in pursuit, to be robbed by a fierce latecomer on blurring wings. Abby looked again at Joe, downcast. "I was at my worst last night. Don't know why I couldn't stop drinking. Sometimes there's a black hole I try to pour myself into. Scared hell out of poor Luke. Among others. What do I do now, Joe?"

"The best advice I can give you is to go for a thorough checkup."

"Another tour of the body? Those multimillion-dollar machines whining and clicking, creeping over me and looking through me . . . I always feel like I'm being prepped for a high-tech burial. We've been there, Joe. Luke and me. I've got a nice-looking backbone. The vertebrae are crisp and clear. There's no dark snake wrapping itself around my brain stem. Luke sends a little bottle of my blood out once a month for analysis. Guess what? I'm healthy, my weight's under control, I don't think about the indignities and the discomfort very often, the occasional bedwetting when I'm not punctual about sitting myself on the john, the—nightmares. I just don't let myself think about all that. Abby's a very positive thinker, except for those times when her black hole appears. Tell me honestly: would I have died last night if I hadn't had prompt medical attention?"

Joe walked to the edge of the porch and leaned against the railing.

"I don't know. You might have strangled on your own vomit."

"Why was I vomiting, if it was a seizure?"

"I don't think you had a seizure. It was more of an extreme allergic reaction."

"To what? I've never been allergic to insect bites or stings. Nothing stung me anyway, did it?"

"I didn't see a place on your body where you might have been stung. But—I wasn't all that thorough in examining you; I deferred to Dr. Thomason, of course."

"Food poisoning? I ate some ribs. So did everybody else."

Out of ideas, Joe shook his head. The girl from Lillian's kitchen appeared diffidently to remove their trays and glasses. "Miss Abby," she said, "after I clean up would you be needin' me for anything else?"

"No, thank you, Keneesha. Call the Barony when you're ready to go and have someone drive over to pick you up."

"Yes, ma'am."

When Keneesha returned to the house, Abby propelled herself by hand to the edge of the porch, stopping beside Joe.

"So I'm a medical puzzle."

"To me, you are."

"Do you think Luke could have missed something?

I know, there are people who don't think much of his abilities. There were suits brought against him when he practiced in Beaufort years ago—but a lot of doctors get sued, don't they?"

"I'm afraid so."

"Seems to be the guiding principle of the legal profession these days: to err is human, to litigate, divine. But I have complete confidence in Luke. I've always had confidence."

"I don't know of any reason why you shouldn't."

Instead of feeling reassured, the confidence she had professed began to slip away like an armload of sand.

"Could you examine me, Joe? Luke has everything you need, doesn't he? I'd feel better. I really would."

"I can't, Abby. If I undress you, it will be to make love to you."

She said, after a quick explosive laugh that seemed to take her breath away, "I'm not ready for *that.*"

Joe shrugged amiably, folded his arms in a show of comfort, and watched her.

Abby said, her loss of breath resulting in a precariously light head, "That was—a scary thing to say."

"You mean it's scary to think about."

She laughed again, and looked perplexed. "You know how to get inside a person's mind, don't you?"

"It's a knack I have."

"Well—I am scared, Joe; must be one of those deficits you mentioned that can't—be dealt with. So I guess we ought to leave it right there."

"No problem, Abby. Why don't we break out some of that gear I saw inside and go surf-casting."

"Me too?" Her cheeks reddened with pleasure. "Hey, I haven't done any fishing since—well, I guess it was—shoot, I don't even remember."

"Then we're not going to waste another minute."

TWENTY-SIX

Abby returned from the beach house at ten-thirty and rode her little elevator, which (she liked to say) was almost as slow as capillary action, to the second floor. Her hands were puffy and red and still weak from the action of fishing with a ten-foot graphite rod, side-casting her lures beyond the surf and popping them back with quick movements that eventually brought her two puppy drum and several speckled sea trout, which Joe released, along with his own numerous catches. The fish seemed to be jumping out of the water at them, hitting both spoons and live bait until the last light of sunset faded from the clouds. It was the most excitement she'd had since she'd given up going to the NASCAR races at Darlington Speedway. She fished in waders and a waterproof parka from one of the sturdy wooden deck chairs Joe had carried from the porch to the foam line. Past dark they had lingered on the beach around a driftwood fire, sharing a pot of warmed-over Frogmore stew and playing gin until the wind rose to scatter their cards: kings, queens and grinning jokers floated to oblivion on the brimming tide. Her back and shoulders ached from the demands of surf-casting; her hair was a salty stiff tangle, there was salt in her eyebrows and sand, unfelt, between her bare toes. With his back against a tree trunk as thick as a fallen temple column, scoured smooth and bleached white by sun and surf, he'd made a chair of himself for her, so that her head rested in the hollow of one shoulder; his hands were lightly clasped beneath her breasts.

"Maybe," she'd said, gazing half-asleep at the firelit tumble of waves, "what I need is a black cat bone."

"What's that?"

"A black cat bone is part of the Root Man's medicine. Stronger than any force in nature, because its powers are supernatural. An old-time Gullah Root Man who owns a black cat bone can undo any evil, cure any spell. He can raise the dead, or put a wandering spirit back in its grave. Expel demons from the bodies of the sick or crippled."

"Your creative mind is spooking you. What got you started on demons?"

"Maybe instead of a rational explanation, my trouble is irrational: a hex. Did you study hexes in medical school?"

"Our resident Root Man was on sabbatical that term. Tell me where, and I'll hunt up a black cat bone for you."

"Don't bother, you're an unbeliever. You can't buy a black cat bone, it wouldn't have a lick of power to it. You have to make your own. Ask Lillian. She knows how it's done. You have to catch yourself a black cat by the dark of the moon. Completely black, no white foot or little white spot under its chin like most of them have. Then you heat water in a big black iron pot on the stove until it comes to a full, rolling boil. Throw the cat in alive. The cat will stand up on its hind legs and talk like a man, but in a language no living soul has heard before. Then, when the cat is good and boiled, you put the remains in a burlap bag and carry it to the sea.

*You wait for the tide to go out, then cast the cat on the waves.
All of it will be carried with the tide out to sea. Except for one
bone, which will come right back to your hand. That bone has
the power you seek."*

Abby stopped at the door to Lizzie's room on her way
down the second-floor hall and knocked. Lizzie didn't
respond, but the door wasn't firmly latched and the
television was on inside. She pushed the door open.
Lizzie was lounging in pajamas on the trapunto spread
of the four-poster bed, listening to rap music on her
headphones, watching TV and leafing through a teen
magazine at the same time. She'd munched her way
through a bag of potato chips and drunk half a pitcher
of Lillian's grape-juice lemonade. She took off the
headphones when she saw Abby.

"Hi. Where've you been?"

"At the beach."

"Who with?"

"Joe. I moved him out of the Planter's House. He'll
be staying in the beach house for a while."

"He will?"

"Elizabeth Ann, is something wrong with your
ears?"

"No. That's great." Lizzie sat on the edge of the
high bed, one bare foot lapped over the other, studying her. "Did you all have a lot to talk about?"

"I guess so. You're acting funny, what's wrong?"

"Nothing. *You* look tired."

"We did some surf-casting. My back is killing me.
I'm going to do my nightly routine, then pop into the
tub for a soak. Could I ask you to help me wash my
hair and then give me a rubdown?"

"Sure."

Abby rolled into the bathroom that she and Lizzie
shared. It had been rebuilt and enlarged with space
taken from a big closet Abby didn't need, to make matters of personal hygiene as easy as possible. There were

so many chrome grab bars with slip-proof grips that the bathroom had the aspect of an indoor jungle gym. The bars provided easy access to a toilet seat raised to a convenient height, eliminating one of the more difficult problems of transfer for a paraplegic. There were easy-to-reach dispensers for the plastic catheters she used three or four times a day to completely void her bladder and cut down on infection, and another dispenser for latex gloves. A long time ago she had numbed her mind to the procedure she'd learned in rehab for emptying paralyzed bowels, one of her Activities of Daily Living, or ADLs. The concave washbasin and counter accepted Abby and her wheelchair like a piece of a puzzle. So did the whirlpool bath.

Undressing herself completely took time because of the lined underpants she always wore; she had to peel them off while hanging like a chimpanzee from a grab bar. Before she had decided to lose an extra twenty-five pounds, lifting her own weight had been damned near impossible. With her tedious toilet out of the way and the latex gloves disposed of, she ran water in the tub and set the whirlpool timer. Tonight she had spasticity again, the left leg this time. Muscles alive but out of control, governed by some upper motor neuron defect. The spasticity, although she was used to it, was powerful and eerie and always gave her goose bumps. But the involuntary exercise was responsible for the health of her muscle tissue, keeping her legs supple and strong.

When the spasticity ended she lifted and plopped herself down in the roiling water and relaxed with her neck in the grip of a flotation pillow that kept her head always above the water level. She called to Lizzie.

"Is Luke home yet?" she asked, when Lizzie came in.

"No. He called from the gun club earlier. I didn't tell him you went anywhere. I said you were working.

Frosty wants you to call her about the miniseries Spelling wants to do, and the signed limited editions.''

"Okay. How was *your* day?"

Lizzie said with a shudder of angst, "I'm never gonna learn the Chopin in time for the fall recital! Why did Charlene have to send our piano out to be refinished?"

"Don't ask me; Charlene just does things without consulting anybody. If the piano's not back soon, we'll rent one."

Lizzie took off her pajama top to wash and rinse Abby's hair with the shower extension. Suds from the shampoo ran down Abby's shoulders and reefed around her breasts; she cupped them in her hands, holding them up to be rinsed too.

"You have the most beautiful tits," Lizzie said wistfully, playing the light spray back and forth, symbolizing the not-to-be-expressed yearning in her own breast with this attentive laving, then holding the shower head close to rinse Abby's tender nape, working her drenched hair the wrong way to get all of the conditioner out. "Look at me; bubbies is all there is." She despised them with a downward glance, those little gum-colored protuberances that dominated without beautifying her chest. "I think I need implants. But I guess that would look funny if I didn't have any hips to sort of balance them."

Abby came back from a pleasant lull to realize she'd been asked to comment on an ever-present subject between them. "Stop worrying, Lizzie. Everybody has awkward phases growing up."

"I'll bet you didn't."

Abby grinned in an exaggerated way. "See my front teeth? Well, one of them used to go this way, and the other went *that* way. I looked like a razorback hog. I mean I wouldn't open my mouth in seventh grade until they were straightened."

"I think you need to shave under your arms," Lizzie said critically.

"Would you get my razor for me, hon?"

Abby liked reading aloud to prepare for her own, dictated work; after Lizzie rubbed her down thoroughly with a light oil that Norse had recommended and helped her into her pajamas, Abby picked up *Bleak House* and Lizzie stretched out facedown on the bed beside her. After five minutes of skullduggery in and around the High Court of Chancery, Lizzie was fast asleep.

Abby smiled and put the book aside, picked up her tape recorder and pressed Rewind, to hear what she had dictated during her last work session.

There was no cassette in the recorder. It bothered her. Frosty had always been faithful about returning the tape after she transcribed a night's work, so that Abby easily could pick up the strands of the story she was weaving. Frosty's lapse was a major inconvenience for Abby. Her choice was to wake up Lizzie and send her stumbling off into the night to retrieve the tape from the workroom, or go herself.

Lizzie's face was slack in dreamless sleep on the other pillow. *The hell with it,* she thought, a little irritably. With her latest novel high on all the best-seller lists she was far from under any contractual pressure to deliver the new book, which she had titled *The Flame and the Fox:* a romance, like the others, this one set in the time of the French and Indian War. Her impulse to get to work was ebbing, although this was almost a monthly thing, like the painless, punctual menses that reminded her of her healthy unusable uterus. Abby worked at her trade regardless of the level of inspiration involved, happy when the words poured freely, grumpy and disconsolate when they came haltingly out of a blanketing fog.

Although her head was clear tonight, her lungs refreshed as if she'd just completed a hard swim, she couldn't remember much of what she'd written lately. The names of characters slipped from her grasp like the fish Joe had pulled from their hooks and waded into waist-high surf to release. The story was vague in her recall, its plotlines twisted into ambiguities. Maybe instead of trying to dictate she ought to review some of her research, which was contained in two thick loose-leaf binders on the table beside the queen-size brass bed. But more reading didn't appeal to her; her eyes felt gritty from long exposure to sun and wind.

Having decided to do nothing, Abby folded her hands below her breasts, then let them slip over her belly and down to her navel; from there it was only inches, four inches at most, to what she thought of as the Barrier: an invisible line just below the abdominal wall where feeling didn't exist: and down, down to the lips of her vagina—"surrounded by a little garden in the valley of her thighs, plump, firm, and so well set for love's great tournament." Villon's old lady had lamented for her lost youth, but at least had been sensually fulfilled, had enjoyed the divine pleasure of vaginal orgasm. Abby's own garden, closed and sere. A sensual limitation, perhaps, but she knew that, erotically speaking, all humans were polymorphs. Abby raised her hands to her breasts, always so sensitive but now excruciatingly so. A lovely distraction today, she thought, stroking her nipples as surrogate for the man she desired: a character come to life from a pile of pages, driving all of her other creations right out of her head. You are not fair, Joe Bryce. And this is *too* distracting, what am I up to, anyway?

She could have watched him for hours: he surf-cast in the English manner, holding the long rod vertically instead of like a javelin, then swinging it perpendicular to his body with the lure far away, bringing it close again and behind his head, finally swinging it out in an arc with the butt hand pulling and the hand on the reel pushing to accelerate the lure like a lazy golden bullet, sending it nearly five hundred feet over the breakers. (Abby gasped and gasped again, and lifted her fingertips from nipples that felt as if they were going to burst into flame.) He wore a bulky sweater and waders for fishing. The lines of his body were obscured by the clownlike apparel, but she easily imagined him as naked as a Greek discobolus: his precise, rhythmic movements, the wheeling power of his throw. (Now a feeling of ease, of lassitude spreading slowly from the still-prickling swollen nipples like thin sweet oil across the skin, she was floating, buoyant, aware only of sensual joy, it was like not having a body at all.) It would be nice, Abby thought, to invite him to swim with her. . . .

"Abby? Are you awake?"

Her nipples were apparent beneath the cotton pajama top. Abby crossed her arms over her breasts and said, "Hey, come on in, Luke."

He opened the hall door. He had a bag of Dunkin' Donuts with him.

"Oh, no! I hope you ate most of those yourself."

"There's a couple of buttermilk, a glazed and a jelly. Charlene had the rest. With her metabolism, she can gorge and not gain an ounce."

"We'll save the jelly for Lizzie in the morning, she likes those best. I'll take buttermilk."

Abby reached for one of the twin trapeze bars suspended thirty inches above her low bed and sat herself up. Thomason sat on the edge of the bed and handed a doughnut to her, munched on one himself. He was dressed sportily, in a shooting vest with emblems of the clubs he belonged to, smelling of old powder and gun oil. He had shaved early that morning, and stubble was showing in the creases of his chin like bits of mica.

"There's a lot of color in your cheeks tonight," Thomason said approvingly.

"I went surf fishing. By the way, I lent Dr. Bryce our beach house for a few days."

"You did? I thought he was on his way home." He brushed sugar crumbs from his lips and took her free hand to count her pulse.

"Not yet."

Thomason nodded, as if he found that informative. "Well. Maybe he'd like to go up to Florence with me tomorrow for the polo matches."

"I'm not invited?" Abby said, putting on a sulk.

"Sure you are. If you feel up to it. You've never showed much interest in the game."

"It made me nervous watching that time. I was afraid you'd get hurt. I just feel like I should go out more."

"Can't see any harm in it." He was silent for twenty seconds, counting. "Pulse is way fast. Been exerting yourself?"

"No, I was just lying here thinking. Exciting thoughts."

He yawned, overlooking the invitation to pry. "Want me to put Lizzie in her own room?"

"No, leave her here. She kicks and I wake up and remember to move my ass around, and I don't get half the pressure sores I used to. Do you like him, Luke?"

"Who's that?"

"Joe."

He had risen to go; he sat down again, running a hand over his jaw. His crimped pale lips pressed together thoughtfully. "Oh . . . on short acquaintance, he seems like a personable young fella."

"He's more than that." Her smile was bliss; her eyes rolled to the tray ceiling, half-drunk with intrigue, womanly secrets. "Much more."

Lizzie stirred in the bed and sat up slowly, saturated with sleep. She stared at Lucas Thomason's face without recognizing him, winced like a testy angel and plunged back to the sanctuary of her pillow. Abby placed a hand on her shoulder, feeling tremors, as if in her sleep Lizzie was running from something stark and unfriendly.

"Abby—am I allowed to be frank here?"

"Of course, Luke," she said, lowering her eyelids a little, still staring at the ceiling with its painted tin intaglio panels, flecked with spurts of light from the candelabra fixture overhead.

"We both know you have a highly impulsive, romantic nature, which in part accounts for your success as a novelist—but which has not been to your benefit in the past."

"Do you know? It's been thirteen years since I've loved anyone like I loved Paul Huskisson."

"You were running away with him to get married the night the two of you got run over. Which is what I mean by impulsive."

"No, Luke. We were on our way to the Beaufort Holiday Inn to spend the night together. Marriage wasn't in the picture yet."

"Tantamount to being married."

"Well, it didn't happen, I was a virgin that night and I will be a virgin when I die. Luke, I'm finally ready to let Paul go."

"I'd call that a mixed blessing," he grumbled. "If you're thinking of falling in love with Joe Bryce."

Abby laughed, quite happily.

"You don't 'think about it,' Luke. It just happens." She turned her face toward him and said chidingly, "It's sure happened to *you*, often enough. What was it I heard you say once? 'The vicious circle is a little band of gold'?"

He had to smile. "If that's not God's own truth. But Abby—I don't think I could survive seeing you suffer again, the way you suffered when Paul finally died of his head injuries."

"You look scared to me, Luke. What is it? Do you know something about me that you don't want to tell?"

"Absolutely not, that's poppycock. But I don't have

the answers right now, so naturally I'm concerned about what happened last night."

"You'll find the answers. Someone will. In the meantime I only want to be happy, and not think about Paul, God rest him, and not think about dying myself. I would be very happy with Joe."

"You're assuming a hell of a lot, Abby! He just wandered onto the place a couple days ago!"

He moved away from the intimacy of the bedside, crossed to the two windows and a vacancy of sky in which his emotions dwindled while maintaining status, like a few vigilant stars.

"No, Luke," Abby said softly. "I'm not assuming. I'm a gimp. But that doesn't matter to Joe. I've seen it in his eyes. He touches me, and I'm whole to him."

"What's gonna happen—all over again—is that you'll have your heart broken. And I'm telling you, Abby, as a doctor, as a man who has looked after you and loved you since you were a ten-year-old child, in your condition you won't be able to stand it!"

After a long silence in which he studied his fears like images in a witch's mirror, Abby issued a soft command.

"Luke, come here to me."

When he was standing at the foot of the bed gazing sorrowfully at her, Abby said, "Who am I?"

"You are the little girl who will always be the light of my life."

"And you know that I love you."

"I know it," he said tearfully.

"And you would never interfere with what happiness may be left to me."

"Don't, Abby. Don't put that burden on me."

"I have to have your blessing. It's no good otherwise."

Lucas Thomason wiped his eyes and clenched his hands.

"Let me be happy," Abby pleaded. "For a little

while. I need you both. Be wonderful for me, Luke."

"You know I never could deny you. I never had the heart."

"I've been knowing that all my life," she said gratefully. "Now say it, Luke. Please."

"All right. If Joe Bryce is the one—then he's welcome here. And you will never hear a word from me against him."

"Bless you, darling. I love you, Luke."

"All I ever cared about is your welfare. God strike me if that isn't the truth."

"I think you're a great man," Abby said, her eyes bright with pride. "I've always thought so."

"I hope I live to be worthy of your respect. I'm gonna try my hardest to get us moved to the governor's mansion."

"It's a done deal," she said confidently. "Kiss me good night, Luke? I'm feeling a little tired now."

"Surely." He went to her side of the bed and kissed her. "Abby, there's something I ought to tell you—speaking as your doctor now."

"What is it, Luke?"

"Thanks to my own carelessness I'm short the steroids you've been getting. I'll call first thing Monday and order more, but I don't expect the shipment before the end of next week. There's always the possibility of a flareup that could have a permanent effect, leave you worse off than you are now. So I don't want you overexerting yourself."

"I'll be careful." She raised her head; her lips lingered on his cheek. "Thank you, Luke. Thank you for everything."

During Lucas Thomason's half hour with Abby, Charlene had undressed and crawled into his bed to wait for him; sleep had overcome her. He made every effort to leave her asleep as he took off his own clothes, but his presence had changed the atmosphere in the bedroom; a subtle pressure weighing on her glossy skin caused her to roll to one side and open her eyes. She saw first a naked hip and dangle of balls, his penis rising in jerks to a stiff salute. Charlene raised her eyes to her husband's face.

"My God," she said. "Did you just kill somebody?"

TWENTY-SEVEN

*Joe awoke at the crack of dawn in the beach house, dis-*oriented after a night of heavy sleep, wondering for a few moments just where he was and what he was up to. The smell of the sea, a long rush of surf on the nearby sand, mild vertigo as he tried to sit up: the sensory apprehensions led him to think he was aboard the *Dragonfly*. His head ached dully, there was a stiffness in his shoulders and arms. The muscle-memories were of surf-casting, not sailing; and a firelit image of Pamela Abelard's beguiling profile came to mind, with memories of laughter and good feeling. She had felt free to exhibit a barbed, spontaneous wit. *"Most literary readings,"* Abby had said, prompted by an undefined pique, *"are a fine example of a dog returning to its vomit."* And, of a mercenary college chum who had left school in her freshman year to marry a paper-company executive well into his fifties: *"She entered into marriage with her meter running."* It was all lined out too quickly, with a nice backhand and then an approving grin that was all

over her face when she realized what she had said, to
have been scripted and stored for a social occasion. He
had observed that there also was a streaky, unacknowl-
edged bullying side to her nature, outgrowth of pain
and deprivation, that would become more of a problem for everyone as she got older. Abby played what
was probably a long-running game of emotional chess
with those closest to her. It made Joe uneasy to remember that, for the first time since he'd gone haywire at
the consciousness-expansion session in Marin County
years ago, he'd given so much of his hidden self to a
woman in a situation where the possibilities of physical
reward were limited. Kissing an upstart ear, the softly
throbbing hollow of Abby's throat, he was never without the sad knowledge that half of her was permanently dead, in spite of the unexplainable episodes of
spasticity that plagued her. His body reacted, all the
same. His testicles were full and warm; his penis rose,
and sulked unsatisfied, cramped within layers of clothing against the unfeeling small of her back.

He was on the second floor of the beach house, in
one of three bedrooms furnished as plainly as a bar-
racks. A deep freestanding tub with a walnut-and-brass
rail around it took up half of the bathroom. His face
in the dulled mirror over the basin looked smudged,
half-finished, as if Flora Birdsall had begun to make
good on her threat to erase him.

A long run on the beach was the best cure he'd
found for morning megrims.

Outside he encountered fog, wispy as a steambath,
with a darker bank of fog out to sea like a stalled tsu-
nami, in which the disk of the sun was as pale as the
pith of a lemon. There were knee-high wavelets along
the shore. He jogged just out of reach of the muted
surf on wet packed sand, able to see less than twenty
feet ahead. A barefoot woman appeared, wearing cutoff jeans. Her skin was sun-blackened, the texture of
beef jerky. She was bent over as she worked the beach

for shells with a child's play shovel. Her posture accen-
tuated a hump of fat, like a buffalo's hump, on her
upper back. She had several casting rods spiked into
the sand, lines rippling in the dark water. They eyed
each other, strangers in the mist. There was something
wadded and mucusy about one of her eyes, while the
other flared, like a brief electrical storm, savage in its
blueness. He smiled peaceably at her and stepped
around a stranded blob of jellyfish, then avoided a
yards-long tangle of kelp, agile today, not as clumsy as
when he had stepped on the ampule of epidural steroids in Dr. Thomason's infirmary. . . . Something agitated the skin on the back of his neck, like a mosquito
perched there. The separate images kept circling in his
mind: the aging woman digging in sand, the drug safe
in the infirmary, his carelessness. If there was a connection, he didn't get it. He slowly upped his speed
until he was running at a pace sustainable for miles,
past the looming decks of a beachfront community,
where the flotsam of civilization reappeared in discouraging mass: the so-called disposable baby diapers,
foam cups so durable they would still be around when
the sun winked out forever, soft-drink cans and baby-
food jars, watermelon rinds picked clean by gulls and
crabs, a soggy paperback book. The first law of nature
seemed to be the more people, the more crap. When
he came at last to a wide swash he couldn't cross except
by swimming, he returned to his starting point.

Most of the fog on shore had dissipated, the sun had
risen above the low-lying fog bank. Joe found Abby
waiting in Rolling Thunder, hooded, bundled up
against the morning chill, facing out to sea on the
porch of the house, her face warmly alight, as if
someone were holding a lantern just above her head.
Her eyes were meekly closed; she showed a trace of a
smile. He heard a far-off ringing of church bells.

Abby didn't react when Joe came panting up the
four flights of steps from the beach to the floor of the

porch; he didn't take his eyes off her, wondering if she'd "done a fade," in her words, and was watching them both, from a spirit-level vantage point in the space beyond the porch railing.

Intent on Abby, he tripped over a floorboard that needed hammering down, staggered, caught himself just as his right foot came down on a paper cup left from their meal the day before. He squashed the cup flat. *Sorry, Doctor.*

Sorry, Dr. Thomason, but you're a damned liar.

Abby had opened her eyes and was laughing at his ineptness when he looked up from the paper cup and stared at her. She stopped laughing abruptly.

"What is it? Did you hurt yourself?"

"You're perfect," he said vaguely.

She laughed again, puzzled. "What?"

"I said, you're perfect."

"I'm not, but thanks anyway." When his intent expression didn't change she turned her face away, as if she couldn't bear to be teased. "Stop, Joe. What's with you this morning?"

"Abby, how long have you been on steroids?"

She looked blank for a few moments. "Uh . . . why?"

"Just tell me."

"Are you always like this before you've had your coffee? You would have to ask Luke, because I don't know."

"Well, is it a few months?"

"Oh, longer."

"A year or two?"

Abby reached up and pushed back the bronze-colored hood of her designer sweatshirt. "A lot of years. Different types of steroids. Luke says they're for—"

"I know what they're for. To arrest inflammation of the spinal cord. So you haven't had any problems."

"Joe, look, I've been in a wheelchair for thirteen years, goddamn right I've had problems—"

"But nothing serious enough to put you in a hospital, nothing life-threatening."

"Not unless you count Friday night. What's on your mind?"

Joe sat on the porch railing opposite her. "Too early to explain. I have to do some thinking."

"But you *will* tell me."

"Of course I will, Abby. Give me a little time."

They were both quiet, for almost a minute. She wouldn't let go of him with her eyes; she was searching for trouble.

"I have to ask some questions," he said finally.

"Dandy. Could we have breakfast first? Nothing fancy, I can manage biscuits, omelets, and pan-fried ham. I'll bet you're starved after all that running. And we've got a terrific day ahead of us. I hope."

Joe showered and washed his hair in the oversized bathtub while Abby coped with the problems of a kitchen laid out for the convenience of the able-bodied. She'd asked, before he went upstairs, for a list of cookware in hanging cabinets and items stored on refrigerator shelves that were beyond her reach. A couple of things she forgot, but decided not to let the inacessability of a whisk and a measuring cup put her in a bad mood. She blended eggs and milk in a steel bowl in her lap, thinking about her teen years in Beaufort, when she'd often prepared weekend meals for Luke. His second marriage over with, thank God, just the two of them in the centuries-old frame house on Bay Street near the bridge to Lady's Island. He'd had some wry reflections on matrimony following his costly divorce from Teddy, who had thought that marriage to a doctor was the answer to a hypochondriac's prayer. *"One marriage is inevitable, two, understandable; but after that the marrying kind are simply throwing caution to the whims."* For fifteen years he'd stayed off the well-trod path to the altar, then along came Charlene—

blond, in her luscious prime—and Luke promptly forgot his own sensible advice, coming on to her like a rat in a booby-trapped maze. Not that Charlene didn't have her good points—but Abby wasn't in the mood to give herself a pop quiz this morning. Joe had her concerned, because obviously *he* was concerned.

Abby sighed. Prying information out of doctors before they were ready to give it was an exercise in futility. Her left leg flipped out unexpectedly, knocking over the bowl in her lap, foaming yellow egg going all over herself and the floor. She was in tears when Joe came into the kitchen, cheeks shaved and gleaming, hair with its cache of tiny silver needles neatly brushed.

"I just—it doesn't—so frustrated—I can't *stand* it sometimes."

"Go ahead and scream," he said.

"Huh?" She looked up at him, his image swimming in great orbs of tears.

"You want to scream. Let's hear it. Don't hold back. Blow out my eardrums."

"Boy—you don't know what—you're asking for."

"Do it."

Abby screamed. At him, at all the standing smugly superior asshole indifferent people she'd wanted to bring to her level for so many years, God damn them all! If they only *knew*.

"*Go*, angel," he urged her, falling to his knees in front of her, and never mind the slippery egg. "That's only half of it. Again."

She screamed again, delighted, spraying spit that seemed to delight Joe; he leaned into the force of her scream, an expression very like joy transforming his face. He screamed back at her, "You're not *hiding* any more, are you?"

"No!" She choked; her breasts heaved. "How do you know so much about me? How do you know—what I feel?"

"I hide too, Abby."

"Not you. Oh, no. You've never had a second's doubt about anything or anybody in your whole life."

"Sure I have. We're all alike. Everybody's got a story, and most of them ain't pretty."

Two prolonged, taxing screams, bloody murder to anyone passing by on the beach. CRIPPLED NOVELIST BLUDGEONED IN LOVE NEST. She looked spent, but not tormented. He got up to wet a kitchen towel and gently wiped her reddened, glazed face. Abby tried to duck her head, to keep her eyes on the floor. He wouldn't let her.

"I wanted to do this—for you," she said hoarsely. "I wanted to make your breakfast and pretend—"

"No pretending," he said, with a firm shake of his head, "about us."

"But—that's all it *can* be, it's all a fantasy of mine. I know better."

The moment passed when he might have objected; chagrin quieted her. He used the towel he'd wiped her face with to clean up the spilled egg and milk. Her right leg began to march, quick-time, in place, pumping up and down erratically. Abby sat back in Rolling Thunder, hands clenched, eyes closed. Joe watched the episode of spasticity until it ended, a slight frown on his face.

Abby began to twist uncomfortably.

"God, now my shoulder's cramping."

Joe untied the running shoe on her right foot and took it off.

"What're you doing?"

"Let's try something." Her feet appeared to be in good shape, not fattened by fluid buildup; the skin was healthy and dry. "Do you use an extremity pump?"

"Five or six nights a week for a couple of hours, when I'm writing. There's a small compressor that's automatic, I don't have to do anything but wear the boots."

He elevated her foot and began to massage the sole, close to the toes.

"I don't know why you're doing that," she complained. "It's useless. The wires are down, Joe."

"Down, but not cut, according to your doctor. Contusions and inflammation of the spinal cord can be tricky. Nothing shows up on a scan, not even an MRI. But the damage is obvious. How's your shoulder cramp?"

"Well, it feels better," Abby admitted. "Can't be the accupressure, because I don't feel a thing. You could cut my foot off right in front of me, and I wouldn't feel it."

After twenty more seconds she said with a slightly exasperated smile, "Okay, the cramp's gone now. Thank you, but I don't believe you proved anything. I think all those ancient Oriental remedies are hoaxes anyway. I've had needles stuck into my nerves so many times—"

"In the wrong places, probably," he said, retying her shoe.

"Dr. Joe, what's going on in your head?"

"I'm still trying to put something together. The fact is, I'm out of my depth here, Abby."

She nodded glumly. Her head stayed down.

He clapped his hands once, as if commanding a hidden rheostat to bring her back to brightness.

"Your coffee's perked. What do you say we get going with breakfast again?"

TWENTY-EIGHT

The Pandora's Bay Polo Club traveled in a caravan to Florence, South Carolina, on Sunday morning: horse trailers, Winnebagos, vans, station wagons, a mobile blacksmith's shop. Two dozen horses made the trip. Polo is a sport that tires horses quickly: the outdoor game calls for at least thirty minutes of galloping action, divided into a minimum of four periods, which are called chukkers. The field is three hundred yards long and a hundred and fifty yards wide. Polo horses are routinely called ponies, but some of them are former thoroughbred racehorses, desired for their stamina and strength.

Lucas Thomason and his trainer took five horses to the match on a gentleman's farm outside of Florence, and all of them had thoroughbred lines.

"I've got better than forty thousand tied up in my string," he explained to Joe as they were tacking up under the shade oaks at one end of the playing field. "But that's nothing. We had a touring Argentine team come through last month, they whipped the daylights out of us. Their captain, I think his name was Hernandez, said he wouldn't take a quarter million for his best ponies. They all could do one-eighty turns on their forelegs. It's an eye-popping sight—those flashy Latin ponies all but standing on their heads reversing field."

"How long have you been playing?"

"Took it up about three years ago," Thomason said, pulling on his boots. "Basketball was my sport in college, but for pure action polo is king." He glanced away from Joe. "Walter Lee!"

"Yes, sir."

"I don't like the way that new boy is wrapping Blue Dorado's forelegs. Does he know what he's doing?"

"He come highly recommended. But I'll check those wraps."

Thomason reached for knee guards in his trunkful of equipment. The team's captain, a federal judge named Whitney, was already suited up and mounted. He walked his horse over to them. Thomason introduced Joe, and winked before saying, "Joe, you ever see such an uninspired hunk of horseflesh in your life?"

"Now, don't you start in on Hung Jury," the judge said complacently.

Joe looked the horse over. He was big and ungainly, probably into late middle age, more than a little swaybacked, with a somnolent expression and a pigeon-toed stance. His testicles were his best feature, which no doubt accounted for half of his name. Joe smiled noncommittally. "What's his secret?"

"His secret is, he's a polo-playing fool, and out there looks don't count. Timing does. Instinct. Speed. And he has a deep-seated desire to ride every other horse comes his way clear off the field. I traded a '56 Mustang car in pristine condition for Hung Jury, and I never have had a minute's regret. Lucas, we've got our work cut out for us today. A couple of Colonel Oldfield's nephews are down for the weekend from Washington and Lee, and they've got seven goals between them."

Thomason nodded. There were dull grumblings of thunder in a hazy sky. It was sultry in the grove of trees, and the air was filled with fat autumn flies; Hung Jury swished his tail irritably, and looked around at his rider. Thomason rose from his camp chair and reached for his white helmet, called for his best pony. But Walter Lee was already leading Diacono, the big black gelding, toward him. "Let's get at 'em."

Two hours later he was driving east, alone, in a downpour. His right shoulder ached; from a fall he had taken when one of the overeager college boys had crossed his line and caused the least surefooted of his ponies to tumble. No serious damage done to horse or rider, but he was still mad about the foul. He drove his Dodge Ram pickup left-handed at a moderate speed, on secondary roads through an unfamiliar part of the state. He was looking for a farm he had visited only once, thirteen years ago. He regretted having to go there again, but the necessity was plain.

He missed the cutoff road in the hills and was in North Carolina before recognizing his mistake. Turned back, found the right road, followed it past little ramshackle roadside stands deserted in the rain with hand-painted signs advertising strawberries, pecans, sweet potatoes, honey. But this was primarily tobacco-growing country. Some of the old tobacco barns showed up in woodlots and fields—tall, narrow structures with little porches and small chimneys, almost all of them abandoned now in favor of automated gas-curing houses.

He had slowed to twenty-five miles an hour. There was no other traffic on the narrow state road. Through waves of rain a Pentecostal Holiness Church appeared at a crossroads, and he knew he was in the right place.

He turned left, went to four-wheel drive on a laborious
stretch of slick unpaved lane, pools of red water standing everywhere, and made his way to the farm buildings on one side of a large pond. Frame house with a
red tin roof, sprawling equipment shed with tractors
and cultivators under wraps, a curing house for tobacco standing next to a big old-fashioned stock barn.
There was a farm truck with a stake-sided bed parked
beneath a roof between the barn and the curing house.
Plenty of room under cover for his own truck.

He parked there and looked back at the house a
couple of hundred feet away. Big blank windows, no
panes, no shutters. No interior lights relieved those
rectangles of darkness. Thomason frowned, because he
had made sure he was expected.

He kept watch through the back window of his truck.
Before long a figure appeared on the small porch of
the house. A red umbrella popped open. The umbrella
bobbed toward him across the barn lot; bowed legs in
denim showed beneath the scalloped edge of the umbrella.

Thomason rolled down his window partway. The umbrella, streaming rainwater, filled his line of sight momentarily; then it was collapsed. He saw the face of a
young man with a tattered haircut, deeply hollowed
eyes, a little stubble on his upper lip and bony chin,
an air of destitution and ignominy.

"Are you here for Mr. Phipps?"

Thomason nodded. He didn't know the young man.
There'd been another much like him, when he'd last
come to the farm. Mr. Phipps harvested them, one at
a time, from the side of the road, from shelters for the
homeless, from local jails.

"If you will wait in the barn, Mr. Phipps will be at
your disposal shortly," the young man said slowly, as if
getting the message straight had meant a hard feat of
memorization.

Thomason nodded again. That was Mr. Phipps for

you. His home was his sanctuary. He did business in
the barn. And Thomason never called socially on Mr.
Phipps.

When the boy was on his way back to the house,
Thomason took a lockbox from underneath the seat
and placed it beside him. He dialed the combination
lock, opened the lid and took out a well-sealed, letter-
size manila envelope a half-inch thick. This he placed
in an inside pocket of his hacking jacket.

He got out of the cab of his truck and stood beside it, clipping the end off a ten-dollar cigar, which
he proceeded to enjoy in the dampness and late-
afternoon gloom. It didn't make his shoulder feel any
better, but it dispelled the chill around his heart; the
good smoke released him from the feeling he'd had
for the last couple of days of being pinned into a corner.

Mr. Phipps appeared to be taking his sweet time; but
it was Sunday, after all, and possibly he was showing a
touch of resentment at being disturbed on the Lord's
Day. Or perhaps the October rain was giving him
twinges. Arthritis and old bullet wounds could do that
to a man.

When he had finished a third of his cigar, Thomason
let himself into the barn.

There hadn't been an animal, not even a rat, inside
the clean barn for nearly twenty years. Mr. Phipps was
allergic to animal dander. Instead he used the large
space as his studio. Mr. Phipps was an amateur painter
of real distinction, who painted only one subject, on
oversized canvases.

"Jesus Christ," Thomason muttered, looking
around. A work light was on, supplementing the watery
light of a dark afternoon that came through high windows on all sides of the barn.

The suffering eyes of the crucified Savior looked
down at him from numerous angles in the spacious
barn. Large-scale paintings of Jesus were racked, sus-

pended on wires from the rafters or simply stacked by
the dozens against the walls. His work was not just calendar art; Mr. Phipps was a symbolist, and his paintings
were packed with images of fishes and angels and
golden calves. An unfinished canvas, ten feet long, lay
on the floor surrounded by paint pots, brushes and the
pads Mr. Phipps wore while working on his knees.
Thomason reckoned that Mr. Phipps was one of those
painters, like Picasso, who do something interesting
once, then keep on doing it until you despise them
for it.

He strolled around, growing edgier by the minute,
while waiting for Mr. Phipps. Near the sliding steel
doors that had replaced the old barn doors there was
a Harley-Davidson motorcycle beneath a dust cover.
Beside it was a shrouded pickup truck. From the shape
of it beneath the Dacron cover Thomason thought it
could be the same Diamond T pickup that Mr. Phipps
had cared for so meticulously for all of his adult years.
He wondered if the impact with human bodies on a
warm September evening in Beaufort, thirteen years
ago, had damaged the pickup. But he was supersti-
tious, and wouldn't touch it, fearing a shift in polari-
ties, a reversal of the flow of good luck that had
sweetened his life since that nearly disastrous night.

"Good afternoon, Dr. Luke."

Mr. Phipps spoke softly, not wanting to startle him,
but Thomason flinched anyway before turning to the
door on the opposite side of the barn.

"Good afternoon, Mr. Phipps. Still feeling the pinch
from foreign-grown tobacco?"

"The Lord has surely put us all on trial," Mr. Phipps
said, with a thoughtful frown.

They approached each other slowly across the barn
floor, Mr. Phipps with noticeable effort, as if his knees
threatened to lock on him at every step. Mr. Phipps
was wearing a blue suit coat and trousers, subtly mis-
matched as to color, the scuffed black shoes that he

might also have been wearing at their last meeting, and a cheap white shirt. Somewhere on his person, Thomason knew, he carried a nickel-plated revolver with a two-inch barrel, though his warring days with the Bureau of Alcohol, Tobacco, and Firearms were long over. He was a man of medium height, with large bones and strong shoulders. He had a wide, densely fleshed face—not sagging with fat, but well shaped, with a hard jawline and a cleft chin. There was a deep white dimple in his left cheek when he smiled, which was nearly all the time. His teeth were first-quality, his eyes—one of them glass, but a fine piece of work— pale gray, his forehead nearly unlined but showing a thin jagged scar from deep inside his hairline to one divided eyebrow like a bolt of inspiration leaping from the attic of the brain to potentiate the seeing eye, which had the quality of distilled spirits bubbling in a fleshy cauldron. The only real change in Mr. Phipps was his curly hair, which had gone from dark red to gray and thinned somewhat since Thomason had last laid eyes on him.

They met, just outside the cone of light illuminating the unfinished crucifixion panel on the floor, exchanged compliments on the excellence of each other's appearance and wishes for continued prosperity.

"Still picking buckshot out of your right leg? There was plenty I couldn't get at, operating as I was on a kitchen table, and with the light none too good; but they didn't threaten your prospects for a full recovery."

"The last piece of lead that I recall worked its way out about a year ago."

"No problems with the old spreadin' adder?"

Mr. Phipps lowered his head slightly and gave it a shake, as if he had been embarrassed since childhood by references to his monumental phallus, once slightly damaged by the shotgun blast referred to. He quietly changed the subject. "I hear you'll most likely be running for governor in the next election."

"It looks that way. If I make it through the primary, I can count on tough opposition from that Cheraw lawyer the Christian coalition has been cultivating. Not a blemish on his soul, and it's a known fact that the sins of the father were too old-fashioned for me."

"No man is without a blemish or two."

"The trick is to find out where the bodies are buried. And if you can't find a buried one, you come in with a live body, a sweet-looking country girl born out of lechery and schooled in deceit, who can lie her way past the Pearly Gates. There's a measure of villainy in every do-gooder. People know that. You're disappointing the voter if you don't give him a scandal to wallow in. So I may be calling on your good offices."

"But that's not why you've called on me today," Mr. Phipps said, with the unvarying smile that, depending on how one's emotional currents were running, could become unnerving. Thomason had learned to screen it out.

The nose of Mr. Phipps twitched slightly, inquisitively; Thomason produced a twin of the cigar he'd been smoking outside.

"My compliments, Mr. Phipps."

Mr. Phipps looked with faint apology at the cedar-colored, seven-and-a-half-inch double corona cigar in its glass case.

"Oh, no, I never have smoked. It's bad for the heart, and bad for the lungs. Isn't that a medical fact, Dr. Luke?"

Thomason shrugged. "Man is nothing but a creature of habit."

"Yes, sir. That's what has always kept me in business. Other folks' bad habits."

Mr. Phipps moved his head slightly to gaze at the painting of the Crucifixion on the floor. He flexed his right hand, as if he'd noted some detail that needed improvement, and was anxious to pick up a brush. It was only one of a few hints of genuine emotion he'd revealed to Thomason, even on those widely separated occasions when he'd lain in wait, shot-up and exhausted from loss of blood, for the doctor to come and probe and disinfect and stitch him back together, with never a report to the authorities. Which, for any licensed physician, was a felony punishable by a jail sentence. This was the bond between them. Mr. Phipps had once recollected, unbidden, while in a haze from anesthesia, that he had killed thirty-six of his fellow human beings—men, women and children—for money, beginning when he was thirteen years of age, and had earned a total of exactly seventy-two thousand, three hundred dollars and sixty-four cents. This was one of many contradictory traits, for him to know the sum of his cold-hearted labors to the penny. It shrank Thomason's balls to think about the murdering Mr. Phipps, coexisting peacefully with the artistic Mr. Phipps, and the Mr. Phipps who recited passages from Scripture aloud to the wanderers and jail bait he brought into his home, while baptizing them with seed from the spreading adder.

"I noticed you still have that old Diamond T truck. The Rolls-Royce of pickups, isn't that what it was called?"

Mr. Phipps looked up politely. "It's in fine running order. No need to get shed of anything that still does the job for you." There was a brief disturbance on the surface of his otherwise impenetrable calm. Thomason understood.

"Miss Pamela Abelard is one of the best-selling novelists in the world today. I don't think I need to describe to you the rewards of her celebrity. Would any of this have been possible if she'd thoughtlessly married that boy, subordinated her life to his while raising their children? Not likely. It was one of those misfortunes that turn out for the best."

"I take pains with my work, Dr. Luke. It was a clean hit on the boy, and she was at least ten feet away. But her back was turned when I drove into him. He had seen me and was just beginning to run. His body was lifted from the road and thrown against her. Looked to me like his head struck her just above her waist. Any higher, of course, and her skull bones might have been shattered."

"I found two of his broken-off teeth embedded in her back. The police drew up a diagram of angles and trajectories, and came to the conclusion it happened just the way you recall. I've never held you responsible for that twist of fate."

"Yours is truly a forgiving nature, Dr. Luke."

Thomason thought the moment appropriate. He withdrew the envelope from the wallet pocket of his jacket and handed it over. Mr. Phipps smiled as if he had been remembered on his birthday.

"Slip this into your Bible. It'll be much comfort to you, some winter's night when the tobacco business has not been up to your expectations."

"Thank you, Dr. Luke."

"Speaking of the Bible, Mr. Phipps—if the meek inherit the earth, who will tell them what to do with it?"

Mr. Phipps turned his head a fraction; the scar on his forehead took on light, a thin glowing filament of hardened tissue. His smile wore on, wisely.

"I don't believe either of us is truly concerned about that. Am I leaving today?"

"As soon as possible, Mr. Phipps."

"Do you have a name for me?"

"Her name is Frosty Clemons." Thomason hesitated, blinking, his gaze removed from the other's face, unfocused as if he were silently recalculating odds that would have meaningful effect on the rest of his life. Then he said, with no further hesitation, having renewed his confidence in the extraordinary talents and good luck that had kept Mr. Phipps unjailed, unsuspected and thriving in this the fifth decade of his murderous career:

"And his name is Dr. Joe Bryce."

PART **THREE**

All through the dark the wind looks for the grief it belongs to.

—W. S. Merwin, Night Wind

TWENTY-NINE

Late Monday morning, Joe picked up a substitute Laredo at the rental car agency in Nimrod's Chapel and headed south to Charleston, an hour's drive away.

Sunday's poor weather had dissipated and the fall day along the coast was brisk and sunny. Far out in the Atlantic, hurricane Honey was located around the Tropic of Cancer, moving in a northwesterly direction at approximately twelve miles an hour, with dangerous winds up to two hundred fifty miles from her center: a large, sprawling storm. Assuming that Honey would continue on course, she would pass just north of the Bahamas in about two days, then continue on to landfall in the U.S. around Cape Canaveral, Florida. But this was still problematical, as there were no oceanic superhighways for hurricanes to travel; with a pause or two and subsequent course changes, Honey, like many tropical storms before her, could head north on a curving track between Bermuda and the east coast of America and blow herself out over the colder waters of the North Atlantic.

Joe had never visited Charleston, so with an hour at his disposal before meeting Laddy Langford at the restaurant the plastic surgeon had recommended, he wandered through the old coastal city and was smitten. According to Abby, Charleston had been the richest city in the nation in the eighteenth century. First the Civil War, then the disaster of the great earthquake of 1886 had impoverished most Charlestonians, who should have known from a previous earthquake that they had cast their lot in a jinxed location. They were still recovering from the most recent visitation of epic bad news, Hurricane Hugo. Rebuilding took time, where preservation committees stringently demanded exact replacements for old-world materials such as roofing tiles first brought to this country two hundred years ago. But on this Monday in October the city of Charleston, tissue wrapped in heat-tinted Southern cloud, was a lot like heaven ought to be. A little of the Côte d'Azur in its pastel makeup. The harbor was as calm as a bookshelf aquarium. Tourists were in town for the fall viewing of cloistered pre-Revolutionary homes. No one seemed to be in much of a hurry, as if leisure were a birthright here. There were those people, Joe thought, looking over the small tasteful shops and sidewalk cafés, who were hell-bent to give a bad name to everything. Pornographers. Fashion designers. Fast-food franchisers. But the citizens of Charleston had so far conspired to keep the city's good name, maintaining a livable place of architectural distinction, some of it out of plumb from monster winds and higgledy-piggledy.

"I love coming to Charleston," Laddy Langford said over lunch, which they took at an Italian café on Meeting Street, "especially when they pay me for it."

"How long have you been here?"

"Since Saturday. My quartet sang at the Barbershop

competition over the weekend; came in third. Now I've got four days of lectures at the Medical College before I head back to Atlanta.''

Joe's other guest for lunch, a neuropathologist named Nick Portuguese, asked him, "Are you thinking of settling down in South Carolina?"

"I've been tempted," Joe said.

"Laddy said you were a marine architect."

"More of a hobby than anything."

"Married, Joe?"

"Never got around to it."

"I used to be, but I liked sex too much to stay married.''

Nick was a dark, compact, fur-bearing man with more gold chains than a sidewalk peddler. He had an eye for every woman who walked by them where they sat outdoors, his rating system a smile that ranged from sympathetic to elegiac.

"Did you know that forty-nine percent of all married men still masturbate?"

Laddy grinned.

"Shocking," Joe said. "And how many women?"

Nick ordered a second double-malt whiskey from the waiter. "Statistics are unavailable. Probably all of them." His eyes followed a couple of lissome teenagers past their outdoor table. "Look at that. So near. So ready. The female is at her freshest and most appealing when she is untouchable, as a matter of law, by those men like ourselves who have the experience, wisdom and sensual refinement to most fully appreciate them. Life is truly not worth living today."

"Something's bound to turn up," Laddy said soothingly.

"Sixty-four percent of teenage girls have had sex by the time they're seventeen. Funny how none of them ever sat by me in one of my classes."

"Statistics fascinate," Laddy said; his deep voice

sounded entombed. "They say more than they mean, and mean less than they say."

"Of course. No area of investigation is so circumscribed that it cannot support hives of statistics. Statistics create light without heat, a metaphysical aura of community. Forty-seven percent of Americans confess to having had one or more paranoid episodes last year, up two and a half percent from the previous year. Seventeen percent own guns they can neither load nor fire. Thirty-nine percent keep dogs that have never had obedience training. The percentage for children is considerably higher." Nick quivered, following with his eyes a tall redhead in a deerslayer jacket to her table. "Jesus. There she is. Right out of my Fenimore Cooper fantasies. What if I told her I could happily spend my nights licking corn-dodger crumbs off her mons veneris?"

"I'll get her over here and we'll find out," Joe offered.

"Wait," Nick said, putting a hand on Joe's arm as he was getting up. "It's only one o'clock in the afternoon; and I'm not drunk enough."

"Why don't we deal with Joe's problem before we deal with yours?" Laddy suggested.

"Why not? The paraplegic with the curious symptoms? Is she gorgeous, Joe?"

"Very."

"No names?"

"Not yet."

"So tell me about her."

Joe explained what he knew of Pamela Abelard's condition, and Dr. Lucas Thomason's course of treatment.

"Right away I have to wonder about the steroid protocol," the neuropathologist said, and Laddy Langford nodded in agreement. "Steroids, whatever proprietary names they go by, have notorious side effects, even short-term. Cushing's syndrome includes swelling of the face, a hump of fat on the upper back, outsized appetite and the kind of lunatic mood swings that used to get sufferers confined to Bedlam. Laughing, weeping, violent rage, abject depression. But your lady is fair of face and not subject to such fits. More of an enchanted princess, who falls into swoons now and then. Except for the episode a few nights ago, when she convulsed and you thought she was going to die.''

"It was damned scary."

"You've observed spasticity. What about pain?"

"Either she's learned to sublimate so that she doesn't pay attention to it, or pain is absent.''

"Not likely, if the spinal pain tracks weren't severed. Amitriptyline might give her some distance from the pain, but it won't shut it down. Because, in the case of most paraplegics, pain is apocryphal: the brain is happiest when it's processing information from all over the body. Cancel that flow of information and the brain gets anxious and, in one of its more mysterious moods, sends intense pain to the vicinity of the unresponsive site. Sort of a neural wake-up call. Her legs are no longer useful, for whatever reason, but the brain refuses to concede.''

Their lunches came then: seafood tortellini in garlic cream for Joe, which Nick looked at enviously while he was served plain linguini with a side of breaded veal cutlet, and gnocchi with tomato sauce and wild mushrooms for Laddy Langford. Joe and Laddy had Sicilian red with their meals; Nick finished his second malt whiskey and thereafter drank ice water.

"Should have ordered the pizza," he said, after sampling his linguini. "God, I love pizza. Fifty-one percent of married men over forty admit to having fantasies involving cheap motels, young prostitutes in stiletto heels, and pizzas with extra cheese." He sipped ice water to cool his imagination. "By the way, what was your lady drinking the night she convulsed?"

"Vodka on the rocks, mostly. Is that a clue?"

"No," Nick admitted.

"But you don't think she's on steroids."

"I'd have to see her; but from what you've told me, there's not much chance. Her country doctor is shooting her up with something else."

"That he wants her to believe is steroids."

Nick nodded uncomfortably. "If there's deception involved, it brings us close to some serious illegalities. She ought to be examined by somebody good. And right now, in my opinion."

"I'm trying to get her to do just that."

"She's resisting?"

"She has, or says she has, complete confidence in her doctor."

"Does anyone care what I think?" Laddy Langford said, smiling. "Of course I only run a chop-shop. But I know a lot about human weaknesses and vanities."

"Go," Nick said.

"It may be possible that she likes being paralyzed."

Portuguese nodded thoughtfully. Laddy looked at Joe, who said, troubled, "I don't know her that well."

"She has spasticity, apparently without pain. She could willfully be denying herself the effective use of her legs. And, let me add, in subconscious collusion with the man who's caring for her."

"She was involved in a serious accident. Her fiancé was killed. Those are the facts."

"It was a hit-and-run," Nick said. "What does she remember about it?"

"Nothing."

"Do you know if she had psychiatric counseling?"

"No."

"It could have been helpful," Laddy said. "Particularly if she was harboring any suspicions that she might have been able to do something to prevent her fiancé's death."

"She survived," Nick said. "And paraplegia was the

compromise she made with her sense of guilt. I think the name for it is hysterical conversion reaction.''

Joe shook his head. "I really have problems buying into this.''

Nick said, "I have a credo that ought to be engraved in bronze over the doorways of every health-care facility in the world. 'There are no limits to the perversities of human beings.' You should have stuck around the medical profession, Joe. If nothing else, the practice of medicine keeps your shit-detector in good working order.''

"I don't think it was a sense of guilt that caused her to convulse, turn red all over and otherwise exhibit a severe allergic reaction, I want to know what's in those syringes her doctor keeps emptying into her system. If he's not treating a persistent inflammation, what is he treating?''

Nick looked at Laddy, and rubbed his eyes, thinking it over.

"Do you have a sample?''

"I know where I can get one.''

"Why do I cringe at the sound of that?''

"You wouldn't be breaking any laws or compromising medical ethics. You won't be deposed into the next century. The sample turns up in your mailbox at the hospital, tomorrow or the next day. You send it up to the lab along with whatever else you send on a daily basis to be analyzed. Then, let's say Friday of this week, same time, we have lunch again here and admire the lovelies, and you give me an oral rundown on substance X. In the meantime, I'll persuade Ab—my lady—to come into town for a three-day stay under the supervision of whoever you recommend to me now.''

"Petersen. He's the best I've ever worked with.''

"Can you have her booked right away?''

"What name?''

"Pond. Holly Pond will do."

"That's a very interesting alias."

"It was my mother's stage name," Joe said. "She used to be an exotic dancer, in New Orleans."

THIRTY

A Chicora County school bus was dropping Lizzie at the gates to the Barony when Joe returned from Charleston. She looked around at the sound of his horn; her grumpy expression lightened at once and she lugged her book bag over to the Laredo.

"Hi, where've you been?" Lizzie said, settling into the front seat beside him for the short drive to the house.

"Charleston."

"Oh. Who do you know there?"

"A physician friend of mine from Atlanta is delivering a series of lectures at the Medical College. We had lunch. How was your day?"

Lizzie slumped in her seat. "Awful," she mourned.

"That bad, huh?"

"Somebody did a snot rocket all over my combination lock. I'm pretty sure I know who, and if he doesn't let up I'm gonna punch him in the eye." Lizzie hunched her narrow shoulders. "I did the wrong assignment for geography. Then I farted in gym class, and everybody knew it was me.''

''I've had days like that.''

Lizzie swung a fist sideways and banged him on the bicep. ''Shut up. You have not. Everybody's making fun of me all the time.'' She chewed anxiously on her lower lip. ''Now I have to practice the *piano*. If we got it back. Charlene said it had *scratches*. She just runs all over everybody in that house, does what she pleases, and Abby thinks it's fine. Did you read in *Newsweek* about that ten-year-old girl who flew solo across the Atlantic? I wrote a paper for English about her. I hate writing. Abby got all the talent in the family. School is such a waste of time. I knock my butt off for A's but nobody gets low grades anymore, even if they're dumb as chickens, it's bad for their self-esteem. Anyway, I should be *doing* stuff with my life. What if I sailed solo around the world? I'll bet nobody my age has done anything like that! I'm a good sailor. My stepfather taught me. Of course that girl had a copilot, an adult, with her. So I guess I'd have to have somebody with me, who could do repairs and stuff.'' She gave him a look over one hunched shoulder. ''You're a good sailor, aren't you, Joe?''

''Yes.''

Lizzie squirmed herself upright in the seat, hopefulness expanding in her breast like a large balloon, filling with the cheery winds of her imagination.

''Why don't we do it then? We've got a boat! Big one. Luke doesn't use it anymore since he took up polo, it's just rotting away down by the bay. We could leave as soon as school's out next year. Can we sail around the world in three months? Doesn't matter, I could do my schoolwork by satellite! It would be such a great learning experience, don't you think?''

''Hey, Liz.''

The balloon burst; she gasped forlornly. ''You think

I'm just a stupid kid. You wouldn't even kiss me back. I looked up *perdition* in the dictionary.''

"What did that tell you?"

She didn't answer until he had parked the Laredo with half a dozen other vehicles on the motor court. They sat together in silence for a few moments.

"I guess," Lizzie said slowly, "I wouldn't have respected you very much if you had—if you tried—"

"There are all kinds of useful learning experiences, Miss Liz. Some you don't recognize until they're long over with."

She nodded, looked at him, smiled in a weepy sort of way. "I really didn't have a very good day. Did you?"

"Let's keep this just between us, but I think we're making progress where Abby is concerned."

"Oh. Ohhh! *That's* why you had lunch with your—"

"I'm trusting you, Lizzie," he said, with a stern note of caution.

"Sure! I won't say anything. When do you think you can tell me about what you're gonna do?"

"In a couple of days."

"Really? Oh, that's great news! I need to get something to eat. I'm starved. All they had for lunch today was noodles with this urp on it, and the tomatoes in the salad weren't ripe. I hate that. Would you like me to make you a peanut-butter sandwich?"

"I'm fine, Lizzie."

"Where're you going now?" she asked, as she got out of the Jeep.

"To find Abby."

"If the piano didn't come back I'll see you all later; otherwise it's practice, practice, practice," Lizzie said, throwing her book bag over her shoulder and trudging up the steps to the house.

The workroom doors were open and he heard Abby as he approached.

"I don't know how you could be that careless, Frosty."

"I don't either; nothing like this happen before."

"You probably misfiled the tape."

"I think you're right about that; the problem is, there's hundreds of tapes to go through to find the right one. I'm truly sorry, Abby."

"Oh, well. I wasn't in the mood to work tonight, anyway. Are there more letters to sign?"

"No, they're all taken care of. What do you want me to say to Grant when he calls back?"

"Tell him I understand how the Hollywood types feel about giving novelists creative control—"

"I think what he said was 'It's easier to get an elephant to tango.'"

"I at least would like to have some say about who they cast in the miniseries, regardless of TVQ and all that."

"Maybe it's negotiable," Frosty said, as the telephone rang. "Here he is now. Do you want me to tell him you think Rachael Karey should play Abigail?"

From the doorway Joe saw Abby grin. "Tell him the idea positively knocks my dick in the dirt."

She turned her head as Joe knocked. "Hey, come on in! I was just brushing up on my Hollywood agent-type talk. Those people are hysterical. In every sense of the word."

Frosty glanced at Joe, failed to return his smile, then turned her back at her desk to devote herself to conversation with the agent.

Abby was surrounded by cartons and packages, including a stack of bulky mailing envelopes that contained copies of her books. There was an opened tin of homemade cookies in her lap.

"Here, have one of these," she said to Joe. "Every other month this woman in North Dakota bakes them for me. Molasses and raisins and nuts, and are they ever tasty."

"Fan worship?" Joe asked, helping himself to a saucer-size cookie.

Abby nodded. "This month alone I've gotten hand-made jewelry from an Indian social worker in New Mexico, a wood-carving from the Ozarks—just exquisite—and dried flowers from Oregon. I send them hardcover books and try to say something worthy of their generosity. Joe, could you open that big box for me? Frosty didn't have the chance."

Joe used a pair of scissors to open the lightweight box. He lifted out a fedora-style straw hat, pale yellow, ornamented with tiny ceramic flowers.

"Isn't it gorgeous?" Abby unbound her hair and let it fall, tried on the hat immediately, tilting it this way and that. "I used to be a nut about hats. Haven't bought one in years. Look, it even ties under the chin for the beach." She posed for Joe. "What do you think?"

"Wear it. Let's go take some sun."

"Yeah, I need to get out. Frosty? Later."

Outside she asked him, "Where've you been all day?"

"I went for a long drive. Did you go swimming this morning?"

"Yes. By the way, Norse has his jaw wired shut. You must have hit him with a Buick."

"I could strut around and say aw shucks. The fact is I don't feel very good about what happened."

Abby was searching through a ratsey bag. She squinted up at him. "Joe? Must have left my sunglasses inside. Dear heart, would you mind—?"

"I'll be right back."

In the workroom he found Frosty with her head in her hands. She heard his footsteps but didn't look up. There was a fizzing glass of Alka-Seltzer on the desk.

"What's the matter, Frosty?"

"Just my afternoon headache."

"You ought to try one of those little headsets, if you spend a lot of time on the telephone."

"Good advice. I'll look into it."

He put his hands gently on her shoulders. "I could loosen you up in no time."

Frosty's hands parted. She gave him a wise untrusting look.

"I'll bet you could. Just take your hands off me, please."

"Sorry. It's more than a headache, isn't it?"

"Don't know what you mean."

"I was at the Lost Sea Turtle the other night."

She sat back slowly in her squeaking office chair. "Know that. I saw you with your little friend you made there."

"Wasn't anything to it, Frosty."

"Just a quick boff, relieve your tensions?"

"I wonder why you don't like me, Frosty."

"Haven't give the matter all that much study."

"You think you see right through me. You don't see a thing, Frosty."

She drank some of her Alka-Seltzer, sighed and patted her trim stomach.

"Maybe you just don't have much use for men," Joe said, pursuing a sore subject.

"Could be you're right about that. So what?"

"I'd like to see you when we have more time to talk."

"No way," she objected, with a simmering malevolence.

"How about tonight, say ten o'clock? What's your address, Frosty?"

"Don't you be coming to *my* house."

Joe looked around, and saw Abby's Revo sunglasses on one of the round tables of Jamaican wood. He crossed the workroom to pick them up.

"Ten o'clock, Frosty. It's a small town, I won't have any trouble finding out where you live."

Frosty smothered an Alka-Seltzer belch. "You come around, my daddy Walter Lee will be on the porch with his shotgun across his knees."

"Better see he's in bed early," Joe advised, "unless you'd like to include him in the conversation."

"Just what the hell do you *want*?" she cried.

"I want to save Abby's life. Don't you?"

Frosty was not the fluttering kind, but for a couple of moments she was back on her heels, uncertain of Joe or of how to reply. Then she came back at him, almost harshly.

"I've been told it's not my business! Whose side you on, anyhow? You doctors stick together, just as cozy as ticks in a dog's ear."

"I'm not your ordinary-type doctor."

Abby was calling him, faintly, complainingly, from the garden. Frosty, responding to an uncontainable agitation, walked toward the workroom windows, reversed herself, came, reluctantly, closer to him, at the same time raising her hands breast high in a gesture that could have been protective or a surrender.

"What's she got? What is it she could die of?"

"I don't know. That's why I need the ampule you handed off to Reggie the other night in the parking lot at the Sea Turtle."

One hand fell, the other crept to the base of her throat, pulled at a slender gold chain there. She looked angry, more at herself than at Joe.

"Daddy was right. I never—but I—you see—" She made a difficult effort to compose herself. "You don't know what she's been like, the past few weeks. When she dictates, it's like her brain is all jumbled up, and what's on the tapes is worse nonsense than that *Finnegans Wake* I had to read in college lit."

"Must be why you can't find the tape the two of you were discussing this afternoon."

"Yes, I'm keeping it from her. Just don't want Abby to know. What would that do to her anyhow?"

"I think you made the right decision, Frosty. What you need to do now is make a decision about me."

Abby called to him again, a certain plaintive longing, that might have been intentional fun on her part, in the two-note extension of his name: *Johh-ohhhhhh.*

Frosty said, her words unsteady on a high-wire of emotion, "Her head was whirling all afternoon long. Said to me, 'I think I got a fella.' Don't know when— I seen her this happy." She wiped across her forehead as if cleaning a slate. "Okay. Ten o'clock. You *can't* come to my house. Daddy would know, and I don't want to upset him worse. I'll come to you." Joe nodded. "Abby put you up at the beach house, she said. This is Monday, so the Sea Turtle be closed. I'll have to locate Reggie. He used to rent a room in town, but now I believe he's staying with some musician friends in a double-wide up around Murrell's Inlet. Better make it ten-thirty, eleven o'clock, I got some driving to do."

Joe put out his hand. Frosty just looked at it.

"No reason for us not to be friends."

"Maybe that comes later," she said.

THIRTY-ONE

Abby was in conference with one of the gardeners, a tech-nical discussion about how much dolomite to apply to the French hydrangeas to change the soil pH factor and turn a select few of their abundant blooms from blue to pink when they reappeared the following summer. There were sounds of implanted sprinklers gushing to life around the perimeter of Bermuda lawn, and sharp steel blades snip-snapping rhythmically as two more gardeners trimmed ivy growing in a thick spiral around the trunk of a chinaberry tree. Nearby a brown bird settled into the basin of a trickling fountain, puffed out its speckled breast and began beating its wings against the surface of the water like a fat happy child splashing in a wading pool. Still, the wild green of summer seemed to be outliving itself; there was, in brilliant mesmerizing distances and cool cloud formations, the sense of another season about to slide into place.

"Lizzie said you had a boat," Joe said, when she smiled to acknowledge him.

"Yes, we do. That was Luke's hobby before he took up polo—and politics. I don't think either of us has gone sailing for at least three years." She looked mildly regretful in recalling this lapse. "Time passes, and you somehow forget a few of the things you've always enjoyed. I guess the *Wayfarer*'s in poor shape now. I don't think Luke has been keeping her up, he never mentions her anymore."

"*Wayfarer?*"

"He wanted to name the boat after me, but I balked. Original, huh? There's probably a million old tubs out there on the briny deep named *Wayfarer*. Do you know anything about boats?"

"I've been around them for almost half of my life," Joe said. "Let's have a look."

"What's it worth to you?" she said, with a flippant, come-on grin.

Joe leaned over her and past the brim of her new hat and kissed her. Almost upside-down, he murmured, "People will talk."

"I don't care who knows I'm happy. Kissing's funny, isn't it?" He turned his face a little and they were eye-to-eye, the blue and the gray, with little flecks of amber liveliness showing in her irises like the fizz in ginger ale. "I mean, maybe three times in my life I've gotten a real buzzola from kissing. Do it again?"

He did it again. Each of them smiled as their lips touched.

"Your face is turning red," she told him, and blew on his cheek as if to cool it.

"You're keeping me in suspense."

"Buzzy," she said. "Definitely buzzy, like caterpillars are walking up and down my spine, all the way to the Barrier."

He straightened, and rotated his shoulders to loosen a couple of muscles.

"Sex is funny, too," she said, leaning toward a bush bulky with roses the color of orange marmalade and with a fingernail flicking away a blackly-spotted and withered leaf from an otherwise pristine branch. "What little I know about it."

"What do you know about it?"

"I had a boyfriend, who died. Basically all we ever did was fumble around with each other. I was usually too nervous for it to be very exciting. I watched a porn video once. That was funny; the *size* of him, he should have been in a circus doing it with ponies. And then it made me so sad I could never look at another of those again. What's great sex like, Joe?"

"Great sex is when you don't feel afterward like you've been changing a tire."

Abby flicked her face in his direction as if at the too-near approach of a stinging insect, then looked away deliberately, her lips drawing tight. "I guess I didn't ask that question for you to make it sound like a dumb question."

"Maybe I don't know what it is to really make love to someone."

For an instant she saw clearly through what had sty-mied her, made her half-afraid of his maleness and the physical responses that would come so naturally and urgently from him, and which were beyond her capa-bilities: the expression mattered, not the mechanics. So much bother about sex. It was neither a circus nor a feat of endurance; loving was all, whatever solutions they applied to their needs. Abby raised her eyes.

"Push me," she said, and when he seemed unsure of what she had in mind, she explained, "The path to the dock is bumpy and I could flip Rolling Thunder, so I need a guiding hand. That's all I meant."

It took Joe the better part of half an hour to untie the rain-toughened sailor's knots and uncover all of *Way-farer*, where she sat on blocks and under a zinc roof at

the end of a gently sloping launch ramp into Pandora's
Bay.

Forty-three handcrafted feet of teak and mahogany,
with a classic sheer, cleanly designed and built in the
days before fiberglass and Airex and computerized
flow patterns. The keel made for the shoal waters of
the East Coast, a four-and-a-half-foot draft. Late fifties,
early sixties, he guessed. A deck-level center cockpit
allowing for a broad clean aft deck and probably generous aft quarters below. She was not suffering too
greatly from time ashore. Dry rot was his first concern;
aboard the ketch he found a ball-peen hammer in a
lazarette tool locker and worked his way carefully
around the hull, hearing, in most of the places where
he tapped the planks, a reassuring *ping* of good health.
He finished this part of his inspection in an exhilarated
mood. It had been more than a year since he'd run
his hands across fine wood so beautifully shaped and
cunningly fitted. The shipwright was unknown to him,
probably long gone from the scene; but his craftsmanship was immortal.

He was sweaty and smudged from accumulated dirt
when he dropped down from the foredeck and said to
Abby, who had waited with patient good humor for his
mania to subside, "Want to go sailing?"

"What? She looks pretty sick to me."

"Three or four days, max, she'll be in her glory
again. I'll need some help doing the scut work. There's
some pitting in the chrome over the rub points which
can be buffed out. The decks have to be sanded and
recaulked with black silicon. I need to cut out some
bad places around the transom and refit with good
mahogany planking. The sails are Dacron and there
are spots of mildew, not enough to seriously mar their
looks. The diesel is a four-cylinder Perkins that ought
to be okay if it was put up properly. I'll need a few
things from a good marine-supply store; I think I saw
one in town."

"You did. By the Lost Sea Turtle. They're probably closed now, but we can go in the morning. You must really know boats. I'm relieved there's no bad damage. I don't feel so neglectful anymore."

Abby stared past Joe at the chop on Pandora's Bay. There was a good wind at his back, where his shirt was wet and sticking to his skin. He heard Lizzie hailing them and saw her heading in their direction with Bruiser keeping her company. In skimpy running shorts and a tank top she showed the fleet finesse of an athlete; her thin legs looked polished and purposeful as pistons while she ran.

"Paul had a little sailboat," Abby said. Wind tugged at the brim of her hat. "What do you call them, Sunfish? Nothing you'd want to take very far out in the Sound. We'd sail up to the Coosaw, or hug the shore all the way to Fripp Island." She looked up at Joe slowly, as if her mind were being pulled, rudderless, into troublesome depths. "It was such a simple, beautiful time."

The pale yellow hat flew off her head; Joe snatched at it, getting nothing but air. The hat went skittering and tumbling across open ground and into a stand of widely spaced pines as Lizzie and then Bruiser detoured to chase it down. Abby turned to watch, stiffening in her wheelchair as if another convulsion were beginning. Her auburn hair blew into her eyes and looked fiery in the sun that struck her full in the face.

When Lizzie stooped to retrieve the motionless hat, Abby screamed.

"No! No! No!"

Lizzie, her back to them, looked around briefly, then picked up the hat.

Abby turned violently again, facing Joe, looking through him. She pushed a hand up through the hair covering her forehead, exposing the hairline and a long thin scar there.

"Bleeding."

"No, you're not. What is it, Abby?"

She grimaced and slumped forward, still holding her head, lightly rubbing the all-but-invisible scar, as if it were suddenly too tender, after years of dormancy, to stand much pressure.

"What is it, Abby?" Joe asked again.

"I don't know. If I can explain. I felt as if—I was chasing the hat myself. Not running. I was being pulled toward it at terrific speed, fa-falling out of control through black, black space."

"Where did that scar come from?"

"The accident. When I was—run over in Beaufort." She grimaced again, squeezing two tears from her eyes. "It *hurts*," she complained.

"There aren't any nerve endings in scar tissue," he said, carefully taking her hand away and holding it, looking at the site of the injury. From the size of the scar it had been a shallow tear, but scalp wounds could produce a frightening quantity of blood.

"That's all you remember?"

"Yes," she said, cold and trembling. "Make it go away, Joe."

"Make what go away?"

Lizzie came up to them slowly, holding the hat, her cheeks brick red from exertion, sweat in the hollows of her eyes. She had a spot of dried peanut butter at one corner of her mouth.

"Abby?"

"I'm all right, sugar."

"Here's your hat."

Abby shook her head, not looking at either of them.

"Thank you. I don't want it anymore. It's b-bad luck. I shouldn't have been wearing that hat. Because then it wouldn't have happened. I would have seen it coming, and I could've *stopped* it."

Her voice, compressed by grief, was so small and tinny it might have come from the mechanical voice box of a doll. Lizzie looked at Joe, startled and upset.

He smiled reassuringly at her, and squeezed Abby's limp hand, trying to bring some warmth and life to it. "You don't have to think about it now."

After a few moments Abby cleared her throat. "I'm not thinking about it. It's just *there*. Like superstition: nothing to see, just something to fear."

"A daymare," Lizzie said in a fragile voice, then made an attempt to smile. She put her own hand on Abby's shoulder, then in an agony of compassion embraced her cousin, her forehead against the back of Abby's neck.

Sounding more like herself, Abby said, "I haven't had a drink for three or four days. Would one drink hurt me?"

"I'll okay that," Joe said.

"You don't have to mother me, Lizzie."

"I'm not, and shut up," Lizzie said, clinging to her.

"Luke and Charlene are doing some kind of charity thing tonight. Why don't we take Joe to the Skipper's for dinner?" She looked up at Joe, revived by the prospect of an outing, eyes losing their pall. "It's this unbelievably tacky place on Calisto, up on stilts beside a creek, and you think it's going to fall down when the wind blows hard. Pitchers of beer and lobsters so big they serve them with a chain saw. We'll have a party. And Lizzie, guess what? The *Wayfarer*'s going to sail again, thanks to Joe."

THIRTY-TWO

When Frosty Clemons came impatiently out of the house to find out what progress Walter Lee was making, she saw that he had removed what might have been the guts, kidneys and liver of her minivan (for all she knew about it) from beneath the hood and spread everything on a square of paint-clotted old tarp protecting the floor of the carport. He was washing parts of this and that in a coffee can filled with naphtha, holding up to his work light and examining with a leisurely eye each newly cleaned piece of metal.

"Brought you a cold drink," she said, setting the can on the plastic seat of a child's play chair.

"Uh-huh."

"Kids are settled down, but not asleep yet."

"Okay."

"What's that you got there in your hand?"

"Fuel injector."

"Did I tell you I needed to be out of here forty-five

minutes ago? What about that leak you said I had, made the temperature shoot up?''

"Hose clamp. I fixed it. Frosty, there's two kinds of automobile batteries nowadays. The kind you just leave alone, and the kind you need to add water now and then.''

"Oh. Which one do I have?''

"Add water.''

"I suppose that's not working either.''

"No, your battery's okay. Only three of the cells were dry. But that's why she was hard to crank.''

"So when can I have my van back?''

"Give me about another hour and a half.''

"Huh!''

Walter Lee looked up at her from the padded mechanic's dolly he was sitting on, wiped his hands on some waste and massaged an aching knee.

"Long as I'm about it, might as well give you a regular tune-up.''

"Daddy, when you go to the hospital for an emergency appendectomy, do they do a heart transplant at the same time, in case you might be needing a new heart someday?''

"Seems to me you complained all last week how you were stalling out on idle, had to keep giving gas at a red light with your foot on the brake?''

"I guess I did,'' she said with a shrug, and looked at Walter Lee's car, a twenty-year-old Chevy in need of a paint job that was parked under the buzzing streetlight by the front gate. "I know you had a long day, and I appreciate you paying attention to my van. Maybe I could borrow your car for the night?''

"Help yourself. I ain't going nowhere except to bed.'' He reached for his Pepsi and drank half of it in three swallows. "Where you off?''

"Oh, Reggie and me are cooking something up for

Saturday night at the Sea Turtle. It's extra bucks, Daddy, and I need music in my life."

"How far you going? Maybe you better put gas in." He reached into a side pocket of his overalls and tossed her the keys.

"I'll fill it up," Frosty promised. She went back into the house for her purse. She listened for sounds of activity in the twins' room, heard nothing suspicious, and left quietly. In the carport she gave her father a kiss on his rugged forehead. "Look for me around midnight."

The paint job on Walter Lee's car had oxidized to a pale sage green, and there were places covered only by gray primer where he had plugged holes and filled in dents. Not much for looks, but the sedan was tidy inside and the engine, after starting, was as quiet as a fine watch. But she knew from the other times she'd borrowed it the Chevy was a gas hog, even with its engine tuned.

Awtry Avenue, the street on which Frosty lived with the girls and Walter Lee, dead-ended at a slough off the Corday River. In the other direction, at the corner of Awtry and Second Street, several blocks from downtown Nimrod's Chapel, there was a Church's Fried Chicken on one corner, the Deliverance AME chapel diagonally opposite, a vacant lot that contained several cars and a couple of trucks with sun-faded FOR SALE signs behind the windshields and, across from the unlighted lot, on the northeast corner of Second Street, a convenience store that sold a cut-rate brand of gas called Zoom!

There was a blinking red light at the four-way stop. Frosty paused in Walter Lee's Chevy for a camper with Maryland plates to go by. She glanced at the collection of vehicles on the informal used car lot. Most of them had been there for a while, getting dirty and attracting no buyers. A recent addition was an old but apparently well-cared-for pickup that faced the intersection, parked with its bumper at the edge of the narrow sidewalk. Black, with a long, pointed hood, and, surprisingly, tinted windows, a customized touch. She wondered if Walter Lee had seen it yet. He might be interested. She'd have to mention it to him, although there was no sign visible with a number to call.

Frosty crossed Second and turned right onto the concrete apron of the convenience store, pulled up to the pump that dispensed regular leaded. She added ten gallons, put up the nozzle and hose and went inside the convenience store to pay.

The franchisee of the Zoom! outlet was also the minister of the AME church, who had seven children. Five of them worked at the convenience store on a rotating basis. Frosty knew them all. Tonight Zach was behind the counter, wearing a white short-sleeved shirt and dark trousers. He played several musical instruments and had recently moved up from the teen choir to the adult choir. He had a fine baritone voice.

"How're you tonight, Frosty?"

"Right as rain, Zach." In truth she had a tension headache, and she suspected, from a cramp she'd had earlier while dressing to go out, that she was about to get her period.

"That's pump number four? Be twelve dollars and twenty-one cents." Frosty made a face. Zach said with a quick sympathetic smile, "It's mostly taxes, you know. Daddy says we got to pump nine thousand gallons a week to show a profit outside. Inside sales are what keep us in business. Anything else for you tonight?"

"Pack of this Wrigley's spearmint." Chewing gum helped her cope with tension. There was a box of tampons in the van, but she didn't want to go back for it. She dug down to the bottom of her purse and found a lone tampon in its wrapper. *Now or later?* she asked herself.

"That's seventy-eight cents, so your total with tax is thirteen-fifteen." Zach made change for a twenty.

Later, Frosty thought. The onset of her period might not happen until early morning, and she was almost an hour late getting on the highway to Murrell's Inlet.

"Good night, Zach."

Frosty left the convenience store and returned to the Chevy. The windshield could've used a cleaning, but she let that go too. She got in, started the engine, opened her pack of gum and drove east on Second Street, still concerned about whether she was doing the right thing in placing any kind of trust in Dr. Joe Bryce. *Trust.* She trusted in Jesus and she trusted her father Walter Lee. All other men were suspect by reason of their maleness. Two of them in her life, both musicians, had proclaimed their love and picked her pocket. A third had fathered her children and run off to Chicago with an editor from *Ebony* he had met while she was vacationing in Charleston. It only lasted a few weeks, but Delmus was still hanging around up north. Let him stay there. Enough was enough. And that Joe Bryce was just too good-looking to be attracted for very long to a crippled woman. Something about him, in spite of his profession, his selfless good works, didn't feel right. Frosty had perfect pitch when it came to music; somebody humming off-key two aisles over in the supermarket affected her like fingernails on a chalkboard. Her disappointments in love had sharpened her pitch where men were concerned. Dr. Joe Bryce was off-key. Putting his hands on her when she hadn't done a thing to encourage him, like he was *claiming* her. Never mind how it felt, all the locks on her emotions springing open as if he were some kind of sexual Houdini. He was just too used to getting his way with women.

Frosty had a cramp, lasting a dozen seconds, that almost took her breath away. She chewed gum furiously, concentrating on the road. Light traffic heading south, only a single pair of high headlights behind her, truck of some kind, a sedate driver like herself. Never more than a mile or two over the speed limit. Always be cautious, obey the laws, pay the taxes on time, stay out of debt, filter the drinking water and avoid romantic attachments; so many ways you could screw up your life without half-trying. Invite the demons of bad luck to pick at your carcass. She remembered a discussion of the luck factor in a psychology course she'd taken as an undergrad at Furman. "Bad luck," said the lecturer, a puckish little man with a startling red goatee, "is a matter of poor preparation, less than optimum diligence and insufficient clarity of vision. And then you just happen to be standing on a manhole cover when the sewer blows up." Amen, brother. It was a miracle, she thought, that she'd had the nerve to raid Dr. Luke's infirmary and take the ampule, then coolly cover up evidence of her theft. But righteous anger had driven her to it. Abby was in danger, and helpless to protect herself.

Her vagina was getting wet. Her time again. Dismayed, Frosty peered ahead, looking for a gas station. But she was on that long stretch of highway between the Intracoastal Waterway and Chicora State Beach, now closed for the night. There were no towns or commercial establishments for another six miles.

Anxious not to stain her underpants and a nearly new pair of jeans, Frosty slowed, looking for the first northbound exit to the state beach.

Almost missed it. Braked hard and made the turn. The paved road gave out after a couple of hundred feet, where the gates across the shell road that went down to the public parking and beachside facilities were padlocked. She stopped, the headlights of the Chevrolet illuminating the red CLOSED sign on one of the silver-painted gates, and a stand of longleaf pine fifty yards down the road. Then she turned off the headlights so as not to be conspicuous to anyone passing on the highway.

The quickest way to accomplish insertion of the

needed tampon was simply to get out and hunker
down in relative privacy behind the front bumper of
the Chevy. She looked in the mirror and saw the lights
of an eighteen-wheeler passing. There was some tur-
moil in her stomach; she didn't feel like leaving the
car in a lonely place with a single sodium vapor light
burning on a pole beside the gate. As if her menses
would attract creatures unknown from the dark of the
woods and the sea beyond.

The Chevy sedan had a bench front seat. Frosty put
her feet up, her back against the left-side door, and
unbuckled her jeans. She liked them tight and usually
she had to lie on the floor of her bedroom to wriggle
into them when they were freshly laundered. The
denim, on her body for several hours, had a little more
play to it now. She tugged the jeans and the panties to
midcalf, looked to see if there was any staining, then
lay down a little more in the seat with her thighs open
and tore the wrapper from the tampon, which she held
just above her eyes.

She was looking almost straight up when the window
above her head was shattered with a baseball bat, covering her with glass. In screaming she swallowed some
of it. More glass glittered in her compactly shaped
dome of curly hair as she struggled to sit up. She was
seized by an arm like steel in blue cloth that smelled
faintly of mothballs, an arm that crossed her throat and
pinned her solidly back against the door. There she
was held, choking, her convulsing lips and throat lac-
erated by granules of glass, while his other hand sought
the lock and opened the door. It swung open slowly,
and she was dragged across the bench seat with it, leaving a thin smear of blood on the seat cover. Her legs
were pinned together by the gathered material of jeans
and underpants, but she lashed about wildly in an effort to escape.

Looking up, she saw his wide face and blunt coun-
tryman's features, the bead-shaped, pinkish light above

the gate repeated on each convex surface of his own glasses. He went slowly down on one knee as he continued to drag her from the car, now holding her powerfully by the throat with his left hand, pushing down until the edge of the seat was across the small of her bowed back and her head was only inches off the pulverized shell of the road. The underside of the steering wheel dug painfully into her pelvis.

Unable to bear the lack of expression in his eyes, Frosty moved her head by inches in his grip, until she was looking past his knee at the front-end chrome of the pickup truck that had crept, lights off, to within a hundred feet of the Chevy. It seemed familiar to her, but her throat and lungs were bursting, she couldn't think where she might have seen it before. But it didn't matter. She closed her eyes and wished for a moment in which to embrace her children, to kiss her father, *one moment please*. And knew it would not happen.

THIRTY-THREE

Dreaming, Joe found himself in a strange house by the sea, and in possession of a letter from his mother.

dear one
would've typed this but the keys of my type-
writer stick together with old cinnamongum which
reminds me I have lost another tooth yes I know
neglect is not the answer but supposing the sea is
calm tomorrow   creatureless   then all I ask
but if you are well the address to which you must
write as I may be wanted by thought police (they
never tell you until too late) forgetting the assassination angle for now please observe the fictitious
me and kindly obliterate postmark   for which I
thank you in advance although by the time you
read this may be as fraudulent as the old black
woman who reads palms by the cemetery wall
yet has no answers either despite (I'm certain)
knowledge of the bird smaller   than the kitti-

wake that swims to the chambers of the heart
which with a little thought might then appreciate
the greed of Death   or if it doesn't mean cancer
than obviously I can still see my handprints for as
long as the sea lies low and freezes   freezes
knowing I am calm and perpetual in spite of the
pain being no good lately that you already know
about from my last letter (sealed with a kiss) because the implications deny remorse and the supermarket cash registers don't work right since I
am always sixty-four cents or seventy-two cents
short   is no fucking (oops) laughing matter and
sometimes the fever like a ghost I wake up to
but what about your own clichés   which I am
willing to forgive any time any city will meet you
just give notice and send a hundred for expenses
which you have to admit I am worth it   and
perpetual   tomorrow the sun its treasure of
venom   the sea (see?) transparent but creatureless at last   you will come to find your Holly
won't you because my dear the little swimmer
birds only nest in abandoned hearts and the truce
shall make us free

He woke up naked and in a sweat; something
seemed to catch up to him in the long void between
dream and reality, flicking vehemently past his face—
nothing solid or identifiable, but dark as dread. He
heard the sea, ending its long course to the shore in
a tumbling wave, and another sound out there, a car
door closing.

Mother?

He got out of bed and fell, wobbly, to his knees; he
had a cramp in one calf.

Massaging the muscle, he made his way gimpily to
the windows of the corner bedroom, which faced east
and north. The plantation shutters were open; the
moon rounding to full, a matter of days, solitary in the

black sky, its luster crowding out the stars—his heart
was wild in response.

The rented van was parked on the narrow road that
ran behind the beach house. From there it continued
on, a dwindling sandy track, to the colonies and en-
claves lying to the north along the strand.

It had to be late, but he didn't know the time. He
still couldn't think about anything except the imagery
of the dream, provoked by the language of the letter
his subconscious had written, and the finality of that
car door closing. (Drove away and left him; and now,
if she lay dying in some undisclosed place, of what use
was his forgiveness?)

He was too awake, too shaken, to think of sleeping
any more. He pulled on a pair of shorts and a cash-
mere sweater and went downstairs.

In the intervals of silence between the smash of
waves he heard, he thought, the engine of a car or
light truck, a receding sound as someone drove north
on the rutted track on the marsh side of the dune.

Several bottles of Killian's Red in the fridge. He carried one out to the front porch. Looking north, he saw
taillights, brightening as brakes were applied, then fading. Too far away for him to tell what kind of vehicle
it was.

He hadn't bothered to lock the Laredo. He had a
couple of pulls on his bottle of beer, then walked barefoot down to the road behind the house.

Not easy to tell by moonlight, but the Laredo appeared undisturbed where he'd left it.

Maybe they'd been county cops on beach patrol, or
fishermen getting a very early start. Joe yawned, leaned
against the Laredo and finished his beer, wondering
what to do with himself for the rest of the night.

There were a dozen movies on satellite TV: he
couldn't concentrate for long on any of them. A handful of actors who would always stick in the mind, but
the majority would have been more entertaining if they

were stuffed. He went outside again to wait for the dawn, uneasy, wondering if he should have approached Frosty Clemons, who had failed to show up as promised. Afraid of him, of a late meeting at the isolated beach house? He'd detected some of that in her hostility. It could require months to sort out a relationship with someone like Frosty. She would keep taking him, whip in hand, over the jumps, the neurotic thickets and emotional stone walls in her life. Every orgasm won from her like a few yards of battlefield. War was merely orgasm, on an apocalyptic scale. Churchill might have said something like that, except, if the biographies had him pegged right, he never gave much thought to sex at all. . . .

Joe didn't want either to fuck or fight with Frosty Clemons. It was just that time of night. He couldn't explain the worry he felt, the sense of being observed by enemies he hadn't met. He expected to sleep poorly in wooded, rustic places, or in cities—the best of them were fretful, snarled, distempered, their dark streets like large graves unfilled. But he'd seldom spent a restless hour within sight of any sea.

Regardless of what Frosty's feelings or misgivings might be, there was another way to obtain a sample of the drug Thomason was injecting into Abby; he could withdraw some of it from the implanted reservoir. For that he'd need her cooperation. But if she said anything to Thomason—

Joe had another Killian's, because the first one hadn't touched him in any way, and returned to the track of the moon on water, thinking about Luke the physician. Who, according to his current wife, had skidded through medical school on a banana peel, and who, according to Abby, had enjoyed an undistinguished career littered with malpractice suits as he slowly prepared himself for a second career in politics, based on Abby's considerable financial resources. Nothing seriously against him so far: maybe his personality was designed for the political game. Like most opportunists, he had an acquisitive nature. Blue-ribbon women, a handcrafted ketch, horses, guns, the friend-ships of powerful men. He was cynical, but with wit and aim. Probably you could have a laugh at his expense, but he'd bill you for it later. And the bill would come wrapped around a rock. His ministry to Abby bordered on possessiveness. He was lying about a course of treat-ment. What did he know that he didn't want Abby to know? Something about Thomason was so deeply fraudulent it cooled the marrow of Joe's bones. Be-cause he recognized how alike they were: cheats at heart, with the self-righteousness of vengeful children.

Lucky Abby, so unaware, like the snowblind angel that guarded her workroom. If Joe's machinations saved her life, then she might well turn against Lucas Thomason, depending on how badly the good physi-cian had misdiagnosed her case, then turn to Joe for solace, the love she needed. People who live in glass houses might as well leave the door unlocked, Joe thought. *Come on in, Abby. See all of me there is to see, in glass rooms with no furnishings.*

By ten o'clock in the morning he was well out of that self-lacerating mood. He had run two miles on the beach, swum in the dawn breakers, treated himself to a monster breakfast of eggs and waffles at the IHOP in town, and shopped for tools and materials he needed at the marine-supply store. A couple of the Bar-ony's gardeners had helped him hose dirt off the *Way-farer*, and he was running a sander on the aft deck, wearing only protective glasses, a pair of ragged denim shorts and deck shoes, when Charlene Thomason showed up. He turned off the sander.

"I saw you working down here when I got up this morning," she said. "From my bedroom windows."

"How are you today, Charlene?" She was wearing work clothes herself: old sneakers with frayed laces, faded paint-streaked jeans, a white T-shirt with an inscription between her nipples in lettering the size of the smallest print on an eye chart. A ratty old Plantation straw hat kept the sun off her pale face.

"Oh, okay," she said with a shrug. "Luke's schooling polo ponies and Abby went for her swim. I could help you." She smiled hopefully. "I can run a sander and use tools. I'm a real good painter too." She shrugged again. "I don't have anything to do."

"Come on up here."

He gave her a hand as she reached the last step of the aft ladder, pulling her over the grab rail. He smelled gin on her breath. Maybe it was her mouthwash of choice after brushing in the morning.

"What's that on your T-shirt?"

Charlene looked down. "Oh, it says, *'If you can read this you're too fucking close.'* " She blinked solemnly at him, a little owlish in the full morning sun on the deck. "It's, you know, it's a joke," she said, as if she couldn't be sure. She looked down at the deck. "You've got a lot done already! Good job. Do you have the stuff to recaulk?"

"Over there by the cockpit. If you can finish this job, I'll get to work mitering some odds and ends of mahogany I picked up this morning."

"We used to go sailing a lot. I loved to sail. I took lessons. I know how to tie good knots. Then I guess Luke just got tired of it. He gets tired of everything, sooner or later. Maybe that'll happen with polo, before he gets kicked in the head."

"Do you worry about that, Charlene?"

"No." She had a way of looking at him, as if she were delivering her life into his hands. Whatever her sexual history, he thought she was probably a good person who had learned that to be good meant taking a lot of lumps. It was knowledge that had made Charlene bitter, but had not turned her mean, a trait that might have meant salvation at the expense of everyone else

who passed through her orbit. Instead she seemed
doomed to drown in a bottle, at the end as blank and
becalmed as a fetus in alcohol; or to become one of
those pallid pathetic nervous wrecks who kept the needle docs in Ferraris. "No, I think he'll come out all
right. He always has."

She was, to his surprise, a tireless worker. She put
on welder's gloves to spare her nails and attacked the
shabby decking, and by two o'clock she had all of it
sanded and the aft deck nearly caulked. Her T-shirt
was transparent with sweat. She went below to change
into a one-piece suit she had brought with her, walked
down the ramp to Pandora's Bay and plunged in. One
of Lillian's girls had appeared with a hamper of sand-
wiches, potato salad and cold drinks. When Charlene
returned from her brief swim, they sat in an oblong of
shade cast to port by the roof of the boat shed and had
lunch.

"It's about all that's keeping my mother alive," she
said.

"What's that, Charlene?"

"The idea of me being in the governor's mansion.
It's like payback time to her, getting even with all the
people who ever slighted her in her life. I don't know.
I can't think that way. You want to know something,
Joe? I've just spent four of the happiest hours of my
life, working with you on this boat. When I thought I
was just going to get up this morning and get drunk
before lunch."

"I'm glad you came by."

"I'm glad *you* came by. Joe, I can't be the governor's
wife. I get—panic attacks when I let myself think about
it."

"It might not be that bad," he said cautiously.

"What I want to do is find a little house of my own,
one that's not in very good shape, and just tear into it
and build it up again, every inch of it, by myself. I really
would be good at that."

"I know."

"But I'm not—not good at living without a man. The idea gives me a panic attack too."

"Charlene—"

"Charly. Would you just think about it? I can be very, very, *very* good for the right guy. I know it."

"Let's don't."

"You can't really be serious about Pamela, though. I mean—for the obvious reason? Look at me, and—look at her."

"It isn't sex, Charly."

"What, then?"

"Fate, or something."

"Oh, yeah." She was hugging herself, rubbing a goose-bumped arm up and down. "Like karma. I never did understand that. I had my horoscope done once. I had planets in all but two of the houses. That's supposed to mean I still have a lot to learn." Her mouth turned down. She rested a cheek on the back of one hand. "It's easier just to do a line, or take another drink, and say fuck it."

"What are you so afraid of, Charly?"

"Him," she murmured, her eyes squeezing shut on tears.

"Why?"

"I can't tell you. Unless you promise to—take care of me. The fate you're talking about? The reason you came here? Well, maybe *I'm* the one, and not Pamela."

Joe didn't say anything. She looked at him reluctantly, as if she expected a scolding.

"But if it's nothing, if *I'm* nothing, just tell me."

"Charly, you make me sad, and unhappy for you."

She took a couple of deep breaths, ridding herself of a dense cloud of despair.

"I guess that means—you like me, or you wouldn't feel anything. Just bored, or whatever."

Joe nodded, and smiled. She hitched up her shoul-

ders, lifted her head, looked at the *Wayfarer* with a romantic eye.

"Luke would probably give her to me, if I asked.
Sailing always made him a little nauseous. You know
what? I didn't get a pre-nup. My mother was *so* furious.
But Luke said, let me see if I can get this right, he said:
'Men of means who sign pre-nuptial agreements are
like kidnappers agreeing to pay a ransom to their hos-
tages.'" Charlene's mouth curled in bewilderment.
"He's always coming up with something like that. You
can't argue with him. That's why I get frustrated? Once
I had him, you know, by the short hairs, I should have
held out for a pre-nup. But I was scared to be alone. I
guess that's always going to be my downfall: scared to
be alone."

By five o'clock that afternoon there wasn't much doubt
that Frosty Clemons had disappeared in Walter Lee's
old Chevy.

Lucas Thomason spent much of the afternoon on
the telephone, talking to the commander of the South
Carolina State Patrol, the Chicora County sheriff and
the chief of police in Nimrod's Chapel. Abby argued
for private investigators. The police weren't going to
work very hard, she said, until there was some evidence
that Frosty had met with foul play.

"Which I very much doubt," Thomason said. "True,
she's gone off somewhere, and she ought to have been
thoughtful enough to get in touch and let Walter Lee,
let you, as her employer, know—"

"She's also my best friend! And I think I'm *her* best
friend. And this is not *like* Frosty."

"Well, you know, there is that one person in her life
who still has the most influence on her, whether anybody, including Frosty herself, cares to admit it. You
know who I'm talking about. Her ex-husband."

"Delmus? They're still married. She never went
through with the divorce proceedings."

"You knew him well, didn't you, Lillian?" Thomason said to the housekeeper, who, along with Joe, was taking supper with the family.

"Yes, sir. My sister-in-law Bertie raise him from when he was four years old."

"He was a devil with women, I've been told."

"That's the truth."

"Where's Delmus at now, Detroit? Do you think if he called, Frosty might drop everything and go back to him?"

"Luke," Abby said, "Frosty has better sense than that! After all the abuse she took from that man . . ."

Thomason was looking at Lillian, with his crimped, eager, pushed-out smile to encourage her opinion. The center of attention, Lillian put down her salad fork and picked up a napkin, touched it to her lips. She looked at Abby in a kindly manner, then glanced at Joe, seated next to Abby, and touched her lips again as if blotting out any excess of emotion.

"I allow," she said, in a voice that was only a tone higher than inaudible, "it ain't a common-sense thing."

"No, it's not," Charlene seconded, not much louder than Lillian.

"What are you all talking about?" Lizzie demanded. "Do you think Frosty went to Detroit and didn't tell anybody?"

"Wouldn't have to be Detroit," Thomason said. "Delmus is a musician. Maybe he's on the road, and gave Frosty a call to meet him somewhere, up or down the coast."

"Frosty is the mother of four-year-old twins," Abby objected. "She wouldn't just go off and leave them."

"She left the girls in Walter Lee's care," Thomason pointed out. "She certainly wouldn't want to say anything to her daddy about Delmus, which would only serve to get Walter Lee riled up. And her sister's over there now. The twins are in good hands. Abby, it hasn't been twenty-four hours yet. I think as soon as Frosty gets her head back on straight, she'll be on the phone crying and full of apologies. So don't you be too hard on her when she does call."

"No, of course I won't, but—I just can't help having bad feelings."

"It's your creative bent, to dramatize these little inconsistencies of human nature. Cut Frosty some slack, and try to be understanding. Meanwhile the police are on the lookout, and they'll probably turn up the car in a motel parking lot, in Myrtle Beach or Hilton Head." He smiled around the table. "It'll all turn out for the best, you'll see. Lizzie, would you mind going to the kitchen to ask if the girls have any more hot biscuits back there?"

THIRTY-FOUR

Abby said she felt like driving, so they took the Suburban van equipped for paraplegics to the Clemons house on Awtry Avenue. It had been months since she was behind the wheel, and she made a few errors in handling on the lightly traveled roads of Chicora Island that had Joe gritting his teeth, but by the time they reached the causeway to Nimrod's Chapel she was more confident, working the hand controls smoothly while steering with her left hand.

When she had parallel-parked without crumpling any fenders she let out her breath and said, "See, I told you I'd get us here."

"The Lord be praised."

"I'm glad to know you're not an atheist," she said tartly.

"Allah be praised as well."

"Are you sweating like that on purpose? I'm a *good* driver."

The streetlights had come on against the dark green

of magnolia trees and the evening sky, which still held
a faint blush of pink. Some shirtless boys were playing
basketball at the end of Awtry Avenue, scuffling and
trash-talking. Abby locked Rolling Thunder down at
the foot of the steps to the porch, and a young assistant
pastor from the AME church set his paper-plate
chicken dinner aside to fetch Walter Lee. He came
from inside the house, which teemed with relatives and
friends, with his suspenders dangling. He wore a clean
white T-shirt with a gold cross on a chain centered over
his breastbone. His gray hair looked teased and he
seemed preternaturally awake, as if he had just walked
through a thunderbolt. He started to sob as soon as he
saw Abby.

"Walter Lee, I want you to stop that," she said, lifting up her arms to him. He hobbled down four steps
and knelt beside the wheelchair.

"I can't help it. I just can't help myself. I know it's
something bad. Why she be gone all this time without
a word to anybody? Oh, sweet Jesus, I know it's
something bad!"

"Have faith in the g-goodness of the Lord, brother
Walter," the assistant pastor said, stripping a leg bone
with his teeth.

Abby held Walter Lee's galled head against her
breast, glancing at the yellow minivan in the carport.
"When did you see her last, Walter Lee?"

"About a quarter to nine last night. She ask to borrow my car, said she had to meet with that Reggie fella
she sing with sometimes at the Sea Turtle Café."

"Reggie? Have you tried to get hold of him?"

"The police. They talk to him, up in Murrell's Inlet.
Say he didn't see her, last night or this morning neither. It's something bad. Nobody can tell me different." He sobbed again, tearlessly; he had cried himself
out.

"We're not going to think those thoughts, Walter
Lee. Frosty will come home. Can you tell me if she was

seeing anybody, you know, from the church?''

"Oh, no, she didn't have no man. There wasn't no man for her, after Delmus."

"Speaking of Delmus—"

Walter Lee sat back on the first step, hands locked between his knees, head downcast and swaying slightly. "I don't know how to get in touch with him."

"Walter Lee, I'm hiring the best detective agency in Detroit to locate Delmus, and find out what he knows about this. Frosty might have been talking to him again."

"All right. All right. I hope it's Delmus. No-account that he be. I hope that's who she gone to."

"You have to be brave, Walter Lee. Frosty knows how to take care of herself."

"Oh, Lorrrddd," he moaned.

"How are the girls?" Abby asked, wanting to distract him.

He reacted slowly to her question, as the light and human warmth their presence provided reached his half-petrified heart.

"Jus' fine. They ain't too worried; but they don't understand why their mama ain't home yet." He wiped his haggard face with a handkerchief, looking first at Abby, then at Joe. "This the worst thing that's ever happened to me. I'm so scared. Look how I'm shaking. I just don't know what to do next." He recoiled from the possibility that nothing could be done, and blinked at her. "Miss Abby. This is so thoughtless of me. Can't I get you a cold drink of something while you sittin' out here?"

"I could do with a Coke," Joe said promptly. "Abby?"

"I guess so," she replied, frowning at him.

"I need to use the bathroom, too, if you don't mind. Walter Lee, could you show me the way?"

"Surely," he said, getting painfully to his feet. "Come in, Doctor."

There were a dozen people, Walter Lee's support group, in the small living room, most of them watching TV while they ate Church's chicken from take-out boxes. A satellite picture of Hurricane Honey was on the tube: swirling rings of color from yellow to the dangerous red of the strongest winds near the center. Honey occupied a very large area of the South Atlantic. According to the TV weatherman, the storm had momentarily paused, as if considering a change of direction while gobbling more energy from the tropic sea. The outer ring of clouds extended nearly to the northernmost Bahama islands. Joe knew there would be winds of at least thirty-five knots on the fringe of Honey, with gusts to fifty knots. At sea winds of that velocity produced fifty-foot waves, with the top eight or nine feet blowing off.

Walter Lee led him down a short hallway past the children's room. They were in their pajamas, watching a Disney animated movie on the VCR, with two older girls baby-sitting. One of the twins began jumping up and down on her bed when she saw her grandfather, calling him.

"This is my room," Walter Lee said, "and cross the hall is Frosty's room. Looks like somebody using the bath right now."

"That's okay. I wanted to talk to you privately."

Walter Lee looked around at him in alarm. "Why?"

Joe hesitated, wanting to be very careful about what he said to Walter Lee.

"I need to talk to Reggie. He may call you. If he does, will you get me a phone number where I can reach him?"

"Why?"

"All I can say is, it's very important."

"Is this—doctor business?"

"Yes, it is."

"And Frosty—Frosty have anything to do with your doctor business?"

"Walter Lee, I saw Frosty yesterday afternoon. I don't know where she is now, or what might have happened to her."

Walter Lee said, with utmost suspicion, a dangerous look in his eyes, "But she *does* have something to do with your doctor business."

"She took an ampule of medication from Dr. Thomason's drug safe and gave it to Reggie for safekeeping. She wanted him to have it analyzed when he goes into the hospital for treatment later this week. I can't wait that long. For Abby's sake, I have to know what that drug is, and right away."

Walter Lee had been shocked into silence. His expression was hell scraped raw as he gripped Joe by the shoulder, almost sending him to his knees.

"Let *go*, Walter Lee!"

"How do you know what Frosty did?"

"She told me. She trusted me. You have to trust me too, Walter Lee."

Walter Lee pressed him against the wall. "Dr. Luke—he knows Frosty stole from him?"

"No. I don't think so."

"You didn't tell him yourself?"

Joe's right arm was going numb from the pressure of Walter Lee's fingers.

"*No.* He's a bad doctor. I wouldn't let him bandage a cut finger, let alone try to take care of a paraplegic. Frosty knows it. She did what she did for Abby's sake. Ease up, *God*, before you break something."

The big man's fingers suddenly had no strength. His hand slipped away. He seemed near to collapsing.

"I *warned* that girl. I told her, 'Frosty, you will bring down misery and suffering on our heads if you don't mind your own business.'" He clawed at the side of his face with worn-down nails, as if the prophesied misery had taken hold there like a skin cancer. He stared at Joe in fear and dismay. "Who are you? What did you come here for?"

Joe rubbed his shoulder, staring into Walter Lee's eyes. "I need for you to help me find Reggie."

"Try the Sea Turtle."

"He's only there Thursday through Saturday nights."

"The police found him okay. Ask them."

"I can't do that. I can't go to the police."

Walter Lee passed a hand across his mouth; suspicion burned in his eyes again.

Before he could say anything, the assistant pastor of the AME church, who had stayed outside with Abby, found them and said with an excited stutter, "C-come quick. Something's ruh-wrong with the lady."

Abby was sitting bolt-upright in her wheelchair when Joe ran out to the porch. She had a white-knuckled grip on the arms of her chair. She was gasping for breath. She turned frightened eyes on Joe.

"I'm—all right. Now. Yeah. All right."

"Abby, what happened?"

She had begun to breathe easier in the moments since he came outside.

"Damnedest thing. I was talking to Reverend Moseby. Then. It was like I. Forgot how to breathe."

"What do you mean?" he said, holding her cold hand.

She started to laugh, perplexed and frightened. "Joe, I mean—I could *not* draw breath! As if a computer suddenly shut down and wouldn't obey my commands." She continued to breathe hard, blinking; she might have been counting each precious draught of air, taking in too much, just in case.

"That computer is in the brain stem, Abby." It scared him to say it.

"But I'm okay now." She looked up at Walter Lee. "Sorry to be such a bother." She began to cry, but protested, "It's okay. I'm not going to lose it, mon. I'm just a little nervous."

"I'm taking you home," Joe said, keeping a lock on his own case of nerves. He also looked at Walter Lee, who appeared to be stunned by Abby's distress. He clenched and unclenched his callused hands, then nodded abruptly, the meaning clear to both of them. Whatever doubts he still had about Joe, he would try to find Reggie.

"Well," she said, as Joe was driving them back to the Barony. "That's life with Abby. I can promise you, it won't be dull. As long as it lasts."

"You're going to be just fine, Abby. My personal guarantee."

"Joe, you look so grim. Smile for me. That's better. Now, listen. We aren't going to tell Luke about this."

"All right."

"It might not happen again. Maybe I psyched myself out in some way."

"Sure."

"You don't have to agree with me; just lie a little more convincingly. Joe, I don't want to go home tonight. The bathroom on the first floor of the beach house was done over for me. I won't be any more trouble, I promise. But I want to be with you."

"That's good. Because I'm never going to be very far away from you, from now on."

THIRTY-FIVE

By midnight Joe was nodding off as they played another hand of rummy in the beach house. He'd lost the last six hands, and more before that.

"Want to quit?" Abby asked him.

"No, I'm okay. Maybe I'll have another cup of Twinings. Cards just don't seem to be coming my way. I'm usually a better player than this."

"You can't beat my luck," she explained, without lording it over him. "It's not a streak. I'm lucky all the time. Did I tell you I won eight out of ten NFL bets Sunday? I ignore the point spread and the weather and who has the best arm and bet my hunches. My bookie owes me four big ones. Luke says if he's governor he'll never approve of a state lottery because I'd win *that* every week."

Joe yawned. "Sometimes you lose. You still owe me ten for the bet we made about one of your characters."

"That's right, I do, and I always pay my debts. But I never carry any money. Frosty'll give it to you out of petty—'' She looked away, her smile changing to a grimace. After a few moments she said, ''Do you think I should call again?''

''Getting late, Abby. Walter Lee has the number here.''

''Joe, c'mere?''

He stretched, back muscles a little sore from the hours he'd put in on the *Wayfarer*.

''Do you want me to move you?'' he asked, facing Abby, his hands on the padded arms of Rolling Thunder.

''Yes. Not just yet. Look me in the eye, now. Joe, you're half out of it and there is no way you can outlast an insomniac, particularly one who has her mind made up that she better not ever go to sleep again.''

''Abby, listen to me. It's only a little over an hour to Charleston.''

''I know that. And I said to give me some space while I—''

''You're not being sensible.''

''I don't care! You have no idea how much I hate hospitals. And they won't let *you* take care of me there.''

''I'm not qualified even to consult.''

She began breathing too rapidly again; he put a hand on her cheek to soothe her. She had on a sweater and there was a stadium blanket across her lap, but still she felt much too cold.

''*Qualified*, bullshit, you're the one I want near me, doesn't that count for anything? If I'm gonna die I just want to be home when it happens!''

''But you're not going to die.''

''Then don't make me think about it. Could we just lie down and hold each other? That's what I want most. I want to watch you sleeping. And if anything—goes wrong, I'll pinch you and wake you up.'' She made the best of a smile that still looked tortured. ''I mean, if I need CPR, it's better if I'm already lying down, isn't it?"

"That's one of the dumbest things I've ever heard. Abby, I'm sorry. I'm tired and you're not rational and I think I'd better call Luke."

She grabbed his wrist. "You said you weren't going to let me out of your sight from now on! I know you didn't mean forever, but just tonight, *tonight*, please."

Her expression was tough and obstinate, but the hysteria that gave her strength was about to spew from the pressure cooker of her emotions. He sighed and closed his eyes and leaned his forehead against hers, willing her to be calm.

"Okay. Tonight is six hours long. I'll catch some sleep, at dawn we're on our way, and you don't have any more to say about it. Deal?"

"I'll think it over."

"Comes the dawn, I'm loading you into the van whether you like it or not."

"I'll scream all the way. We'll have state troopers strung out behind us for a mile. Roadblocks. They'll lock you up for kidnapping. Don't think I won't press charges."

He looked fierce without being angry. "You can't bully me, Abby, like you do the rest of the family."

"We'll see," she said confidently, her cheeks scarlet from the verbal punch-out.

Joe brought two mattresses from the second floor while Abby was using the downstairs bathroom. He spread sheets and added blankets. When Rolling Thunder reappeared Abby looked approvingly at the arrangements, and looked at Joe. She was wearing a white terry bathrobe with blue trim over a Duke T-shirt and what she called her "puddle pants."

He lifted her from the wheelchair and positioned her on her right side, a small pillow for her head, pillows at other pressure points. She didn't give directions. He was gentle and a little awkward, as he might be with an infant. He should have children, she thought. He would be good with children. She wondered why some woman hadn't already marched him to the altar, at gunpoint if necessary. Her good fortune that it hadn't happened.

Joe silently covered Abby with a blanket and lay down facing her, close enough to feel her breath, lightly scented with mint toothpaste, on his face. She asked him for a hand to hold. His eyes closed in thirty seconds.

"See? I always win," Abby murmured.

His face was everything to her, more fascinating than the ancient suns that filled the black of night. If it came to that, in the very near future, she wanted to take his image with her, complete in every detail, for all eternity. She believed in some sort of continuation, a resting place for the soul out of the cumbersome body, like a tree in a meadow where no storms come. *Hopkins?* A long time since she had read the good English poets. Too involved in her own work, which now did not seem of great importance. She had forgotten how to breathe; it would happen again. Her lips were often cold, but they were tingling now: a recurring symptom of something-or-other. Assassins of the heart were everywhere, drifting homeward in the final season of her blood. She felt a heavy, serpentlike stirring of terror that she suppressed by kissing his hand. The only happiness greater than this would be to touch his naked body, to caress him, to be caressed in return.

His lips had parted in sleep. She watched a slowly swelling bubble of saliva at one corner of his finely chiseled mouth, where the chisel had slipped and left an errant mark. *All men possess in their bodies a poison which acts upon serpents; and the human saliva, it is said, makes them take flight as though they had been touched with boiling water.* The bubble burst when she nudged it with her little finger. She put the finger in her mouth and sucked. A little saliva for the serpent. Abby left the finger there, nursing. She listened to the sound of the sea. She was barely aware of her slowed and regular breathing, of her own eyes closing contentedly. "Love you," she whispered. "G'night."

Paul Huskisson was an athletic boy of twenty-two, in his first year of law school at the University of South Carolina. His hair, already beginning to recede, was the color of the blush on a peach. He had shy brown eyes but the sturdy outthrust chin of a born competitor.

The night they were both grievously injured, he was home from Columbia for the weekend, Abby had not yet left to begin her second year at the University of Virginia. The Huskisson house on Bay Street in Beaufort's Historic District was being repainted, and the rest of his family was at their summer house on Hunting Island. Paul had taken a room at the Holiday Inn. They had agreed, without actually having a discussion about it, that she was going to spend the night with him there.

A storm was threatening when they left the garden party at the home of Abby's best friend from high school, soon to be a bride. It was not quite dark, the sky kingfisher blue, and in the west, solitary, the evening star. The storm was coming from the other direction, off St. Helena's Sound. Thunderheads solid as cathedrals, the peaks and domes still lighted by the sun, seething gold and royal purple. The wind was picking up along Pinckney Street, also part of the Historic District, beginning to move the dense crowns of old liveoaks. The air beneath the trees was heavier, summery, flavored with jasmine and roses and the breathy murk of the nearby river. Lightning struck from the darkest clouds like fangs in a snake pit. The amplitude of the thunder suggested that there was enough time for them to walk seven blocks to the Holiday Inn without getting drenched in a sweeping down-pour.

Abby's mood couldn't be called ambivalent. So many different moods flashed through her like the distant lightning: she was giddy and apprehensive, eager to make love but not certain she wouldn't chicken out or otherwise spoil it for him; stunned by the responsibility of pleasing Paul while assuming a commitment that couldn't be fulfilled for at least two years. She had drunk champagne at the party, and eaten crab cakes. Already she had a rumbling stomach. He had kissed her breasts on several occasions, but what would it be like, fully naked in bed with him? The thought gave her goose bumps, and put heat in her groin. She sensed just how concerned *he* was. Maybe it was the wrong night, maybe they weren't fully ready for each other, but it was going to *happen.*

They were walking down the middle of the street, moving to the side whenever a car came by. Some high-school kids in a flamed, Hawaiian-orchid street rod cruised by and made semi-gross remarks which she almost answered with the finger. But two of them crammed into the topless snarling coupe were the younger brothers of Abby's friend Diane Persons. They knew not to go too far with their adolescent taunting. The wind began to swoosh through the big trees as they approached King Street. Abby and Paul were talking about the behavior of friends at the party: who was drinking too much, which bridesmaids-to-be had developed crushes on the groom's attendants. They held damp hands, bumping together companionably as they walked. Abby wore a chiffon party dress and a hat with a big brim. Her straw handbag, with her nightgown and other essentials tucked away in the bottom, was in her free hand. She accused Paul of directing admiring glances at a demure dark beauty who had earned a colossal reputation at Beaufort High. Three broken engagements already, and she hadn't given back any of the rings. In the old days, Abby said judgmentally, she would have poisoned husbands for a living.

The closer they came to the Holiday Inn, the clumsier and more incompetent Abby felt. She stepped on Paul's foot, almost tripping herself. Her cheeks burned. Paul smiled and wanted to smell her breath. Abby pushed him away, not entirely a good-natured push.

The wind gusted and her big hat blew off. She whirled in exasperation. The hat had sailed against a wrought-iron fence in front of the Timyard house.

Abby looked around; Paul was laughing, making no attempt to retrieve her hat for her. Don't be a goof, she said furiously. The wind was turning her hair into a mare's nest. Would you get my hat for me, please? He shook his head. I want to see if you can walk that far in a straight line, he said. I am not drunk, she said. How did this get started, anyway? You said I wasn't faithful to you, Paul answered, still smiling, but glumly.

There was a moment when they looked at each other and it seemed as if they might have a real quarrel brewing and it would be all over with them before it had truly begun.

Her heart cringed at the thought; no, not what she wanted. She loved him, she loved him. Time to give in. Abby walked deliberately to the fence, where her beribboned hat with the wide brim trembled, pinned there by the wind. She heard the rumble of a powerful engine behind her, coming out of nowhere, and almost looked around; but she knew it was Jimmy Persons in his show-off car again, and she wasn't going to give any of them the satisfaction of knowing they were annoying her.

The hat crept up the fence and blew over the iron spikes before she could get to it. A clap of thunder almost obscured the noise of the car's engine, and the sound of Paul's laughter at her predicament. God damn that stupid hat, on its way to the lily pond in the side yard. Now what was she supposed to do?

She stood with hands on hips by the six-foot-high
fence, annoyed by nearly everything, but particularly
by the accelerating growl of the engine in the car coming up the street.

And, inspired by a sense of foreboding—Jimmy was
going too fast on that narrow street, didn't he have
better sense?—she started to turn her head.

Out of the corner of her eye she saw Paul flying
toward her from the front of a black truck with a long,
high hood and no headlights showing. There was no
sound of impact. It was as if he had taken a running
start and gone off a springboard and had his arms outstretched to tackle her. And just as all this registered
and her muscles began to tense the top of his skull hit
her like a rusty cannonball in the lower back, lifted her
off her feet and out of her lemon-yellow Capezios,
drove her into the fence with such force both collarbones were shattered and her left shoulder was broken.
Her head was torn open at the hairline by one of the
blunt black spikes that crowned the fence, and her
skull was fractured.

In spite of Abby's injuries, it was a long time before
she lost consciousness. And she wasn't aware, until the
medics arrived, that she was on her knees with Paul's
body lying across her lower legs, a weight that held her
upright and slightly angled against the fence. By then
rain was beating down but still there was so much
blood in her eyes she could only see blurs of lights and
moving shadows. She had swallowed blood from her
scalp laceration, her lips were glued and her tongue
was thick with it. She had stopped screaming but she
wanted to scream, once more, so loudly that Paul
would have to hear her, and wake up, *wake up* . . . !

When Joe sat up with a start, he saw that Abby was no
longer on the mattresses with him.

Rolling Thunder was right there, its small Confederate flag drooping, but Abby wasn't in her wheelchair either.

He got up slowly, looking around.

The first floor of the beach house was, except for the bathroom, open space, with no partitions between the living room and the kitchen and dining area. The bathroom door stood open. Moonlight through the salt-glazed porch windows illuminated every corner. Abby was gone.

Joe rubbed the sleep-blur from his eyes. Panic touched his breastbone like a claw.

"Abby!"

Not that he expected a response; the house felt empty to him. He looked at the front door. It had been closed, but not locked. Now it was half open.

He cupped a hand around the dial of his wrist watch to read the time. Twenty after two. The hair on his forearm rose as if he had been magnetized. She had dragged herself outside, somehow without waking him, as quiet and methodical as a turtle, dragged herself across the porch and down to the waves of the sea.

Barefoot, Joe ran out of the beach house, his heart firing like a shotgun at the full moon.

Down to the sea, but not in. Seventy yards from the house Abby lay on her back at the foam line of the retreating tide, white-robed, like a sleeping pilgrim. One knee drawn up. Her left hand flung out, as if she had fallen a long way out of the sky to drift downward, weightlessly, the last few crucial feet, landing with no discernible impact.

He couldn't be sure that she wasn't dead until he bent over her, lifting her head and drenched hair from the depression made by the swirling shallow waters around her. Sand in her left ear, grains of sand on her blue lips. The outstretched left hand and forearm were half-buried. A small yellow crab scuttled out of a fold of her soggy robe. Her nipples beneath the transparent T-shirt were like the pupils of dilated eyes.

Her heart was beating; she breathed through parted lips. He shook her and she gasped, swallowed hard.

"Paul."

"Abby, it's Joe."

He brushed the sand from her lips. She moved her head, wincing, and looked up at him. The blankness of the moon.

"Wha—"

The sea shuffling in and out. A chill went through her upper body. Her teeth began to chatter.

"Where—?"

"You're on the beach. I'm taking you back to the house."

She was a load to lift, from her dead cold weight and the added weight of the soaked terry robe. Kneeling, he stripped it off her. Half-naked, she shuddered violently again, her gaze wandering. What had taken her to the edge of the sea? Maybe she'd been looking for her black cat bone.

"S-saw it," she said, with a convulsive jerk of her head, the words spurting out of her like something half-swallowed. "Was here."

Joe worked the wet T-shirt off her body, exchanging it for the long-sleeved striped rugby shirt he'd been wearing.

"Saw what?"

"The truck. H-hit Paul. Was here. Oh, God! Him t-too."

"Who, Abby?"

"The driver. He was h-here." She raised her right hand, pointed limply. "Standing over there. W-watching me. That's w-when I f-fell down."

"You did what?"

"F-f-f—"

"You mean you were standing up?"

"Uh-huh."

"Abby, you were dreaming."

"N-no. I w-w-walked."

"From the house?"

"D-don't know—how f-f-far."

Joe looked at the packed sand nearby, from which the tide had receded. Even by moonlight he could make out the imprint of quarter-inch-deep footprints, intaglios from her small bare feet.

"What the hell?"

"So c-c-cold," she complained. "Help me."

Joe picked Abby up in his arms, still looking at the small footprints. There was no strength in the arm that hung around his neck, and although she was racked by shudders her legs were immobile. In the drier sand above the high-tide line it was not possible to distinguish other footprints. Nor could he locate what would have been the obvious trail made by her efforts in dragging half of her body across the beach.

The mystery of it had him trembling too, his own chill enhanced by the cold weight he carried back to the beach house, staggering at every other step in the deep sand on the sloping beach.

Through the sounds of his own heavy breathing he heard something coming out of sight on the narrow road on the other side of the dune and behind the house, its peaked roof a shade darker than the night-time gray of the moon-luminous sky. The upper windows that faced the sea had a pearly sheen. So did the eyes of Pamela Abelard, gazing up at him with a drowned lack of expression.

"Poor P-Paul," she said. "P-Paul is dead."

He wanted to keep her talking. "You said a truck hit Paul. What kind of truck was it?"

"Old pickup. Black. The same one I saw . . . tonight. It came back. Why?"

At the top of the dune, near the boardwalk and long wheelchair ramp, the lights of another truck bouncing along the track from the direction of the Barony flashed in his eyes: half a dozen lights, including four mounted above the cab of the truck. He turned away.

The truck stopped beside his rented Jeep. Joe started up the ramp to the house.

"No! Bring her to me!" Lucas Thomason called.

Joe stopped; Abby stirred in his arms.

"Is that Luke?" she asked weakly.

"Yes."

"Why . . . is he here?"

"I don't know. I didn't call him."

Thomason ran up the boardwalk, black against the explosive glare of truck lights.

"What happened? Is she all right?" He came up to them, the laces of his untied sneakers flopping. His thinning hair was feathery, uncombed, his triangular eyes still puffy from sleep. He put a hand on the side of Abby's throat, staring at her face.

"Luke," she said, "d-don't be mad." Her teeth chattered again.

"Hypothermia," he said. "Let me have her, and get a blanket from the house. Bring it to the truck."

Joe handed Abby over to him and jogged into the house. He pulled the blanket off the makeshift bed and took it down to the road. Abby was slumped on the passenger side of the cab, chattering as if she were seated on a block of ice, some saliva on her lower lip. Her expression was dangerously dull. She tried to form words. He wrapped her securely in the blanket as Thomason got in behind the wheel of the Dodge truck.

"How long was she in the water?" he asked Joe.

"I don't know. I was asleep."

"Asleep? How in hell did she get down to the beach?"

"She says she walked."

Thomason gave him a look of scornful antagonism.

"That's not very funny. I won't be needing your help any more tonight."

"She belongs in a hospital," Joe said.

"I'll decide that."

"Doctor, you could lose Abby."

"Thanks to your complete lack of judgment and negligence in caring for her. Is it too much to hope I won't be seeing you again? Good night, Dr. Bryce."

Abby stuttered something unintelligible. Her eyes appealed to Joe.

Thomason hit the gas and backed up, wheels spinning, throwing out a torrent of sand and shell. Joe had to turn away to shield his eyes; his naked back stung from bits of sharp shell. The Dodge truck headed back to the Barony.

Joe watched it go, still trembling, but fiery inside from anger and the knowledge that in truth he had not done a very good job of taking care of Abby. In spite of the fact that something extraordinary seemed to have happened to her. He could only hope that she would get through the rest of the night with Thomason at her side. In four or five hours, when he'd had time to think and to explore the beach at sunrise, it would be his turn.

In the beach house he boiled water for tea on the stove, turned on the television. Hurricane Honey had moved north instead of hitting Nassau, and now was two hundred fifty miles southwest of Bermuda. The red eye of the satellite imager, the center of the storm now rated as Category Three, was irregular, shaped very much like the hourglass on the underside of a black widow spider deep in its web.

THIRTY-SIX

At eight-thirty, Joe found Lucas Thomason taking breakfast on the veranda of the Barony with Spence Labèque, his campaign manager. Spence had the sleeves of his dress shirt rolled up, an opened attaché case on a wrought-iron chair beside him.

After a preliminary scowl Thomason waved in Joe's direction.

"Mornin', Dr. Bryce. Kindly allow us a few minutes here to clear up our business. Annabeth, give the doctor some juice and coffee."

The chubby brown girl presiding over a serving cart smiled at Joe and poured grapefruit juice for him. He retired to a bench at the other end of the veranda, looking out over the still-misty garden to the glittery calm of Pandora's Bay. Any westerly move by Honey in her huge web of swirling clouds would change the complexion of the day quickly, but for now it was tranquil and sunny, with only the slightest hint of a chill in the morning air.

Thomason was in a pettish mood, his voice rising and falling according to the aggravation that Spence Labèque's opinions or arguments visited upon him. A couple of times he rattled dishes on the half-inch glass tabletop with a pounding fist.

"I *know* he's a war hero; you can't go to any function in this state without his Goddamned medals poking you in the eye! But he's also a snake in the grass. Personally I don't trust any man who sings his own praises as seriously as if they were the national anthem."

A little later he disparaged another possible candidate for lieutenant governor by saying, "He's nothing but a pissant version of Jimmy Carter. There is no success for the humble, Spence. If there is, they don't deserve it."

Presently Lebèque gathered up his papers and took his leave with a strained smile at Joe. Thomason remained hunched over the table wearing reading glasses and leafing through a speech in a blue binder until suddenly he looked up and around at his other guest. He gestured for Joe to join him, scratched his already-perspiring head where his hair was thinnest and said, "More coffee for both of us, Annabeth."

Joe took a seat opposite Thomason.

"Good morning."

"Good morning. Any of that corned beef hash left, Annabeth?"

"Yes, sir."

"Give some to Joe. How do you like your eggs, Doctor?"

"Easy over."

Annabeth went off to the kitchen. Thomason took off his half glasses and put them aside.

"Sorry about my temper last night. I was more or less snatched out of a sound night's sleep."

"Did he call you?"

Thomason looked hard at him. "Did *who* call me?"

"Abby said something to me about a man being on

the beach with her. She didn't describe him. This morning I found some boot prints—about a size twelve, approximately where she said he'd been standing.''

Thomason shook his head in annoyance.

"Nobody called me, sir. When I say I was snatched from sleep, it was a nightmare that did it. A nightmare in which Abby lay dying. Very real to me. I'm not usually afflicted with nightmares. So I got up and went looking for her.''

"How did you know—"

"I'm not a fool, Doctor. I knew she had to be at the beach house.''

Joe nodded. "I have a lot to tell you. How is Abby this morning?''

"She was asleep, thirty minutes ago. Exhausted, but I think she'll be all right, if her spine doesn't flare up.''

"I'd like to see her when she's awake.''

"Don't think that's the ticket, Joe. She was in a highly agitated state a few hours ago. What I want for her now is bed rest, and *no* visitors. I even chased Lizzie out of her room. Lillian will sit with her today, call me if I'm needed.''

"I want to say again that in my opinion Abby should be in a hospital.''

"I wish you would believe me,'' Thomason said earnestly, with no malice, "that hospitalization would not be in her best interests. I know that she talks a good game, keeping up her spirits, but the truth is that Abby is easily frightened. She doesn't cope well away from her home.''

"She had a dream of her own, about the accident. I think the experience was so intense, so harrowing, that in a fugue state she got up from my side last night and walked seventy yards to the edge of the ocean. It's the only way she could have gotten there, unless someone came into the house and carried her out. But Abby also thinks she walked.''

"I'm really astonished to hear you say something like that, because it is clearly a medical impossibility. She has not stood erect without assistance or taken a step for thirteen years."

"Has Abby ever said anything to you about forgetting how to breathe?"

Thomason looked at a yellowjacket that had ventured close to the table.

"I don't understand what you mean by—"

"Her words. We were at the Clemons house last night. Abby was on the walk in front of the porch. I went inside with Walter Lee for a couple of minutes. A preacher from the neighborhood church she was talking to alerted us. Abby said she hadn't been able to draw a breath for—it might have been half a minute. She said it was just as if she forgot how breathing worked."

Thomason, without comment, fixed his eyes on Annabeth, who had emerged from the kitchen with a tray and covered dishes on it.

"Abby was also complaining about a tingling of her lips. She says that's been going on for some time."

Thomason dismissed this information with a slight wave of the hand.

"There are so many symptoms, I couldn't relate them all. Some real, some probably imaginary. Not that Abby's a hypochondriac, you understand. Left to her own devices, she handles her disability very well." His triangular eyes contracted in quilted folds until there was only a gleam of a gaze, diamond-hard. After Annabeth served them and left them alone, he said, "Have you tried to have sex with Abby? That was the purpose of her being out there with you last night, wasn't it?"

"No."

"*No* to having sex?"

"I don't see any reason why I should answer that, or what it has to do with our major concern."

"Her lips get a little blue, they tingle, sometimes she can't get her breath. Hysterical symptoms. Want to know what I think? She doesn't know how to deal with you. Her emotions getting all stirred up, the, uh, sexual excitement. Abby has her routine, you understand, that she's accustomed to, that is both beneficial and stabilizing. You come along, her—let's say, her *concentration* is shattered; all right, let's also say she's convinced she's in love. There goes her stability. So she's sleeping with you, having all kinds of disturbing dreams, crawling out to the beach—"

"I didn't see any evidence of that at all."

"You never saw Abby on her feet, did you?"

"No."

"Then it didn't happen. It *did not happen.* Pure and simple."

Thomason reached for a toothpick in a glass container, and, holding his left hand to cover his mouth, picked at food impacted between back teeth with the other hand. A sudden gust of wind lifted a linen napkin from the table and blew it across the veranda. Then the air was calm again. Joe watched his untouched coffee cool. Thomason hunched his shoulders and looked thoughtfully east, toward Pandora's Bay and the ocean beyond.

"What I believe, that storm out there's gonna turn itself around and bust us in the chops a couple of days from now."

"It might."

Thomason had begun to parcel out little silences like a miser counting silver from his purse.

Eventually he said, "Charlene tells me the two of you have been working on *Wayfarer.* Reckon I'm at fault for letting her fall into such a sorry condition. Thanks for your efforts."

"Thanks for your hospitality."

More silence. Another little puff of wind, seemingly out of nowhere. A small yellow-breasted bird was blown over the veranda wall and veered away from where they sat.

"Yes, sir, the winds of change are picking up. November of next year I expect to be a very powerful man in the sovereign state of South Carolina. Don't mean to brag, but I don't think there's a single thing that can stop me."

"Congratulations," Joe said. He uncovered some warm raisin toast and buttered half a slice, although he had a knot in his stomach he didn't want to add to.

"Can't stop the wind from blowing, can't stop the way a man and a woman feel for each other."

"No, you can't."

Thomason looked at Joe over his joined hands.

"You feel for Abby the way she feels for you, Joe?"

"Yes, I do."

Thomason breathed out as if from something intolerably heavy pushing against his chest.

"Well. I told Abby I never would say a word against you. I meant that."

"Thank you."

"But I never made any guarantees about your personal safety, should you hurt her in any way."

"Dr. Thomason?"

"Sir."

"You don't have to convince me that you're a cutthroat son of a bitch. I knew it the first time I laid eyes on you."

Thomason smiled in that curious, injured way of his.

"Having reached this point of understanding in our relationship, I don't suppose I need offer you money in order to leave us to the peace we ordinarily enjoy."

"*Abby's* money? Huh-uh."

"I sincerely want to believe your integrity has spoken for you. If not, it's wise to remember that greed is the little bit of arsenic in one's daily bread."

Joe had had his fill of demeaning looks and barbed epigrams. "When can I see Abby?"

Thomason leaned back in his chair, yawning, hands clasped behind his head, not looking at Joe, not looking at him as if he'd never so much as heard his name, or knew that he existed. It was a chilling display of utter contempt by a man without fear, pious toward his every fault, strong in his sinecure. Joe's anger simmered, but he was cautious. The most plausible men, those with no apparent ragged edges or inconsistencies of personality, had to be watched as closely as you would watch a wasp's nest slowly building under the eaves of your house.

"Oh, I expect long about four o'clock this afternoon she should have her nap out."

Charlene was already at work on the *Wayfarer*, her blond hair in two milkmaid braids and partly covered by a Sherwin-Williams painter's cap as she applied primer to the sections of mahogany hull Joe had replaced yesterday.

"I wasn't sure you were going to come," she said with a couple of quick looks, like stones skipped across the surface of a pond, to assess his mood. "So I got an early start. My aerobics class starts at eleven. If I don't stick with my aerobics, my buns and my morale go all to hell." She stopped painting and looked hard at her brush. "I think I need to trim this again. It's my favorite brush, but it's starting to shed." She stuck out her lower lip and blew at a nearly invisible strand of platinum hair that was loose and annoying her. "I heard there was a big commotion with Pamela early this morning. Is she sick?"

"Nothing too serious," Joe said.

"Luke sure was in a bad mood when I saw him."

"He still is."

She shrugged. "I just try to stay out of his way. *If* I see it coming. With Luke, you don't always see it coming."

"How long have you been married, Charly?"

She stepped back and looked critically at the work she was doing. "Seven blissful years." She took a cutting tool from a loop of her painter's coveralls, advanced the razor blade a fraction and set to work trimming stray bristles from one side of the inch-wide paintbrush.

"Did you hear him get up in the middle of the night?"

"Luke got up? I guess not. I was in my own room."

"You didn't hear the phone ring?"

"My phone? No. Luke has a couple of different lines in his room. I don't even know what the numbers are. He doesn't think I need to know." She raised her eyes. "Why did you ask that?"

"I think someone called him about two, two-fifteen this morning to tell him that Abby was at the beach house with me."

Charlene's eyes widened a little. "She was?"

"I've been trying to persuade her to check into a hospital, Charly."

"You just said it wasn't too serious."

"The fact is I don't know."

Charlene's cutting tool slipped and she winced, dropping the paintbrush. She looked at the damage to her left thumb. "Damn! Cut into the nail." She held out the thumb to him. A drop of blood had formed, matching the shade of her nail polish.

He held her hand and blotted at the blood with a clean handkerchief. The cut was minor. He pressed gently to stop the bleeding. Charlene stared at him.

"I don't usually remember my dreams," she said. "But last night I dreamed we were together, in one of those hot-air balloons. Sailing through the sky, like, a hundred miles above the earth. It was so peaceful. We sailed through some really beautiful clouds. Then you were outside the, what do you call it, the basket, your arms outstretched, floating right alongside the balloon. But just out of reach. I tried to pull you in. But you said, 'No, it's easy, you can do it.' I wouldn't, though. I couldn't climb out of the basket. I was too afraid of falling. And gradually you got farther and farther away. That's all there was to it. It was really a lovely, peaceful dream, except for my being afraid at the end.''

Charlene unwrapped her thumb gingerly and looked at it. "Stings a little," she murmured. She held him tightly and bowed her head over their joined hands.

"I heard voices after I woke up," she said. "Below my windows, on the veranda. Luke was with someone. I could hear them talking, but I don't know what they were saying."

"How did he sound?"

"He wasn't angry or anything. It was just a discussion. Didn't last long. Luke thanked the other man. Then he said, 'Good night, Mr. Phipps.' And a little after that, I heard Luke's truck."

"Mr. Phipps?"

"I'm sure that's what Luke called him."

"Do you know who he is?"

"No. I've never met anybody with that name, and I'm good about remembering names, you have to know every single girl by name at the pageants, or they think you're a stuck-up cunt."

Charlene raised his hand to her lips and gently bit a knuckle.

"I saw you looking at me yesterday, you know, when my T-shirt was all wet."

"I probably was. You're hard not to look at, Charly." He spoke truthfully, knowing all the time he had pushed the wrong button, as if he were in an elevator destined to crash.

Her face opened to him like the face of a derelict, thieving child.

"Joe, I'm all loose inside, I feel like I haven't had a man for ten years. I cleaned up down below before you came, opened all the portlights. Can't we just go down, go down, and pull the hatch closed after us, and I'll make love to you?''

She bit her knuckle harder and breathed deeply. He didn't try to pull his hand away He felt desolate, yet responsive. Charlene came closer in her baggy coveralls, pressing against him, pressing his shoulders against the curved hull of the *Wayfarer*. Then her mouth covered his. Her kiss was greedy, a fiend of appetite; she bolted him like a dog at its dish.

When they both had to pause for breath Joe looked away from her half-closed eyes and saw Abby in Rolling Thunder, stopped fifty feet away from the boat shed. He put a hand on one of Charlene's thick braids and tugged, and she turned her head.

There were tears on Abby's face, little crystal drops in the sun. but she said in a clear, precise tone of voice, "The State Police found Frosty's body two hours ago. Would you mind very much driving me into town?''

THIRTY-SEVEN

Abby rattled ahead of him in Rolling Thunder; Joe walked behind. She went recklessly fast, as fast as the four-speed motor would take her, along the serpentine brick paths, over the mossy speed bumps, wiping at her eyes with her free hand, so many tears—as if it were raining, but only around her face, within her solitary soul. Through the garden and around the house to the motor court she raced; he felt as if he were chasing her. Charlene had stayed behind, like a pillar of salt.

Next to the blue minivan Abby stopped with a suddenness that tipped her forward. Then she collapsed, huddling in the chair, racked and coughing up her grief.

When she could speak she said, not looking at him, "I thought you cared about me."

"I do care."

"Charlene—"

"I was a little slow to duck, that's all."

"Then—"

"All Charlene wants is a way out of here, Abby."

"You must have encouraged her."

"I tried to keep it friendly. It probably came across as encouragement."

Her breath escaped her like bubbles breaking from the gaseous depths of still water.

"Abby, I had my feet on the ground, and I wasn't about to lose my head."

"I know how Charlene is. But I never thought—I don't *want* to think about it now. Let's go. Please. I have to get this over with."

"Where's Luke?"

"In his car, the Cadillac. He has a meeting somewhere. His cellular was busy, I couldn't raise him."

"Are you sure you're up to this?"

"They wouldn't tell me anything on the phone. I have to know."

The small lobby of the one-story State Police post in Nimrod's Chapel was filled with dark faces around Walter Lee, who sat slumped to overflowing in a molded plastic chair against a concrete block wall. He moaned as two women took turns sponging his face with the handkerchiefs they were wetting down in a drinking fountain.

"I want to see Frosty. Where they taken my baby?"

Members of his support group backed away when Abby rolled slowly toward him in her wheelchair. She picked up one of Walter Lee's hands from his lap and held it against her cheek. His pugilist's battered eyes opened redly.

"Killed her, Miss Abby! Broke her neck and stuffed her in the trunk of my car. Who knows what else they done to her before?"

"Oh, Walter Lee."

He roused himself from the torpor of grief and began to shout.

"Who can tell me? Ain't there nobody here can tell me who killed my baby?"

A uniformed black woman and a plainclothes detective wearing a blue-striped dress shirt with a collar that was one size too small came out of an office nearby; the uniform introduced herself to Walter Lee, who was rolling his head from side to side in his agony.

"I'm Sergeant Oney Boston, and this is Lieutenant Esco Rich from the state Law Enforcement Division? You have our deepest sympathy. I wonder if we could—"

"Where's Frosty? Where you all taken her?"

"She's at Coleridge and Laster funeral home, Mr. Clemons."

Walter Lee trembled, his bloodknot eyes standing out in his head.

"Oh, God! They gonna have to cut her up in that place?"

"Mr. Clemons, I think you might be more comfortable inside, and we need to ask you a few questions."

Abby let go of his hand.

"Go on, Walter Lee," she said quietly. "Help them find who did this."

"My head. My head just splitting wide open."

"I'll get you some aspirin," Sergeant Boston said. "And we won't keep you long."

"Where did you find her?" Abby asked.

Rich looked at her politely and said nothing.

"I'm Pamela Abelard," she said sharply. "Frosty has worked for me for the past six years."

"The novelist?" Rich said. "My wife sure does admire you. She has all of your books."

"Could you answer my question, please?"

"Yes, ma'am. The car was parked off Japonica Island Road, with several other cars that are usually left there; the people who live on Japonica Island take their boats back and forth across the inlet, there's no bridge or ferry—"

"I know. How long was the car there?"

"We're looking into that now."

"Do you think that's where it happened, where she was murdered?"

"No, we don't. The window on the driver's side was smashed, completely destroyed. There was glass inside the car, but not on the ground outside." Lieutenant Rich glanced from Abby to Joe, who was standing behind Rolling Thunder. Joe frowned slightly and said nothing that might enhance the cop's curiosity.

A couple of relatives, murmuring consolations and encouragement, got Walter Lee on his feet and helped him walk the short distance to the office.

The lieutenant said to Abby, "If it would be all right, I'd also like to talk to you this morning."

She nodded tautly. "Yes. I'm feeling a little woozy right now. I need to go out for some air."

"Certainly, Ms. Abelard." He nodded to Joe, and followed Walter Lee into the office.

Outside Abby paused at the end of the walkway to the building and put her sunglasses on. Her hands were shaking.

"I think I need strong coffee."

"There's a diner down the street."

"Yeah, Donehoo's. It's okay. Could you give me a push?"

"Sure."

Abby had nothing else to say until they were in the diner. She declined to order anything except coffee, then sat forlornly turning a paper napkin into little squares as ragged as her nerves.

"You hear about it happening. It must happen every day. Women are kidnapped from supermarket parking lots and murdered beside ATMs. But Frosty—she's—you don't know her, but she would have put up a fight. Bitten and scratched and yelled like hell. So—I just don't think she was attacked. She must have known who it was, let him get close and then— And if it was Delmus—"

"Her husband? They'll track him down in a hurry."

"I really can't believe it *was* Delmus. Frosty started working for me right after she married him. I met Delmus a couple of times. I liked him okay, although it was obvious he was a lech. Even Charlene complained about him. And that's, what, calling the kettle—"

The mention of Charlene caused her expression to change. She looked stonily at Joe.

"I wonder what Charlene knows about you that I don't know."

"I didn't come on to her, Abby."

Her shoulders fell. She shook her head, woebegone; her loose-fitting sunglasses dropped into her lap.

"I don't think I've misjudged you. And I don't mean to be accusatory. Luke gave me something last night, maybe it was Valium; can't shake it. I think I bit my tongue. One shock after another, and the day's not half-gone." She stared at him, the sun through the window nearest them like needles in her watering eyes. "Where's my little dragonfly? Where's the good luck I'm supposed to have? I'm not talking about money-luck. Maybe that's nothing but a curse after all." She revived herself with a thought that made her smile. "Hey, I know what to do."

"About what, Abby?"

"I need to get a dragonfly tattoo. Like your mother had, on her shoulder? Then it can't fly away, ever."

"My mother was—"

"We'll both get one!" she said. This fancy, the momentary relief from the steel press of reality, enlivened her. "What do you say, mon? You're not chicken to get a little tattoo, are you?"

"Not me," he said, smiling.

"There's a couple of these tattoo artists, the best one's on Ocean Drive in North Myrtle Beach. At least she's there during the summer. Damn, what a great idea!"

Abby was diverted again, by the arrival of a noisy truck in front of the diner.

"There's Reggie!"

Joe saw the familiar muleskinner's hat and a little of Reggie, possibly seated in his own wheelchair in the bed of the five-ton truck, surrounded by numerous hand-carved waterfowl with graceful arching necks that seemed bound for a flea market somewhere. The truck bed had a canvas shade like a Bimini awning over it.

With the aid of a power tailgate Reggie was lowered to the pavement and motored inside the diner. Abby greeted him ecstatically; Reggie parked beside her at the table and they hugged and cried.

"I heard; I came to see if there was anything—"

"I don't know, I don't know how it could have happened, Reggie."

They were joined by a couple of hippie relics name Bill and Nellie, who owned the truck and did the carvings. Straggly beard and straggly blond hair, macrobiotic thinness, bandanas, tinted granny glasses and frayed jeans.

"I had to get something to eat," Reggie explained after introductions were made. "My blood sugar gets low about this time of the day." He ordered waffles, scrambled eggs, sausage and a pot of coffee. Bill and Nellie brewed tea from what looked like dried grass and nibbled from Baggies of seeds they carried with them. Reggie and Abby resumed talking about Frosty. Joe's attention was on Reggie's scruffy JanSport backpack, which was hanging from a handle of the computerized wheelchair, as it had been the night Frosty placed in a zippered side compartment the stolen ampule containing an unknown drug from Dr. Luke's infirmary. Was the ampule still there? If it was, would Reggie think of mentioning it to the cops? Joe wondered where that conversation would lead.

He wanted the ampule himself, and he wanted it

right now. But that was going to be difficult. He couldn't just ask Reggie to hand it over.

An alternative was to steal it, but stealing involved even greater difficulties. Joe was a clever thief with words, but his hands were unskilled.

In addition to the muleskinner's hat he had placed in his lap, Reggie wore a beaded Thunderbird vest over an unpressed blue workshirt, and black trousers. There were three small gold rings in his right earlobe. His narrow shoulders slumped and he looked close to helpless in the wheelchair; his hand movements as he consumed a stack of waffles were more laborious than when he played his twelve-string guitar. Probably there were good days and bad days as the disease wore on, turning connective tissue to wood pulp. But his eyes were bright and attentive. He had the wan, bony, hawk-nosed face of a minor outlaw in a nineteenth-century daguerreotype, photographed with the boys in front of the Last Chance Saloon. In spite of his looks and his ability to assimilate so ably the blues tradition, it became obvious through his conversation that Reggie had the intellect and credulity of a ten-year-old boy.

When Reggie had to go to the bathroom, Joe excused himself a couple of minutes later and followed him.

Reggie had squeezed himself into a stall not designed for wheelchair access. The door was half-closed on his chair, which stuck out into the small bathroom.

"I hate it when they don't have a toilet for handicapped," he said.

"Aren't there federal laws now?" Joe asked.

"Nobody but us ever makes a fuss about it. And there's not enough of us, Abby says."

"How long have you known Abby?" Joe asked, unzipping at the urinal next to the stall Reggie occupied.

"I don't remember exactly. I know we've been good friends a long time. But it's been a while since I seen Abby. Frosty had a surprise birthday party for me two years ago. Abby gave me this wheelchair. You know they cost almost ten thousand dollars? Quadriplegics use them. I'm not there yet. I mean I've got rotation in my left wrist so I can reach all the chords I need to." He managed to sound upbeat about the progress of the appalling, slow-moving, always fatal disease. "Abby said you're a doctor? Is it true that in a couple years at the most that there's gonna be a new treatment for scur roses? I mean that they take each cell and sort of do a housecleaning, so that it stops the—I can't remember the word they use."

"Induration."

"Did you hear anything about that?"

"It isn't my field, actually."

"Are you Abby's doctor now? Frosty kind of gave me the idea she wasn't doing so good."

"I know what Frosty told you."

Reggie was quiet while he labored to move his bowels. "When did you see Frosty?"

"This was a couple of days ago. It's true that Abby has serious problems. She's almost died on me a couple of times."

"Lord!"

"And I don't think I can do anything to save her, unless you're straight with me, Reggie."

"M-me? What can I do?"

Joe flushed the urinal and took his time washing his hands.

He said, in a harsher voice, "I don't know you, Reggie, but I've already done you a hell of a big favor. I've kept your ass out of jail. Talk about no facilities for the handicapped."

"Jail!"

"That's right, Reg. Frosty committed a felony when she stole that ampule of medication from Dr. Thomason, and you're an accessory. Do you know what that means?"

"I haven't done anything!"

"Keep your voice down. And remember what I said. You'd better be straight with me, son, because time is of the essence here. Do you want Abby to die?"

"No!"

"Where's the ampule Frosty gave you for safekeeping?"

"How do you know—"

"Reggie. I'll ask the questions, and all I want to hear from you is straight answers. And if I don't get them, I can have a bench warrant for your arrest in ten minutes. I don't care about *your* ass, son, my only concern here is Abby. You owe her, Reggie. Now do what's right for her. I need that ampule to save her life."

"I d-don't—"

Fear had the effect of a quick-acting laxative on Reggie. Joe backed away from the stall.

"Last chance. I'm walking out the door."

"No, wait! It's—I left it in my locker."

"What locker?"

"At the Lost Sea Turtle."

"Good. Good, Reggie. What time do they open?"

"Five-thirty."

"I'll meet you there at six o'clock. *What* time, Reggie?"

"S-six o'clock."

"Don't let me down. For Abby's sake. And keep this conversation to yourself. Talk to nobody."

"Okay."

"By the way, I think you're a hell of a talented musician."

"Th-thank you," Reggie said humbly.

Outside the bathroom door Joe paused to take a breath. His fingers were tingling. It had been a decent job of intimidation, but he wondered how long it would take Reggie to stop thinking about Frosty and their meeting in the Sea Turtle's parking lot on Friday night, and start thinking about dead Frosty, and what connection her murder might have with the stolen ampule. Maybe it wouldn't occur to him at all. Or maybe some smart state cop, asking a few routine questions, would find Reggie nervous and evasive and take his sweet time pursuing the matter until Reggie blurted something that would put Joe Bryce in a very bad light. But that was the chance he'd been willing to take; now all he could do was wait for six o'clock and hope that Reggie would be alone when they met again.

THIRTY-EIGHT

Inside the cozy tattoo parlor on Ocean Drive in North Myrtle Beach, there was a poster of Ray Bradbury's Illustrated Man with the legend *A Creatively Tattooed Body Is Better Than Being Well-Dressed, Except in a Cold Climate.* The proprietress, however, claimed to have no tattoos at all, not even a token of affection for some defunct lover in an intimate place.

"I'm an artist," she said, and the photographs on display of her clients' extravagant whims—sailing vessels, snarling tigers, the Mona Lisa—reproduced in colored inks on canvases of skin testified that she wasn't bragging. "Did Picasso paint his own face?" She was in her forties, perhaps her early fifties, but looked, in black leotards, as taut and well crafted as a five-iron. She was weathered, coarse, with thick black hair as vain as plumage and frank, amorous Latin eyes—explicitly erotic in expression, the way a bee is sticky with pollen after wallowing in a flower.

She looked up photographs of dragonflies in her

collection of nature books, found one that satisfied them all, then did sketches with colored pencils on a notepad. She served them rosé wine and herb crackers while setting up her apparatus. On her television there was storm news on CNN. Hurricane Honey was waffling in her course, but seemed to be attracted to the East Coast again.

"Oh-oh," Abby said. On the weather map the northeast edge of Honey, the most dangerous part of a hurricane, was still well out to sea but on the same latitude as Savannah, Georgia, not so far down the coast.

"I hope we don't have to go through another one of those."

"It will hit us," the tattoo artist said, her voice low but with the power of superstition. "In less than two days."

"How do you know?"

She shrugged. "I do the charts. Mundane charts. Then I meditate. Nature is subtle beyond one's ability to comprehend. Until she's ready to wipe you out."

Abby volunteered to be first. She sat smiling through the needles, with an occasional wince that squeezed out a few tears. The dragonfly was on the cap of her right shoulder, where she could see it at a glance. She seemed ecstastic when it was done, helping herself to the chilled wine again.

"Your turn, hero!"

Joe took off his shirt and sat on the padded stool. The tattoo artist worked with magnifying glasses like those used by surgeons. She chatted more with Joe than she did with Abby.

The wine got to Abby, and she had to excuse herself. She was in the bathroom for a while. The tattoo artist finished her work and sat back, studying Joe, but not as if she were coming on to him.

"It's dangerous," she said. "What you do."

"Excuse me?"

"But you're not a flier. Or a policeman. I'm not

quite sure why I feel that way. You see, I learn things about people as I beautify them. My fingers reach inside the skin. I touch what is hidden. It's hard to explain."

"A psychic thing," Joe said, with a cool smile.

"You're not impressed," she said, almost indulgently, touching a small mole beside her well-shaped mouth.

"Is this going to cost extra?"

"No." She had a dark and forbidding scowl. "I'm not in love with money. I don't always say what's on my mind. Something compels me now. The dragonflies are little tokens. Ephemera. The fact is, you and your nice lady are soulmates. You have been separated many times in the past, often under tragic circumstances. There is a long, spiraling, intertwining journey through space before soulmates may be' together at last, in peace and the perfect love they crave. I only want to prepare you."

"For what?"

"This dangerous thing," she said, becoming vague as she withdrew a little in contemplation. "You are like a house in flames. A house in flames. Others may burn with you." She shuddered, and closed the turquoise lids of her eyes. "Again."

The net fishermen were seining in the breakers off the black community of Atlantic Beach, attracting a crowd and flocks of seagulls pilfering the remains of gutted fish that littered the sand, which was packed hard enough here to allow Abby easy access in her wheelchair. You could, in fact, drive a good-sized truck up and down this part of the Carolina shore.

"My mother came up here during the fifties to dance to the black music on the jukeboxes," Abby said. "I guess they still boogie and do the shag at the places along Ocean Drive. When I was in high school we went to Fat Harold's a couple of times, but shagging was kind of quaint to us.''

Her hair was blowing in a stiffened wind that filled the air with salt spray and brought out the red in her cheeks. Joe bought two huge deep-fried fillets from a fisherman cooking some of his catch in a big iron pot on the beach; they ate them hot and lightly salted between slabs of Cuban bread.

"You look spooked,'' Abby said, staring up at him and flicking crumbs of bread from the corners of her mouth.

"No, I'm okay.''

"What did you and the nice tattoo lady talk about while I was in the john?''

"Destiny.''

"Heavy, mon. She's sort of a witch, don't you think? I don't mean that in a nasty way. You know, horoscopes and reading palms. Did she read your palm? Did she tell you how many children you're going to have?''

"Ten.''

"You lie.''

"What she said was, you and I are soulmates.''

Abby pondered the implication of "soulmates.'' "Does that mean sex is out?''

"Completely.''

"That had better be another lie,'' she said with a grin. "Does your tattoo itch?''

"A little.''

"I can't believe you went through with it.'' She regarded him with a feline complexity, her pupils small in the light off the sea, brows and lashes beaded with a fine mist; he looked back at her calmly, a little quizzical hitch at one corner of his mouth. "It's deeper than marriage, you know. It feels—occult. Whatever brought us together in the first place, we've sealed our bargain today.''

"Or canceled an old debt.''

She nodded.

"Somehow that seems right. When I looked at my dragonfly, I didn't feel like an ass for being there with a man I've known for less than a week. I felt this huge sense of relief. I felt protected—no matter what becomes of us—protected in this life or the next. How old was your mother when she died?"

The question startled him.

"I don't know that she's dead."

"But you think that she is."

He looked away, over the heads of the shouting fishermen, their flung nets returned with silvery leaping catch. Gulls hovered like seething thunderclouds above the sand. The sea rolled over, and over again.

"Yes, I think she died, soon after she left me in Arizona, I think she was killed for some small transgression in New Orleans, or for maybe nothing at all except that she got on the wrong side of a psychopath who was fixated on adjusting a grievance that wouldn't mean a thing to a normal mind. She was so damned young; twenty-four, twenty-five. She'd had a marriage that turned into living hell for both of them, and a couple of years of hard knocks in a tough town filled with human debris, and she thought she knew what made the world go around. Now I can feel sorry for her."

"And forgiving?"

"I don't know yet. The tattoo lady told me I was like a house in flames."

"Joe, do you know when I was born? September, nineteen sixty-three."

"And?"

"If we're soulmates, like the tattoo lady said—"

"Abby, for God's sake—"

"No, wait, this is *very* interesting."

"Not to me."

"Don't close your mind, Joe. If you believe life is eternal—and I do; forget the bodies we clunk around in for the time we're on earth—life isn't just random or accidental, there's much more to it than one round-trip to earth, then blackness evermore. When the preachers say God has a plan for all of us, maybe they aren't just mouthing ignorant platitudes. Joe, you got through thirty-five years or so without having pictures drawn on your good-looking hide, safe to say you weren't interested. Yet today you didn't hesitate when I suggested the tattoo parlor. What were you doing, humoring me? You can't wash it off in the shower. We're linked until our mortal flesh turns to dust."

"I was definitely humoring you."

"Oh, bull. And don't try to humor me now, this is serious. Maybe I *was* your mother—"

"I think the sun's too hot for you today, Abby."

"—or maybe now I'm just a little blip of her soul, one drop of rain from a cloudburst, nevertheless she's living again in me for a *reason*." Abby paused and touched her lips, as if she felt them growing numb, or was afraid she had spoken beyond the pale.

"I know I'm making you uncomfortable. That's a heck of a big hole you're kicking in the sand, there. Just think about it, Joe. Otherwise there's no rhyme or reason to us. You said it yourself: a debt was canceled today. What made you say that?"

"I don't know." But he felt a twinge of pain, as if a piece of glass from an old accident was working its way through his flesh. "I can't buy into this, Abby. Reincarnation is fantasy. A sick faith, the last refuge of a chaotic personality."

She smiled gamely. "I'm neurotic, not chaotic. I'm a *disciplined* neurotic, goddammit."

"I didn't mean—"

"I'm not sore at you. Listen, you're stuck with a bad concept, that's all. Reincarnation as something to haunt you, an intrusion in this life, the only life you know. Try thinking of reincarnation as a language you're learning, a fresh page of a journal you've been keeping for half of Eternity. Bodies don't matter so much, then. We have bodies to make other bodies.''

Abby looked down at her motionless legs. "Or we have them as punishment," she said. "One more debt waiting to be canceled."

The fading blue sky looked hung with hot cobwebs when they returned to the Barony, after a day that had been too hard on Abby. He saw her upstairs to her room. She was too exhausted to say much more than "Come back later."

Lizzie came in to help Abby with her bath and a shampoo she needed after the afternoon they had spent on the beach. Joe and Abby kissed while Lizzie was laying out towels in the bathroom.

On the stairs Joe encountered Lucas Thomason, who was on his way to Abby's room with a small tray containing packaged syringes, two ampules, a blood-pressure collar and two glasses of red wine. He had a stethoscope around his neck, over a plaid flannel shirt.

They paused one step apart. The tension filling the space between them was like a large, unnamable animal.

"Did the Solumedrol come?" Joe asked politely.

"No. I'm expecting it by Fed Ex tomorrow from Zurich." Thomason glanced down at the tray. "I give Abby B-twelve shots once a week." He didn't explain the contents of the other ampule. "If you'd like to eat, Doctor, they'll fix something for you in the kitchen. The wine is a Stag's Leap cabernet, the best California has to offer, in my opinion. Help yourself."

"Thank you. Is there anything new about the— about Frosty?"

"Well, her neck was broken. She was stripped but not raped."

"That's unusual."

"That she wasn't sexually molested?"

"Why take off her clothes if you don't have rape in mind?"

Thomason's lips crimped together. "I don't know." He looked past Joe at the second-floor gallery, chock-ablock with the work of American Bucolic painters and nineteenth-century portraitists. "I suppose Abby is taking Frosty's death very hard. How was she today?"

"It was a severe shock. But she's tough."

"I meant—did she say anything more about the symptoms you mentioned at breakfast?"

"The symptoms you dismissed?" Thomason's eyes tightened slightly, as if the reminder implied serious disrespect. "She complained a couple of times about her lips feeling numb."

Thomason took that in, nodded, shared nothing of his thoughts, then, with another nod and a slight smile walked past Joe up the steps.

"Good night, Dr. Bryce. It *will* be good night, won't it?"

"I'm driving into Charleston for the evening."

"I see. Well, it's not hard to have a good time in Charleston. Enjoy yourself."

THIRTY-NINE

Dr. Nick Portuguese occupied the third floor of a post-
Revolutionary brick house on Legare Street. Three piazzas, added long after the original house was built,
faced southwest and the Ashley River a short distance
away. There was, as in many Charleston homesites, a
walled garden. This garden was behind a high iron
gate studded with thorns, a style called chevaux-de-
frise. Inside the garden there were palm trees. Nick was
at the top of an extension ladder rescuing a neighborhood cat that had gone in a flash straight up the trunk
of one of the palms and couldn't get down.

When he was back on the ground he handed the
young tabby to a tearstained teenage neighbor.

"I need a shower and a change of clothes," he said.
"Come on upstairs."

They reached the third floor by way of an outside
stairway at one end of the triple stack of piazzas. Nick's
roommate was a replica of Aphrodite but with bigger
breasts and a snaggletoothed grin. She was vacuuming

vigorously in the front parlor, wearing running shorts
and a halter top, listening to classical music on headphones. She took a much better tan than did most
redheads. She was about half a foot taller than Nick.

"NAME'S SHUGGIE," Nick said, over the noise of
the vacuum cleaner; Shuggie smiled and nodded to
Joe. Nick turned on his way to his bedroom to appraise
her from a different angle. "Have you ever seen an ass
sit that high on a female human being? She moved in
four weeks ago. Psychiatric nurse from Hamburg.
Nothing's happening yet, but I think I've got a shot.
Or else I'll have to resume a long-standing dependency
relationship on Elevil and airplane glue. Help yourself
to beer in the pantry, or there's hard stuff if you want
it. Piazza has a nice breeze this time of the day."

Joe took a cold Dos Equis outside and watched the
wide river turn from lava red to twinkling gold.

Nick reappeared in clean safari shorts and a tank top
and some of his gold chains. You could have lost a
ballpoint pen anywhere in the wilds of his reddish
black body pelt. He clutched three more bottles of Dos
Equis in one hand.

"Like the house? Three of us pooled our resources
and bought it last year as an investment. Charleston is
a tight little peninsula, and the really good old houses
seldom come on the market." He seated himself on a
cushioned patio chair and looked at Joe across a low
glass-topped table with a hurricane lamp on it. "I guess
this visit means you got what you wanted."

From a pocket of his blazer Joe retrieved the ampule
that Reggie the blues man had turned over to him at
the Lost Sea Turtle Café. Reggie had made no fuss. He
had been glad to be rid of the unlabeled ampule,
which was nearly filled with a chalky liquid. The question had been clear in his eyes, but he hadn't asked it.
Does this have something to do with Frosty's murder? A question Joe had been trying to block from his own mind

during the hourlong drive to Charleston: but it was like holding a finger in a crumbling dike.

The neuropathologist drank half of his first bottle of beer, looking at the ampule, turning it around and around in his fingers.

"This could be difficult to identify. Without some idea of what it is."

Joe stared at the western sky, now ashes and sulfur.

"If you had a patient," he asked Nick, "who went into convulsions, then later complained of forgetting how to breathe—"

"She did what?"

"That's exactly how she described it. She forgot how to breathe. Her lips were tingling and blue. Today they felt numb, she said. Knowing that she's partially paralyzed, if you heard those symptoms, what would you think?"

" 'Forgetting how to breathe' might indicate a brainstem glioma, or a neural tumor compressing the cervical spine. But the other symptoms suggest toxicity of some kind. And this is the culprit?"

"I don't know yet."

Nick held the ampule up to the light from one of the fixtures on the ceiling of the piazza. A bug zapper mounted near the double plantation doors methodically fried mosquitoes and other night-dwelling insects, its blue light shooting through the contents of the ampule.

"Fibrillation? Elevated blood pressure? Tachycardia?"

"I don't know about fibrillation; yes to the other symptoms."

Nick gave a nod. "Similar to the reaction I had when a timber rattler nailed me at the Philmont Scout Ranch in New Mexico. I was fourteen. It was my first Jamboree. They thought I was going to lose my left leg below the knee."

"But her symptoms come and go."

"You believe she's been getting regular injections of this stuff?"

"I don't know how often. She has a reservoir implant."

Shuggie came barefoot out to the piazza and sat casually in the doctor's lap, draping an arm around his shoulders and picking up a beer with the other hand. Nick tried to conceal the fact that he was ecstatic about the attention. She smiled at Joe. The uneven teeth gave her the look of a voracious street urchin. Her cheekbones were so large they all but pushed her bright blue eyes deep into her head.

"*Mazel tov,*" she said. She tilted her head back and drank most of the beer in three big gulps.

"Reservoir implant," Nick ruminated, watching Shuggie's throat muscles as she drank. "It may be leaking. That could account for the irregularity of her symptoms, again depending on what we've got here. But the possibility of toxic shock—it's a start."

"Maybe we can narrow it down further," Joe said. He rubbed the back of his head in agitation, then got up and leaned against the railing of the piazza, looking down at the gaslit garden. "I think that stuff will prove to be a powerful muscle relaxant—the kind they use for protracted spinal surgery."

"Tetrodotoxin," Nick said immediately.

"What is that?" Shuggie asked, stretching upward in Nick's lap until her breasts looked ready to explode from the tension. She was as playful as a chimp with a bellyful of fermented termites. Joe wondered how the doctor had failed to get her into bed thirty minutes after she unpacked in the spare bedroom. Probably he was one of those lovelorn men who had a tendency to overevaluate every opportunity, instead of simply seizing it.

"Tetrodotoxin," Nick explained, "is a neural poison, extracted from Japanese blowfish. Fugu. Very, very little of it is always deadly. You may have heard about those Japanese gourmands who liked to flirt with death at the dinner table. The great chefs leave a trace amount of poison in the fillet they prepare, enough so the customer's lips get that telltale tingle, and they know just how close they are to the ancestral home in the sky. It's supposed to be better than sex."

"Would anesthesiologists use Tetrodotoxin?" Joe said.

"Probably an analogue. In the synthetic state the drug can be made to act on specific receptors, reducing side effects, and rendering the patient paralyzed at preplanned levels."

"How long would the effect last?"

"Three to four weeks before the paralysis wears off."

"Better than sex?" Shuggie said. "How?"

"Never mind," Nick muttered.

"Does anyone want this beer?" Shuggie asked, looking at the last bottle of Dos Equis on the table. For once, neither of the men was paying attention to her. "What's the matter?" she said, frowning. "What is this talk of poison fish?"

She seemed to be lagging a few sentences behind in translation and comprehension. Nick joggled her on his knee. "Close your ears. This conversation never happened." To Joe he said, "The son of a *bitch*. How long?"

"It may be several years," Joe said in shock.

Nick nodded, slowly.

"She was in an accident, and the spinal cord, let's assume, was damaged in the lumbar region. Severely compressed, but not cut. Resulting in paralysis that could continue the rest of her life, or disappear in a few months with treatment and decompression. It's a medical fact that every patient who has been given a spinal anesthetic feels that he has been cut in half somehow, and his lower half is gone, never to return. The psychological effect is abject terror. The absence of proprioception doesn't mean that the legs are neurally or functionally dead. But there's an existential breakdown. The patient 'loses' his legs as internal objects, what neuropsychologists call the 'imago.' There's a severe perceptual deficit that could be cultivated and encouraged by someone who doesn't want that patient ever to walk again."

"She did walk," Joe said. "Last night. I'm convinced of it." He explained what had happened at the beach house, and told Nick about finding Abby's footprints in the sand.

"Most paraplegics have dreams of walking. In her dream state she was able to actually accomplish it because her mind revoked the condition of *jamais vu*; tricked the body into 'repossessing' her absent legs. I'd say also that her last shot of anesthetic has begun to wear off, allowing for proprioception on a nearly conscious level. We tend to forget that the organism is a unitary system: there's a continual interaction of body and mind. That's probably why your needle doc has been using the paralytic for years, just to reinforce her perceptual deficit. But it also has left his patient open to some potentially fatal consequences—stroke, total paralysis, you name it. He's not an anesthesiologist, so he probably doesn't know what the hell he's doing with that stuff. A miracle he hasn't accidentally killed her off before this. You'd better get her out of there."

"I'll need the proof."

"I should be able to get you a certified lab report by tomorrow afternoon."

"Proof of what?" Shuggie inquired.

"Put this conversation out of your mind, Shuggie." To Joe he said, "One of our anesthesiologists may know where your needle doc is getting his supply. Ultimately it should be traceable to him. An ordinary GP has no business ordering quantities of a paralytic, but it's not against the law."

"I know that."

"So—"

"I don't know how much of the drug is left in her reservoir. But we'd only need to withdraw a tiny amount to demonstrate that he's been deceiving Ab—deceiving and jeopardizing the life of his patient by enhancing whatever paralysis remains with something as dangerous as Tetrodotoxin."

"I had some bad fish once, in the Caribbean."

"That's nice, Shuggie," Nick said, gazing into space.

"It *wasn't* so nice. I was sick for three weeks."

"I'm bringing her in," Joe said.

"When?"

"Tonight."

"Okay. Here's the way I think it should be handled. Sid Petersen will tap that reservoir, with two other doctors witnessing. The sample will be labeled and initialed by everybody, and I'll see it through the lab. If the drug is what you think it is, legal action can be initiated, at the state level, whether your patient requests it or not. That'll keep her out of his clutches from now on."

"Good."

"Why don't you give me a call when you're on your way?"

"I will."

"Oh, you're leaving?" Shuggie said. She got up from Nick's lap and shook Joe's hand with Germanic firmness. "*Auf wiedersehen.* Come back to see us."

"I'll walk out with you," Nick said.

On the sidewalk outside the garden gates Joe thanked the pathologist for his help.

"No problem. Recoveries, or even minimal improvements, are so rare in neurology I welcome the opportunity to help someone who may make it back all the way. So what about Shuggie? Do you think I have a chance with her?"

Joe suppressed a smile. "Bring her a little present. Fix her breakfast. Tell her you see depths of sadness in her. She'll cry. Then she'll fall on you like a dynamited chimney."

"She will?" Nick shook his head in awe. "Women have always been reflections on water to me. Verses in Sanskrit. Mysterious white birds in the sky—"

"Nick, I'm beginning to think you're hopeless. Sex is the court jester in the temple of the body. So lighten up and have a few laughs."

FORTY

Joe heard it first on the car radio during his drive back to the Barony, but the shoreward movement of high clouds delineated by a full moon and more frequent gusts of wind that buffeted the Jeep Laredo had already told him Hurricane Honey had changed course and was bearing down on the Carolinas. The hurricane's speed had increased along with the velocity of her winds, now reported by the hurricane hunters to be one hundred twenty miles an hour at the center, which was two hundred fifty miles southeast of Charleston. The eye of the storm, asymmetrical but roughly forty miles across at its widest point, was plotted to reach the vicinity of Pandora's Bay in less than seventeen hours, at about four o'clock the next afternoon. Honey's arrival would coincide with the high tides for the month of October. An ocean surge of up to eight feet above the normal tide of ten feet could be expected: high enough to wash over the porch of the beach house where he was staying. Evacuation of vulnerable Low Country beaches and islands had been recommended.

The approach of Honey didn't concern Joe. The problems of getting Abby out of the house and to the hospital in Charleston fully occupied him in the hour it took to reach Nimrod's Chapel.

Two conclusions were obvious: he didn't have much time; and the difficulties in neutralizing Dr. Lucas Thomason would decrease in proportion to the risk he was willing to assume. But a confrontation had to be avoided, because, if the drug in the ampule he had turned over to Nick Portuguese proved to be an analogue of Tetrodotoxin, the evidence would confirm that Thomason was, to put it mildly, bizarrely pathological, and probably psychotic in the exercise of his power over the helpless Abby. Charlene sensed, and maybe Frosty had found out for sure, how dangerous such a person could be.

It might have begun, Joe thought, simply and humanly, as a crush on the adolescent beauty growing up in his household. Thomason would have been in his mid-thirties when Abby came to live with him. Sexual maladjustment in adult males—the court jester in the rags and mask of Caliban—was hardly a phenomenon. Neither was the guilt that accompanied unfortunate fixations on the wrong objects of desire. If his sex drive was strong and uncompromising, then emotionally Thomason would have been required to maintain a comprehensive feat of balance: affection for and intimacy with the underaged *adorée*, the need to brutally possess her. Sexual conflicts properly energized could move armies or create masterpieces of art. Condemned to lightless depths of the psyche, the same conflict would inevitably raise appalling monsters.

Joe reasoned that Abby's accident had provided temporary salvation for a tormented man threatened with an unsupportable loss. For a while she had been fully in his care and keeping. Her paralysis would have had a calming effect; he might even have been impotent for a little while, an expectable transference. They probably never had been so close as during those months after misfortune. Signs of Abby's recovery would not have been welcome to Thomason. Realizing she would walk again after all, knowing there would be lovers to replace the dead boy, he metamorphosed from healer to jailer, implemented by rationalizations potentially more damaging to his soul than either guilt or shame.

The moon was gone; the wind blew strongly from the northeast when Joe reached the Barony. From the road that continued through the intertidal marsh to the shore Joe glimpsed the lights of the main house through swaying trees. He felt the drop in barometric pressure in the mended bones of his face. His heart ached for Abby. He drove on.

There was a car he didn't recognize parked on the shell-and-sand road behind the beach house. A lamp glowed in an upstairs room.

He got out of the Laredo quietly and warily, looking around. The sound of surf was loud beyond the dune. A night bird squawked in the marsh behind him. He felt alone in a lonely place, bowed down emotionally from fear and too much knowledge of the evils men do. All crimes were committed in the name of love. And the jester danced on, taking his pratfalls with an insolent leer.

She appeared at the railing of the porch as he was coming up the ramp at the side of the house, her wiry hair blown into an antic shape by the wind off the sea, sparks flying from a cigarette that smelled like cloves. Her affection for coarse black flavored tobacco, which had given away her presence the night Joe and Flora had gone for a walk in the far reaches of the Barony's garden, identified her before she spoke to him.

"Hey, it's just me, Adele Franklin! Thought I'd stop

by for a beer. How're you doing tonight, babe?"

"Not too bad." The last thing he needed right now was company. He had planned to pack up and drive into town, then place a crucial phone call to Lucas Thomason, to lure him away from the Barony. He hoped he could quickly get rid of Adele.

Spume was in the air from the wind gusting off the ocean. Adele turned her back to it to save what was left of her cigarette.

"Getting rough out," she said. "I hear that hurricane's headed our way."

"It could turn north by morning, follow the coast up to New England."

They went into the house. Adele had turned on nearly all of the lights downstairs, and the television. A late-night talk show featured a damsel-harlot with a quasi-religious name whose success had gone beyond the merely phenomenal into the realm of the supernatural. Adele had fixed a snack for herself. On a coffee table enclosed by rattan sofas and chairs there was a plate with crusts of sandwich bread and a half-eaten pickle. A shell ashtray held several cigarette butts.

"Have I kept you waiting long?" Joe said dryly.

"Oh, I've been here about an hour," she told him, with a nonchalant wave of her hand. "Let me get you a beer."

"Thanks. What did you want to see me about, Adele?"

"I thought you might be able to clear up a couple of things," Adele said, opening the refrigerator.

"Look, Adele, it's getting late, and—"

"I'll try not to keep you up. But that depends on what you have to tell me."

She crossed the room to the conversation nook with two bottles of Killian's Red and put them on the coffee table, smiled at Joe, sat on the edge of one of the sofas.

"I don't think I have anything to tell you."

She patted the seat cushion of a chair next to her.

"Come on, sit down. Have a look at this."

From a pocket of her baggy pink cardigan Adele took out a passport and tossed it on the table. She looked up expectantly at Joe.

"It's yours," she said. "Found it when I was going through your things upstairs. Good likeness of you. The entry and exit visas appear to be authentic, but I guess only an expert would know for sure."

"What are you talking about, Adele?"

Adele reached for a pack of her rank-smelling cigarettes and lit one, settled back on the sofa.

"Well, I'm saying this is a phony passport. And your name is not Joe Bryce. And you're not a doctor from Winnetka, Illinois. I was there Monday and Tuesday, and I've already proved *that* beyond any doubt. I was a good journalist once, believe it or not. I know how to dig. I didn't bother with that hospital administrator again; obviously your group bought his cooperation. I just hung around and talked to nurses who had been at North Shore ten, fifteen years, and some of the pediatricians on staff there. My camcorder has a playback screen. I showed them videotape of Joe Bryce from the barbecue the other night. Nobody could identify you. How do you explain that?"

Joe sat down in the chair next to Adele, picked up his passport from the table and put it away. He twisted off the caps of the Killian's Reds and handed one to Adele, smiling benignly. Then he glanced at her open purse, lying on the other side of the table. Unlikely that she was wearing a wire, but there would be a busy tape recorder somewhere.

"Why do I have to explain anything to you?" he said, sounding insulted and exasperated.

"Joe, Joe, now you're not being fair! I've been fair to you, so far."

"Walking in here and searching my luggage?"

"That's journalistic license, babe. What I'm saying is I could have been sitting here with a couple of guys I know from the State Attorney General's office when you came in. See, I don't mean you any harm. I just want to talk."

Joe had a couple of swallows of beer while he studied Adele and tried to decide what her angle was. He thought it might be beneficial to have her a little more on the defensive.

"You were spying on me the other night in the garden."

Adele expelled a cloud of smoke. "Pure happenstance. They don't let me puff away in the house. So I overheard enough of your conversation with Miz Birdsall to know that she's an old friend of yours. Or is it—colleague?"

Joe nodded, almost imperceptibly. "Then you went to the trouble to find out more about Flora Birdsall."

Adele grinned, the brown cigarette lolling in one corner of her mouth.

Joe leaned forward, put his bottle of Killian's on the table, assumed a serious pose with his hands clasped between his knees and gave Adele a long, level look. When she started blinking a couple of times a second, holding herself a little more erect, he sighed as if conceding.

"Because you're a good journalist, I'm reasonably sure that you've put most of it together by now. You just want me to confirm, is that it?"

"What's your real name, Joe?"

"I am who I am, Adele. It doesn't have any bearing on your concerns."

"That sounds like doubletalk."

"There is information which may be relevant for you to have, and which I can confirm, to the extent I'm allowed to say anything at all."

"About your 'project'?"

"You've already come to some fairly specific conclusions, haven't you?"

Adele removed the spicy cigarette from her mouth.

"Damn right. But I don't understand how the CIA has license to get involved in politics on the state level. Their charter specifically prohibits—" She broke off and stared at Joe, in wonder and excitement. "So—that means you're not here in an official capacity."

"You're very, very clever, Adele," Joe said approvingly.

"*Now* I get the connection. And Senator Harkness has something to do with it, too."

"My presence could be in the nature of a favor. If you want to put it that way."

He had been looking around the beach house unobtrusively, and finally he saw it, Adele's small camcorder, inconspicuous inside a glass-front cabinet filled with oceanic bric-a-brac: polished driftwood, lacy sponges, a collection of shells. The cabinet was about ten feet from where they were sitting; the doors stood open a couple of inches.

Adele said, "You're trying to get something on Lucas, put him out of the running for the nomination."

"What I needed to know, I already know."

"How bad is it?"

Joe shrugged. "There are courts to decide that, Adele."

"Jesus," she pouted. "You're not telling me anything."

"I've told you enough."

"You're not doing me any *good*, Joe. I've got a job and my future to think about." Adele smoked furiously for a little while, then leaned toward him. "Okay. Let's lay it on the line, now. Who wants Luke out of the running? Is it Harkness yanking party strings? What is it they're all afraid of? Pull the skeleton out of the closet, and let me take a look at it. Don't be afraid to talk to me; we're off the record here, you've got my word on that."

It might have been a gust of wind catching the screen door and banging it sharply against the jamb;

but the wind couldn't have been strong enough to throw Adele's head violently back against the sofa cushion. Joe was already turning in his chair to look behind him when it registered that the pulpy red spot in the middle of her forehead was a bullet wound.

A gray-haired man in a dark suit came in swiftly off the porch, the revolver in his hand aimed at Joe. He was wearing leather gloves.

Joe's breath turned to ice in his throat. When you're threatened with a gun, it is all you can look at, and sometimes the very last thing that you see.

Still walking toward Joe, the man said, "On your knees."

Joe looked from the bore of the big revolver to the man's face. He had a thin livid scar running from his receding hairline through one disrupted, whitened eyebrow. He had just murdered a woman, but his face seemed as empty of emotion as if he were there to mail a letter. When Joe failed to move fast enough, the man hit him over the ear with his gloved left hand.

The heel of the glove was reinforced with a steel plate, like the toe of a workman's boot. The force of the stiff-arm blow flung Joe over the back of the sofa where Adele Franklin lay gaping at the ceiling with her brains draining down the back of her neck.

Joe lay on his face on a sisal floor mat. The side of his head throbbed as if it were trying to explode. He was conscious, but without the power to move anything but his fingers. When he tried to lift his head he was overwhelmed by nausea. He blacked out for a few seconds, and came to retching and puking.

Someone else was in the beach house. Wearing old but well-cared-for riding boots. Joe could see that much, with his face a few inches off the floor.

"No need to put a bullet in him," Lucas Thomason said. "When he gets done vomiting, I'll give him something that will leave him dead asleep. For a few hours. In the morning they'll find Joe when they come around to make sure everyone's been evacuated off the beach. They'll find him with that throw-down pistol of yours, and with poor Adele; and when they poke around in his rented Jeep they'll find Frosty's clothes. It makes a neat package for the police. Like everybody else, they don't want to work any harder than they have to."

"He saw me."

"Don't be concerned, Mr. Phipps. Midazolam wipes out memory twenty or thirty minutes prior to injection. The other drug I'm going to give him literally dissolves the ego and destroys normal perception. He won't make sense to anyone because his concept of reality will be as full of holes as Swiss cheese. It was the Swiss who came up with this, by the way, as a treatment for severe manic disorders. But the side effects tend to negate the potential benefits."

"Where do you want him?"

"Where he is. Hold him while I get the injection ready."

Joe tried to roll over on his back, but made poor work of it. Mr. Phipps kneeled beside him and put a gloved hand on the back of his head.

"Thomason . . ."

"Yes, Joe?"

". . . Why?"

The doctor stood over him. "Lift his head," he said to Mr. Phipps. "So he can see me. That's good. Hello, Joe."

"Why?"

Thomason pressed his crimped lips together, as if the question required ethical consideration. Then he shrugged slightly.

"Why? Because you wouldn't go away. And because you found out things about Abby, didn't you? That's reason enough, but the plain fact is, I just don't like you."

"Don't . . . give her any more Tetrodotoxin. You've poisoned her. She'll die."

"Tetrodotoxin? Where did you get that idea?"

"Don't . . . shit me. I know."

"Doesn't matter what you *think* you know. Or who you gave the ampule to for analysis. You're out of the equation, Joe, and all that remains is unsubstantiated allegation. No one can ever prove a thing against me."

"Sick bastard."

"Abby and I have a love for each other that is beyond your ability to comprehend. Do you think she would have accomplished all that she has without my care? No, she would have devoted her life to some mediocre lawyer or insurance salesman and never answered the call of her ambition. I made that possible. She's had a richer and more fulfilling life by virtue of her incapacitation than she ever dreamed of when she was nineteen, and infatuated with that Huskisson boy."

"Was it really . . . an accident? Or did you have a means of getting Abby's lover out of the equation too?"

"Son, you don't need to know," Thomason said with mild contempt. He inserted the point of a syringe into an ampule and withdrew half of the contents. "Mr. Phipps, if you'll kindly get a grip on him now, we'll finish our business here."

Joe, at half-strength and with the right side of his head throbbing, attempted to fight. Mr. Phipps took a weak jab on a raised shoulder, then slapped Joe hard, but not quite hard enough to snap the jawbone with the steel-weighted glove. With Joe off-balance and comets rocketing through his field of vision, Mr. Phipps spun him around easily, kicked his feet out from under him and rode him into the coarse fibers of the sisal floor covering. Joe inhaled a noseful of his own vomit. Mr. Phipps held Joe facedown with a knee pushing his spine toward his gut and a hand on the back of his head while Thomason jabbed him between shoulder and collarbone with the syringe, injecting him with Midazolam.

"That will put him to sleep," he heard Thomason say. "It'll take a few minutes."

"I think it should appear he shot himself," Mr. Phipps said, perhaps impertinently; but from his tone of voice when he replied Thomason didn't take offense.

"You don't understand, Mr. Phipps. He came to my home, I am convinced, to take away the one who is dearest to me in all the world. And he was insolent in his assurance that there was nothing, *nothing* I could do about it. A bullet in the soft palate, well, that would be paying him respect I don't feel he deserves. I'm paying him instead with hours, days—a lifetime of disorientation, crippled mentality and incarceration in the foulest institutions this state has to offer. What this other stuff here does, in sufficient quantity, to a man's parietal lobes is a fascinating lesson in the two-edged sword of pharmacology."

The last of his words were indistinct to Joe's ears, like a radio voice two rooms away. He felt the prick of another needle, a belated surge of terror, and bit his tongue savagely. Then he roared up off the floor, taking Mr. Phipps by surprise, and threw Mr. Phipps off his back. Thomason stepped back quickly. On his feet, moving like a drunken samba dancer who has lost the beat, Joe swiped at the syringe hanging down his collarbone and dislodged it.

Before Mr. Phipps could pounce and wrestle him down, Joe stamped at the syringe and crushed it. Then Mr. Phipps smacked him on the tender side of his head again with the loaded glove. There was a searing flash in Joe's brain, like an acetylene torch lighting up. Falling, his eyes unfocused, he saw Thomason stooping to retrieve the smashed syringe.

Then Joe was on his back, blinking up at both of them. He had no sense of how his body was positioned.

His feet might have been twisted under him, or spread far apart. There was almost no sensation in his hands.

Thomason was saying, in a voice that alternately roared and receded unintelligibly:

"No matter. Most of. Gun in his hand   Mr. Phipps can't hurt us   in   the   state   he's"

Joe watched Mr. Phipps pick up his right hand and fit it to the revolver. He felt nothing. Mr. Phipps placed the muzzle against a pillow, and fired a shot. The report it made was a tiny pop to Joe's ears. Mr. Phipps let go of Joe's hand. Without his help to lift the revolver, it lay on the mat, smoking a little, the odor of gunpowder stinging Joe's nostrils. His finger was on the trigger, but he couldn't feel that, either. *Shoot them,* he thought, but the impulse never made it to the nerves of wrist and hand.

Mr. Phipps examined the fat pillow to make sure the bullet had stayed inside. He turned his head and said something to Thomason, who had pinpricks of light in his glass-blue and hollow eyes as he stared down at Joe.

The lamps in the room seemed to be fading into a dense black fog. He heard nothing but the beating of his heart. Then there was one last heartbeat extending to eternity. Ghosts moved around Joe, transparent shapes without identities. He felt a thumb on one eyelid, peeling it up and back. His mother's slim hand on his feverish brow. You're burning up, Joely-Moly. Would you like some ice cream? Strawberry, he said. Then he asked her, If I was ice cream, what flavor would I be? She smiled. Peach, she said. Sweet peach. Then he knew it had to be her, because it was the right answer. She would sit with him and give him spoonsful of ice cream to cool his parched tongue, and he would sleep with his head on her perfumed breast, snub nose pressed against a half-exposed nipple, until he was bathed in her perspiration and his own on a muggy unseasonably warm winter's day in New Orleans, and the fever had burned itself out.

FORTY-ONE

When Lucas Thomason returned to the Barony around one in the morning, Bruiser the Neapolitan mastiff was outside running in nervous circles in the garden and occasionally stopping to bark at something, or nothing, the way dogs will do when a large storm is threatening. The winds were brisk and rising, but as yet there was no whiplash certainty that a killer hurricane was inbound to his home and sanctuary. In any event, his polo ponies were stabled ten miles away from the island, and would be secure. He walked around the grounds, illuminated with hidden floods and Malibu lights along the paths, regretting all the glass in the conservatory Abby had wanted to build; but Walter Lee or one of the boys had had the foresight to stock up on plywood, a stack of four-by-eight, half-inch sheets covered with a tarp next to the tool and potting sheds.

As he was looking back at the house a hundred yards away, the fact of murder, indistinct as an old dream in the brightened angles of the beach house, now struck him in the dark—standing still, his body trembled like a bell. His heart was as hot as an isotope. Bending over, he threw up on the ground.

When he returned, Lillian was on the veranda in her carpet slippers and bathrobe; her pursed mouth held the wages of another's sins.

"What's keeping you up so late?" Thomason asked her.

"Miss Charlene is in the front parlor acting peculiar."

"How do you mean that?"

"She pushed all the furniture to the middle of the room, and she's stripping wallpaper."

He felt so weary he could barely hold his head up. The isotope was still burning in his chest; the arteries of his neck felt swollen, black with char. "The wallpaper she put up last month? Jesus, that was a special order, three hundred dollars a roll if I remember correctly."

"Also she is naked as a peeled egg, Dr. Luke."

Thomason stopped in the kitchen. Gallingly thirsty, he drank water directly from the sink tap.

The parlor was ablaze with light. The Aubusson carpet was littered with scraps and scrolls of wallpaper that Charlene was industriously, perhaps maniacally, gouging off the walls with a steel scraper. She had moved all of the furniture except for the white Italian Baroque Revival piano in one corner, and she was standing on tiptoe on the closed lid to reach an untouched area of the wall near the crown molding, her buttocks clenched from effort. Sweat was running down her back. She panted as she worked, mumbling under her breath.

He picked up a frosted glass from a lowboy and tasted. Piledriver, heavy on the vodka. Glumly he watched her scraping at the wall, pausing to tear off strips of paper, huffing and puffing.

"Charlene, what's this all about?"

Her heels touched down on the piano lid. She turned, almost lost her balance, and glared at him.

"Can't sleep thinking about it. All wrong. I screwed up. Got to get it *all* off, it's driving me crazy."

"Look at this mess. You're too drunk to know what you're doing. Get down from that piano before you fall."

"Go away. I'm busy."

He remembered Charlene on their Italian honeymoon, when she could never be naked enough. Now little bits of flocked wallpaper clung to her elbows, her breasts. "Peeled egg" was certainly accurate. What remained of her pubic hair was like a cruelly clipped vine that had ceased to flower for him. So this was the way it ended, he thought.

"If you're not a sight. You think I want anyone in this house to see you like this?"

"They're asleep," Charlene said sullenly. "What's wrong with how I look? When I had my own 'partment, I always did housework in the buff. You don't like to look at me? You got myopia or something. My tits are still great. My ass the best. Also it's the best goddamn pussy you ever had! What's your *problem*?"

"Women who drink too much disgust me."

"Yeah? Your problem's always been, I figured out, you don't know a damn thing about women."

She was the one who was drunk, but he couldn't seem to keep her in focus. His face was beaded with sweat.

"I do know this much: offhand I can't think of a single woman in history who deserved a Viking's funeral. But plenty of them should have been buried with a stake through the heart."

"Oh, that's *funny*."

What was left of his self-possession vanished in a rising tide of blood; he felt a sense of loss, of time wasted with a woman he had not loved and didn't want anymore. He needed to go upstairs and sit in a pelting

warm shower and not think about anything. But Charlene was like a large awkward plucked bird loose in his
house, violating it. He couldn't tolerate her any longer.

He reached her in two strides and caught her by a
wrist as she was trying to back away from him. He
yanked hard and threw her head over heels from the
piano to the carpet.

"Oh God! Oh God! You hurt me! My shoulder!"

"Shut up." He changed his grip to the other wrist
and pulled Charlene to her crossed feet, pulled her
halfway across the room until she stumbled and fell
again. Then he dragged her on her knees, on one hip,
on her back, dragged her out of the house and across
the brick veranda, with her screaming all the way, Stop,
stop, I'm bleeding! He stopped and said with calami-
tous calm, Walk, or I'll drag you again, and Charlene
got up slowly, whimpering, then stumbled along with
him holding her by the wrist, pleading: Luke, Luke,
don't, I'm hurt, don't hurt me any more, until they
reached the sheds on the far side of the garden. There
he threw her down and there she lay, sobbing, unable
to move, shallow lacerations from her hips to her ankles as if she had been raked, both elbows bloodied,
while he searched for the right key on his ring, opened
the padlock on the toolshed door.

"No, Luke! It's dark in there! There's all kinds of
spiders—oh God, I *promise*, just *don't*, I couldn't stand
it, *please*!"

"You're never coming in my house again."

"I'm sorry! Don't do this!"

He opened the door, then kicked her butt until she
crawled inside on the packed earth floor, squirting
golden urine in the dirt while she batted antically at
her platinum hair as if she were already in the grip of
cobwebs, besieged by the spiders she dreaded. He
slammed the door on this spectacle, on a last glimpse
of Charlene, hardly able to whimper, stunned by the

awfulness of her predicament. He fastened the pad-lock.

Charlene was banging weakly on the corrugated steel walls of the windowless shed when he walked back to the house, feeling relieved but light-bodied, insubstantial, as the weight of the wind against his back staggered him from time to time. They would abide by *his* rules, they would not interfere in *his* life, or they would deeply regret their transgressions.

As he crossed the veranda, Thomason caught a glimpse of Lillian's face at a kitchen window, the round lenses of her glasses flaring from outside light as she turned away, but he did not care for her opinion right now, thank you.

Inside he turned off the lights of a parlor half in ruins, then went to the infirmary and swallowed a fifteen-milligram tablet of Halcion. Drops of sweat had gathered on his forehead, they rolled down his backbone, but his body was cold except for the isotope in his chest; he had a constant need to clear his seared throat without gagging himself.

Climbing stairs was such a chore he had to pause a couple of times, hold fast to the curved railing. He had never doubted his physical stamina but it had been a difficult night so far. The house was awake in the wind, rafters creaking in complaint, a shutter banging somewhere. The Barony had survived many storms as bad as the one headed their way, no need to pack up and move inland. The roof was fastened down with iron straps, and never leaked. The chimneys had been sealed before summer began. The shutters were thick hearts-of-pine. The great old trees gripped the center of the earth with their roots, and they would hold.

He could hold up too, but he was deathly tired, his own roots withered from the heat of the isotope burning in his chest like a condensing star, inconceivably heavy in its smallness. He carried it, hunching slightly, down the second floor hall to Abby's room, and inside, where its glow, like the speed of his ardor, passed through her closed lids and woke her up. Groping, she pushed the book she had been reading—the poems of Yeats—off her breast and blinked at him. *What rough beast . . .*

"Luke."

"Hello."

"Is it late?"

"I think so."

"Did I hear Charlene yelling?"

"It was nothing."

"Were you fighting?"

"She was drunk. Never mind about Charlene."

"Come here and let me kiss you good night."

He approached the bed. Lizzie lay facedown against Abby's left side. The faintly starchy, animal odor of sleepers was comforting to him. Charlene had always worn cologne to bed. Which seemed as unnatural to Thomason as his last memory of her, tossed out, that was that.

Abby was wearing a flannel gown with ribbony shoulder straps. When he bent to kiss her he saw by the tightly focused light of her reading lamp the tattoo on her shoulder.

"What's that?"

She turned her head and said with a smirk of satisfaction, "That's my little dragonfly."

"What—you mean you—had yourself tattooed?"

"I had it done in Myrtle Beach."

"It's permanent?"

"Yes, Luke. I think it's *so* pretty. You don't like it?"

"No. How could you do that?"

"I wanted it. Luke, what's wrong, you're glaring."

"It's—I think it's obscene, to do such a thing to your body." A whore's valentine, cheap as neon. Dismay choked him like an iron collar. "Was it *his* idea? Is that what this is all about?"

She seemed shaken by his use of the word *obscene*, as

if he meant something worse, a moral flaw.

"Yes. Joe has one too. The dragonfly has a very special meaning for both of us."

"This isn't worthy of you."

"It's personal," Abby said, and her teeth came together, her lips thinned contentiously. "Private."

"But there's never been anything to come between us, Abby," he said pleadingly.

"Nothing's come between us, Luke. Why are you acting this way?"

He thought of something he'd heard as a child, from a reclusive aunt who always seemed to be bent over her Bible, a deep crease between her stir-crazy eyes: *"If yesterday was circumstance, today unplanned, then tomorrow comes the reckoning."* Aunt Melva had baby-sat him often when he was a child, and used her switches in response to his bent for mischief. She cut them from hickory saplings and kept them in an umbrella stand in her gloomy front hall. His hatred of her was as raw as turpentine. He undid the fastenings on Melva's toilet seat so that it slid to the floor with her bare ass on it when she sat down. He waited in the tupelo tree at the end of the grape arbor, a walnut in the leather pouch of his hand-carved slingshot, for her to come looking for him. But it was his father who came, and his heart let go of anticipation, stalling in the vastness of his terror. The Old Guy. Paterfamilias. Manners had been an obsession with him, but failed to obscure a steely dislike of the ruck of humanity, his son one example thereof. It took Lucas's father four hours to talk him down, vowing no retribution, but when his feet had barely touched the ground the Old Guy hit him in the mouth with the back of his hand so hard the blow knocked out three teeth. His upper lip was partially paralyzed for months as a result, and funny-looking after that. . . .

"Luke, what's wrong?"

He had climbed down from the tupelo tree. Tomorrow was here and his dictatorial father was long dead, there would be no reckoning. Abby had not moved. There had been no significant change in her condition, and her condition ruled her life. No other man could alter that fact. The dragonfly was a frivolous, foolish thing, but women were entitled to their frivolity. He knew that he would always be in control of Abby's love, and knowing gave him peace.

"I'm all right. I need some sleep. I have to go into town early tomorrow, pick up a Fed Ex at the Planter's House."

"What about the hurricane?" Abby said, listening to the wind. "I haven't been watching TV."

"Coming right for us. But we'll be all right here. We'll lose some tree limbs, a few tiles off the roof."

Abby yawned. "I feel safe. Where's Bruiser hiding?"

"Under the bed in Lillian's room, I suppose."

"Poor old Bruiser."

"Do you need anything?"

"Maybe some Lioresal. My legs have been flopping all over tonight. More activity than I can remember. I woke Lizzie up twice."

"I'll get it for you." He bent to brush his crimped lips against hers. They were cold. He choked off a moment of panic. "Did you feel that?"

"No," she said. "But it's okay. Just something else to live with, I suppose. Gimp legs and gimp lips."

Abby turned her head and looked at the cylinder of oxygen nearby, drew a long and heartfelt breath.

"Do you think Joe's all right at the beach house?"

Just the sound of his name had a grating effect on Thomason, like the ends of a broken bone coming together. "I suppose so. I haven't seen him."

He left Abby and made the trip back down the stairs, feeling so enervated it was an effort to pick up his feet. But the isotope in his breast had shrunk to carat-size.

Lillian, still in her nightclothes, was standing in the middle of the green marble gallery. The wind thumped and bumped against the stout front door.

They looked at each other for several seconds. Lillian had an aptitude for meaningful silences.

"All right," Thomason said finally. "Pack some of her things, sober her up and clean her up. Then call Lonnie or Aldous, see that she gets to the Planter's House okay. That's all I'm going to do, understand?"

FORTY-TWO

By the light of a hurricane lamp on the floor of the toolshed, Lillian worked on Charlene for the better part of an hour. She rinsed old blood and dirt from her tender, bruised body until the water in the pail she had brought with her was rusty brown in color. She had wrapped Charlene in a bedsheet with a fleur-de-lis design and worked on one area at a time, pausing to give Charlene draughts of hot coffee laced with 150-proof rum. This kept her quiet through most of the pain, except when Lillian inadvertently pressed too hard on a deep contusion: then Charlene squawled and cursed her.

Lillian bore the curses without resentment because she knew Charlene's mind wasn't right. She didn't seem to recall what had happened to her. She talked mostly about flying saucers. Her bedroom was littered with books and magazines on the subject. She didn't read anything else, as far as Lillian knew.

Charlene's face was swollen but unbruised. Everywhere else she was cut and scratched, blotchy with purple bruises. Lillian didn't think any bones were broken. Lillian remembered lynchings when she was a girl, and the effect they'd had on her and other children in the Gullah community where she had grown up, near the Carolina-Georgia line. Charlene was on a talking jag, but the pupils of her eyes looked huge and hypnotized. She had the gestures, the insecure whine of childhood. Lillian could deal with the external damage, but not the delusions Charlene was protectively spinning, sealing what was left of rationality in a soft white cocoon of the mind. It was all nonsense, about abductees and alien fetuses in her womb, and mother ships: what movie or movies was all that coming from?

While Lillian was dressing her in soft fawn slacks and a turtleneck cotton sweater, Charlene's outpouring stopped for a little while, although her mouth continued to move, haphazard with unrealized language, and her eyes watered ceaselessly.

"I never was fair to you, Lillian," she said unexpectedly.

"That's all right, Charlene. You just try not to talk so much and calm down some."

"Do you forgive me?"

"It's Christian to forgive; and I ain't a grudgeful woman."

"There's an awful wind outside; it doesn't stop."

"It's going to be a mighty blow."

"What time is it?"

"Long about three in the morning."

Charlene licked her sore flaking lips for the hundredth time. She shuddered uneasily, looking around the toolshed, which was a prefab building about fifteen feet square, large enough to store a small tractor and two riding mowers, and some unused outdoor furniture.

"I don't know exactly when it's coming," she said.

She was brushing her hair, long languid soothing strokes.

"When what coming? The hurricane?"

"No, I mean the Mother Ship."

"Best you not get to talking like that again."

Charlene gave her a look both chastised and cunning. "Oh, I see."

"I don't know what you see, lamb. I can make you a nice bed here on the top of this picnic table for the rest of the night, until I raise Aldous to come drive you into town."

Charlene seemed distraught; her breathing quickened. "Morning? I'm supposed to be gone by then, aren't I?"

"It don't matter. You need to get some rest."

Charlene glanced up at the roof of the tool shed, and hunched her shoulders. "They'll find me here okay, won't they?"   .

"Who?"

"The ones who come from the Mother Ship."

"I—I expect they will. Now what I want you to do is lie back on the table for just a few minutes. I need to go back to the house for bedding, fix you something hot to eat, like soup. How would that be?"

Charlene nodded. "I need to keep up my strength. I have a sacred duty."

"You do?"

She put a hand beneath the bulky sweater, on her belly.

"That's why Luke was so mad, you know. Doctors have X-ray eyes. He looked in my womb when I was sleeping and saw that it was an alien's child I'm carrying. It made him very jealous, Lillian."

"Well, you—just lie down on your back, and think good thoughts, Charlene, because—I know everything's going to work out all right. Bless you."

"Thank you, Lillian. You're so good to me. I don't deserve it."

Lillian took the hairbrush from Charlene's limp hand, put it back in the travel case she'd brought from the house and helped her lie down on the redwood picnic table. It was a painful process; Charlene couldn't put weight on her raw elbows, and her fanny was tender from the scouring bricks of the veranda.

When she was as comfortable as the hard surface allowed, Charlene sighed and her eyes closed.

"I must've killed a billion spiders. I could see their red eyes in the dark. That's what saved me. I beat them with the shovel until they were all dead." The memory of this frantic effort produced a shudder, and a twitching of her lips. "They're all dead now, aren't they?"

"Reckon they must be. You're a good spider-killer. Now, I'll leave the lamp. And I'll be right back. You rest."

Charlene's eyes had closed. She said something indistinct. Then something that sounded like, "Can't be late." Then her body jumped. Lillian stroked her damp forehead with a calming hand, until Charlene's breathing slowed and she snored suddenly, a loud glottal sound.

Lillian closed the toolshed door quietly and shuffled toward the house more than a hundred yards away. The wind was nearly enough to drive her to her knees. She prayed for the strength to get her safely back and forth this long night, but she was frail, and tending to Charlene's wounds had depleted her.

Back in her kitchen, off her aching feet, Lillian slumped in a chair, thinking to rest for just a minute, long enough for her heart to slow down. The minutes passed, then half an hour; finally she roused herself and set about warming a can of consommé on one of the stoves. From her own room she took a pillow and blanket, poured the soup into a thermos and set out again for the toolshed, this time facing the wind, which threatened to knock her down with every step. Hard to fetch a decent breath in a wind like that. She clutched the pillow, blanket and thermos against her chest and pushed doggedly on, moaning to herself.

The side door to the toolshed was banging in the wind when she got there. The interior was dark, as if the hurricane lamp had gone out. But she knew there'd been fuel for hours. Lillian stumbled inside, across the floor, bumped against the redwood table.

There was enough light from Malibu lamps along the garden paths for Lillian to make out the interior of the toolshed. Charlene wasn't lying on the table, and she hadn't fallen off to the floor. Both the lamp and her travel case were missing. Charlene had taken them, and she was gone.

Lord have mercy, Lillian thought. *What next?*

Joe was awake on the sisal mat in the beach house. He was shaking, because the door was open and the air had turned colder as the hurricane continued, at fifteen miles per hour, toward Chicora Island. He had no idea what time it was. The lights were on, but they flickered as the house was pummeled by the wind. Sand and bits of shell picked up from the beach made spitting sounds against the screened windows and the front of the house. The air inside the house was heavy; even though he seemed to be lying on his back, he experienced a little difficulty in breathing. It was even more of a chore to open his eyes; they felt as if some of the wind-blown sand had drifted beneath the lids.

So far all sounds and sensations were identifiable, if not reassuring. He raised his right hand to rub his eyes. This small exertion caused his heart to pound suddenly; he broke out in a sweat. With no evidence to support his fear, he felt that something dreadful was happening, or had already happened, to his body. There was no internal cohesion; he had been reduced, somehow, to a jumble of atoms about to fly apart, and scatter on the wind.

He was in Lucas Thomason's infirmary. The doctor

was there with Flora Birdsall. They had strapped him to the table. Flora looked down at him gravely. When her mouth moved, as if she were speaking to him, all he heard was the ticking of a clock. Thomason handed her a laboratory bottle with a glass stopper. Joe's heart congealed. Flora pulled out the stopper; acidic fumes rose into the air.

Joe raised his head and looked down at his naked body, bound with leather straps. *Don't do it, Flora*, he pleaded.

She started with his left foot, pouring the liquid in the laboratory bottle slowly, almost drop by drop, over the toes, the instep. He felt nothing. Flesh and bone didn't dissolve, they simply disappeared. First his foot, then his ankle, then his lower leg to the knee. Gone.

Interesting stuff, said Dr. Lucas Thomason. *It doesn't leave a trace.*

Don't take all of me, Flora, Joe pleaded. *Leave something!*

But the pouring continued, past midthigh. The leather straps that bound him were not affected by the erasing liquid; they remained in place, still taut, as he disappeared out from under them. That was a clue, he thought frantically, but how was he to interpret it?

With no apparent transition he was back in the beach house. The screen door slapped rhythmically in the wind that seemed to suck the air from the house, creating a vacuum in which breathing was now so difficult he thought he was going to implode.

Something stirred near him. In the dream-interval the lights in the beach house had gone out. He held the lid of one eye open with his right hand, knowing that the left hand was no longer there, it had been erased. Along with much of his body. He didn't feel badly about the loss, because he couldn't remember what it had been like to be whole. Possibly he'd never been whole. Oh, once, when he was a small boy. That didn't count.

"Joe?"

In the oceanic gloom a light appeared to his extreme right side, the flickering flame of a hurricane lamp with a smoke-grayed chimney. There was a wedding band on the hand that held the lamp, and a platinum setting for a large diamond that was missing now.

Charlene kneeled slowly beside him as he opened both eyes. He started and screamed in terror, because half of Charlene was missing. The left half.

"Joe? What's wrong?"

"Go away! Please."

"But I have to be here. This is where I need to wait for them."

He was nauseated by the sight of her, so grotesquely bisected. Even though half of her mouth was missing, she still spoke normally. But he couldn't be entirely sure that part of Charlene was really missing. Maybe she had never been whole either, that what he saw now was all there had ever been of her. Reality and dreaming had been reversed, the laws of perception revoked, thought and space were hopelessly out of whack, and there was nothing he could do. . . .

He couldn't go insane. He was already insane. But that had no meaning, either, in this universe of perceptual disinformation.

"Joe." His eyes were closed, but he felt her hand on him, shaking him.

"Leave me alone!" he cried.

"Wake up."

"I *am* awake. I just don't want to look at you."

I am awake. That was so. Intuition, the ghost in the attic of his intellect, stirred.

"It's something he gave me."

"Who?" Charlene asked. "Are you sick?"

"No. I'm drugged."

His eyes were closed, but he knew that she had risen with her lamp. He heard her walking around, heard her stifled cry of distress.

"What . . . is it, Charly?"

"It's Adele," she said.

Oh, yes. Oh, God. "He shot her. Not Luke. There was another man. It's supposed to look as if . . I did it."

Charlene moaned terribly, then began to cry. He heard her walking around again, aimlessly.

If he had been drugged, then eventually it had to wear off. Even the Tetrodotoxin analogue Thomason had been poisoning Abby with began to lose potency in a week and had to be given to her again and again.

Joe forced himself to sit up. He still refused to open his eyes to inconceivable terrors. He shuddered like a child, and heard Charlene's footsteps as wind from the sea battered the house. Metal deck furniture had begun to fly around the porch.

"I'm not afraid," Charlene said. "I'm not afraid."

"Do you believe me, Charly?"

"I'm not afraid," she said again, her words weighted by an immensity of doom that transcended fear.

Joe opened his eyes, holding his breath as if he were under water. He couldn't find her. Half of the first floor of the beach house was gone. Not blotted out, just missing. He couldn't be sure that it had ever been there.

"Charly, where are you? I need help. Listen to me!"

And suddenly she appeared from his left. Half of her stepping out of the void with the lamp, or half of the lamp, held near her breast. Her appearance, as if she were an apparition, was so shocking that he almost screamed again.

"What's wrong with you?"

"I can't remember. But I'm sure your husband . . . drugged me. I can only see half of you, Charly. The left half."

She stared at him with her single eye, puffed and reddened from weeping. He made himself look at her, and soon it seemed normal, that Charlene was only half there. His nausea subsided. He was able to look down at himself, to verify that half was indeed missing, as he had dreamed. Or else the left side of him had never existed at all. It didn't seem to matter. He began to laugh.

"Half of me?" Charlene said, sorely perplexed. "Stop making things up."

"There's a name for this. But I can't remember . . . half-vision. It's in the brain. . . ." He couldn't think; he was convulsed with jittery amusement, like a child about to fly out of control.

"Stop laughing!" Charlene set the lamp down and began to explore her face with the fingers of her right hand, part of which promptly disappeared. "It's there. I'm all there."

"No, you're not, Charly. But I'm like you. I'm not . . . all here either."

"Goddam bastard! Don't say that!" She lit into Joe. He felt the blows of two fists, but saw only one. He toppled over, and she sprawled on top of him. "Wake up, wake up!"

It was so funny, half of him wrestling half of Charlene, that he nearly became hysterical. Her own terror mounted as she tried to beat the nonsense out of him.

Half-vision. *Hemianopsia*, that was it! The condition sometimes resulted from severe migraine. But in his case it had been drug-induced.

He held her tightly against him. "Charly, let's calm down. I need . . . I don't know, maybe a cold shower would help. Get me upstairs. I've got to . . . Somebody'll come. Sheriff's deputies. They'll take me to jail, and I'll never get out of this fix. *Help* me, Charly."

She lay on his breast, heaving and sobbing, incoherent. He thought he heard her say something about a baby.

"Are you going to have a baby, Charly?"

"Yes! But I can't have it here. It has to be born on the Mother Ship."

"What . . . what are you talking about?"

She told him. All about the voices she heard sometimes when she was under the hair drier at the beau-
tician's in town, the blue-tinted aliens who walked
through her bedroom walls, and the fetus that had
been implanted in her womb. The Mother Ship that
was traveling toward them in the center of the hurricane so it couldn't be detected, to take her and her
baby to a galaxy far, far away. Where Luke could never
find them.

"God, Charly. What has he done to you? To all of
us."

"It's all *true*," she wailed.

"Okay, I believe you. But we . . . we're in trouble.
I've got to start functioning, somehow. What time is
it?"

"I don't know."

"My wristwatch. Left wrist. It isn't there for me. But
you can see it. Tell me the time."

"The time . . . I think it's . . . almost ten-thirty."

"Ten-thirty? So late? Get up. Get up, Charly; the hurricane's going to make landfall in a few hours."

"They'll be here then," Charlene said gratefully.

"In the meantime, we've got trouble."

He sat up, and half-Charlene sat up beside him. He
had to close his eyes then, because he was sure there
was no way he could stand and balance himself with
half his body missing. Even though his rational mind
had accepted the hypothesis that he was hemianopsic,
he had to see his other half to believe in its continued
existence.

And if the left half of him still existed, it should be
simple to prove it. All he needed to do was open his
eyes, then turn his head to the left.

Simple to think about. But it required an excruci-
ating effort of will while fear pounded in his heart like
the rain that was beginning on the roof of the beach
house.

Inch by inch, as he turned his head, more of the

first floor of the house came into view, and fear turned
to exhilaration. He dared to look down, and there was
his left leg and foot . . . his left hand on his knee.
Nearby, an old blued revolver with the butt wrapped
in grimy tape. He lifted his gaze, and found Adele in
the rattan chair, knees apart, her head back against the
chair cushion with the lumpish rusted stain on it.

Charlene's hand touched his right arm. "Joe?"

"It's . . . better now. I think I can deal with it. A cold,
cold, shower, that's what I need. Or a plunge in the
ocean."

"Wait," she said. He turned his head as she was getting up, and as she walked away from him toward the
front windows she became whole for the first time,
since she occupied only the right half of his visual field.
Charlene opened the plantation shutters and looked
out. "No. The water's too high. It's halfway up the
beach already."

"Charlene, we need to do something about Adele.
And the gun. It was fired twice, once with my finger
on the trigger so I'd have gunshot residue on my hand.
But that will wash off."

He turned his head to the left again, relocating the
revolver. As he was reaching for it Charlene walked
over, picked the revolver up before he could touch it
and held it by the butt the way a woman will hold
something nasty she is about put into the garbage. She
looked at Joe, and at the body of Adele. Then she
turned and went to the door, which blew open as soon
as she turned the knob. The screen door bulged snak-
ily inward from the force of the wind against it. Charlene pushed against the frame and more or less fell
outside to the porch, where she hunched herself prim-
itively against the horizontal, slashing rain.

Joe rose inexpertly to his feet, balancing on his right,
taking a quick look to make sure his left was there, or
something that resembled a left foot, then shifting his
weight. He found that he could walk, but with a quirky,

limping gait, overcompensating for what his conscious
mind was still trying to tell him didn't exist. There was
an existential term for the way he felt: "inauthentic."
The conflict between there and not-there used a lot of
primal, survival energy. His heart was overworked, he
was a swamp of perspiration.

Before he made it to the door Charlene, her clothes
soaked and strands of platinum hair wrapped around
and around her face so that it looked like a shelled
cooked egg in a string basket, stumbled back inside
and forced the door shut again. She was still clutching
the revolver.

"What did you do, Charly?"

"You said to get rid of it. I was going to throw it in
the ocean. I played third base on my school softball
team. I could throw harder than anybody." Her voice
quavered. "But not against a wind like *this*."

She leaned against him, shuddering, and Joe had to
turn his head quickly to keep all of her face in view.
Charlene had spoken of a practical thing in a matter-
of-fact voice. But the bones of her skull appeared to
be thrusting through the delicate albumen of her skin;
her dark drifting toneless eyes seemed related to a
deeply seated mania, or dementia.

"I saw lights up the beach road. Blue lights. I guess
they're coming this way. Checking all the beach houses
to make sure everybody leaves. I can hide the gun. But
what should we do with Adele?"

FORTY-THREE

With Hurricane Honey stubbornly on course, bearing 270 degrees and headed for Nimrod's Chapel, the sea islands as far south as Edisto and as far north as Wrightsville Beach in North Carolina had been evacuated. Lucas Thomason was awake early to supervise the boarding-up of the Barony, and he had no time to speculate on what might have happened to Charlene. None of the plantation vehicles, including the Range Rover she usually drove, were missing.

"She sneaked back into the house," he said to Lillian, "and she's hiding herself in one of the old servants' rooms up on the third floor. She'll come down when she gets hungry, or the wind really starts to blow. Have you heard from Walter Lee?"

"His sister say he was at the funeral home all night, sitting up with Frosty. They couldn't get him to go home to sleep."

"I'll stop in when I'm in town and talk to Walter Lee. You're sure we've got plenty of hurricane lamps?"

Lillian nodded, unwilling to look at him. But he'd already had enough of her reproachful gaze. He went upstairs to look in on Abby, who was watching the progress of the storm on the Weather Channel. They had their own satellite dish, which probably wasn't going to make it through the worst of the storm, although it was located on the protected west side of the Barony.

Abby and Lizzie were playing Trivial Pursuit. Abby had circles under her eyes after a restless night. Without even saying good morning she asked if Joe had shown up.

Thomason said, "He'll probably be along. Of course he might not know enough about hurricanes to get his tail off the beach."

"I can't call, there's no dial tone. The lines may be down already. Maybe I should drive over there."

"If you're that worried, I'll go myself."

"Would you, Luke? Thank you."

"Are we going to be all right here?" Lizzie said.

"The Barony's stood fast through some big blows. This isn't the worst hurricane on record."

"It seems to be getting stronger, though," Abby said, glumly watching the TV. Both of her legs were jittering in the wheelchair. She looked as exhausted as if she'd danced all night. He could hear each breath she took. But with barometric pressure falling, it was difficult for any of them to fill their lungs without conscious effort.

Before he was halfway to Nimrod's Chapel a hard, driving rain began, in which trees melted away like root-bound phantoms. At Kirkeby's Corners the lot in front of the general store was packed with cars and pickups as the islanders who were sticking it out loaded up with batteries, flashlights, canned goods, bottled water and candles. As he was making a left turn toward Nimrod's Chapel Thomason thought he saw Mr. Phipps's old Diamond T truck pull out of the store lot and continue east toward the Barony. At least it looked very much like the pickup, but he couldn't see who was driving. And Mr. Phipps, whose business here was finished, should have been home in his seldom-visited corner of Horry County entangled with the captive anatomy of one of his woeful catamites.

Thomason was momentarily concerned. Mr. Phipps had not been satisfied with the resolution to the problem which he, Thomason, had insisted on. Mr. Phipps hadn't wanted to leave Joe alive at the beach house, in spite of the doctor's insistence that so much damage had been done to Joe's parietal lobes he would be dwelling out there on the lunatic fringe for the rest of his life. Mr. Phipps was understandably dedicated to the proposition that no witnesses insured a secure future.

He thought about it, and decided that it hadn't been Mr. Phipps, just a look-alike old truck in the rain. They had been doing business going back twenty years, and Mr. Phipps had always appreciated the wisdom of his approach to the problems a professional man sometimes encountered. Hit-and-run, deadly but untraceable drugs, an attack on a lonely road—those were the safe bets. So a couple of potentially disastrous malpractice suits had never made it into court, due to the sudden unavailabilty of the plaintiffs; Paul Huskisson had not married Abby, and Joe Bryce's suspicions would sound like so much psychotic babble, if anyone was paying attention to him after the first five minutes. Too bad about Adele; but there was no way to know how much Joe had told her. And her unexpected presence at the beach house did provide a more compelling ending to Joe's intrusion in their lives.

There were whitecaps on Pandora's Bay; Thomason had to wait twenty minutes while the swing bridges were open, allowing for a flotilla of pleasure and commercial watercraft heading upriver to safer anchorages inland. Along Front Street in Nimrod's Chapel most of the business establishments were nailing up plywood on the windows that faced north and east, taping other windows. Emergency shelters had been opened at the YMCA and in the high-school gymnasium; these buildings were on the highest ground in the vicinity, but still only about twenty feet above sea level. The storm surge, which was like a huge bubble atop the normal tide, was due around four o'clock that afternoon. It was expected to be as much as eight feet above high tide.

That would be high enough to flood the lobby of the Planter's House Hotel, where he stopped to pick up mail and the package he'd been expecting from the pharmaceutical house of Anderlingen in Zurich. Dependable Fed Ex had delivered it bright and early. Thomason chatted with the hotel's manager, who was overseeing the removal of some valuable lobby pieces and area carpets to the hotel's mezzanine, then returned to his Dodge truck in a considerably better frame of mind and dropped around to the Coleridge and Laster funeral home.

Walter Lee, having had no sleep for the previous forty-eight hours, had finally dozed off on a lyre-back sofa provided for him in the viewing room where Frosty Clemons lay on aquamarine silk in a lacquered mahogany coffin. It was going to be a seven-thousand-dollar funeral, when the weather permitted, and Thomason had already written the check. Frosty looked like a complete stranger without her gold-rimmed glasses. Cinnamon-colored, her broken neck concealed by the high lace collar of the old-fashioned dress they had put on her.

Walter Lee snored, broke off, whimpered in his sleep, shifted restlessly on the sofa. New black shoes, size fifteen, were aligned on the mulberry carpet in front of the sofa.

"How's he holding up?" Thomason whispered outside to one of the relatives, a petite, severely bowlegged woman who wore elbow-length white kid gloves and carried a prayer book.

"He's a broken man," she said, with a gloss of tears in her eyes.

"The girls are okay?"

"They gone to stay with Walter Lee's sister in Sumter till this storm blow itself out."

"Well, I just wanted to stop by, tell Walter Lee we love him and we loved Frosty too, and he's in our prayers."

"God bless you, Dr. Luke."

On the sofa in the viewing room Walter Lee stirred among the floral remembrances and gasped; his eye-lids trembled. He raised his head and had a glimpse of Thomason as he walked away down the oak-paneled and softly lighted hall. He was like the remnant of a nightmare to Walter Lee, who sat up, panting, and stared at Frosty in her coffin.

"Told you!" he said. "Told you, Frosty, you didn't know what you was dealing with."

He put a hand into the wallet pocket of his suit coat. The new black suit was a size fifty-two long, so the re-volver with the two-inch barrel he carried there made no visible bulge when he stood up. Which he did now, and walked achingly across the carpet to go down on his bad knees, holding on to the pistol in his pocket with one hand and sobbing, the side of his face pressed against the lacquered mahogany. It reflected his agony like a dark mirror. Walter Lee sobbed Frosty's name again and again.

"Oh, God! Just tell me the right thing to do. I *know* it was him. But they ain't no bringin' Frosty back. Lord, I just don't know what I has to do!"

Overcome, Walter Lee began to thump his head against the side of the coffin. The heavy, solid blows echoed through the nearly deserted funeral home. The bowlegged little woman stood in the doorway with tears running down her cheeks. She was joined by the funeral director and one of his assistants. But they all stood in the wide doorway and didn't venture in. No one had the nerve to speak to Walter Lee or disturb him in his grief and rage.

The two deputies from the Chicora County Sheriff's Office were wearing yellow slickers with hoods that glistened in the gray sheets of rain sweeping the porch of the beach house. There was lightning in the turbulent gray-green sky. Ten-foot waves were rolling in two-thirds of the way up the beach, with enough power to shake the house on its foundation. Whitecaps were visible all the way to the darkening horizon.

Joe held the door open a few inches, his shoulder braced against it.

"We're just packing up now! We'll be out of here in ten minutes!"

"I'd advise you not to take any longer than that!" one of the deputies hollered. "All the roads and bridges could be under water in the next half hour! How many are you, sir?"

"There's three of us!"

"Is your vehicle operating okay?"

"Yes."

"Better get going, then!"

"We've got power lines down on Hamrick Road!" said the other deputy, listening to his walkie.

They made their way off the porch as Joe forced the door shut. He turned around, face dripping, and moved his head until all of Charlene came into view, sitting on one of the steps to the second floor.

"Charly, we have to get out of here. And we have to take Adele with us." He turned a little more, to where the body lay on one of the couches. They had covered her with a blanket, as if she were sleeping.

Charlene raised her head. "I can't go. I have to wait here. They're coming for me here."

"Charly, no. That's—it's like a dream you had. Nothing's coming but the hurricane. It'll destroy this house."

She shook her head, peaceable but stubborn. "You don't understand. It wasn't a dream. I was awake all the time. They took my nightgown off and I was lying on a table in the Mother Ship. The air smelled good, it was like after a hard rain, so fresh. They did it with a glass rod they put in my vagina. They inseminated me. I'm going to have one of their babies. That shows how much they love and respect me. The Higher Beings would never let anything bad happen to me."

"Please, Charly. I have to get back to the Barony. Abby's in a lot of danger, she has to be in a hospital."

Charlene thought about it. "Why?"

"One of the drugs Luke's been giving her is a dangerous paralytic. It's leaking from the reservoir. A little of it has reached the brain stem. If he injects any more of the paralytic, she'll die."

From the way Charlene was looking at him, Joe knew she didn't follow. Didn't care to understand. She put her head in her hands, squeezing.

"Yes," she said, and then after a long pause, "yes" again.

The house had begun to shake with each violent gust off the sea. It was necessary to speak very loudly to be heard over the droning of the wind.

"Charly, we don't have any more time!"

"Please be quiet! It's important. They're trying to get through to me." She squeezed her head tighter still, fingers digging in near her temples. She moaned softly.

Joe considered his prospects of forcibly removing her from the beach house. Half-blind, with his proprioception dangerously affected, he would have to fight Charlene and the howling bitch of a wind every inch of the way, then keep her in the Jeep while trying to drive. The alternative was to hit her good and hard while she was distracted, right on the button, and knock her out.

He started across the floor, slowly, bumped a chair

in the void to his left, stumbled. Charlene dropped a hand between her knees, watched him cautiously. Once again he had lost half of her to the void. He stopped and moved his head to the required degree and there was the rest of her; she was holding the old revolver that had killed Adele in her right hand, aiming it at him.

"No," she said. "Don't try to make me go with you! My place is here."

"Easy does it, Charly."

"Get out while you still can!"

"Charly, I'm disoriented! Sick to my stomach. I can't make it without you."

"You have to. You'll be punished if the Higher Beings find you here too. Don't come any closer! Luke taught me to shoot. It was the good thing he taught me. The Bad Thing—I don't have to do the Bad Thing anymore, just to make him happy. And he can go to h-hell."

"Come with me, Charly!" Joe took another step toward her. With no change of expression or other warning—but as if her hatred and fear of her husband suddenly had become a more inclusive indictment— she shot him.

FORTY-FOUR

"What are you doing?" Lizzie asked nervously, watching her cousin transfer from Rolling Thunder to the side of her bed and reach for a trapeze bar that was suspended parallel to the bed. The public-utility electricity had been cut off at midmorning as the outer winds of Honey began to howl in earnest around the Barony. Two emergency generators kept the lights and television sets on and the twin refrigerators in the kitchen running, but they weren't powerful enough to operate the air-conditioning units. The air in the closed-up house was sultry, and they both were filmy with perspiration in Abby's room, despite the action of the ceiling fan and a small fan on top of her wardrobe. Abby's face was rigid with concentration as she extended her arms and hung on tightly to the bar.

"I'm getting up."

"You can't—"

"I did, night before last. At the beach house. I was dreaming that I walked—"

"You do that a lot."

"But then I—woke up on the beach, a *long* way from the house, Lizzie! I was standing by the edge of the sea. Alone. Nobody helping me. That was *not* part of a dream."

"What happened?"

"As soon as I—realized what I was doing, I couldn't do it anymore. I fell down. But I'm going to stand up now. I can! I know I can."

"Maybe I should get Luke or—"

"Not home yet. He called on the cellular. He had to take a big detour, there was a live wire down somewhere."

"Joe's not here, either."

Abby looked at the bar above her head, and ventilated like a power-lifter about to tackle a quarter ton of iron. "I don't . . . understand . . . where he could be."

"I looked outside from the kitchen a few minutes ago," Lizzie said, and concluded apprehensively, "You can't see ten feet from the house because of the rain. This is going to be a bad one, isn't it?"

"You scared?"

"Yeah."

"We'll just stick together, Elizabeth Ann. Everything's okay. This house is built like a fort. The shutters are an inch thick. Okay . . . here I . . . *go*!"

Abby pulled up hard, halfway. Her face was splashed with red, her arms trembled. Once her bare heels were off the floor, her knees turned in.

"Liz! I need a . . . butt-boost."

Lizzie kneeled between Abby and the side of the bed and put both hands under her butt, then lifted until Abby, vertical but wobbly, swinging a little from side to side before she settled down on her heels again, gained some control of her situation.

"I don't think—"

"Shut up, shut up, I'm gonna do this! Let go now."

Lizzie, still crouching, dropped her hands and backed up. Abby bit her lower lip, trying not to sway.

"This is hard—oh *God*, this is hard!"

"Why do you want to do this now? There's no place to go."

"Lizzie, I'm—thirty-two years old. And I've still got—*everywhere* to go."

Saying this, Abby released the bar with her left hand. For a couple of seconds she was stable, and motionless; then the swaying began again. She twisted halfway around, clinging desperately to the bar, her face going from red to magenta. Through sheer willpower she managed to align her body perpendicular to the pegged-board floor. She looked at her feet to make sure they were straight and in line with her hips.

Lizzie watched her fearfully. "Don't let go, Abby. Let me—"

Abby let go, and promptly collapsed half on top of Lizzie. A wild elbow caught Lizzie in the mouth.

"*Fuck!* Did I hurt you?"

"Yes," Lizzie mumbled, tasting blood and beginning to cry.

"Lizzie—Lizzie, I felt something! I really did."

"What?"

"The floor! Something's happened, Lizzie. The soles of my feet, my toes—I was feeling the floor!"

"How does my lip look?"

"Just a little cut. Don't wipe it off on your shirt."

"It's your shirt. I borrowed it."

"Oh, well, in that case, go right ahead and get it all bloody."

"Are you gonna do this again?"

"Yes. You're damn right. I'm going to do it again."

In a blinding, centerless, torrential universe, tinted by lightning the color of mortified flesh, hell had been raised to the status of watery limbo.

Mr. Phipps didn't see the gray Jeep Laredo coming

at him on the beach road until it was too late to avoid
a collision.

Neither the Diamond T truck nor the Laredo was
traveling at more than twenty miles an hour. The Laredo was running without headlights. A flash of lightning revealed Joe's face behind the wheel just as Mr.
Phipps took evasive action. The impact was on the
right side of his pickup truck as it left the road and
plunged up to the hood ornament in the rising waters
of the intertidal marsh. Without a restraint Mr. Phipps
was slammed against the steering wheel of the pickup.
The door on his side remained closed. Mr. Phipps hit
his head on the windshield column and lost his glasses.

The impact crumpled the front end of the Laredo;
the airbag on the driver's side of the Laredo protected
Joe from further injury, but he was stunned, and for
a few seconds he couldn't move. The pickup had appeared to him out of the hemianopsic void on his left
side just as both vehicles reached a bend in the road.

He wouldn't have been able to drive at all without
the telephone poles on the right side to give him some
idea of where the edge of the shell road was. In the
gray opacity and screaming wind the sky had vanished
and the earth was half-drowned. Gnarly live oaks and
cypress trees writhed like supplicants praying in a
ghostly cloister at the ending of the world. Lightning
flashed and thunder was so loud it hurt the eardrums.

Charlene's casual shot had scorched his right shoulder like a hot poker and punched out a piece of glass
in a beach-house window. In his last glimpse of her as
he went out the door and was blown off his feet on the
porch, she was still sitting on the stairs to the second
floor with the revolver dangling from her right hand,
as if she'd already forgotten about it.

Sitting in the Laredo, Joe tried to restart the engine.
It started, but judging from the racket under the hood
things were grinding together or flying apart. He
turned the ignition off and opened the door cau-

tiously. The wind caught the door and nearly flung it off the hinges. The cold rain on his unprotected face felt like needles. It wasn't coming from just one direction anymore: the rain swarmed all around him, a maelstrom. He could barely see.

Except for the lightning, he would have been helpless, just another drowner in the quickening hurricane, which at the height of its power could obliterate entire islands, turn old-growth forests to kindling and sweep oceangoing freighters so far inland they had to be torched for scrap. But so much lightning accompanied this phase of the storm that he was able, in spite of the visual handicap, to retain some sense of direction.

Joe recognized, through a streaming cracked window, the shape of the driver in the front seat of the old Diamond T pickup. He seemed to be moving, but it could have been an illusion prompted by the overwhelming, theatrical flashes of lightning. Even when he shielded his right eye the rain was all but blinding. He couldn't be sure that this was the man who had murdered Frosty Clemons and Adele Franklin. He didn't care to take a closer look. His fear was of what lay behind him, a lethal tidal surge; his dominant instinct was to find shelter, and fast.

He'd been on the road in a torrent, the Laredo almost whipsawing in the wind, for several harrowing minutes. He couldn't see the house, but he thought he must be within a few hundred yards of the Barony.

He was crouched with his back to the wind. In half of his visual field there was tumult; in the other half nothing at all. His nerves were at break-point as he set out up the road, not daring or even able to walk erect, totally unaware of what his left foot and leg were doing. Driving had been difficult; walking was a comedy of horrors. Every faltering step invited disaster. And he felt as if he were drowning with each breath he took.

He lost count of the times he fell, and struggled back to his feet. He looked back once, and couldn't find the crashed vehicles on the road. What did that mean? Occasionally, in the hemianopsic void, he thought he saw tiny glowworms, hair-thin and isolated. A phenomenon he couldn't account for. What if he lost the other side of his visual field? He was desperate for clarity, for air and space.

There seemed to be more trees where he was, including some tall pines that were swaying in arcs of sixty degrees or more overhead. At some point he had wandered off the beach road. Now he was in a vale or ravine, where he was protected from the brunt of the wind. Looking up, he saw the crude barrel of a Columbiad cannon and realized how much off course he was. He had reached the old Confederate breastworks on Pandora's Bay. The path from the breastworks went around by the inlet where the *Wayfarer* was, then continued to the cemetery and the gardens of the Barony. The distance, he remembered, was about six hundred yards.

Halfway up the breastworks, Joe had to stop and rest. The glowworms in the void had begun to knit together in a filigree pattern. He didn't know if that was good news, or bad.

Turning his head as lightning pulsed through the flailing trees, he saw Mr. Phipps coming, the gleam of a nickel-plated revolver in one hand. His glasses were awry on his face. He was going from tree to tree, staggered by the maddening, shrieking wind, holding on to branches to keep from being bowled head over heels. It was not possible to tell, from Joe's impaired perspective, just how far away Mr. Phipps was or if, as he turned his head quickly side to side in the glare, he knew where Joe had gone.

Nevertheless Joe thought it was a good bet that if Mr. Phipps did find him, he intended to kill him.

There was an overturned camper truck in the middle of the intersection of Fox Creek and Pitt's Landing roads just past the causeway to Chicora Island, and the tow-truck operator was having trouble deciding how to clear it out of the way. The overhead traffic signal had fallen. Two Highway Patrol cars, blue lights flashing in the windy torrent, and a line of traffic coming off the island made more of a mess of the intersection.

Walter Lee, driving Frosty's yellow minivan, was met by a trooper in a Crayola-orange rain suit. Inexplicably, he also wore sunglasses with amber lenses.

"You're going the wrong way!"

"There's people at the Barony I need to look after!" Walter Lee said, blinking furiously as the rain streamed in through the two-inch gap of the rolled-down window. "Let me go through, please."

"Well, we can't stop you! All we can do is advise that some of the roads are probably impassable already."

"I'll get there! If you'll just move that one car which is blocking me."

"Up to you!" the trooper said, and he plodded, haltingly, like a boxer into a welter of body-blows, toward the parked cruiser. Walter Lee rolled the window up. The windshield wipers were going at maximum speed, sweeping waves of water off the glass, but still it was hard to see more than five car lengths past the intersection.

He heard Frosty say, as clearly as if she were seated beside him and not in a polished box back at the funeral parlor, "Daddy, they will put you in jail the rest of your natural life."

"I ain't afraid of that." He *was* afraid to look, though, to see if she really was there in the yellow minivan. He knew that wouldn't be good news. If he saw her, then it would mean he had gone crazy. And a crazy man was not a purposeful man.

He hunched his shoulders, shivering, and risked a peek to his right. Frosty was still very much alive in his memory, but her ghost was not occupying the other seat in the front of the van. Still, he had heard her voice, and the shock of it continued to tingle his neck bones.

The only other time he'd heard a plain-as-day, out-of-the-blue voice had been at a particularly strenuous though uplifting tent revival, and it had been Jesus speaking. Jesus had said to him, "Walter Lee, I need that twenty-five cents in your pocket you were going to spend on chocolate bars." And then, after he'd dug up the quarter he'd been trying to forget was buried in a deep pocket of his overalls and tossed it into the collection bucket, Jesus spoke again: "And I don't want you looking at those sinful magazines with naked women in 'em no more."

The sheriff's car was backed onto the shoulder of the road, and Walter Lee proceeded.

He had been faithful to Jesus since that night at the revival, true to those he loved and charitable to many who didn't deserve it, only to have his life come to this. Frosty was right. It would mean jail, or worse. Nothing had really changed in the last forty years. Colored still didn't stand much of a chance in the courts. No matter that Dr. Luke was an evil man; he was a white man who had powerful friends.

Walter Lee risked taking a hand off the wheel, and pressed his palm against the revolver in his suit pocket. The feel of it was no comfort to him; he had never liked guns of any kind. He'd never fired a shot in anger, even in wartime. He was a fisherman, not a hunter.

Trembling from grief, Walter Lee drove on, and came to the starving dog.

The sides of the dog had sunk down to staves; its lips were clenched in a grimace of hunger, or fear. Unable to control the momentum of walking, the yellow dog was in the middle of the road, floundering sideways, haunches sinking. And, as Walter Lee slowed, the dog wound up the way it had come: puzzled, vacant; powerless, or unwilling, to go there again.

Walter Lee stopped and sat for a few seconds, look-

ing at the waterlogged cur in his headlights. Then he
took off his suit coat, folded it on the seat beside him.
He got out of the minivan, an arm up to shield his
face, and, staying low, inched his way to where the dog
was lying helpless. There were stinging, pinhead-size
pieces of hail mixed with the rain. Each flare of lightning was as green as granny apples. Walter Lee stooped
with his back to the gale, picked the shuddering dog
up in his arms, carried it back to the van and laid it
on the floor behind the driver's seat. Too far gone to
live, Walter Lee thought. But he reached for his suit
coat, took the revolver out of the wallet pocket and
wrapped the dog snugly in his coat.

The dog looked up at him; its dying eyes were unexpectedly serene.

Walter Lee felt something like the tap of a hammer
at the base of his spine; relief and awe jetted through
him as fresh as childhood blood, and his aching head
felt miraculously cleared. For the first time in more
than forty years, Jesus spoke to him, words that came
not from heaven and with a pealing of heavenly
chords, but from the belly of the yellow dog.

"If you put him in the ground, Walter Lee, how can
his soul come to me?"

Flooded roads, flooded bridges, as he drove toward
the violent middle of the storm, the minivan in two
feet of water part of the time. But it didn't quit on
him. "Don't you go quittin' neither," Walter Lee said,
more than once, to the dog behind him. By the time
he reached the gates of the Barony, he knew what he
must do to put Frosty's soul at rest, and satisfy the Lord
as well.

Lillian had gone from room to room on the first floor
at the back of the house, retaping seams around win-
dow- and doorframes where the wind came through
minute cracks with the hiss of a steam kettle, wringing

out wet towels jammed under the French doors from
the dining room to the veranda.

"Did you find her?" Lucas Thomason asked Lillian,
his mouth close to her ear. "Is she hiding upstairs, like
I said she'd do?"

Lillian pushed a dry towel under one of the doors.
"No time to see."

Thomason put his FedEx package down and
combed his fingers through his sparse wet hair. His
ears were ringing from the pressure of the fulminating
storm. In spite of Lillian's efforts, there was a mist in
the room. "Well, that's where she is," he said again.
"Maybe I'll go have a look for Charlene myself, later."

Lillian looked at him as lightning flashed, wordless
but not without comment.

He blotted his face with a handkerchief. "Any damage so far?"

"No."

"I'll be upstairs in Abby's room! I could use a sandwich when you have time, Lillian!"

"Yes, sir."

Thomason carried the package into his infirmary
and broke it open. He took out the ampule from the
Swiss lab, opened a cabinet drawer and found a syringe
of the appropriate gauge. The lights in the room
winked at a particularly violent gust from the hurricane; Honey was all over the house now, clawing like
a huge, forgotten cat trying to get in. He turned off
the lights, thinking that he would have to refuel the
generators soon to keep electricity on inside. The public utility lines to the house had been disconnected
earlier to prevent back-feeding, adding to the risk of a
disastrous fire if things didn't go as well as he hoped
they would.

He walked toward the front of the house, swallowing
to reduce the pressure on his eardrums. The chandelier in the gallery was trembling; the green marble
floor was a mosaic of watery shadows.

"Luke!" Abby called. "Look at me!"

Glancing up, he saw her, standing—*standing!*—in the second-floor hall twenty feet above him, gripping the railing around the stairwell tightly. Lizzie was behind her.

"Something's happened, Luke! I have *feeling*! I can—"

Mainly with the strength of her arms, Abby propelled herself a little farther along the railing in a mood of stubborn good cheer, her face streaming perspiration, each breath an exclamation of achievement.

Thomason felt his gut muscles cramping from shock. "Now, Abby—don't overexert yourself! And don't depend on that railing to hold you up, it's none too strong—"

Even before he finished speaking he saw the railing buckle as the bolts that held it to the wall pulled loose, saw Abby's look of shock and fear as she moved erratically sideways with the railing, losing what tenuous balance she had been able to maintain.

FORTY-FIVE

Charlene was hungry, so after a while she got up and went into the kitchen to look around. Earlier she had closed the door Joe had left open in his hurry to get away from the threat of the revolver, which she had aimed carefully and with no intent to do serious damage. But there was nothing she could do about the wind and the rain pissing in through the bullet hole in one of the windows that overlooked the porch. A salty mist had invaded the beach house; everything she touched was slippery.

The electricity had been off for a long time, and her hurricane lamp was running out of fuel. But there was so much lightning she had no trouble finding her way around the shaky beach house. Ice cubes in the freezer were melting into a lump. She put the ice in the sink and chipped off some with a paring knife, and made lemonade with artificial mix she found in the pantry. There was an unopened jar of peanut butter too. She drank lemonade and scooped peanut butter out of the jar with her little finger, having her treat without bread or crackers—the way she'd always liked it. But how long had it been, gosh, twenty years since she'd dared to eat peanut butter. All that fatty semisolid oil.

Tasted so good she wondered if she should pack the rest of the jar with the few things she had found in the bathrooms, the liquor cabinet and Adele's big handbag to take aboard the Mother Ship when it arrived. Adele wasn't going to need her hairbrush or emery boards. Too bad her lipstick was the wrong shade, but Charlene had taken that too, thinking the color might look different in a better light.

She also found a spare battery pack for Adele's camcorder, but not the camcorder itself.

It was getting harder to wait. No television, and the low pressure within the hurricane had clogged her sinuses and closed her ears, deafening her. Just as well; the shriek of the wind would have been hard to bear at full volume.

Now and then the house rocked, as if it was about to slide off its foundation, and Charlene cringed. *What was keeping them?* Any minute now, probably, they would come flickering through the walls, never less than two or more than five, and surround her, glowing like the low flame of a gas-stove jet, eyes slanted and pupilless within their misty auras. She never knew what to say to them—well, face it, the first encounters had so terrified her she was tongue-tied. Until she came to accept the fact they meant no harm. Leaving her in her bed on their first visits, merely touching her all over with appendages that resembled leafy stalks of celery until she was so thoroughly covered with a mucilage-like liquid she'd had difficulty scrubbing it all off in the shower afterward. Twice Luke had slept through these visitations, two feet away from her; but they weren't interested in him.

Charlene walked the floor of the beach house, trying not to be impatient. There were some old decorating magazines on one of the bookshelves. None she hadn't seen before, and the light was too poor to read anyway. Almost the middle of the afternoon, but the day had never really dawned. She picked through some sea-shells on a higher shelf, coral fingers mounted on ped-estals, and found Adele's camcorder draped in fishnet, partly hidden behind a big crusty starfish.

Charlene undraped the camcorder and took it down from the shelf. The battery was dead, but she remem-bered the spare battery in Adele's purse, which was at the head of the couch where her dead body lay under a beach blanket decorated with leaping blue porpoises.

With nothing else to do, Charlene changed batteries and sat on the floor holding the camcorder in both hands, waiting for the tape to rewind. Then the show began. The light had been good. First there was noth-ing but furniture, including the couch on which Adele was now laid out; then Joe and Adele appeared and began talking. That wasn't interesting because the au-dio playback was set too low, and Charlene, not all that familiar with camcorders, couldn't remedy it. But soon something happened. Adele's head snapped back, and it was clear on the videotape that she'd been shot, be-cause the back of her head more or less exploded. It was like the president's head in the open car in Dallas the year Charlene was born, the crude frames of film everybody had seen a hundred times. Joe looked back, getting out of his chair. Then a man in a dark blue suit with a gun came into the picture, which wasn't a bad picture at all in spite of the distance, color values were just fine. The man hit Joe and knocked him down. And after that, who should appear but—

Charlene watched the tape until it ran out on a tab-leau of Joe, drugged and motionless on the floor, and Adele, equally motionless, the two of them like char-acters in a play that had ended without applause or a descending curtain. When the small rectangular screen went blank, Charlene rewound and watched it all again, this time wondering what had been in the syringe Lucas Thomason emptied, or nearly emptied, into Joe's neck. He always liked his needles so much. She had a touch of the flu, he wanted to give her a needle.

When she became bored, just after the shooting in the third replay, Charlene shut the camera off and looked at Adele. The house shook and she felt a little dizzy from concentrating on the camcorder screen. She got up and put the camera on the couch with Adele, between an arm that had been stiff but was now softening again and her side. The shriek of the wind pierced Charlene's clogged ears, alerting her. It was a different pitch than she'd become accustomed to. There was a steady barrage of God-knew-what against the front of the house and the nylon screens that protected the windows. Pieces of shell, flotsam, coral; even fish, dredged up by the action of the huge rollers rising steadily to the level of the porch.

Several panes of glass had been cracked since she'd last looked out. The heavy screens were laden with kelp. It now seemed as if the house were being picked up, a few inches each time, then slammed back on its foundation. All she could see outside was one huge black cloud rising from the heaving waters like an undersea mountain.

Charlene had never seen anything like this, but there could be no doubt that the world was coming to an end, preceded by moaning and howling in which the body blanched and shrank to a nub of bald, primal fear. The Mother Ship had to come *now*. At any moment the beams of blue light would shine through the walls, penetrate downward from the roof and coalesce into familiar heady shapes: the Higher Beings. She crept across the sisal floor covering on knees that had begun to bleed again and picked up her travel case. She held it, shivering, against her breast, too drained to move again. Terror was shutting down her vagus nerves. Charlene was like an animal in the jaws of a predator that had pursued her all her life and, inevitably, had at last run her to ground.

Shelter of any kind was preferable to the battering he had to endure in the open, so when Joe reached the *Wayfarer* he pulled himself aboard and crawled to the Lexan bubble over the midships cockpit, which, fortunately, he hadn't removed while making repairs. The forty-three-foot ketch was trembling on her keel blocks. The roof of the boat shed, heavy-gauge corrugated steel, had already been ripped away by the wind and crumpled around a live oak. Waves rising up from the normally placid inlet of Pandora's Bay broke over the stern. With his right hand he slid back the panel of the moisture-clouded bubble that provided access to the deck when the boat was at sea, and lowered himself inside. He was quick to close the bubble, but in a matter of seconds the cockpit was soaked from the driving rain.

He slumped against the padded backrest, gratefully relieved, for now, of the intolerable burden of the wind. With little visibility and half of his vision missing, he could easily convince himself that he was no longer on land but riding out a force-eleven gale without mast or helm. He wondered what the anemometer would read, what the seas would look like in a monster storm. He already had the vertigo that would accompany the lift and helpless plunge of a small boat down the backs of hissing, forty-foot waves. His imagination, he thought, wanted him diverted from the reality of a situation even more dangerous. The *Wayfarer* was drydocked with a windbreak of cypress and mangrove behind, a woodlot of mixed hardwoods and pines on two sides. He had seen, as he struggled to reach the boat, trees of less than a foot in diameter uprooted like weeds. The *Wayfarer* had a sturdy hull but a direct hit by the trunk of a large tree like a cypress would smash it to splinters. Never mind what would happen to the Lexan cockpit bubble.

His safety was moment-to-moment, a matter of luck, and the nearness of the hurricane's front wall. *How much longer?* he wondered. If the full force of the hurricane was just now making landfall, it was inevitable that the *Wayfarer* would be swept away.

Lightning. And something out there on the tapered foredeck, clinging to it—crooked branches of a tree, he guessed, or a large dark animal of some kind. He turned his head to bring more of it into view. It would have to be a raccoon; they had the capability of climbing and clinging. Whatever it was, it was very nearly helpless in the screaming wind. Yet, as Joe watched, the animal seemed to be moving, inching from handhold to handhold—cleats, stanchions, forward hatch cover—toward the cockpit bubble. Resolving, after a long suspenseful minute, into Mr. Phipps, his suit coat pulled up around his head, arms foreshortened, black leather gloves on his hands, all of which accounted for the humped, misshapen look of him.

Joe hadn't given any thought to Mr. Phipps since he'd seen him near the breastworks; such was the hold the hurricane had on his mind and emotions. Now he couldn't be sure that what he saw was real, as if his mind, weakened like his body by vertigo, had taken refuge in hallucination.

To make the hallucination worse, much worse, his drug-affected vision had begun to play even stranger, surreal tricks. The right eye, which all through his ordeal since waking up in the beach house hours ago had provided a normal visual field, was blurring now, from stress and irritation. The blurring was made worse by the opaque nature of the rain on the Lexan bubble. At the same time, in what had been a hemianopsic void, the filigreed, wisp-thin strands of light began to form a pattern, a mosaic of geometric shapes, so that the bubble around him began to look like a perfectly halved section of a geodesic dome—but flat, crystalline, without dimension.

He blinked and turned his head to the right.

Surprisingly, half of Mr. Phipps reappeared within the mosaic as he crept against the wind toward the cockpit. Motionless for a few moments, his lips pulled flat against his teeth, eyes nearly closed, the mosaic half of Mr. Phipps became dimensionless also, a figure composed of hexagonals and etched on glass. But his left hand and left leg continued to move, the hand reaching slowly for a vent near the front of the cockpit as he pulled himself across the top of the teak trunk cabin. The teak provided a lot of resistance even in the sheets of rain that swept across the shuddering boat.

Except for the slight movements of his head, Joe sat motionless and fascinated in the rear of the cockpit. He couldn't be sure, despite flashes of lightning, that Mr. Phipps knew he was there. He might only be seeking the best shelter he could find, as Joe had done.

With his grip on the vent secure, Mr. Phipps rolled to his left side. His right half moved too, in Joe's mosaic vision, but in a discontinuous stuttering fashion, the action broken into a series of flash impressions, so that when his hand came up with the nickel-plated revolver in it, for Joe it was like watching a jerky old black-and-white silent film.

Confused by what his brain was telling him, and not telling him, Joe dwelled on this curious breakdown of space and time without processing the imminent danger.

Mr. Phipps fired a shot through the Lexan bubble. It missed Joe's head by a couple of inches. The immediate high-pitched scream of wind through the exit hole behind him galvanized Joe. He threw himself off the seat and to his left to avoid impaling himself on the helm mounting from which the wheel had been removed to storage.

The companionway doors were padlocked. He had

less room to manuever in the cockpit than a gerbil in a cage. Crouched on the sole, he wouldn't be a target again until Mr. Phipps hitched himself closer— another few feet against the wind that was trying to tear him off the deck of the *Wayfarer*. His position was precarious but Joe's was impossible.

There was a miscellany of tools in the cockpit locker beneath the bench seat. Joe felt inside the locker and picked up a chromed winch handle eighteen inches long. Then he risked rising from his knees to try to get a glimpse of Mr. Phipps without also catching a bullet full in the face.

Mr. Phipps was off to his right, gun hand outstretched. With the wind and rain in his face his sight lines were narrowed; and apparently he had lost his glasses. Visually they might almost be even, Joe thought. But Mr. Phipps didn't have to be able to see well to pull himself to the cockpit coaming and fire methodically down into the cockpit until Joe was dead.

His only hope was to go after Mr. Phipps before he could come any closer.

With the winch handle in his right hand, Joe groped for the sliding panel on the port side of the bubble and moved it back. Pushing his head and shoulders out of the bubble was like being beaten with the stream from a high-pressure fire hose. He wormed his way far enough through the opening to grab a cap-rail stanchion with his left hand, and used it to pull himself, flopping in the huge wind, onto the two-foot-wide portside deck. The mosaic of his hemianopsia was still in place, his right eye blurred. He lifted his head a couple of inches off the deck and saw Mr. Phipps lying motionless with his head down between hatch covers in front of the cockpit. The wind billowed his suit coat like a small dark sail. They were both pinned down. Joe realized that if he tried to stand he would immediately be blown off the *Wayfarer*.

But he had to do something about Mr. Phipps, or get shot.

He began to creep on his belly, following the curved cap rail. The wind was at his back, wanting to pick him up and bowl him forward to the pulpit. His left hand and arm ached from the strain of holding on as he moved from stanchion to stanchion along the half-height trunk cabin on which Mr. Phipps lay spread-eagled, his feet braced against the low curved grab rails. He was less than three feet away. Joe raised his head and saw the face of Mr. Phipps, half of it a pensive mosaic, the other half as alive as earthworms: gray, contorted from tension. His gloved hand moved on the teak surface of the trunk cabin, and the muzzle of the revolver came around slowly toward Joe.

Joe let go of the cap-rail stanchion, rose up and hammered at the revolver with the steel winch handle, knocking out the cylinder and disabling the weapon. In spite of the glove he wore, the blow also broke Mr. Phipps's trigger finger and crushed half of the knuckles on his right hand.

In the next instant Joe went tumbling forward in the wind, over the foredeck to the pulpit, where he was wedged painfully against the shrouded mast and the pulpit railing, crammed as tightly as a big cork in a jug.

Mr. Phipps had turned himself around on the trunk cabin. There was an aura clinging to the mosaic of Joe's hemianopsia, like the afterglow from a nearby flash of lightning. But he couldn't see much of anything with the rain driving full in his face. He had only painful glimpses of Mr. Phipps making his way to the pulpit, black suit coat billowing like the Jolly Roger.

A shroud line had come untied in the gale and was whipping across Joe's face. He couldn't get his arms unpinned. The *Wayfarer* had begun to buck up and down in the drydock cradle. At each jarring motion the shrouded mast and sail loosened. With his feet under him, Joe was able to twist his left arm and hand free and grab the line that was lacerating his cheek and ear. He wrapped it once around his hand. In a brilliant flash that accompanied a tree toppling only about a dozen feet away, Joe glimpsed the looming black wall of the tidal surge, racing up the narrow channel of Pandora's Bay.

And Mr. Phipps was there, with the winch handle that Joe had dropped, clutched in his left hand.

Somewhat protected from the wind by Mr. Phipps's broad back, Joe ducked inside the intended blow as the winch handle slashed down through the rain. He rammed the top of his head under Mr. Phipps's chin, coming up nearly hard enough to break the man's neck. Mr. Phipps sagged against the shrouded mast, his mouth spilling blood and shattered teeth. Joe pounced on him with the end of the shroud line and wrapped it around Mr. Phipps's neck—twice, three times, yanking the line tight. Then he fell to the deck, knowing the tidal surge was almost on them. The forward hatch cover was eight feet away. A couple of days ago he had removed the chromed catch fitting to clean it. There was a gasket around the hatch that resisted his frantic efforts to pry it open. The sound of the wind had sunk to that of a low organ note, endlessly held. Over this sound he heard the black surge coming like a freight train.

Joe felt around on the deck for the winch handle, found it near where Mr. Phipps was on his knees trying to dig the shroud line out of his neck with the gloved fingers of his working hand. Joe jammed the handle through the gasket. The hatch cover sucked free of the vacuum created by the low pressure of the hurricane and flew back on its hinges. He wriggled around and dropped down into the small forward cabin, pulling the cover down with him, as the tidal surge swept across the *Wayfarer* and lifted her from the cradle. The hull, deck and bulkheads groaned as if she had collided with a supertanker. But most of the seams and joinings held.

Dismasted, out of control, moving faster than she ever had under sail, *Wayfarer* was borne on a fifteen-foot wave through the hurricane air toward the Barony.

FORTY-SIX

Lucas Thomason said to Abby, with a necessary gravity of tone but not lecturing, "You can do yourself some *serious* damage if you don't listen to me! You're days overdue for your steroid shot. If your spinal cord flares up, then you could be paralyzed all over your body, not just in the legs."

But she was not in a state to listen to him, or anyone: she had done something rash and unwise, had nearly fallen fifteen feet to solid marble, a potentially fatal fall (Lizzie's quick hands had pulled her weight off the poorly anchored railing, and Abby had gone backward instead of headlong to the gallery floor), and she was so blanketed in bitterness and disappointment at her failure she couldn't speak. She lay on her bed, breathing hard, with eyes fixed on the slowly swinging light fixture and trapeze bars that cast multiple shadows on the apple green walls and stamped-tin ceiling. The thick walls and shutters of the house accepted the full force of the wind and stood fast, but the house was not airtight; there were whistlings and moanings from every sliver of space around window- and doorframes, the house breathed as if it had lungs.

The lights were failing as the twin generators gulped gasoline. They needed to be refueled, by hand. Thomason had placed the ampule, which had arrived that morning from Switzerland, and which, in his hurry, he had not relabeled as Solumedrol, along with a packaged syringe on the Jacobean turned table beside Abby's bed. He looked at the paralytic, wondering if he should try to fill the implanted reservoir now, or give Abby a little longer to cope with her failure to take even a single step on her own. The despairing mood she was in, her long-standing hatred of needles—probably he should give her an oral tranquilizer first to settle her down.

Lizzie came out of the bathroom. "Can you do something about the lights?" she asked worriedly.

"Yes, I'd better take care of that. I'll be a few minutes. Sit with her, Lizzie. I'll send Lillian up with some cold Dr Peppers." He moved closer to the bed and blotted Abby's forehead with a tissue. "Or would you rather have a Sprite, Abby?"

Abby breathed harshly and didn't respond. Her hands were still clenched at her sides.

Lizzie edged onto the bed beside her and covered a rigid fist with her own hand. There was a sudden loud pounding downstairs: a sound of hazard, or threat. Lizzie jumped, her eyes blue sparks in a woefully flushed face.

"My God—what's that?"

Thomason frowned. "Somebody at the front door. I'll see."

"Maybe you shouldn't let them in," Lizzie said. "It could be a trick, you know, somebody pretending to be stranded when what they've really got in mind—"

"Don't let your imagination get the best of you, Lizzie," he said, but then he decided she had a point.

He smiled reassuringly at the girl and left the room.

In the hall outside Thomason paused to pick up a lighted hurricane lamp Lillian had left there—the gallery lights were now at a fourth of the wattage they had been a few minutes ago—and went to his own bedroom. From a compartment of a small English secretary he took out a compact eight-shot automatic and tucked it into his belt under the sport shirt he wore outside his pants.

Downstairs he responded to the frantic knocking at his door.

"It's Walter Lee!"

Thomason opened up. Walter Lee, soaking, stumbled inside, his black trousers muddy to the knees. Thomason forced the door closed again, and turned.

"Walter Lee, what—"

Walter Lee had his revolver out, pointed at the doctor's head.

"Look me in the eye. I said look me in the eye! And swear you didn't have nothing to do with killing my baby!"

"For Christ's sake," Thomason said, and threw the hurricane lamp at him.

The lamp exploded against Walter Lee's chest as he jerked his face aside and fired a shot, wildly. He fell to the floor, hands beating frantically at the burning kerosene, delicate flames that floated around his torso and head like an aurora. His clothing and even his skin was so wet the flames puffed out before they could do him serious damage. But he had lost his revolver, his impetus, his moral posture.

Walter Lee lay with his back against a wall, smoking and moaning, as Thomason retrieved the revolver. His own gun was in his other hand. He looked around quickly. Kerosene was flaming all around him, on the green marble floor where it couldn't do real damage. None of it had landed on the vulnerable walls or stairs.

"Oh, God, I'm blind!" Walter Lee screamed. "I can't see, help me!"

Lillian came from somewhere with another lamp and knelt protectively over Walter Lee. She looked back at Thomason, the rage of her race imbuing her with a bitter, brutal majesty.

"If you shoots him, then you just as well shoot us both."

"Lillian, get up from there! I'm not gonna shoot Walter Lee. He's gone crazy in the head, that's all. Accused me of killing Frosty. Now, that's *crazy*." There seemed to be a shortage of air in the house; he filled his lungs by gasping, but his head spun dizzily, he was sick of unpleasant surprises. He stuffed the guns behind his belt. "I don't think he's too bad off. His eyes probably got singed. I'll get some saline solution from the infirmary."

Lizzie was at the head of the stairs, screaming along with Walter Lee.

"What happened? What HAPPENED?"

"You get back in there with Abby," Thomason ordered. "He'll be all right." Lizzie's face was twitching out of control. "Don't you get hysterical on me, young lady. Do what I tell you."

He took the other hurricane lamp and was halfway down the hall to the infirmary next to the kitchen when he heard an ominous thundering sound—but deeper than atmospheric thunder, with a chilling liquid resonance—beneath the furious wind. He had a couple of moments to reflect on what it might be while his balls gathered tightly toward his groin and hairs sizzled on the back of his neck. Then the storm surge off Pandora's Bay, a crest of fifteen feet moving at perhaps sixty miles an hour and carrying with it everything from cemetery grave markers and aboveground coffins to the sheds and gazebo that had been in the garden to uprooted or snapped-off trees, reached the house.

The impact was like a bomb going off, followed by

smaller but still massive thuddings and jolts as the contents of the surge were flung against the brick walls nearly as high as the roof. Shutters at several windows and the plywood sheets nailed over the French doors of the first-floor dining room were breached with loud rendings and reports of glass shattering. Something forbiddingly heavy had crunched through the plywood and jammed itself into the fifteen-by-twenty-five-foot dining room with enough force to buckle interior walls, creating gaps in the house through which all of Pandora's Bay was now flooding.

Seconds after the surge assault on the Barony, the lights went down for good.

Thomason had managed to stay on his feet and not lose his grip on the lamp. By its light he reached the infirmary and forced open a door that was hanging up in the jamb. Lizzie's screams resounded through the darkened house. He stood in the infirmary too dazed to think as black water swept in over his knees. Panic seized him and he waded out into the hall without remembering or caring why he had gone to the infirmary in the first place.

There was a swift current against him—the water surging at his hips, still rising—and wind in his face, but he had to see what Honey had wrought at the rear of the house. Severe structural damage could mean an impending collapse of his treasured home. The Barony, its history, the pretensions of its owners: the bitch hurricane had no inkling. She stomped everything flat in her path and moved on. A simple bird's nest high in a tree probably had better hope of surviving such winds.

Something sleek and black came toward him, swimming frantically, and instinct had him pointing his automatic before he recognized the head and popped, frantic eyes of Bruiser the mastiff. Bruiser bumped against him, making terrified yipping sounds, and was swept on down the hall in the direction of the front

parlor and gallery. Thomason pushed against the tide,
through pots and pans and bobbing bottles, to the
kitchen. He held the lamp up to see furry bedraggled
creatures and glinting eyes on every elevated surface—
range tops, counters, window ledges. He shuddered
and waded waist-deep toward the dining room.

In the doorway between kitchen and dining room
he stood braced against the swirling waters with the
lamp held high, staring in disbelief at the *Wayfarer*—
the forward two-thirds of the ketch, wedged into and
taking up most of the space of the room, its keel resting on the remains of a mahogany dining table so long
and heavy six strong men were required to move it,
water beginning to ripple over the cap rails and decks.
The immensely valuable crystal chandelier imported a
century and a half ago from a Hapsburg palace lay, its
many gold branches half-denuded like a discarded
Christmas tree, on the foredeck.

And there was a body, hanging down from the pulpit
of the *Wayfarer*, the head and shoulders submerged,
swaying on a length of line running tautly over the
pulpit rail from the shrouded horizontal mast. He
couldn't see the face, which was under water, but the
smallish puckers—like a child's finger-pokes in a brick
of lard—from old pellet wounds that starred the partly
bared buttocks and lower back were perfectly familiar
to Thomason, since he was the one who had done the
extractions many years ago.

While he was trying to account for the presence of
the now-dead Mr. Phipps aboard the *Wayfarer*, then
staring at the hole in the ceiling left when the chandelier was torn down, the forward hatch cover opened
slowly and Joe Bryce, wet head gleaming in the light
reflected from the remaining crystal facets on one
branch of the fallen chandelier, looked toward Thomason's lamp.

For a few moments they stared at each other. Then
Thomason nodded, as if the bizarre occasion called for

this minimum amount of ceremony. He fought the lassitude of shock and the urge to yawn, aimed his automatic and began firing.

At the first shot Joe's head disappeared as he slipped
back down into the forward cabin. Thomason lowered
his aim and began firing into the hull. When the slide
locked open, he dumped the automatic and reached
for Walter Lee's revolver. He was about to empty that
as well; then it occurred to him that the revolver might
not have the punch to carry through the *Wayfarer*'s mahogany planking. He replaced the revolver. The water,
still surging, was above his waist now; his stomach muscles cringed at the coldness.

He had observed that only the wide veranda doors
and some framing stonework had been taken out when
the *Wayfarer* slammed into the house. The Barony had
absorbed the best Honey could throw its way, and
would stand. The water, not wind, was the real threat.
Four feet high, and rising. Time to get back upstairs.
He would wait for Joe Bryce there.

Joe came up again through the companionway hatch,
in darkness, not wanting to use the flashlight he had
taken from a nav-station compartment. It would light
up the cockpit bubble, which was still in place, like a
crystal ball.

Instead he felt for the port-side sliding door and
eased it open. The cockpit was flooded, and the cabin
below was filling rapidly. He crawled out onto the side
deck against the incoming tide. It was painful work.
He was bruised all over from being thrown around the
cabin as the *Wayfarer* rode the storm surge from Pandora's Bay to the house. And now he was inside the
house, half-drowned but functioning. And, possibly as
a result of the jolting and the cold bath, his hemianopsia had vanished.

He lay still in inches of water on the flooded deck.
The lamp had disappeared from the dining room. By

flashes of lightning he gradually assured himself that Thomason wasn't lurking there like a hunter in a blind for the rising water to wash Joe out of concealment. He had counted two shots, and heard a few more thudding against the hull. Which didn't mean anything. He didn't know how well Thomason was armed. He only knew the man intended to kill him.

But he had to get moving, while he still could. The water was lapping halfway up the cockpit bubble now, and he was on all fours with his head in the air in order to breathe.

Holding the waterproof flashlight in his left hand, he sloshed around the deck to starboard and lowered himself slowly over the side. With his feet on the floor of the dining room, the water was chest-high. Something clammy brushed against him in the dark, under water. He took a nervous step away, turned and flicked the light, which he shielded with one hand, toward the pulpit of the boat. Saw the hanging body of Mr. Phipps moving slowly, but from the inflow of the water, not as if he were alive. He aimed the light into the water and saw Mr. Phipps's head, an empty broken vessel half the size it had been. The top of his skull had been sheared off to within an inch of his eyebrows, and he had no brains. But one eye, of glass, was still in its socket, appraising him.

Joe shuddered and turned away from the body, gave himself to the wind-driven flow of the water. He kept a tight grip on the flashlight as he was carried, flailing on his back, through the doorway to the kitchen.

His ears popped after a ducking; he caught the edge of a countertop with his free hand and held on. He thought he heard Thomason's voice above the jet-whine of the wind. And Lizzie, almost hysterically shrill. So Thomason wasn't waiting for him outside, nearby in the dark, hanging on for a point-blank shot to Joe's head. He might be on the second floor by now. There was household flotsam all around him. He held the flashlight high, trying to get his bearings. He saw a cottonmouth water moccasin as thick as his own forearm crawling up through the latticework of a floor-to-ceiling wine rack in an opened pantry. How many more like that one had been flushed into the house with the tidal surge? He hoped other snakes would be too busy surviving to bother him.

Once more he went with the flood, as if through a nearly full storm drain, toward the front of the house and the gallery. He heard Bruiser barking.

At the top of the semicircular stairs a hurricane lamp glowed. Halfway up the stairs, three or four feet above the lapping water line, Walter Lee, his face burned and swollen, sat with Lillian, who did what she could for him with cloths rinsed in a basin of fresh water she'd taken from the supply stored in upstairs bathtubs. Walter Lee's chest was heaving as he breathed. Bruiser lay on the step below his feet, soaked and shivering. Lillian looked away as the beam of Joe's flashlight paused on her face.

Joe pulled himself out of the water by the banister rail and sank down next to Walter Lee. Lillian nodded to the second floor.

"He's in Miss Abby's room." He didn't hear her the first time. Lillian leaned over, placing her mouth close to his ear. "He have Walter Lee's pistol!"

"What happened?" Joe asked Walter Lee, pointing to his face.

"Threw a lamp on me."

Joe took a closer look at the puffed blistering flesh on Walter Lee's cheeks and forehead. His eyebrows and lashes were gone, the eyelids swollen. Liquid oozed from the slits that were left.

"Can you see anything?"

"Naw! Not much. It's the same as when they whip you with the laces in the ring, try to cut you blind!"

"Why did he do it?"

"He's a guilty man! Done killed my little gal. He is going to burn in hell for that."

"A man named Phipps killed Frosty. It probably wasn't the first murder he committed for Thomason. But Phipps is dead now."

Walter Lee slumped a little more, grimacing. He put a hand on Bruiser's head.

"Then there ain't no way to prove it!"

"What is it they say—confession's good for soul? I need to get to Thomason. He's been injecting Abby with a dangerous paralytic drug! Any more of it, she could stop breathing in a heartbeat."

Walter Lee tried to peel open a sticky eye. "Then Frosty, she was right!" He dropped his hand. "I ain't no good like this. Can *you* take him, Dr. Joe?"

"I'm going to try, Walter Lee."

"He'll shoot you," Lillian warned. "He don't care. I seen that in his eyes, he come past us on the stair like we wasn't here no more." She thought about Thomason's mental state. "He's locked up in that room with all the life left to him. God help Abby, and little Miss Lizzie! God help them."

Joe looked at the upstairs hall, where rich paintings hung askew on the walls.

He glanced down, at the still-rising, dank water, and a big marsh rabbit with laid-back, drenched velvet ears, swimming, an arrow of current behind its head, through the gallery into the parlor that had been Charly Thomason's pride.

"Abby's in the corner room? Who's next to her?"

"Lizzie, on this end of the hall. Other end is Charlene, then Dr. Luke. Lizzie's room connected to Abby's by a bath."

"Okay. Lillian, what I need for you to do is go bang and holler at Abby's door. Make as much noise as you can! Keep Thomason occupied. Tell him Walter Lee had a heart attack! Anything."

"All right, Dr. Joe."

Joe put a hand on her shoulder, nothing but skin-covered bone. There was no trace of anxiety in her webbed face, only an ingrained acceptance of pitiless nature wrecking everything, and human beings who persisted in bringing this manifestation of God's displeasure down on their heads. Lillian's body was frail and her swollen blocky feet nearly useless, but her eyes were as unbreakable as a family curse.

Lillian rose slowly. He helped her up the remaining steps and down the hall as far as Lizzie's room. Lillian glanced at him, then went on. Joe tried the knob of Lizzie's door. Like other doors in the house, this one was sticking in the jamb. He had to lunge against the solid panels to pop it open.

Lizzie's room was dark and hot. He turned on his flashlight and angled the beam past the four-poster bed to a wall in which there were two doors separated by posters of sullenly posed, snitty, in-your-face rock groups. One door stood open a couple of inches and his light caught curves and angles of misted chrome fixtures, a trapeze bar trembling as the house shook from the force of the hurricane.

During a change in the pitch of the wind, Joe heard Lucas Thomason rambling on in Abby's room. Then Lillian's voice, a contralto tremolo, from the hallway.

"Dr. Luke! Dr. Luke! Walter Lee's in terrible pain from his eyes! You got to help him!"

Joe went quickly into the bathroom, where all the fixtures looked strange to him, either higher or lower than normal, partly enclosed in shiny steel tubing. A prison of sorts, but her sentence was about to be commuted. He clicked off the flashlight after making sure of the location of the opposite, extra-wide door. His hand touched the easy-opening latch handle, and he paused.

"Lillian, I'm looking after Abby now! There's nothing I can do for Walter Lee, the infirmary's flooded!"

"*Please* open the door, Dr. Luke!"

"You just do what you can. I'll see to him in a few minutes."

Joe depressed the handle of the door to Abby's room. He put his shoulder against it, expecting the door to be warped in the jamb. Instead it opened easily, and he went stumbling inside, one hand going to the floor in an attempt to maintain his balance.

He had a glimpse of Lizzie kneeling at the foot of Abby's bed, Abby on her right side facing the shuttered windows and with a sheet over her. There was a hurricane lamp on a little table beside her bed, the gleam of a syringe on a tray.

Ten feet away Lucas Thomason turned from the unopened door to the hall, peered at Joe with a look of mild consternation and then, swiftly, annoyance. He pulled Walter Lee's old revolver from his belt. Lizzie cried out at the sight of blue steel, the proposition for violence it represented. Abby looked back awkwardly over her raised right shoulder.

Joe shouted at Thomason, "What are you going to do, kill everybody in this room? That's what you're up against now!"

"Joe!" Abby yelled. And Lizzie yelled his name too, and then Thomason said, with annoyance scraped aside by something as stark as a surgeon's knife, leaving him with no more expression than still water, "Just you."

The door to the hall was smashed off its hinges; the weight of the solid oak door, with Walter Lee on top of it, rode Thomason down and pinned him to the floor.

"Oh, God, oh my God!" Abby cried. "What are you doing to him?"

Joe picked up the revolver from the floor, glanced at Lillian in the hall. Lillian nodded and edged inside, around the door and Thomason with an arm pinned under him and trying to breathe. Lillian smiled at Abby.

"Everything gonna be all right with you now, lamb. You'll see."

"Let him up! Walter Lee, what are you—you're hurting Luke!"

"He has something to say to you," Joe said. "Walter Lee, just sit tight."

"He was gonna shoot Joe," Lizzie said. "He was just about to shoot him!"

"What is going on here?"

Joe picked up the ampule and the filled syringe from the tray.

"Did he give you any of this?" he asked Abby.

"No! He was about to. Those are my *steroids*, Joe!"

Joe said to Thomason, who had turned his head and, still helpless beneath Walter Lee's weight, was staring up at him, "*Are* they steroids, Dr. Thomason?"

Thomason said nothing. His jaw was working. He coughed and winced from pain. A froth of blood appeared on his lower lip.

Joe kneeled down and placed the tip of the syringe in the hollow of Thomason's jaw, below the left ear.

"If it's nothing but steroids, then it can't do any harm if I inject a little of this into the muscle here. Can it, Doctor?"

Thomason's jaw went on working; his throat muscles were tense, his visible eye bright with pain and hatred.

"How're you doing, Walter Lee?" Joe asked.

"No problem," Walter Lee said, reclining on the door. "I'm comfortable."

"Broken ribs," Thomason said. "Let me . . . up, I can't breathe."

Joe's thumb came down slowly on the plunger of the syringe.

"Do you see what I'm about to do here, Doctor?"

". . . Don't!"

"Why not?"

". . . Kill me."

"What? The steroids you've been giving Abby all

these years? How could those hurt you, if they're supposed to be beneficial?"

Thomason's lips moved, soundlessly.

"Okay," Joe sighed, "an autopsy should determine why what was good for Abby turned out to be lethal for you."

"Son of a bitch. Fucking son of a bitch."

"What's in the syringe, Dr. Thomason?"

"Parahydratoxamin."

"Analogue of what?"

"*You* know, you son of a bitch."

"Abby doesn't know," Joe said, and, while maintaining light pressure with the point of the syringe under Thomason's jaw, he looked up at Abby. Lillian and Lizzie had helped her to sit up in bed. She was staring at Joe and pinned-down Luke, her bluish lips apart, blankness creeping into her eyes.

"Oh, Luke."

"Tell her!"

"Analogue of—be careful, don't penetrate the skin with that syringe, one drop is enough to—analogue of Tetrodotoxin. Blowfish poison. Used in—complicated spinal surgeries. Paralytic. Complete block from the site of the injury down. Just let me up from here, I'll walk away. No harm done. For *our* sake, Abby. I only did it—for us."

"Oh, Jesus," Abby moaned; a sound so filled with excoriating pain Joe couldn't bring himself to look at her.

"Don't blame me. I've loved you since . . . you were ten years old. I didn't want . . . for you to ever . . . leave me."

"GOD, NO, DON'T MAKE HIM SAY ANY MORE."

"Just let me go," Thomason said to Joe, as if he'd heard his cue to press a winning argument. "She'll walk again. That's the important thing . . . wouldn't you say? I'll never come back. I swear it."

"You got Frosty to answer for," Walter Lee said.

"And Paul Huskisson," Joe added. "Go ahead, Thomason, finish this."

"My ribs are broken," he pleaded. "Lung is punctured. Let me up, I'm . . . smothering."

Joe said, "Did you pay Mr. Phipps to kill Paul Huskisson and Frosty Clemons?"

Thomason's face clenched furiously, the skin drizzly with an evil sweat.

"Leave me . . . with nothing, is that it?" he said, as if it was just sinking in that he had been disinherited by an unkind Fate. *"Abby."* He tried to move his head enough to catch a glimpse of her face. "Abby! I've always taken care of you . . . the best I knew how. You can't believe what he's saying! You *don't* believe it, do you?"

Abby sobbed in Lillian's arms. Lizzie sat recklessly gnawing on a thumbnail with a look of protected vacancy, as if the horrors of the moment were sliding off her psyche like drops of mercury on a mirror.

"Let me up!" Thomason demanded. "Let me go to her."

"You're never going to touch her again," Joe said.

Abby began to scream.

Thomason's face stiffened at the sound of her anguish. He coughed again, and fresh blood spotted the floor. Joe saw it, and decided Thomason was probably right about the punctured lung.

Still holding the syringe in his right hand, Joe looked around at Walter Lee. He was drained to the marrow, unnerved by the demon released but unexorcised in the stifling air of the room.

"He's had it. He won't hurt anybody else."

Thomason, his body compressed and immobile beneath the door, flexed the fingers of his right hand and suddenly jerked his head up, toward Joe's hand and the syringe he was holding. The needle slipped into soft tissue, meeting no resistance until it penetrated the tough casing of the carotid artery. The sud den movement put pressure against Joe's thumb, and most of the Parahydratoxamin, intended for the reservoir in Abby's lower back, rushed into Thomason's bloodstream.

His life was over in seconds. Unfortunately for those who had to watch it, the spasms that snapped his bones and joints and turned his skin a glowing red went on much longer.

FORTY-SEVEN

The small hospital in Nimrod's Chapel was crowded in the early hours of the day that followed the passage of Hurricane Honey to the north and east. Honey left behind devastated barrier islands, wetlands, maritime forests, and old coastal towns. A lot of "developed" beachfront land got undeveloped in a hurry, as rows of houses simply disappeared in the violent winds and tidal surges. Solid concrete piers were torn up by wave action or crumbled by wind-driven rain, bridges inundated or swept away. Homes and buildings of all types of construction were left roofless or totally collapsed. So many cardinals, robins and blue jays were stuffed into the spaces of chain-link fences that the downed and twisted fences looked like carnival bunting. But a species of parrot native to the Canary Islands, having flown more than two thousand miles within the eye of the hurricane, was spotted by a birdwatcher unharmed but cranky in the belfry of a country church sixty miles northwest of Nimrod's Chapel. Farmers who staked down chickens to keep them from being blown away found their birds intact but completely naked, without a feather between them. A live porpoise, six feet long, was discovered in the living room of a house on Pandora's Bay after the tidal surge swept through it. Power was out, up and down the coast, and would be out for more than a week. The habitats of red-cockaded woodpeckers, wild turkeys, red wolves, three already-endangered species of turtles, numerous shore birds, marsh rabbits and fox squirrels were severely disrupted. So were the lives of all the people in the hurricane path. A few were missing, a few were dead, others were hospitalized for treatment of everything from heart attacks to snakebite to accidental electrocution. Damages, when the various authorities got around to adding them up, would be in the billions of dollars. Yet Honey was not the strongest hurricane to hit the Carolina coast. Hugo, with winds of up to 168 miles an hour, had been even more punishing.

At Joe's insistence, what was left of the Parahydratoxamin in Abby's implanted reservoir was drained by a doctor named McClard, who didn't have time for all of the questions he promised to ask later. He initialed the ampule in which he saved the anesthetic and locked it up in the hospital's safe. They made room for Abby in the nurses' lounge of the new pediatric wing of the hospital, to which she had contributed nearly two hundred thousand dollars a couple of years ago.

Lillian sat in a chair beside the bed on which Abby had been strapped down, dozing and soaking her crippled feet in a pan of Epsom salts. Abby was restrained because of episodes of spasticity in both legs; the involuntary activity of the muscles was strong enough to throw her to the floor. She had not closed her eyes nor uttered a sound for at least ten hours.

Joe hadn't closed his eyes, either, but he was exhausted from the ordeal of getting them all out of the

Barony and into Nimrod's Chapel, once the floodwaters had partly drained from the back roads. Lucas Thomason's four-wheel-drive Dodge truck was the only vehicle operational after the hurricane; the storm surge had carried Frosty Clemons's yellow minivan two hundred yards into the partially cleared lot that was to have been Thomason's practice polo field. But the late Dr. Thomason had chained the rear axle of his pickup to the magnolia tree in the center of the motor court. There was a chain saw in the tool locker in the back of the truck, and Joe had cut a path for the five of them along treacherous roads filled with debris and downed trees. Almost all of the live oaks had survived the hurricane winds, losing limbs but not coming out of the soaked ground; but pine trees and water oaks were piled twenty feet high in places.

He knew a little about post-traumatic shock syndrome. Abby might come out of it soon, or (there were cases, going back more than twenty years, patients warehoused in VA hospitals) never. He had almost no voice left, but he tried talking to her.

"The paralysis is going away, Abby. Another week or two, then some time with a physical therapist, you'll be walking again. As well as you ever did. The rest of it—"

He paused to rub his eyes, to wait for a flicker of understanding in her own wide-awake eyes, as silvery-gray and blank as aluminum in the weak emergency lighting of the hot little room. A casement window was open, water dripped outside; the air smelled of salt and dank rotted marsh. The stars, unmoved by the disasters of a medium-sized planet in what would be, from a different perspective, a galaxy hardly worth mentioning among its titanic neighbors, were bright in a cleared sky. Somewhere a mournful cock was calling for the sun to visit their devastation as chain saws coughed and roared spasmodically throughout the town. A National Guard genny pounded away in the parking lot of the regional hospital. Lillian's white head, hairpins sticking out every which way, nodded toward one shoulder, then jerked erect. She smiled meaninglessly, all speckled pink gums behind charcoal lips: her teeth were in a pocket of her dampish shiny dress, spotted in places with pluff mud like a leopard's pelt. She resumed dozing in her chair.

"As for the rest of it," Joe went on, "I know it will take a while. And probably no one could ever explain why Dr. Luke did this to you. I guess—" His own head nodded from weariness, and he had to think hard about what he meant to say. "I mean, I *know* there are feelings that a man has for a woman that are so powerful—if they go bad, they turn into something—as close to evil as human beings can get. And I know— there are lies that can't be forgiven."

He smiled humbly and reached out to smooth down one of her saturnine eyebrows; his thumb grazed her eyelashes and she blinked, but it was pure reflex. No other muscle moved in her face, as if she had willed herself to follow Dr. Luke's protocol beyond his death. But maybe she truly didn't know about that; another act of the will. As if she had decided to lie in suspension forever, waiting for him to reappear. There was no obvious perspiration, but her skin had a liquid sheen. And a little saliva had trickled down from one corner of her taut mouth.

Joe reached for a tissue on the bedside tray and wiped it away, feeling a cringing of his heart. "I wish," he said, "I knew how to deal with the feelings I have for you." He smiled again and put a hand over his eyes, holding back tears, tears of repentance and failure.

There was no place for Walter Lee and Lizzie except in the hot crowded corridor outside the overburdened emergency cubicles. Walter Lee had had his burns treated, and one eye, which had taken a jot of flaming kerosene that resulted in a blistered lid the size of a bumblebee, was covered with a gauze pad and criss-crossed strips of tape. On the little bench they shared Lizzie was hunched up against Walter Lee's side in a cardigan sweater long enough to cover her knees, a nearly-empty can of 7UP in one hand. She looked list-lessly at Joe when he came toward them through the seated elderly and the whining children in their moth-ers' arms. Sweetish medicinals stung her nostrils, and the jaded bouquet of old blood.

"Abby okay?"

"Still out of it, Liz. How're you, Walter Lee?"

"Hongry."

"Me too," Lizzie said.

"I wish I could do something about that. There's not even a bag of potato chips left in their vending ma-chines."

"Thank you, Dr. Joe. We'll be all right. Wonder do the telephones work yet? I need to get in touch with the girls."

"No, I don't think they're working." They heard the sound of an ambulance pulling up outside under the damaged marquee of the emergency wing. "Walter Lee, we need to talk. It'll take a little while yet, but sooner or later the police will be around."

"Yes, sir, I expect they will. But what is there to say? I mean, Dr. Luke had a heart attack and died. We all witnessed it."

"That's right," Lizzie said, looking up at Joe with the cool of a polished liar.

"Wasn't nothing you could do to save his life."

Joe sighed. "Maybe you shouldn't jack around with the cops, Walter Lee."

Walter Lee showed a weary, cynical half-smile.

"Frosty dead. Dr. Luke, he dead. What we got to care about is the living. Get Miss Abby well, on her feet. Sure, they ask their questions. Me, I don't know a thing. What am I supposed to know? I just work for the man, that's all."

"What am *I* supposed to know?" Lizzie said argumentatively. "I'm a kid."

"We bury the dead now, Dr. Joe. We get on with things, best we know how. Miss Abby gone need us. We gone need her."

"You make it sound so simple."

"Plenty tragedy to go around, this day. Everybody got their own concerns. All the bad is done with for now. We'll abide." Walter Lee paused, and Lizzie scrunched herself a little closer to his side, her eyes closing. One of his big hands covered her shoulder. He looked up in the poor light with his unbandaged, iodine-colored eye, and offered Joe his other hand.

"I hope this finds you in agreement, Doctor."

Joe shook his hand. Walter Lee looked content.

"What you got in mind for yourself, Dr. Joe?"

"Well—" They were bringing someone in, quick-time, on a gurney, two paramedics angling the injured man toward an already-occupied treatment room. Joe leaned against the wall to get out of the way. "I think I'll have a drink of water, then find a place to sit down and catch a few winks."

"You done a powerful lot for all of us. That will be remembered."

"Thank you, Walter Lee."

After a few moments Lizzie stirred and looked around the bulk of Walter Lee at Joe walking down the hall toward a cooler that dispensed bottled water. He joined the line waiting for drinks.

"Where did Joe say he was going?"

"Didn't exactly make that clear," Walter Lee said gently. "You get yourself some rest now."

"I will." She closed her eyes again, yawning. Walter Lee's chin dropped by degrees toward his chest. Seconds, or perhaps minutes, later, Lizzie gave a start and looked up, bleary-eyed. She looked down the corridor to where she had seen Joe last, in mud-caked khaki clothing taken from Lucas Thomason's wardrobe, patiently waiting his turn in line at the water cooler. He wasn't there anymore. Lizzie frowned. There were a lot of people outside under the concrete marquee, the lights of police cars and ambulance reflecting off the taped glass doors. She thought she saw him, making his way through the milling paramedics and rescue volunteers, hands in the pockets of a hunting jacket, walking away from the hospital. She started again, as if she were about to get up from the bench; then Walter Lee's hand grasped her a little more firmly.

"No, Lizzie," he said.

"Joe is—"

"He figure it be time for him to go, honey."

"Go where? He could stay with us! Abby needs him."

"He done her a miracle already. Maybe what he needs now is time to work out his own life, find a direction for himself."

"Do you think we'll ever see him again?"

"Can't say."

Lizzie swallowed a protest and thought spitefully, as she was to think many times in the coming days of confusion and anxiety over Abby and their temporary homelessness, through two funerals and a police investigation that hit the front pages of newspapers everywhere in the state and made her at least peripherally notorious when school resumed, *It isn't fair of him.* And then as more interesting speculation about the man called Joe whose identity could not be verified came to her attention, her resentment lessened, and she began to fantasize about who he really was. The police, having reviewed the tape found in the camcorder at Adele's side in the only house on the beach not demolished by the hurricane, wanted him, for questioning only; they looked for him, as they looked for the missing Charlene Thomason, but they found neither. It was speculated that Charlene had drowned, one more tragedy not to be accounted for until eventually her fleshless remains might be discovered in a tangle of uprooted trees along the shores of Pandora's Bay, or in the ever-shifting river sands farther inland. As for Joe—he was as elusive as a secret agent, a master criminal . . . an auroral ghost afloat on solar winds.

For months, while the cleanup at the Barony progressed (the house and Abby's workroom had to be stripped down to the studs to get rid of the infusion of salt water and pluff mud that contaminated all wood and insulation) Lizzie alternated between nightmares and dreams of a guardian angel who appeared at her bedside and spoke to her in the voice of Joe Bryce, offering solutions for the tribulations of the day she had taken with her to her pillow. In his last appearance the angel, more human in aspect than in earlier dreams but still not fully recognizable, bent to kiss her on the lips, and Lizzie awakened with a sob, a welter of emotion in her nicely expanding breast, a cramped abdomen and fresh blood in her vagina: she was a month from her fourteenth birthday. The mystery of Joe Bryce persisted, but her own interest had begun to wane as the fashions, fetishes, crushes, pubescent intrigues and daily gossip of her first high-school year kept her occupied. Elizabeth Ann Abelard was growing up.

EPILOGUE

The snowflakes are perfect.
The stars are perfect.
Not us.
Not us.
We are here to ruin ourselves and to break our
    hearts.
And love the wrong people and die.

—John Patrick Shanley, **Moonstruck**

The Beermans, Jerome and Grace, were from California. They had rented a ten-room villa overlooking Magen's Bay on St. Thomas in the Virgin Islands that went for seventeen thousand dollars a month with a two-month minimum during the December-to-April season. The amenities included a full staff of servants, and Joe, who owned a piece of the realty company that had leased the villa to the Beermans.

After the holiday season was over, the Beermans became bored with the social prospects of the next two months and decided to take a cruise. It was a busy cruise season, and the best of the oceangoing palaces that sailed the Caribbean during the winter were solidly booked. Grace Beerman appealed to Joe, who spent a couple of days prying deluxe accommodations for two aboard a Carnival ship out of an executive of the cruise line. The exec required a promise of some costly favors to be paid at a later date.

Joe left Charlotte Amalie at the lunch hour on an

intensely blue day and drove cross-island to Magen's
Bay to give the Beermans the good news in person.

Jerome Beerman had worked for a couple of hours
that morning, and was lying down when Joe arrived.
Jerre was a screenwriter who specialized in megabucks
action movies. He generally took a year to turn out a
hundred and twenty pages of dialogue that contained
every conceivable variation on the f-word. For his success in having mastered an art form which, he modestly
conceded, ranked well below jailhouse tattoos and the
designing of paper airplanes, Jerre was paid in the
neighborhood of two million dollars per script. Not
counting residuals, which could add up remarkably for
movies that grossed—worldwide, baby—half a billion
dollars or more, depending on the current appeal of
the male sexpot assigned to star in each picture.

Jerre was a very pale, thin little man with dusty-
looking gray hair and a bad case of emphysema; he
had begun to smoke at the age of ten. He got around
with the help of a portable oxygen pack he wore on a
shoulder strap that kept him breathing through nasal
cannulae, but in all respects he was as slow as an un-
wound watch. Grace was in her forties. She wore heels
nearly all the time, which raised her to an even five
feet. Her body was trim and erect from punishing exercise routines designed by a personal trainer. She had
a fetching mane of brunette hair with white streaks
that looked painted on. Her face had gone under the
knife so many times she now had the glossy puffed-up
appearance of the designated robin at a worm farm.

Grace met Joe at the door of the one-story, Italianate
villa, and he bent down to receive the kiss that brushed
across his lips in a teasing, soulful way. She was wearing a two-piece skater with a bandeau top over perky
breasts that could hang on to the top nicely, without
the detachable straps to hold everything up. The short
skirt revealed all of her honey-gold thighs. A sheer
chiffon shirt embroidered with little golden anchors,

which she wore unbuttoned over the white skater, billowed in the trade wind that swept through the front-to-back open gallery of the villa, situated a hundred feet above a private beach and the glittery turquoise sea.

"You're in time for lunch!" Grace exulted. She was as vital as her husband was drab. She couldn't walk ten feet without throwing in a girlish pirouette. Her hand gestures claimed every crumb of attention from those she worked hard to enthrall.

"I'm skipping lunch this week," Joe explained. "Too many Christmas cookies."

Grace presumed to doubt him by pinching him above the beltline.

"Don't be ridiculous! You're fit as a fiddle. And dear André has gone out of his way in your honor—*sopa di yuana*, and some of that marvelous *keri keri* his mother taught him to make. Papiamento is such a *fun* language. André's been teaching me. Do you speak any Papiamento?" Joe shrugged; a few words. "Come, make me happy for once." She peered at him as if from behind a small cloud that had scudded across her horizon. "You are going to make me happy, aren't you?"

She was all over him, chatty and affectionate, on their short walk across Italian limestone to the gusty veranda where the oiled teak luncheon table, partially shielded from the wind off the sea by bamboo shades, had been set. A pair of blue-and-red parrots in a cage began croaking for attention as Grace and Joe were seated by a houseboy who had that underlying tone of dark malice which island visitors interpreted as surliness. His attitude was commonplace on all the islands, where the only natural resources were those that drew hordes of white tourists expecting a week or two of fantasy living while being catered to by blacks living at or near the poverty level.

With no fanfare Joe took the blue envelope contain-

ing the prized cruise reservations from a pocket of his
linen jacket and laid it before Grace Beerman. She
snatched it up and read the good news, which called
for another round of kisses—which she left her chair
to deliver, wrapping her small strong arms around his
neck. For a few minutes she sat in his lap, and they
were eye to eye.

"I don't know how I can thank you," Grace said
breathlessly. "Joe, you're straight from heaven."

"I was happy to find a way to help."

"Jerre's going to be thrilled."

"Is he having lunch with us?"

"Well, you know; it's such a chore to get him to eat
anything. And he really spent too much time at the
word processor this morning. He said he was on a
roll."

"Good for Jerre."

Grace disentangled herself and with a sliding of fingertips across his cheek left Joe for her own place at
the table. Wine was poured by the houseboy, a Chianti
as light and sparkling as the air around them. Grace
picked up the envelope again, speculatively.

"This will mean some shopping. Are you free this
afternoon, Joe?"

"I'm afraid I can't."

"Oh, *damn*. I wanted your opinions. You have such
good taste, without being at all *'GQ'* and fairy-faddish."

"You have a week before the ship arrives in San
Juan," Joe pointed out.

"Another day, then. As for tonight—" She leaned
forward, elbows on the scalloped top of half-inch glass,
hands joined, taut chin on her hands. "Joe, it's been
so boring for me since Peg and Hunter left. I mean,
without your *friends* there's just nothing to *do* here."

Joe smiled in commiseration.

"So I thought we might have a wonderful evening,
just the two of us. Wouldn't you say our relationship

has reached the stage where we don't have to tiptoe around the subject of sensual gratification?''

''Probably.''

Grace lifted her glass of wine. She had a slightly outthrust, toothy smile.

''Good. Because my glands are quivering like warm jelly. I am literally *desperate* to fuck you.''

Joe smiled again, acknowledging her desperation.

''I can't help wondering how Jerre would take it. You and I.''

''Oh,'' she said, with a little conspiratorial moué, ''we've already discussed that. Jerre, as you know—well, what can I say? He's been so gal*lant* about this perfectly awful, tedious business of dying, but dying he is; I've done my best to make him happy, and he's very appreciative. He likes you quite a lot, because obviously you've read a book or two; God, where we come from, nobody can even *spell* Sartre. You've been a good listener when Jerre's had the breath to talk, and also you've been so, um, maddeningly discreet about not making any moves on me. He suggested just the other night that you're more or less wasting your time with that little real-estate business of yours, that you'd be a natural at the Hollywood game.''

''The Hollywood game is all backhands. I've spent some time there. But I never had much use for trendy restaurants where nobody can get a table unless he tests positive for hubris. I'm not a fire-in-the-belly type. No, thanks, not again.''

Grace brushed windblown hair from her face and said good-humoredly, ''I can't believe that someone with your panache can be really happy in what amounts to a tropical ghetto. I've had the sense that there's great sadness in you, Joe. Naturally I want to know all about it. Pillow confessions are so good for the soul.''

"Gracie, there was a time when I'd have given up my front-row seat in hell for you."

"*Was* a time? Oh, heavens, am I about to be rebuffed?"

"I like my life," he said. "I've bought into the firm, and I don't watch the clock. I sail, I swim, I fish. I say my prayers at night."

"I hope you're not going to tell me you're some sort of defrocked priest, clinging to the ideals of celibacy."

"Far from it."

"Is it the little brown sloe-eyed creature in your office? The one with the cunning braids and the uppity ass?"

"Miranda's boyfriend is getting his Ph.D. in marine biology at the University of Miami. And I wouldn't play around with the help."

"Well, can you remember the last time you got laid?"

Joe thought about it, and laughed.

"Maybe it was around this time last year. I'm not sure."

"We are both *long* overdue. The last time I made the attempt with Jerre, all I did was blow in his ear, and he convulsed."

And thus it had started, so many times before; and he knew how it would go from here, if he desired. She would be ravenous, desperately full of gemütlichkeit, she would fall in love with him, then dig in her nails in a different kind of desperation. The husk of Jerre Beerman would soon fall from the earthly vine. Grace would be worth, depending on how sharp Jerre had been about avoiding probate and the IRS, say six to eight million. He could pick Grace clean with his eyes closed. A man who knew how to take his time with a woman could take her for everything else. And he'd been the best. Lottie, Adrian, Clare, Magdalene, Sarafina, a dozen others—if you pressed them, in spite of heartbreak they'd admit it. Joe had been the best.

He could feel a lustful twinge or two looking at Grace Beerman; but there was nothing he really wanted from her.

"Let's be friends, Grace."

Her lips pressed together; she sighed, and it turned into a tremor.

"I'm not so bad, though; am I? It's just that the timing's wrong, or something."

"For me. The truth is, I'm still trying to get the hang of being a reformed bastard."

After his leisurely lunch with Grace Beerman Joe looked at a property on Bolongo Bay that its owner, a British rock star whose albums no longer sold, was eager to be rid of. Architecturally the villa was interesting, but with too many exterior plantings that kept the sun away and promoted mildew inside. The plumbing was wrecked, windows were broken, there were stains on the grass cloth walls that looked as if guests had vomited repeatedly on them, and the terrazzo floors were blackened and ashy in places, suggesting that the rocker or his guests had enjoyed their driftwood fires indoors. With a cleanup and substantial pruning of the purple bougainvilleas and sea grape outside to enhance the view, Joe thought the villa might list at a million-two.

By the time he had completed his assessment and taken some Polaroids it was a quarter to four, and he decided against returning to town. He drove through the rush-hour traffic in his Land Cruiser past Lindbergh Bay and the airport to the West End, then down a private road in Perseverance to the cottage he owned that overlooked an anchorage so small it had no name, and no significant beach to attract developers. There he docked his treasured thirty-one-foot Hallberg Rassy motor sailer.

He fed the cats, Branca and Poor-Eye, stripped and went comfortably naked down to the end of the dock past some roseate terns peaceably occupying a couple of pilings. He plunged in and swam straight at the sun, as far as the reef five hundred yards offshore. Back at the cottage, he drank a beer in the shower and another on the deep piazza paved with quarry tile. Bamboo shades defused the power of the setting sun, which at this time of the year lit up every comer of the small rooms inside. The cottage was poured concrete and required little maintenance: he could push the solid, island-made, termite-proof furniture to one side and hose the place down in twenty minutes. He had Scarlatti in a minor key on the stereo and was thinking about throwing a steak on the outdoor grill for supper when a good-looking schooner came into view beyond the reef, traveling east on diesel with sails furled.

Forty-eight or fifty feet, at least forty of those feet at the waterline, meaning she was built for speed. The hull was flared widely near the sheer, useful in preventing the schooner from burying her bow at more than eleven knots. The handsome deckhouse was split at the mainmast. He couldn't make out the helmsman against the glare of the sun, now close to the horizon, but he wanted to see more of the regal schooner, and reached for his binoculars.

The yacht was seconds from disappearing behind a forest of red and black mangrove to the left of his anchorage when he brought it into sharp relief. A woman with a good figure and flying sunset-tinted hair had the helm. She was wearing a sweatband on her forehead. Sunglasses obscured a third of her face. She had a companion, half-naked, broad-shouldered, who appeared to be tinkering with a jib winch from one of the twin cockpits. Nothing unusual about either of them. Young, rich, with leisure time to tour the islands in their superb boat for several weeks or months of the year.

The man in the forward cockpit turned and said something to the woman, who changed their heading slightly just as Joe's view of the schooner was obscured. But the transom had come around enough for him to read the name and home port.

She was the *Dragonfly*, out of Nimrod's Chapel, South Carolina.

There was a lot of partying going on aboard some of the impressive yachts taking up every available slip in the Crown Marina of St. Thomas harbor. Three big cruise ships, marvelously alight like a wandering city, were anchored at the West Indian pier. The ships and pleasure boats and resorts made up the rich crust clinging to the undernourished economies of islands everywhere in the Caribbean. The U.S. Virgins were bustling, overbuilt and suffering from the demands of tourism. St. Thomas had too much traffic on inadequate roads. Drugs and AIDS were a problem. Pollution of once-pristine little bays had begun to kill off the coral reefs and foul formerly dependable fishing grounds. Pregnant women from island nations all over the Caribbean were flying in to have their babies born on U.S. soil, thus insuring them citizenship and causing great strain on V.I. medical facilities. The crime rate was up, with muggings and break-ins crowding the police blotters. It was no longer safe at night in most of Charlotte Amalie or on any of the island's beaches.

Given time, Joe thought, it would all resemble south Florida. These days life seemed to be a succession of things that were bad for you, and some pretty sunsets. But as long as the sun was hot and the sea was blue and the tradewinds sang in the riggings away from the mendacity and the tawdriness, there still must be some promise left in the world.

The *Dragonfly* was moored stern-to in slip F-18, show-ing lights below. The gangplank was down. Quiet aboard, except for the homey sounds of someone washing pots in the galley sink. He loitered on the dock for several minutes, admiring the craftsmanship. Hard to tell by the dock lights just how well she was kept, but *Dragonfly*'s teak decks were uncluttered and salt-free, the brightwork in the stern had no traces of corrosion. A great boat: trim, seaworthy and well-loved.

He listened to music from adjoining vessels—every-thing from little O'Days to huge oceangoing cats far from Southampton or Marseilles—to the salsa and the disco and the rockabilly; he heard laughter and ice cubes popping into glasses beneath a nearly full moon the color of Edam cheese. And rationally decided he'd seen enough and needed to go quietly away. Because, by this time, she must have her life in order, and be well loved by someone who deserved her.

And yet she had named her schooner *Dragonfly.*

He was still wondering about that when she came up on deck, barefoot, wearing khaki shorts and a yellow Polo shirt. Her tawny hair was tied behind her head. She had a Walkman CD player in one hand. She was as thin and wiry as a distance runner, so tan her eyes shone like hot rivets above prominent cheekbones. She took a deep contented breath and looked around and saw him on the dock fifteen feet away. She smiled.

"Hi, there."

"Hi," Joe said. "Just admiring your boat."

"Admire all you please. She is one damn serious boat, every inch custom. Wish I could give you a tour, but not without permission."

"I understand. Who are you crewing for?"

"Pamela Abelard. The novelist. I guess you've heard of her."

"The name rings a bell."

"Abby's my second cousin on my daddy's side. I'm

Wanda. Abby went into town a little while ago with my better half to see if the replacement burners for the Luke got flown in yet. We've been mostly without a stove since we left Grand Turk."

"How long have you been cruising?"

"Seven weeks. We picked up the *Dragonfly* in Lauderdale. It's about over for Donnie and me. She's certified seaworthy now, and Donnie's got to finish his damn dissertation."

"What are Miss Abelard's plans?"

Wanda gave him a less-admiring reappraisal. "You'd have to ask her."

"Maybe I will." Joe smiled and nodded and walked back along F dock to shore.

After looking into the Hard Rock and a couple of other places on the waterfront, he found her in the upstairs bar of McAvity's Islander with Wanda's husband, Donnie. There was a large, rough-looking yellow dog that might have been part Irish wolfhound sitting next to her barstool, snacking on plantain chips. McAvity's loud reggae band was on break, which Joe counted as a blessing.

Abby's hair was different, cut short for cruising, bleached blond in streaks during long salty reaches. She wore a blue silk camp shirt and matching trousers, white woven sandals. Her thick eyebrows and stuck-out pixie ears he would have known anywhere.

He walked over to them. The dog turned its head, looking up at him with a bouncer's eye for potential trouble.

Joe said, "You still owe me ten dollars."

Abby's lips parted. There was a firecracker flash of recognition followed by darkness, the deliberate cloaking of her emotions. He thought she'd probably been expecting something like this, running scenarios in her mind. She continued to look straight ahead, at his reflection in one of the pier glass bar mirrors mounted on a liquor lazy Susan the size of a wagon wheel.

Donnie did look at Joe. He was a husky linebacker-type with white-blond hair fizzling on his freckled crown and a peeling Roman nose that had met a few stray elbows during his athletic career.

Abby said drawlingly to Donnie, "Man comes up to me in a bar. Says I owe him ten dollars. What do you think I should tell him, Donnie?"

"Why don't you let me tell him?" Donnie suggested.

"Hi, Donnie. I'm Joe. You can go now."

"Man says his name is Joe," Abby said, still staring straight into the mirrors. The bad bar lighting didn't flatter any of them. Joe's pewter-gray hair had a purplish tinge; her mouth was deeply bracketed and looked sullen. "That's one thing we know about him for sure. Or do we?"

"I could probably get the two of us a booth," Joe said, glancing around the crowded bar. "I know the owner real well."

Abby turned to Donnie. "Do you have ten dollars?"

"Sure." Donnie looked perplexed, but he dug into a pocket of his plaid Bermudas and passed the sawbuck to Abby. She turned the other way then, and looked Joe in the eye as she gave him the money. He could tell she'd had a couple of drinks, maybe three, and still couldn't hold her liquor.

"I don't ever want it said that I don't pay my debts. How about you, Joe—Joe—?"

"Maczerek," he said patiently.

"That sounds like it might be an actual real name."

"So my mother told me. It's all she left me with, a long time ago. My name, and a five-dollar bill."

"I wonder if you've ever gotten over that."

"It's a topic for discussion. How well people get over things."

"What language are you two talking?" Donnie said with a bewildered smile.

Abby drew a slow breath. She said with a glum smile of apology to Donnie, "I guess I need to talk to him alone. It's okay. I used to know him. I'll be along in a little while with Chloe."

Joe caught McAvity's eye and arranged for the trysting booth in a palm-fringed corner that usually merited a fifty-dollar bribe. But there was a favor involved, a negotiation Joe had handled and that concerned the pubescent daughter of two irate Atlantans intent on closing McAvity down. The kid had had a thing for Rastafarian musicians.

McAvity fussed over them for a few moments when they sat down, then took a second look at Abby's face and departed swiftly. The large yellow dog named Chloe sat obediently at Abby's right hand and munched on plantain chips.

"She'll eat anything," Joe said approvingly.

Abby's taut expression softened slightly. "Walter Lee found her during the hurricane. She was all but starved to death, a pathetic bag of bones. Chloe and I sort of— recovered together. Now where I go, she goes. And Chloe doesn't take any shit from man or beast."

"How is Walter Lee?"

"He's making it okay. The twins were his salvation, after Frosty—I honestly don't know what I'd do without him. Or Lizzie, either, although she can be a royal pain sometimes. Sixteen is a rotten age, as I remember."

"Charlene?"

Abby rubbed her forehead, uneasy.

"Nothing. I mean—there's never been a trace. For a long time I thought—maybe she was with you, down here somewhere, both of you having a good laugh."

The memory of the pain this absurd conclusion had cost her returned; she scanned the surface of the table as if it were a poison-pen letter she'd written to herself.

"I left her at the beach house," Joe said. "Because

there was nothing else I *could* do. She had a gun on me and was living out a fantasy about flying saucers."

"Oh, my God," Abby murmured, not doubting him.

"Are you still on the home place?"

"Yes. We moved the coffins out of the garden and back into the cemetery. Junked the *Wayfarer*. Rebuilt the house."

"You're taller than I remember."

"You're a son of a bitch."

A waitress brought Joe a Corsair beer and Abby a vodka tonic. The waitress, a fetching chocolate redhead, smiled fondly at Joe, as if reminiscing. Abby didn't miss the nuance.

"Right at home down here, aren't you, Joe?"

"Shouldn't I be? It's been three and a half years. I do a day's work for my pay. I make out fine. Almost all of my intentions are honorable these days. How did you know I was in St. Thomas?"

Abby drank with a stony face, swallowing hard.

"Research. I'm good at it. I've accumulated quite a file on you. Enough to get me started on my next novel: about a thief, a cheat, and a con man."

"Historical fiction, of course."

"Of course. That's what you are to me. History."

"Cheers," Joe said amiably, clinking his beer bottle against her glass. Abby looked startled.

"Go fuck yourself."

"If one of us could develop a sense of humor, the rest of the evening might go a lot smoother."

"Sense of—? You came to the Barony with one thing in mind—my money."

"Uh-huh."

"You were on the job."

"Yes."

"I looked like easy pickings to you."

"The easiest I ever saw."

"God *damn* you."

Joe sat back in the padded booth and had a sip of beer. She had delivered herself of her accumulated outrage, which he had deflected as if it were trivial, and now there was nothing much for Abby to do but get up and stalk out of the bar. She initiated this move by putting a hand on Chloe's choke collar.

Joe said, "Why did you name that nifty schooner the *Dragonfly*?"

"What the hell difference—? Because it seemed to— because I did have some good luck once, and maybe it was the dragonfly, or maybe it was just some bullshit I was eager to believe because I hated my life and I thought— Your name really isn't Mazcerek, you *still* can't tell the simple truth about anything—"

"It was my mother's maiden name. Check your research."

"I went to Buffalo *myself*. I talked with your aunts, the ones you told me about. I know that part of you is authentic, but—"

"I took her name because I didn't like the sound of Joe Petruska, and I figured it was close enough to my roots. Anyway, I never knew my old man."

"They were lovely to me," Abby said. "By the way, they fixed up the house. With some of your ill-gotten gains."

Joe smiled and offered Chloe a macadamia nut. Abby scowled at him.

"Better not. They're probably constipating. They constipate me. I'm walking okay, but some of me is still a little screwed up, like my bowels—oh, damn, *damn* it, Joe, why couldn't you have stayed with me? I was *months* coming out of it. I was in all kinds of therapy which did absolutely no good until I decided just to chuck everything and sail away—where the hell did *you* go?"

"Arizona. I spent some time with my adoptive parents. I retraced just about every step I'd taken after my mother dumped me in Gila Bend almost thirty-five years ago. Retraced and erased.''

She bowed her head slightly and said, as if she were jealous, ''If I could only do the same.''

Joe sighed. ''You've already started. You're here.''

''No. This was foolish. I know I shouldn't have—''

''You buried Luke, but there's no way you'll lose him. You'd better accept it.''

''I still can't—say his name without getting lockjaw. If I could just get through a week without nightmares about needles—and waking up knowing I'm paralyzed all over again. I guess it's asking too much. When you've been betrayed like I have, you can never trust anyone again.''

It sounded cynical, and rehearsed, a novelist's theme that might well turn into a treasured golden oldie as she aged and steadily, ritually extinguished her humanness. Pamela Abelard, born again at thirty-two, still trying to find out who she was. He was wary of the part she had defined for him in her quest for justification. He had finished his own quest.

''Hey, Abelard.''

His tone startled her. His smile mocked her despair. She frowned.

''Trust your instincts. Start that new book. Put all of us in it. Dr. Luke, and the con man who came to call and was charmed into falling for his victim. Write it; then close the covers on that book and put it on a high shelf, and finally it'll be over with.''

''No, it won't,'' she said tearfully. ''Luke's dead and you're alive but I *don't know who you are*! And I can't write the ending until I know—if I ever will— What do you mean, you fell for me?''

''I think I said I fell for a woman named Abby. She had spirit and humor and was great to be with. I don't think she's around anymore.''

"What—who do you think you're—oh, I see. You're conning me again. You're evil."

"Trust your instincts."

"I don't want to trust my instincts!"

"Then you're conning yourself. And you're beginning to bore me."

"Shut up! I was in love with you, and you *deserted* me. The last couple of years, every good-looking guy who crossed my path, I fell for him. I got deflowered. That's a wretched way to put it, but it's the way I felt at the time. *Deflowered.* Shit. It wasn't any good. Hasn't been . . . I'm a *mess*, Joe!"

"So you came looking for me. But if it's more therapy you're after, forget it. I'm not playing that game."

She clenched and unclenched her jaw. "All right, I know it was dumb! I just wanted the chance to tell you how much I hated you!"

"Sure. What's the other dumb reason?"

"I don't—"

"Last chance to level with me, Abby. I have better things to do with my life than to wipe the nose of a broken-down neurotic has-been writer who forgot how to fight back when things got really nasty."

"You are the most despicable—"

"Abby, it's a simple thing when you don't think about it. And so incredibly complicated when you do. So stop thinking, damn it, and stop gritting your teeth. Do you want me?"

Her mouth was open, her throat locked as if she were choking. Chloe looked around at her, and whined.

Joe reached across the table and blotted the first couple of tears that appeared on Abby's glossy tanned cheeks.

" 'Lovers and madmen,' " he quoted, " 'have such seething brains, such shaping fantasies, that apprehend more than cool reason ever comprehends.' "

Abby stared at him. The corners of her mouth tweaked. Her lips trembled, and he thought with a twinge of hope, *Hey, maybe* . . . And then she laughed, loud enough to turn heads in McAvity's Islander, that uninhibited contralto roll-out-the-barrel, from-the-gut laugh of hers.

"Oh, my God," she gasped, when she was able to talk. "Somebody call the cops!"

"Labyrinthine plot twists that grab readers instantly…Farris piles one Grand Guignol moment on top of another with **unerring** dexterity, a **keen** knowledge of human nature, and a **wicked** sense of humor." —*Publishers Weekly*

"It is quite simply **the most intriguing suspense story I've ever read**, with a genuinely absorbing central character who is a baffling mixture of the normal and the supernormal—as is the whole book. **You simply can't stop reading it.**" —Thomas Fleming, author of *The Officers' Wives*

"*Dragonfly* is undoubtedly **the best work by John Farris to date**….Highly developed characters, a tightly woven plot, and heart-stopping suspense. **It's time John Farris took his place alongside the bestselling authors writing today.**" —Sandra Scoppettone, author of *I'll Be Leaving You Always*

"Don't start reading *Dragonfly* on a weeknight, unless you plan to go to work the next day looking like a zombie." —Douglas Preston and Lincoln child, authors of *Relic*